Flight of th

Paul Muller

Tournesol Books

An Imprint of:

The Pen Press Ltd. London

PRINTING HISTORY
First Edition

First published in Great Britain
by Tournesol Books – an Imprint of
Pen Press Publishers Ltd
39-41 North Road
London N7 9DP
www.penpress.net

ISBN 1 904754 45 7

A catalogue record for this book is available from the British Library

Printed and bound in Great Britain

Cover and Typography

The text was formatted and set in 10.5 point Times Roman and other fonts by the author. Cover art is also by the author, motif inspired by the image, "Parthenon and the Greek Flag" www.fotosearch.com. Both fighter aircraft are Eurofighters. The RAF plane is in official black UK livery following a photograph on the Royal Air Force website (2004). The Greek fighter and the C-17 cargo aircraft are represented with traditional markings.

About the Author: See last page.

Dedication

Pheidias (Phidias) son of Charmides: circa 490 BC – circa 430 BC
Universally regarded as the greatest of Greek sculptors.
He designed the towering statues of Athena in the Parthenon in
Athens and that of Zeus at Olympia in the mid 5th century BC.
He and his student-successors, among them Alcamenes and
Agoracritus, also designed and created the Parthenon Marbles.

Foreword

This is a work of fiction. The names of all characters, companies, clubs, and private organizations are the products of the author's imagination. Any resemblance to other persons, living or dead, is unintentional and coincidental.

The venues, public agencies named in the book, and quotations from official sources are real, though in the author's view, some of them are more difficult to believe than much of the fictional content. The political issues are those of today, and the resolutions suggested here are most certainly in accordance with the author's opinions.

The author gratefully acknowledges major contributions to both the content and the editing by his wife Sara Gill Costelloe. Without her intimate knowledge of Greece, Greek culture and language, this book would not have been possible. Kathy Kidd, Rosemary Latham, and Patricia Wiley were our lead readers. Their extraordinarily perceptive comments materially improved the work during author's edits. Other readers included: Diana Bishop, Alma Bethany, Margaret Cooper, David Crow, Judy Higley, Christine Powell, Jacques Schönbeck, and Malcolm Scott. I also thank Clifford Jaques for his expertise in matters of computer security and the full erasure of hard disks. No work of this kind can aspire to professional standards without the strenuous efforts of a gifted professional editor. Thanks are not enough, but I do thank mine, Karen Scott: karen.scott@virgin.net.

All errors in the manuscript are the responsibility of the author.

Pattaya, Thailand   Winter 2002-2003
Lauzerte, France   Summer 2003 to Spring 2004

Prologue

The British Museum is the best possible place for the Parthenon sculptures

"The range of the British Museum's collections is worldwide. They cover millennia of human history. Here the visitor can move from Egypt to the Aztecs, from Africa to Greece and Rome, from ancient Britain to ancient China. The collections provide a uniquely rich setting for the Parthenon sculptures as an important chapter in the story of human cultural achievement and civilization. It is this story, which the British Museum exists to tell.

The Parthenon itself has been much damaged since antiquity. The restoration of the integrity of the building is thus an unachievable goal. Only about 50% of the original sculptures survive in a state fit for display, of which about half are in the British Museum. The other half are (sic) in Athens already.

A select group of key objects, to which without doubt the Parthenon sculptures belong, needs to be permanently accessible to the museum's visitors who come here expecting to see them. To lend these objects would seriously impair the museum's ability to fulfil its core function for the visitor.

The British Museum is a truly universal museum of humanity, accessible to 5 million visitors from around the world every year entirely free of entry charge. Only here can the worldwide significance of the Parthenon sculptures be fully grasped."

Neil MacGregor, Director, full text, press release & website (2002)

Why the British Museum cannot and does not want to lend its Parthenon Sculptures

In 2003 the British Museum celebrated its 250th anniversary.

Many millions of people from all over the world have found enjoyment and meaning in the galleries and study rooms of the museum, and many generations of curators have been privileged to serve them.

Thomas Bruce, 7th Earl of Elgin, who has been unjustly defamed by the campaign for the restitution of the Elgin marbles, deserves his place in history along with other diplomats whose collections came to the museum. Such men saw their embassies abroad as opportunities to promote public understanding at home of the ancient and modern cultures they encountered on their travels.

We are indebted to Elgin for having rescued the Parthenon sculptures and others from the Acropolis from the destruction they were suffering, as well as from the damage that the Acropolis monuments, including the sculptures that he did not remove, have suffered since.

The Parthenon sculptures are now one of the greatest treasures of the British Museum and they have been the heart of its classical collections since they were acquired in 1816. The gallery in which they are housed has been described as "one of the central places of earth". They are among a select number of objects in the museum that are intrinsic to its identity.

[There is] urgent need in Athens of a proper building for displaying the many sculptures of the Parthenon and other treasures that are currently lumbered in storerooms. These include fourteen blocks of the west frieze that were removed, much damaged by weathering, from the Parthenon in 1993 and have not been seen by the public since then. Other sculptures are currently left on the building and suffer the same damage. If symbolic gestures for 2004 are called for, there could be none better than Greece making sure that it properly displays what it already has.

Meanwhile, the British Museum's sculptures are where they will remain, in the museum's own purpose-built gallery, where they are displayed free for all.

Greece has recently given up previous attempts to challenge the British Museum's legal ownership, which is in any case unassailable, but still seeks possession of them by attempting to pressure the museum into agreeing to a loan. The museum has neither the power to agree to such a loan nor does it wish to offer its assent to a proposal which is transparently against the interests of the many visitors who flock to the British Museum from all over the world and is contrary to the liberal principles which the museum serves.

Dr Robert Anderson, Director, British Museum
        Excerpts in context from press release and website (2003)

Dramatis Personae

Helena Katsis (Kat), Greek ex-intelligence officer "*Pandora*", 42
Spiros Anguelopoulos, Greek, 52, confidant of top politicians
Irini Baynes, English-Greek, 25, writing PhD thesis, Greek Sculpture
Achilles, Irini's large, white, green-eyed cat
Peter Ryan, British south-side London promoter, 29, student at LSE
Adam Blix, 23, American at Imperial College, in quantum computers
Andreas Hadjis, owner of Greek delicatessen, Bloomsbury, London
"*Charon*" (codename) the Spymaster, Greek intelligence
"*Cassandra*" (codename) female intelligence officer under Charon
"*Pluton*" (codename) male intelligence officer under Charon
Dr Geoffrey Hayward, curator (director) of the British Museum
Darley, coffee shop waitress
Jamie Peters, of the *Sunday Times*.
Paul Alberts, foreman of Marbles' copying team, British Museum
Miss Naomi Marks, Art student, sculptor, Slade School of Art
Steve Walters, her colleague, engineering degree, aspiring sculptor
Dr Denis Potterton, Irini's supervisor at the British Museum
Benjamin Pearson, international attorney in London
Jane Fowler, stenographer
Andrew Sims, attorney & chief legal officer for the British Museum
Miss Marie Cox, mature saleslady in the British Museum shop
Rodger Artwright, independent expert on early Greek artefacts
Dr Manolis Seferis, curator of the Parthenon Museum, Athens
Robert Goodwin, Minister of Culture (et al) of the United Kingdom
Prime Minister of Greece (unnamed)
Prime Minister of the United Kingdom (unnamed)
Sir Archibald Grosvenor, British financier and donor
Sir Robert Mansfield, head of MI5, the British Intelligence Service
John Fiske, young agent in MI5 (British Intelligence)
Mikko, dealer in special "underground" electronic equipment
Emily Stone, assistant keeper of the manuscripts, British Museum
Trevor Green (Trev), friend of Peter Ryan from "south of the river"
Baby Jim, his strapping, manly son
George Travers, working on Quantum Computer Project with Adam
Detective Inspector Blake
Georgina Hardy, cleaning lady, British Museum

PART ONE

Chapter 1

Are you In or Out?

The Journey of a Thousand Miles begins with but a Single Step

Mid June, London, England

"I'm in!" Irini bubbled. "I've got the job in the museum. What did you want to see me about so urgently, Helena?" Irini had come directly from her final interview, down the British Museum's wide steps between the classical Greek columns, across Russell Street, and through the Victorian frosted, curlicued glass and mahogany door of the Museum Tavern.

"We're going to nick the Parthenon Marbles for Greece. We need you. Are you in, or out, for *that*?"

To Irini's incredulous stare Helena continued offhandedly, "Lift, steal, filch, purloin, pilfer, pocket."

Irini stared dumbfounded at her new closest friend and mentor. Yet flashing emerald eyes betrayed a cascade of brainwaves behind them.

Under Helena's tutelage Irini was emerging from her chrysalis of typical youthful insecurities. A few weeks back Helena would not have dared such a bold-faced challenge to her new friend. But she had sensed in her a deeply suppressed yearning for extravagant adventures, and played to it.

Irini decided that she could not yet trust herself to respond levelly to Helena's new challenge, so she changed the subject. She idly stroked Helena's hand, and smiled endearingly. "Thanks for encouraging me to make that impossible job application. It's my dream come true."

"You rated the position. My small contribution was simply to notice the fact."

"No, Helena, your profound insights into people's souls were hard won by twenty years in the Greek spy game. Thank you for sharing them with me – truly – appreciated."

"Intelligence Service, *ma cherie*; we don't admit to spying anymore, eh?"

"Certainly, if you say so. I do seem to remember the odd tale, from your very own lips, and not that long ago, about this company's secrets lifted, another's protected. Sounded pretty spyish to me."

"Industrial espionage – "

"My dictionary defines 'espionage' as 'spying', *n'est-ce pas.*"

"*Touché.*" Helena mused to herself that her protégée had acquired sharp teeth of late. It was a necessary part of the process, so she smiled and nodded; a fair point conceded.

The two had first met in the refectory of the London School of Economics. The LSE was arguably the pre-eminent university of the social sciences in the world. Helena's patient efforts to encourage Irini had sprung from a personal revelation, arising slowly from deep within herself. Despite her outstanding past career, Helena was suffering her own insecurities, the first time for her in such a life – hardly an affordable luxury in the spy-trade.

She had deliberately taken her 20-years-of-service early retirement to clear the cobwebs and seek a different life – something satisfying in the social sciences as a mature student at the LSE – but instead had failed to shake off a looming obsession, indeed a treacherous criminal enterprise of supreme difficulty. She had tried – God knows, she had tried – to sublimate it with books, class papers, and new friendships, Irini among them.

However, the subject under discussion with all three of her new friends inevitably came around – and her mental fixation always returned – to the *Marbles*. The fact that they shared her passion on the subject hadn't helped divert her. On the contrary, they often offered their own deeply emotional cries of outrage, and they weren't Greek. Except for Irini who had a Greek mother and a Welsh father.

Had Helena secretly hoped the subject would fall on the moral ambivalence of deaf ears, and so let her off the hook? Their unexpectedly passionate agreement and support for the developing vision of lifting them from the museum had deeply moved her, and shocked her with a fresh insight. Could it be that the motivation for her new life had always been to free herself for this specific vision, made reality?

This fresh awareness had awakened her three mornings ago, and she had not slept since. Helena was not in the least tired, and felt more alive than at any time in a life of living beyond herself.

Her depth of experience was such that to entertain the idea was tantamount to a certificate of potential feasibility, the essential first-step in any mission by her old service, NASA or any other cutting-edge enterprise. Over the three days this had morphed into the realization that this was her manifest destiny.

Helena was only mildly surprised to note from her friend's mutating facial expressions that Irini had accurately read most of these thoughts, in her view one of the highest skills of sensitivity. Each was learning from the other, and Helena knew that it had to cut both ways for their relationship to mature.

Irini realised that this had always been much more to Helena than a mere fantasy. Then she found her own voice again. "I do feel your passion … rather as the blind man hearing his deaf son, as if we had read each other's thoughts. It feels both real and intangible." Irini understood something else without having to hear it from Helena's lips. She was not alone; there were others to be involved.

Helena answered the implied question in the silent dialogue. "Two others here, and at least one back in Greece." Helena was being less than forthcoming, for she had not yet proffered a hint to her Spiros back in Athens. Was she afraid? Certainly, both by her feelings for him, and for the enterprise. Was she willing? When the time was right. Was that an excuse? Probably.

Indeed, she had not yet made that leap with her other two new friends here in London. Irini was the test case. The weakest link? By no means, yet perhaps she was the most vulnerable, emotionally and professionally. They had to have an insider, but her cocoon had only recently broken open, and it was asking a great deal of her 25 years. And equally of Helena's 42, with her self-promotion to spymaster. What would hers, hard-boiled old Charon, say to all this? She was afraid to let his face appear before her, as the obvious answer would confront her writ sternly upon its gaunt contours.

Irini was beginning to sense her predicament, and theirs. Yet in that brief interval of only a few minutes, her subconscious self had already made the choice. Irini's thirst for adventure had won out on a unanimous decision of that one indomitable side of her inner self against all the others.

Having followed most of this, Helena relaxed. With an acceptance in hand, or at least inevitable as she sensed it, there were only two or three to go. It was a start, and more than she should have hoped for.

Helena beckoned to the proprietor who obligingly came around the polished mahogany bar, wiping it clean with his ever-present cloth. He tucked it in his. belt, smiled broadly at his new and attractive client, took up Irini's hand and when he sensed her ease, kissed it lightly. "Charmed."

"Irini. Likewise."

He turned to Helena. "I have passed on your messages and packages as requested." Then back to Irini, "Until we meet again – did I hear that right – 'ee-ree-nee'?"

"Yes, thank you, well done!" Irini laughed softly without coyness.

"So, soon I hope." He smiled, and wiped his way among other tables and along the bar, engaging one and all with smiles of recognition punctuated in many cases by the knowing winks of a barman's shared secrets.

That evening, in a specially modified basement flat, Helena awaited the arrival of her putative team. None of them had met the others, and the two young men did not have the slightest inkling that she was recruiting them for the Heist of the Century – if that was the appropriate word – for she was no longer in anybody's service save her own.

Born Helena "Kat" Katsis, of Greek parents in Athens, she initially studied law there under some pressure from her attorney father. A follower she was not and after completing her first degree in criminology, entered directly into the Greek civil service, choosing a career that offered risk and intrigue.

It would underestimate her strengths and personal reserves to assert that she had left because of being burned out. There were those who said that behind her back, but many of these were either jealous of her extraordinary talents, or sorry to have lost her from the service. If there was any germ of truth to burnout, it was in deciding that one life was not enough for her, and that she could aspire to create and live another.

In the Middle East she would be described as a sabra type: medium height, strong body, silky-smooth brown skin, slim ankles, with long legs for her build, perhaps her best feature. She dressed to show this off, including stylish clinging trousers at work, and in the evening, full-length skirts with long slits in a seductive eastern style. She moved with an energetic gait, in long, confident strides, conveying forcefulness in all of her physical mannerisms.

She dyed her natural black hair a light brown, and usually wore it in waves to soften her strongly ovoid face and high forehead. This balanced widely spaced, deep set, commanding, luminous brown eyes, with green flecks that caught the sun and bright lights, the glints of passion, and sudden mood changes that crossed them like clouds passing over the moon.

Helena had the typical Greek respect for their ancient culture, adoring Aristophanes for his wit, irony and humour; and equally Sophocles, revelling in his dark side and the hard realities of history. She also entertained the sardonic thought that today's politicians would do well to take more careful note of the altruistic aspirations in the *Socratic Dialogues* of Plato.

Yet she identified equally with the fiery partisanship of Kazantzakis in his recent books about struggles and the quest for freedom. She saw herself as a crusader, and it was the rare undertaking, whether of an hour, or a year, that failed to draw this flavour of commitment from her.

Helena had acquired a strong sense of social justice, yet nobody duped her. More significantly, she rarely fooled herself. Her passions could overcall good judgment for a time, but a healthy restraint had been earned by hard experience. She would not have survived long in her world otherwise – one she had played in for keeps, taking on some of the most dangerous assignments available on her watch, fully demanding of all her skills and charms.

Uncomfortable and unexpected though it was, she had recently been forced to admit to herself that danger was a drug she needed in life and relationships. Was this another hidden motivation that had brought her to this moment?

Her secure digital mobile telephone chimed, and she keyed the necessary codes. A face bloomed to life on the tiny hand-held screen. "I'm at station alpha, all clear."

Helena stepped to the computer console, and commanded the hidden camera outside to scan the street. There was nothing untoward visible, so she pressed "transmit" on the mobile, "Come." She watched on the monitor as her visitor entered the narrow alley leading to the basement flat she had designated "Safe House One". Was she being too cautious? Was it too early to worry? They didn't have a team yet, never mind a plan, but she did have a dream that the others had joked about with her for several months. So far it had been nothing more than the kind of banter that entertains university students – she smiled inwardly – of any age. Given a fair wind, this would all change tonight.

Adam Blix, Blitz to his good-natured enemies, descended the short flight of steps, casting an appealing smile into the security camera. Helena made one more scan of the street, then pressed the release. He bounced down the remaining steps, and bounded into the room. The energy of youth, she thought to herself, yet his seemed more like that of a six-year-old than an adult of 23.

He crossed the small room, and kissed her cheek-to-cheek on both sides, bending forward to accommodate his six-foot two-inch frame to her. He was one of those in-between types, almost too slender, yet his square forehead and strong chin outlined a face in good balance, topped by a shock of wavy fair hair.

"So, what's up, Doc?" His Americanisms grated on some, but she had come to like them. In any case they came with the package, and she knew well enough to take it that way. She also recognized that he was a bit of a loose cannon, and controlling him could be part of the challenge. She welcomed it, and him, because he was the best, and she had learned that they always came up trumps in the end if anyone could.

He was a loner by preference, the product, as she saw it, of growing up in a typically chaotic home of two working parents in a city like New York. At age 12 he had worked out a secret coding algorithm for sending messages between computers that governments couldn't crack and selflessly sent it out on the Internet; their best-laid plans thwarted by a child. This was just the start, and he went on to graduate from the prestigious Bronx High School of Science, then across the Atlantic to Imperial College, University of London. Helena knew that he was now working on his PhD, as the youngest member of the world's leading research team in Quantum Computing.

"Okay, Helena, what's this cloak and dagger business all about? Secret notes and strange packages from bartenders instead of meeting you directly." He waved a small piece of paper under her nose. "Do this, do that, turn right, turn left, wait here, memorize the codes for the new digital super-secure mobile phones that came in the box – actually I liked that bit – but was tempted to just walk up and knock."

Helena fixed him with a pair of glittering eyes, halting him in mid-breath. She punctuated each word with a stab to his chest of her strong index finger. "Don't – you – EVER – question – a security matter with me – never – ever – again. Gottit!"

Adam paused for one eye blink. "Okay."

She knew him well enough to accept his apparently light acquiescence as a binding contract, and she probably would not need to mention it again. She served him his favourite drink, gin and orange juice, and he sat down in one of four identical armchairs circling a modest, round table.

The mobile phone chimed again, right on the quarter-hour she had allowed between the appointed times, and she repeated the same admission procedure.

"Mister Ryan, I would like you to meet Mister Blix." She had intentionally made the introduction initially formal to set the mood for serious business. Adam jumped up and warmly shook his hand.

Peter's eyes flitted around the room, missing little, and then relaxed a notch to smile a bit warily. "Peter Ryan. It's a pleasure, Mister Blitz." Adam winced. He suddenly realized how tiresome his nickname could be and that it would probably be accidentally rediscovered many times.

"Blix, Adam Blix." It had come out exactly like Ian Fleming's legendary line.

"Sorry, mate." Peter apologized with a strong clap on the shoulder, everyone sharing a chuckle.

Helena recalled her first meeting with him across a refectory table at the LSE. He had caught her attention on earlier occasions by being one of the volunteers who guided the blind or disabled students.

He was nearly thirty, offered an engaging smile, a stud earring in the left ear, and a tattoo just peeking out under the right cuff of his denim jacket. The fully shaven head of his youth had been moderated into a closely cropped crew cut. This focused attention on the profile of his unusually mobile face, which had captivated Helena from the beginning. It amply illustrated his ready wit and acerbic sense of humour. He was of average height, but well founded on sturdy legs with forearms of considerable strength. He would not have quite passed the physical for a job as a bouncer, but anyone who discounted him in a dark alley would be unpleasantly surprised. Perhaps this was the inevitable result of two years in the army, and later stints as a lorry driver and warehouseman on the rough south side of London.

It was his membership in the Transport and General Worker's Union, courtesy of a sensitive convener, that had brought him to the LSE on the Trade Union Studies program. She also knew he had *promoted* the odd lorry load from time to time in each of his three past careers.

Helena understood both his background and his ongoing transformation. Although he had readily agreed with her that the Elgins were a travesty of misplaced morality, and shown many other signs of a burgeoning maturity, she knew he was also the toughened product of his background, and would fill the roles she had in mind for him.

She thought he had been lucky to stay out of trouble. He therefore demonstrably possessed that essential additional quality that augmented all the others – the one that couldn't be taught and was perhaps the most vital of all – he was lucky.

Helena's next guest transfixed the two young men. "Miss Irini Baynes, Adam Blix and Peter Ryan."

"Charmed." Adam could not help staring at this apparition of loveliness, which fortunately she didn't see, having turned to shake Peter's hand.

"Enchanté." Peter was delighted to try out this expression from his French studies for the first time. It fit perfectly his feelings at that moment.

"Irini." The word echoed in the long corridors of Adam's nether brain, and a hot flush surged like a Thames tide to the top of his head. He was sure that Irini would notice, but she simply smiled warmly to each in turn, and sat down in her chair.

The men certainly noticed that she surpassed many contemporary models, neither so thin nor under endowed. Her nose was perhaps slightly longer than she wished for in the mirror, but it ended in a turned-up expression promising an up-beat personality, a persona she was endeavouring to accentuate. The forehead and chin were straight and square, the eyes frank and spacious. She wore her straight auburn hair bobbed short for comfort and practicality.

Was she too good for her 25 years? Irini wouldn't have agreed, yet Helena had pegged her with extraordinary internal strengths, and a certain vulnerability – more than a little fear of succumbing to deep personal or physical attachment.

Irini was not a cold woman. She smiled frequently and deeply, enjoyed the company of others in public, and was not put off by the fact that every male, and some women, thought about coming on to her for a date. She had acquired the rare skill of being able to employ a thick skin, without the overt forms of rejection that many extraordinarily beautiful women learn early and rarely outgrow. She was therefore welcomed in most gatherings of both intellectuals and party-types, could comfortably enjoy either, and they her.

Her credentials, a postgraduate diploma in the history of art at the Courtauld, London University, and her PhD thesis underway on the origins of Greek Sculpture, had proved worthy enough for the British Museum.

The thought had occurred to Helena that despite this she may have been selected over others by the museum because she was part Greek, perhaps a little friendly reverse discrimination due to moves afoot to placate the Greeks, short of actually returning the Marbles.

Irini took straight orange juice, Adam his usual orange blossom, made light at his request, and Peter a Newcastle Brown. Helena sat down last with her one allotted gin and tonic. "I think we may need these. Cheers." A chorus echoed her.

She looked straight at Irini, the question between them hanging unspoken in the sudden stillness. Irini replied cautiously. "I was hoping for a lifetime career here in London, as you know. Perhaps in a museum, or even *the* museum, or maybe journalism or television."

Helena was reassured because she had used the past tense, thereby suggesting that a favourable decision was still in the offing. Helena keenly felt the magnitude of the sacrifice she would have to make for a country she had certainly visited, and admired, but was not her own. Irini acquired dual citizenship by birth, but had exercised her choice in favour of the United Kingdom at the age of eighteen, and had lived most of her life in London.

Irini didn't trust herself to speak again, so she merely nodded to Helena, and set her face to a brave new future, one that a few hours before would have seemed so bizarre as to be without a shred of credibility.

The two men were now openly perplexed, and Helena reassured them with a benign smile that was anything but. "All of you know me and my background well enough, and I assure you that it is real. So perhaps a few words from each of you at this point might help us get acquainted. I will feel free to comment if you leave out any of the more interesting bits."

Adam, ever the optimist, and a bit of a showman, made a good job of it. He got Irini to laugh herself half out of what was some sort of melancholy or at least concern about something important and unresolved. Meanwhile, he was trying to solve the puzzle.

Peter used his wit and light touch to carry off a tough assignment. Helena was sure she was right to force them all to blow their own horns. It brought out an extra helping of humility, and muted their natural youthful hubris. This was another necessary step towards creating a team of the supreme quality needed for such a challenge, rather than a loosely knit group of strong individualists. It was a tightrope walk, because both of these personal qualities were essential to success – but they had to be in balance.

Irini could have said almost anything because the two lads were all eyes, entranced and involved.

Then, suddenly, Adam thought he had it, catching the gold ring as the merry-go-round of his mind came around. "God, Helena, you're not serious?" He already knew the answer before she returned just the flicker of a nod. "We were all just kidding, joking around, like everybody does; it's part of student life!"

Peter hadn't quite caught the drift, but then it hit him as well. "You're not – you *are* serious, aren't you?"

"I have never been more serious about anything in my life."

Helena swivelled the 21-inch computer monitor around beside her so that everyone could see. It felt like the old days again as she clicked the first slide onto the screen from within the obscure depths of *Microsoft's Presentation Manager*.

She paused to look inside herself. This was the last chance to turn back. They would be giving up lives in the United Kingdom, she certainly hoped not literally, but undoubtedly as a viable country of residence. She knew that Irini had seen this from the first instant in the Museum Tavern that morning.

It would be the most notorious crime of the young century, and maybe back another 50 years to the Great Train Robbery. They probably wouldn't be hunted down as assiduously as if they tunnelled into the Bank of England and lightened the load in that institution – although this was an idea that would certainly have appealed to both men! They would be barred from the UK if they succeeded. If they failed, they would not be able to *leave*, and the accommodation wouldn't meet steerage class standards.

Her mind echoed, "*It's the old days again for me.*" This sharp truth shuddered through her. She loved her new academic world, the friends, and colleagues. Wouldn't this inevitably force her back into the old game, indeed as Spy*master*? Could she limit this to a brief diversion in her new life plan? Would she want to? The fear of losing the new world she had set out to create gnawed at her gut. This inner conflict was far more upsetting than the physical risks that undeniably lay in wait for them.

Helena set her jaw in resolute acquiescence. "The first slides are your brief C-V résumés." She clicked through them at a leisurely pace. "The first real meat here is your potential roles and duties, should you agree to take the assignment."

Adam smiled thinly, and not just to conceal his irregular lower teeth. "Where have we heard *that* one before? Helena, does your tape self destruct?" He was referring to the TV show *Mission Impossible* that was on reruns yet again.

"And one wonders if 'impossible' isn't the operable word, Helena." Peter added, but he leaned forward and cast a serious eye on her hard-won plans.

Helena eyes crinkled. "Well, we'll just have to see, and take it one step at a time." The slide on the screen read:

Personnel and Roles

Helena Katsis – Command and Control, Strategic Planning
Irini Baynes – Inside Jobs, Reconnaissance, Contacts
(and Diversions in the museum)
Adam Blix – Defeat museum Security and Technical Support
Peter Ryan – Logistics, Lift Team Recruitment and Command
S. A. – Command & Control (Greece), Finance & Resources
Others Only if Absolutely Necessary

File: OpEl Ver1.02 NoHD-Save Encrypted: GammaBlix-3.27
Page 5 of 41

"So that's why you asked me for the latest encryption release, eh, Helena?"

"Absolutely, Adam. Nothing but the best on this heist."

"Well, a lot of people have worked on it since my day." Adam spoke wistfully, as if he were an elderly emeritus of something or other. On reflection, Helena saw more than a germ of truth in that image.

As he had said to her only a few days earlier, "Sure, I had my day, and it was a hell of a fun ride, but you know it was nothing special, the *average* twelve-year-old knows more about this sort of thing than I do now." Yet he still felt a justifiable pride in the fact that the system had been named after him.

"And you are using a removable disk, nothing on the hard drive. By the book, Helena."

"I had the best of teachers." At this, Adam did blush slightly.

Irini had been smiling enigmatically all through this exchange. "So what was all that then, about my 'Diversions at the museum'?"

Adam and Peter, the latter particularly, could not conceal knowing smiles.

"I think we all may have rather different ideas about the kinds of diversions that may be required of me in the museum." She didn't really mind, and gave this reply tongue in cheek, pert nose raised defiantly.

Peter had been looking at Adam quite intently. "The jobs assigned to me are right up my street, and most of the others too, I

12

s'pose, but that's a pretty heavy load on Adam's shoulders, eh? 'Defeat museum security' just like that!" Peter snapped his fingers. Helena nodded, "Yes, that's the key – no pun intended." Adam shrugged. "Yes, well, it all depends. Some are easier than others. With Irini inside, we can have a look-see." Helena then touched on some of the issues that had fired their earlier discussions.

Reasons and Rationale

Justice
History
Retribution
Pricking Egos
Deflating Pooh-Bahs
Entertainment

File: Op ElVer1.02 NoHD-Save Encrypted: GammaBlix-3.27

This would have been called "Justification Summary" on a mainstream project, but this was hardly that, and Helena had amused herself with headings that resonated for them.

As to justice, Helena and Irini had decided that it boiled down to whether or not the Parthenon Marbles were a special case. The museum claimed with some justification that a general repatriation policy would empty the great museums of the world. Yet they, and others, felt the Marbles were special for many reasons, ranging from the questionable motives and profit made by Lord Elgin, through their unique symbolism for western civilization, to elemental patriotism.

Historically, the Acropolis and Parthenon in Athens were arguably the first major monumental embodiments of western civilization. The history was emotionally compelling, and not only to Greeks. All three had earlier agreed with Helena on this point.

Then they had a bit of fun with the last four items, joking a bit like old times, a welcome break in what they knew was serious business.

This led naturally into a discussion of the more detailed political arguments and the positions taken publicly by the British Museum and government officials. This was a full page on the screen:

The Position of the British Museum vis-à-vis the Elgins

1. The range of the museum's collections is worldwide.
2. The visitor can encompass all times and cultures in one place at the same time.
3. Preservation here has been better than that in Greece.
4. The museum has an obligation to present all collections intact – A loan would detract from that obligation.
5. Everyone expects to find the Elgin Marbles on display there. The Parthenon Gallery is "one of the central places of earth".
6. Elgin is defamed in attempts to repatriate the Marbles. He was just one of many Ambassadors wanting to promote understanding at home of the ancient and modern cultures they encountered on their travels.
7. The sculptures are "where they will remain": They *admit* they do not want to loan or repatriate them!
8. If symbolic gestures for 2004 and beyond are wanted then the Greeks should build a decent museum for what they already have.
9. We are making exact duplicates in marble to put in it. Implication that Greece should be satisfied with the copies.

File: OpEl Ver1.02 NoHD-Save Encrypted: GammaBlix-3.27
Page 16 of 41

Adam, as always, went to the logical heart. "The first three are simple facts with no bearing on the issues."

Irini chose perspective. "The Greeks, like the Spanish, have only recently been able to form stable and relatively prosperous democratic governments, and accede to the European Union as valued members. It isn't fair to make that comparison."

Helena did not entirely agree. "It is to our shame that we have only recently taken account of these preservation issues."

"That small truth does not a *mezes*-feast make, does it?" Irini added.

"Four and five are bollocks!" Peter exclaimed, visibly angry. "Self-serving bastards. The *centre of the earth* as they put it, if it's anywhere in this, it is high on the Acropolis in Athens."

Helena found it immensely endearing that he could feel so strongly about a place he had not yet visited, but she understood why this agreed with his broadening perspectives.

Irini tipped her head and garnished it with a sly wink. "I agree that treasures were taken from many places for our national museum, and others, but that doesn't make it right. The Elgin history is tainted in my view, as some members of Parliament pointed out in about 1816 when the government agreed to pay him off, and send the spoils over to the British Museum. I don't believe that this gives the museum the sole right to hold them." A sheepish look crossed her face. "I know I should be supporting all this as a new employee of the museum, yet I can't bring myself to defend such rubbish. Peter was right, it is self serving, and the real arguments must be found elsewhere."

Peter snapped, "Helena. The last two offend me personally, and I suspect they are offensive to the people and government of Greece."

The room was silent. Helena switched off the computer, and gazed from one to the next. There was a palpable uneasiness in the room.

The dam burst first in Peter. "Bloody hell, Helena! You've known all along the sting in the snake's tail that's squirming around this table – and it isn't a little one."

Adam took up the cudgel. "He's right. What the heck happens to us *afterwards*, even if we are successful? We certainly know what happens if we are not – and, I'm not sure the first isn't worse than the second?"

Peter shook his head. "It's what we called a 'no win' proposition, down by the docks."

"Well," Helena replied with the only answer she had been able to think of after six months of rehearsals for this very moment. "This is a *Greek* drama, and you all know what is required of *our* heroes."

Peter was no expert on this subject, nor was Adam, but Irini understood precisely what Helena meant. She knew deep down that it was up to her to make the point, if she was ready. It was her last chance, and the moment of truth for all of them.

Through her close friendship with Helena, Irini had sensed that missed chances were the worst disease of later life, the one mistake that ruined everything else. If she had a chance for love but didn't take it, nothing would ever be in balance again. Or equally, if she ran away from the risk of becoming a nameless casualty in such a worthwhile battle, then self-doubts would poison the rest of her life. There was no real choice for her. Everything must be risked at the cusp, which always arrived unbidden at the most awkward moment.

Irini looked Peter straight in the eye, then Adam, and gave her answer to Helena's conundrum – and for her, that of life. "Sacrifice is the essence of our humanity. We would always regret missing this moment and our chance to make a difference. Believe me, and as the ancient Greeks well knew, regret is a slow, painful death, far worse than a lifetime in the shadows of prison bars."

The two men knew that her sacrifice was greater than theirs. For her it wasn't a question of risks or a win-lose situation.

Irini continued implacably, her conscious mind now firmly made up. "There are three possible paths at this crossroads, not just two. We can win our quest, lose our quest, or run away from it. The last is a *fatal* loser; the regrets would destroy our lives. The second is uncomfortable to be sure, but it's not fatal. The first is also in many ways unpalatable. We will need the courage to make new lives far from here, in a fresh world of our own making."

Irini turned to Helena and confirmed for the third and binding time that day, "I'm in."

Helena intentionally did not look at the other two, and busied herself with the removable diskette and computer housekeeping.

Adam felt he had the easier of the decisions remaining, and didn't want to pressurize Peter, so kept his counsel. Helena noticed this, and her respect for him notched up.

Peter had stepped into the unknown only once before in his life, when he walked across the ancient causeway over the grand moat towards Angkor Wat. That single day had been his epic turning point. It had led to a new life, uncomfortable though the transition had been, and as he sensed they always were. He now realised that the life you need and want cannot be known in advance. To reach it you must yield to the temptation of the quest, for it may not pass your way again. Irini was right. They didn't have a choice if they were to live. Another quotation inscribed on something he had seen recently came back to him. *Dum vivimos, vivamos.* "To live, *live!*" He turned to Irini. "Thank you." Then to Helena, "I'm in, all the way."

Adam, taking Irini's hand on his left and Peter's on his right, was then free to close the circle of Ouroboros, by saying, "Freedom or Death. I'm in."

Chapter 2

Advance into to the Past

After a Thousand Ships, what is One More for a Helen?

The next day

The plane was poised for takeoff on the wide, open runway at Heathrow Airport, and Helena was debriefing herself on the final scene at the safe house. The serious faces of her young partners as they closed the circle made a moving moment, and Adam's quotation from Kazantzakis, the title of her favourite book and personal battle cry, brought a lump to her throat. Then another uncomfortable feeling surfaced – was she risking them to serve her own needs? Worse, was she using them?

The brakes were released, and her thoughts switched to the reunion with Spiros. Helena tensed her body so as to sense fully the eternal thrill of acceleration at takeoff, that amazing upward thrust that for her had never palled. It always made her think of sex.

She wondered for how long that would still enthral, between her and Spiros, or with another yet to come? Would it outlive the wonder of takeoff, or vice-versa? There was much shared experience, as both joys and sorrows had bonded them, so that when they met, they could use the language known only to them, imbued with special meaning, the common reference points, the unique shorthand of love.

She was confident of her ability to present the case for the conspiracy in the way most likely to appeal to him. She knew that unpredictability had an enormous appeal, which kept him young at heart and on his toes. He sought to use his wealth and influence for worthy causes, but particularly those that were just by his lights. If it smacked of the unusual or dangerous, so much the better to spice the *stifado*, the Greek stew, of life.

She smiled as she recalled one of his favourite anecdotes. He'd got even with a particularly tiresome, self-righteous adversary, who had put his foot wrong just once too often, "a real stinko" as Spiros had put it, eyes twinkling.

On this gentleman's return to Beverly Hills from a high-level business trip, he stood transfixed in horror and incredulity, when he saw his elegant, white mansion dripping from portico to swimming pool, in what he later learned was best-grade, agricultural, liquid pig slurry.

As he stood there with his jaw resting on his chest, the deep-throated rumble of the United States' largest propjet cargo aircraft, the C-130, drew his eyes upward. It was flying so low that he instinctively ducked as it made its final bombing run. The slops splashed across the driveway, as he dived for cover in the hedge, and it had to be the only thorny one in the garden. His suitcase, dropped in his haste to escape, had been buried in it. Helena was never quite sure about Spiros and his stories, because he did have a tendency to embellish them, so perhaps this part was apocryphal.

The Federal Aviation Agency instituted a major investigation, for such goings-on were most certainly beyond the pale. It turned out that this target was not of the inner brotherhood. He had made enemies, the President himself included; indeed he might have ordered the same treatment if he had had the power (or the guts he later admitted to Spiros). So nothing really came of it, and the pilot was never publicly identified. Spiros had privately claimed to her that he was a Greek air force Colonel.

He would always conclude his story with the words, "At least it was good for the garden," then a wink and a satisfied smile, "my silver lining to this particular practical joke. Vengeance is sweet for the perpetrator," and holding up a dramatic finger, "it can be smelly for my victim." Spiros had only rarely reached into his arsenal for such punishments, but he always insisted that the source be unknown, a ready explanation to hand, and always the silver lining.

Helena couldn't help snorting a laugh out loud, noticed by two others sitting in her row. She smiled an apology, but the image persisted in her mind, for Spiros had actually shared this anecdote with that very same President later in his retirement – and, she suspected, the Greek Prime Minister as well.

Helena appreciated the fact that he reserved his most elegant remedies for those who needlessly attacked people who were under his protection, or who had done him selfless service.

Helena had refused Spiros' kind offer of a First Class upgrade, but had taken the usual free Business Class seat, always available to her through their close friendship with the President of Olympic Airways. This provided an opportunity for her to work in comfort on the preparation of the written dossier she intended to present to him.

Her fingers flew across the notebook computer, facial expressions running the gamut of emotions as each point was analysed and justified.

She was determined to keep the paperwork between them as clear as possible with a detailed analysis of potential difficulties and weak links, along with the expenses and team backgrounds. And always with special emphasis on the ever-critical single points of failure that she well knew were the most important.

She fell asleep in her seat, and shortly after that her laptop computer ran out of juice, and shut down, the screen blanking. She began to relive in snatches of memory, her impressions of Spiros and the complexities of their relationship.

Spiros Anguelopoulos was far more than a player of expensive practical jokes. His wealth had sprung somewhat improbably from the establishment of a biscuit factory just after World War Two by his father. Nobody at the time thought that this venture, the first of its kind, stood a chance in Greece. There were few pre-packaged goods at all on the market shelves, and biscuits were not among them. Through dint of good management and luck, the more reliable of the two in Spiros' view, his father had achieved a modest fortune.

When Spiros took over at the age of only 31 he diversified into tobacco, a perhaps regrettable yet unquestionably profitable staple of Greece. He bought farms in Greece and Thailand, and controlled the whole process through to the finished products spinning off the mass production lines in Xanthe. He had never tolerated middlemen in any of his businesses since. "From cradle to grave, and you're always one up on the others."

He was ten years older, with a touch of the attractive father in it for her. He was very proud of his leather bound tomes, in what he lovingly referred to as his library, though he rarely cracked open anything other than an *airline read*. He particularly loved spy thrillers, and this was another attraction because Helena had been in the game. While she wouldn't allude to any detail that might compromise a colleague in the service, she could weave her own tales, and entrance him for the whole of a Sunday without any difficulty, and he was a man who could hold his own with Presidents and Prime Ministers.

Spiros moved in top government circles as a friend of many in high places, and believed that this was often a stronger bond than if he had actually been in government. He was a source of contributions, contacts, and the ability to get things done, openly or clandestinely, inside or outside the normal channels. This often made the critical difference for those in power. He was certainly a notable eminence *grise*.

As such he was perhaps the most effective facilitator of his day in Greece. On a personal level, his sunny, open, good-humoured personality made him desirable and accessible to members of both sexes, young and old. The young, whom he often employed or guided to serve the needs of the older establishment, both respected and trusted him personally.

His word was his bond in all such undertakings. His self-respect and pride, his *philotimo*, was strong even for a Greek, and everyone knew, friend or enemy, that when necessary he could be totally ruthless. If he set in motion such a course of action the targets would understand that their days were numbered. Sometimes such a nemesis would go into exile without the need for direct action. In other cases Spiros told stories that sometimes chilled her, names changed to protect the guilty.

She knew he was an expert on Greek poetry, and had noticed that only these leather books in his library showed signs of wear on the spines. She sensed that this was the yearning side of his nature, perhaps his deepest hidden need, one that he himself had not yet put his finger on. A yearning for what, neither of them could yet say – it had come up many times in pillow talk. Maybe this was the key to reaching him in her present quest.

Spiros waited impatiently to meet her at the airport, having extricated himself from a high-level meeting, frankly thankful for having such a good excuse.

His large head was balanced by a strong chin, coupled with a permanent smile. It was an accident of genetics that his lips turned up instead of down. He had no doubt that this was a built-in advantage in dealing with people, and often quipped that hadn't everyone noticed that all successful used car salesmen shared this trait?

His nose was "classic plus" something that bothered him in his youth, but he later decided that "it loved him". He was otherwise a typical Greek middleweight, tending to a slight corpulence, "useful fat with muscle" as he sometimes put it, not without justice. His hirsute genes were in evidence, giving him the irresistible long eyelashes and classical Greek curls.

Meeting a lover, like Helena, had a powerful rejuvenating effect on him, and anticipation had produced many pleasurable thrills more reminiscent of his twenties than his fifties. He was repeatedly elated then frustrated as he watched the arrivals from London file through the sliding doors. They popped open and closed with each gaggle of eager arrivals, and he didn't know which opening would reveal her.

At last he saw her, with her radiant smile, warm and tangible in his embrace. After several bear hugs and amorous squeezings, he remembered to present to her, with a touch of mock formality, one delicate gardenia. He knew she shunned the predictable, as he did – the ubiquitous, obligatory large bouquet for VIPs, or offered to the returning wives by errant husbands.

She took a long, appreciative, lingering sniff of its perfume, and then tucked it meaningfully in her bosom with a mischievous light in her dark eyes. She linked arms with Spiros, who took the cue, and guided her as of old towards the limousine.

Seated with drinks in his penthouse suite overlooking Athens from the heights of *Lycevetos*, he leaned towards her and whispered softly, "*Agape mou*."

"I love you too."

He sensed that there was more to this visit than the possibility – perhaps probability as he hoped at this moment – that they might take up where they had left off several times before. This was not a negative evaluation in any sense. That had been the nature of their lovership, on for a time, when they could, then off again. Every reprise so far had carried the deeply satisfying benefit of freshness, and one could always hope, against experience, that it might continue forever. Their love was of that kind, the belief in its foreverness.

Helena had read this in his face, and he knew she had. "Well, no time like the present." She clicked open her briefcase, and withdrew a removable computer disk. "Your grey box where it always was?"

He led her by the hand into what was his study, but he always referred to it as The Library. It was a dark Aladdin's cave in stark contrast to the luminous, soaring glass panels that revealed Athens and the Acropolis spread out beyond. Spiros could have owned a palace here, but chose this superb yet rather more modest place because it had the best view in Athens. He also had his own private island, which they had visited on several earlier romantic interludes. Considering what she had in mind, she felt this was singularly appropriate as the command and control centre "East".

The printer whirred, plop-plopping the printed pages of her prospectus into the basket. Spiros grabbed a stack, and reclined in his form-fitting, lazy-boy chair. His persona instantly changed to "all-business", and he read each page carefully, sometimes re-reading, occasionally taking a swipe with an orange highlight marker. The document was substantial, and while he read, Helena went out to make tea, rolling the tea trolley back laden with the sweets she knew he loved. There were plenty in both the fridge and freezer, and she had laid them all out geometrically on a large plate. The baklavas were crisp and oozing honey. The kataïfi were the real thing, honey-soaked with chopped almonds. And finally, profiteroles with the whipped cream interior left partly frozen from the freezer, topped in this case with brown-sugar frosting instead of chocolate.

She felt that a sugar coating for her ultimate disclosure to him might prove beneficial. Helena had been initially confident that he would at least give her audacious idea some consideration. Faced with the reality she could not suppress the cold chills of rising doubt. The moment had arrived as she sat down on his chair's armrest, and slipped a small sliver of baklava into his mouth.

"Well, my golden one, you've got a hell of a team put together here. I'd give them decent odds on the Crown Jewels. Isn't a page missing?" He was thumbing through the now dishevelled wad of papers fanned out in his ample hands. "So – what's the play?"

She smiled and remained silent, truth to tell at this moment unable to verbalize the answer because she had been overwhelmed with emotions that drowned out everything else. She was no longer there in the room, but off in another place, one she had before reached only after passing the point of total exhaustion in lovemaking and once or twice in the service of her beloved Greece, life in the balance. She could only manage a feeble, "Guess."

This annoyed him slightly, because he didn't like guessing games, but then he felt her uncertainty. He had seen it a time or two in her before, when she thought she was in over her head in the intelligence game, and he felt satisfaction that she still had this confidence in him. He knew she hadn't really been in too deep, but when the worm turned, or the unexpected happened, she could be prone to feelings of insecurity. He had found that a wise word or two, with maybe a little help from him behind the scenes, had always been enough for someone of her calibre.

Spiros had a strong intuitive mind, and he reviewed what might have committed Helena to this degree, rather than trying to work it out logically. And so, an idea – a wonderfully frightening idea – insinuated itself into his consciousness. He cocked his head, with just the hint of a grimace. She read him, and replied with her face, for she was still unable to speak and be certain her voice would obey.

His first reaction was shock at the thought, then disbelief at the audacity, and finally settled on amazement at the concept. "You're not serious?" Nevertheless he knew that she was.

Now the ball was on his side of the net, as she handed over the missing page, the Mission Statement. It always came first, this tactical exception only proving the rule. Spiros opened his capacious mouth, and Helena shoved all the rest of a whole baklava in, like posting a packet. She thought it was an appropriate image for her other offering, now clenched tightly with knuckles whitening in his strong hands. He was almost able to swallow it whole.

"Giff me ten minutes." With this, he began reading the document again, beginning with the appropriate page one.

Helena was in a self-imposed torment of the damned as she waited outside in the salon for the ten minutes of eternity, that became thirty. She had touched on the law as a possible career, but could not remember if a long or a short jury deliberation was a good or a bad sign.

She feared the worst when Spiros came out of the library. He had the most serious expression she had ever seen on his face. "Damn," she thought to herself, "I should have done this some other way."

Then, inexplicably, Spiros knelt down in front of her, took her hand, and kissed it. He was weeping! "I am your Knight, my Queen. My Fortune, My Honour, and My Life are yours to Command. My God, Helena." He rose and thrust his fists to the ceiling, obviously feeling he could actually punch through it some five metres above his head.

"THIS is what I have waited my whole life for. *Eee mira mas. Mira.* **MIRA.** YES. *This* is our destiny!"

Helena flew into his arms, and he swept her up off the floor, padding solidly across the polished teak, then up the stairs to the bedroom. He tossed her lovingly yet firmly into the middle of the bed. It was obvious to her that he was in an altered state of consciousness, perhaps an unpredictable one. She was ready to make love with him, but wondered now if she had overplayed her hand!

Her unmatchable first love had been with him, with all the delightful uncertainties, faux pas, and ultimate coming to terms with being transformed from a girl into a woman. The position reversed in the later evolution of their relationship. He was the solid businessman and confidant of Prime Ministers. She was the youthful, keyed-up spy, risking herself every day in a dangerous game, and her approach to lovemaking with him could be frenetic. These were the contrasts that had forged strong bonds of passion, and yet in each iteration of their sexual relationship, had also forced them apart. Theirs was in this sense a classic *get away closer* love. Certainly much more drew them together, than any centrifugal force could ultimately oppose.

He was tearing off his clothes literally, and having trouble with the trousers, for the reason in this instance that he was an extremely well endowed man, not a negligible point in his favour when it came right down to it. She bounced herself off the side of the bed, and came around it to him. "Spiro. Spiro."

"Ow!" Now he had done it, caught some tender bit in the zipper. Helena kissed him, softly, languorously.

"Damn!" He really had done himself an injury. Then he sat down on the bed and started to cry once again. There was no hesitation. Helena was instantly installed as the loving mother, at least for a precious few, needful minutes.

When he could speak through his sobs, he said one of the most wonderful things anyone had ever said to her. "I was dying, Helena, and you have resurrected me as surely as Lazarus."

"Scholars are not so sure about that, you know." She whispered the accompanying laugh, and blew it into his ear.

"Helena, I'm feeling my age. Call it a mid-life crisis if you must side with the unhappy shrinks and dim-witted philosophers of our age. I know that my life is more than half over, at least as a strong, healthy man and mind. I have the fatal disease we are all born with, the terror of aging. What have I left behind? What legacy do I leave for the world? More important, for history – the history we as Greeks

25

worship like no other nationality. Can you begin to feel the power of the gift you have brought to me this day? I love you more than life."

Helena kissed the tears from Spiros' face, and began to massage his eyes, as she eased him down on the bed. His strong legs hung over the end at the knees. She knelt down and took off his shoes and socks. "See, the trousers come off much easier if the shoes go first." He chuckled. "I feel like a teenager again, my first time."

"Let's make it like that for both of us. Softly, oh so tenderly." She matched her actions to the words, beginning by massaging his feet and the knotted calves of his lower legs. The tension dissipated in a few minutes, a long time on one plane, and just a quiet moment in another.

He had come down from Mount Olympus, and she could slip his zipper without inflicting any further injury. The trousers came off easily now, and he sat up on the bed, but she pressed him back down. The remains of his shirt lay on the floor, so with the underpants away as well, he was at her mercy, and she granted it with absolution.

"Do you have any oils; candles; incense?" He nodded at a cabinet in the corner, and in a trice, two flames were dancing on the bedside tables with joss sticks beginning to perfuse the room with jasmine. She drew him up for a moment, turned down the bed underneath, and invited him to lie down again. He brushed a kiss on her left breast as he eased himself back. This burned like fire, then transformed itself into a shout that echoed back and forth, to and from the nape of her neck.

While on holiday in Thailand, they had taken advantage of the basic Thai body massage, a full two hours of oily bliss. She did her best to reproduce every pressure point, stroke, and nuance. She wouldn't have earned her diploma that night, but they weren't counting the points.

In the end he was fully in a trance, rippling small orgasms moving from one centre to the next, outlying points working just as effectively as a light breath at his centre of pleasure. "Okay," she whispered in his ear at last, "let's take a shower."

He had a good one with four pulsating, horizontal nozzles to supplement the standard overhead, and he returned reluctantly from that other realm of the mind to which she had sent him. If this was death, he had thought more than once on his journey, then I'm not afraid of it any more.

Helena made tea, and brought the rest of the sweets back upstairs. They fell upon this sugary feast as though it was a full course of *mezethes*. "Act two," was all that Spiros said.

He didn't give the Thai massage, for he didn't want the necessary second interruption that use of oil would require. Instead, he played on his Helena of the Thousand Ships, as upon the ancient Greek lyre, sotto voce. The tips of fingers, the turn to the nails, one or five or ten, the tongue, lips, and legendary nose were all pressed into service, often in concert.

Then the butterfly-tongue for the best part of an hour, and she was away, flying out of her body, leaving it far behind, as she later confessed, laced with tears, for the first time in her life.

To bring her back, and then reach the ultimate release, he made love to her in a way he had never done before, softly, slowly, side by side, face to face, legs crossed over. The rise and fall of their subdued passions, ebbed and flowed like the tiny tides of the Aegean Sea – but then the moon was full and a storm was blowing up. And thus it was finished, light clouds scudding across Selene's face, even as the candles gutted down and cast their extinguished shadows across Helena's.

Chapter 3

The Links are Forged

It is an ill intention that has no benefit, but it may be concealed.

Spiros had awakened at his usual early hour despite a full night. He drank his black coffee while watching the top of the Acropolis catch early pink rays as the sun rose above Mount Hymettus. By 6AM he was at his desk, keying furiously into his computer. He had Helena's files from the previous day, and was both whipping them into shape, as well as adding his own summaries and other details that she had understandably not addressed.

Summary Plan

Infiltrate the British Museum and defeat security
Lift the Marbles (check numbers and weights)
Fly them out? Other methods? Aircraft, pilot, logistics
Get team clear. Legal: call Benjamin? Staff, PM, others?

Note: I know this looks simple, but it isn't.

Her prospectus was rapidly becoming a finished project plan. The more he wrote, the surer he was that it could work. He also knew that this was not the same thing as deciding, as they must before actually going ahead, that it would *probably* succeed. He was determined that this level of confidence would be reached whatever it took in terms of resources: financial, physical, and human. There were major contributions he could make that would materially reduce the risks and advance the cause. Part of his job on this morning was to define his own role, and that of others whom he could safely involve.

It was clear that only a few people could be trusted with this secret. It was hot, and would all too easily leak. The screen was showing the personnel list:

He reached for a CD, dropped it into the small player beside the computer, and hit "play". The mellifluous voice of Maria Farandouri singing the ballads of Theodorakis filled the modest room most pleasantly.

He reflected again on last night. His real life had begun with Helena, shortly after his father's death, softening that blow and opening his eyes to new horizons of thought and lifetime aspirations. They had both gone around the track several times, in different personas, but between them, what went around always came around. He had feared that the previous time would be their last, derived as much from his own thoughts of inadequacies and irrelevance as any impression he had got from Helena. Now his life had come full circle, and he could see how to close his personal circle of Ouroboros – perhaps with her as well – permanently?

Without this he knew he might have chosen to quit this planet on an earlier flight to eternity than might be scheduled. Until last night, he had suffered agonies of terror at the prospect of growing old, alone, without a legacy. His younger brother had certainly carried on the family name in the Greek tradition, but Spiros had always known that marriage and family were not for him. He knew he had been

29

right, but that still left a yawning chasm of recrimination, irrational though he knew such feelings were. It was like the person ill-treated by another, who still felt guilty. It may be natural, and unavoidable, but that didn't lessen the pain.

He closed his eyes and sat back as "*Strosse Toh Stroma Sou*", or "Lay Down Your Mattress" by Theodorakis played out. From a distance, it changed into a stereophonic duet. He didn't remember it that way.

Helena touched his closed eyes, and began to massage his face, all the while singing along with the recording. It was their song. She knew it went something like, "Lay down the mattress, for two, for you and for me, so that we can embrace." That had been their first time, literally a sun bed cushion laid out on the sand, in a dark cove below that restaurant long ago, under the starry summer sky of Crete.

Spiros hastily switched pages on the screen because he didn't want Helena to see what he was working on until later. They adjourned to the dining area in the grand salon. The sun was now streaming in through the wide windows looking out on Athens. Helena felt, once again, the power over her of the simple fact of the brilliant, living daylight of Greece. It was the exact opposite of the oppressive, dull, overcast that with few admittedly glorious exceptions depressed the skies of her nevertheless equally beloved London Town.

Spiros served the brunch with a flourish, and sat down, tête-à-tête. "I have a function this evening that I simply cannot avoid." Narrowing his eyes, he continued, "It could also be useful to you, especially in the altered circumstances. I know you like a touch of the high life and glamour, now and then. It is a reception to dedicate the new Parthenon Museum, with all the luminaries of government, industry, embassies, and," he concluded with one of his sly, ironic smiles, "*even* a few archaeologists, professors, and the other lower echelons of academia." She knew that Spiros would far more gladly spend an evening with the latter, yet was often forced by circumstances to make the best of one with the former. It was in this way that true power was exercised, certainly as he employed it.

Helena had hoped for a rerun upstairs in the afternoon, and she suspected that Spiros had as well, but he said quite firmly that he had to work the whole day at the computer, and make, "a few phone calls". She was disappointed, but had seen this before with Spiros, an unavoidable part of their relationship.

So she made the best of it, and spent the afternoon out shopping, and then passed by the Benaki Museum to catch the special exhibition "Constantinople's Glorious Past" with its Byzantine artefacts, part of a new series of cultural exchanges between Turkey and Greece.

Arm in arm Spiros and Helena walked from the limousine to the entrance of the new Parthenon Museum, which although a modern addition to the Acropolis complex, blended in surprising harmony with the bare shining rocks and the jagged forms of the ancient city's base. They looked up to the Acropolis itself, the High City, true to its name looming above them. The Parthenon's linear form was floodlit against the night sky, a stark paradox of strength and vulnerability.

Helena remembered its turbulent history, in particular, when the explosion of the Turkish arsenal housed within its very walls almost fatally wounded it. They stopped involuntarily, their recent discussion in the forefront of their minds, gazing in silence and stretching their sensibilities as if to hear the message locked in its stones. Helena was suddenly deeply moved as she became acutely aware that this was Holy Ground, an attempt of her fellow man over two thousand years ago to reach up to the ineffable, and touch the face of God. This was a hallowed sanctuary, one that had been desecrated, pillaged, and sacked.

"This is so often forgotten by us." She breathed softly, then reflected that under the tramp of tourist sandals and the clicking cameras, the polished stones told only the story of lost hopes, humiliation, misunderstood and outmoded ideas. Then she brightened in herself. It was only the original Marbles, with their energy and beauty of form intact, which could, together with the remaining columns at the site and housed in this building, recreate the original message from this long-lost past. In a somewhat sombre mood they climbed the stairs to the second level and entered the brightly lit reception.

It was a lively, colourful scene, yet with a strong undercurrent of expectancy. Expensive perfumes wafted on the air, blending with the natural aromas of roses, gardenias, and jasmine, which had been generously dotted around the room to soften the hard outlines of the empty gallery. Snatches of music could be heard from a small orchestra playing selections from well-known Greek composers.

Sequined bodices sparkled in random synchrony with their movements as they passed underneath the ceiling lights shining directly down. Diamonds glittered on soft curves of flesh. Starlets, in their more demanding latest fashions, stood in contrast to the senior wives who had opted for fluttering, flowing, concealing lines. A few of them knew, or had been advised, of subtle ways to emphasize any feature that was for them still worth calling attention to.

Helena herself was wearing a simple, elegantly cut, full length, black Balmain gown, a gift from Spiros. It was pleasingly décolleté, and the side slits showed just the right amount of her slim-ankled legs. Her golden light brown hair had been swept up in a chignon for this formal occasion, revealing the handsome profile of her lithe shoulders.

Spiros was in his element. He loved a vibrant reception when presented in good taste, and the speakers had something worth listening to. It also gave him a useful chance to hobnob with his peers. Resplendent in his dinner jacket with a slimming dark blue cummerbund, as strongly recommended by Helena, he moved deliberately to and fro among the guests, his face shining with the effort.

From afar, Helena spotted her old spymaster, Charon. His tall, very slight figure and cadaverous face were unmistakable. He had an elusive aura about him, which made him attractive to women, but he also instilled in them a sense of fear. His unblinking eyes would flicker over one's face, reminiscent of the explorations of a lizard's tongue, curious and unpredictable. Helena's unease with him on a personal level was tempered by her deep professional respect for his astute mind and courage.

He acknowledged her with a slight bow, and came over to speak. He took her shoulders in his hands, and embraced her formally, cheek to cheek kisses on both sides, the slight abrasion of his scaly skin brushing against hers. He then stood back at arm's length to look at her appraisingly. "Helena, my dear, how well you look. Retirement obviously suits you."

She wished she could make some equally positive remark about him, but she noticed that the lines on his face had deepened, and his skin had a pallor that is often associated with serious illness. She replied instead about missing the old life, sometimes, yet her change of direction was working out well. She was discomforted by the thought that this was already out of date.

Her attention was drawn, as inevitably in his presence, to the unique, gold necklace with a heavy pendant he always wore. She thought to herself that it was rather like the chains of office worn by thousands of officials all over Britain, from the mayors of small villages, right up to the Lord Mayor of London. She felt that in this case it was both powerful and sinister.

She knew that the circle of Ouroboros, the snake swallowing its own tail, was part of Greek legend. Intriguingly, many other cultures had adopted it, some long predating the Greece of Pericles, as in Egypt, China, India, Central and South America. It was not mentioned in books she had recently read, suggesting the existence of a worldwide civilization capable of trade and travel in the tenth millennium before our era. She thought to herself that maybe it should have been. His example was solid, the snake thick instead of the thinner examples more common on Greek pottery and Egyptian papyrus. The amulet was of substantial mass – the span of her palm – and the chain was a heavy one in the geometrical Greek key-pattern. She thought that tonight it seemed to weigh him down, rather than buoy him up as it had in the past.

After a brief interval of muted conversation, Charon stepped away, "*Sto kalo*", his final benediction. It was a common enough salutation in Greek, and the equivalent of "God be with you" or "goodbye". Yes she felt that he had imbued it with a deeper meaning. It was touching in one who had seen so much evil in his working life.

The gong sounded the statutory three times. Reluctantly the audience gave up circulating around the room and the useful meetings, re-acquainting, and other contacts between colleagues, friends, and the odd lover. The generous buffet of Greek nibbles, a full meal for some of the guests, had also been irresistible to many.

The museum was sited on a modest elevation, and this upper floor of the two had high windows all around, affording a view of the floodlit Parthenon above on the right, and the newer city of Athens to the other compass points. It was devoid of any displays of antiquity. Helena knew that this would become a simulacrum of the Parthenon's interior, with reproduction Doric columns on the sides, and the roof forming triangular transepts at each of the narrower ends. So it would be like standing in the original building before anything was added to the inside, and thus provide plenty of floor space for the major items on display.

Members of the audience were finding their seats in the far end of the hall. In front there was a raised stage on which the VIPs were jostling good-naturedly for their chairs, laid out as in all such gatherings, by the strict requirements of diplomatic protocol.

Spiros led Helena to a seat in the centre section of the first row of spectator's seats, kissed her hand, and said, "I'll have my eye on you." She knew he didn't mean this in the sense of keeping tabs on her, but because he did not want to miss a moment of contact from a distance. Spiros then proceeded to the dais, and took his seat.

The participants had now organized themselves from left to right. Helena knew most of them by sight. There were six chairs, three on her left occupied by the British contingent, and three on her right for the Greeks. The Prime Minister of Greece occupied the first right-hand chair. Gold-rimmed spectacles bridged a broad olive skin face, topped by neatly brushed-back, thinning grey hair over a high forehead. He was of a medium build, and always formal in manner, possibly partly to compensate for his modest stature. Perhaps the most remarkable feature was his beautifully expressive hands, always perfectly manicured, which he used to great effect when speaking.

To her right of the Prime Minister was the curator of the new Parthenon museum, Dr Manolis Seferis. He was in his early sixties and evinced a scholarly persona, perhaps his defence against a hard world. He had a permanent worried expression on his narrow face, as if perpetually looking for some lost object. His friends sometimes teased him that this was the appropriate visage for an archaeologist, but he could only manage a fleeting smile to replace the habitual frown. He was respected in archaeology and was a capable administrator, functioning as such now in his early retirement.

Her very own Spiros Anguelopoulos occupied the third, rightmost seat.

The Right Honourable Robert Goodwin, the Minister of Culture for the United Kingdom was placed by protocol next to the Greek Prime Minister. He possessed a fulsome round face lined in evidence of geniality, and a slightly receding chin. In his mid-fifties, he was a popular politician. In his *Honestly Bob* column in one of the London tabloids he dispensed justice, opinions, and condign punishments for certain overreaching Mandarins in easily digestible doses. This helped to conceal an ambitious and intelligent politician with the necessary ruthless streak.

Goodwin was thinking about how happy and proud he was that his wife was in the audience, for they enjoyed travelling together. Her analyses in private for him, seen from her point-of-view, were often hilarious. She was a good mimic with a cruel sense of humour and the bizarre, and it helped him to relax afterwards, reminding him not to take himself too seriously. "Would that all politicians had a wife like you."

Dr Geoffrey Hayward, the curator (and director) of the British Museum, was a somewhat ebullient figure, in contrast to his Greek opposite number. His paunch had developed gradually along with his diminishing academic enthusiasm and the growth of his need for power and prestige. His native Yorkshire undertones, which he took the trouble to disguise, could still be heard by a discerning native listener, but would probably merely please the Greek ear as honeyed.

Sir Archibald Grosvenor styled himself the playboy, but he had a serious side when dealing with money. He was both grasping and generous, the latter gift having brought him here as the English half of the philanthropic support. He was very confident of his boyish attractiveness despite the fact that he was approaching fifty. The lines on his face had been ameliorated (some wags claimed) by repeated Botox treatments. He had an irritating high-pitched laugh, which one heard rather too often, as he always sniggered at his own frequent jokes.

Grosvenor, in contrast to Goodwin, was happy that his wife was *not* in the audience, having been called to New York for some function or other in her domain. He predatorily scanned the audience, selecting a short list of likely candidates, to be winnowed down to a single winner, according to which of them later responded most positively to his questionable charms.

The Prime Minister rose to the podium, and rapped on it with his knuckle, amplified by the microphone, to call the convocation to order. He made a brief introduction of each guest, and then handed over to Dr Manolis Seferis, the curator of the new museum, with one of his ballet-like gestures.

Dr Seferis spoke in English, then Greek. "Mister Prime Minister, Doctor Geoffrey Hayward, my fellow colleague whom I thank personally for coming here tonight to say a few words, and our strong financial right arms without whom none of this would have been possible (he directed a hand to Sir Archibald Grosvenor and Spiros), excellencies and honoured guests.

"In a few minutes, our Prime Minister and the British Minister of Culture will cut the traditional tape, and open this museum. Everyone here will know the strong bonds we Greeks feel for our history and heritage. Sometimes I fear we dwell too much upon it – that we lose touch with the hopes all civilized peoples around the world have, and should have, for the future. I believe it can be as great or greater than our past.

"As arguably the world's first democracy, we have suffered the ups and downs that many innovators must live through to come out on the other side. We were among the last of the European States to achieve a solid and lasting democracy. Yet we are moving forward, forgiving the past where we should," he nodded to the audience, and Helena realized that this was to the Turkish ambassador seated on her left, "and hoping for the same in return." The ambassador was nodding in agreement.

"This museum and the artefacts to be housed here, both originals and reproductions, is an honourable link to our past. I do also suggest that it can be much more than that. It is my hope that in this monument to our past, a glorious one to be sure, we will find the guide to a greater future. That we might accept our past as in the past, a respected heritage, but at the same time move into the future with the same confidence that Pericles had in his, which was the brightest light in the world for three hundred years, and carried the hopes for a better one two and one-half millennia right down to the present day.

"Counting from our accession to the European Union, which was in my view the second dawn of Greece, three hundred years from now will be a good start. I hope that the physical foundations we have laid for this building, and what it will house, can inspire us to continue laying the social and political foundations for our second renaissance.

"I now have the great pleasure and honour to introduce my counterpart, Geoffrey Hayward, whom I personally thank for his generosity and that of his government in their contributions to this museum, and our greater goals." Uneasiness rippled through the audience and many shifted their positions, some merely to achieve greater comfort as was to be expected; yet many others were expressing their discomfort at a different irritant.

Hayward spoke in Greek then English. "Thank you." He paused, knowing full well what the disquiet signified, and gathered his strength to allay it if he could. It was not an easy moment. "Every civilized man and woman in the world of today remembers and respects the Greek heritage that my colleague has rightly reminded us of."

"Then give us back our Marbles!" It was a clarion call from the back of the hall. A hush fell over the room. The Greek Prime Minister rose, no doubt to apologize, as the heckler was led away. To his credit the speaker offered the back of his hand to stay the Prime Minister's advance. He also apparently knew that to present the more natural palm of the hand was contrary to local customs.

"I was about to say that there were also apologies to be made by others, ourselves included, and the record will show that I, personally, the Right Honourable Minister of Culture seated here, and others in Great Britain have done so frequently, in respect of the matter that our departed guest has just mentioned.

"Further, I accept that my colleague on this dais has equally recognized that these are not simple matters. I represent, in my present office, the interests of the British Museum. Any successor could do no less. The Greek government has rightly accepted the legal position of my museum as to ownership, but I do *not* rely on that here tonight. There are historical and cultural arguments on both sides. We have cared well for your heritage, and I emphasize my recognition that this is your heritage, a history that has perhaps been more influential in creating the Europe as we know it today, than any other single example.

"It is for these reasons, and others relating to our honour and yours in such matters, that my government, aided by the generosity of leading citizens with an interest in culture," he was acknowledging this time the two outside men on the dais, "have tried to go an extra mile, or kilometre," he smiled at the small joke that still separated his island from the rest of Europe, "to meet as best we can, the undoubted legitimate needs of the Greek people.

"That is why your artisans and ours are labouring in the British Museum, to make precise copies of the Parthenon sculptures and panels in marble from the same Pendeli mountain that supplied the Parthenon that towers above us, the pre-eminent symbol of European civilization in my opinion and that of many. They will come here to Greece in three months time for display first in Thessalonica, then here when that exhibition is finished in under a year's time.

"Which brings me to the second point. The Greek Orthodox authorities have agreed, for the first time in history, that the Treasures of Mount Athos may be placed on display outside of Greece. They will go first to Thessalonica as I have mentioned, and then will come to London for a special exhibition at the British Museum, there to be seen by the wider audience they richly deserve. This unprecedented event will be the most important my museum has hosted for many years, perhaps the most significant in the long history of our national museum.

"This cultural exchange, which my colleague here and I proposed, and the Prime Ministers negotiated, which includes production for the first time of accurate reproductions of my museum's holdings of the Parthenon Marbles, by precise computer engraving through actual tracing by touch upon the originals, carved in the same marble, I suggest with respect, is the best that can be achieved.

"I hope that even our earlier speaker from the audience, and those who are understandably sympathetic with his position, will come to agree that this compromise is honourable for all concerned. I think I can speak for both Prime Ministers in this. Thank you for your kind attention."

There was a pause of deathly silence in the hall. Neither speaker had expected applause, for it was not such an occasion, but this was significant. The Prime Minister rose from his chair, and made a deliberately slow crossing to the microphone.

"I appreciate the candour and restraint of both museum curators, and thank them for their remarks." He paused, swept his hands around the room, and then to the heavens above. "But ... there are issues yet to be resolved. Everyone in this room knows it. I have today taken the decision that this hall will remain empty until the Elgin Marbles come here, as we have proposed, on permanent loan from the British Museum or through other equivalent..."

The audience erupted with shouts, applause, and a standing ovation. This was not for the Prime Minister or anyone on the platform. It was given out of respect for the absent guest, the heritage of Greece, felt by all present to be part of her birthright: the missing Marbles.

The moment eventually passed. The wine, champagne, and liquor flowed copiously, loosening tongues and libidos as it always does. The Greek voices got louder, the British quieter and more calculating. Helena wandered along the left wall, towards the far end with its triangular pediment, and then back along the right wall towards the same triangular aspect in the rear where they had entered this simulated Parthenon. She noted with satisfaction that this would be a suitable, protected venue for the Elgins from London, reunited with the originals that Greece still possessed.

If they succeeded, all of the extant original pedimental sculptures and bas-relief plaques (metopes), which previously graced the Parthenon, would rest safely inside, displayed at floor-level to permit close scrutiny by visitors. A full set of the copies would be mounted on the inside of the linear pediments atop the Doric columns along the side walls, in place of the original friezes, which are badly damaged. The sculptures would be set in the triangular pediments at the ends under the apex of the roof. They told intricate stories of Greek history, and the fantasies of the gods. It would be eminently satisfying to see them here, in the city of their creation, and only a short distance below their birthplace on the Acropolis above.

Another set of copies would be remounted on the outside of the restored Parthenon itself as they had been in the beginning. There was current academic debate about whether or not to attempt a restoration of the friezes, which were originally arrayed around the inside, from the controversial and fragmentary remains.

So they would, with a fair wind in the sails of her new Ship, the Thousand and First, have the best of both worlds, ancient and modern, originals and accurate reproductions, resident here in evidence of the birthplace of European Civilization.

Her attention returned to Spiros, who as usual was in intense conversation, hands and body as important as the spoken words. She had noticed him with Charon earlier, and this time he was one-on-one with the Greek Prime Minister in a quiet corner. Their hands had ceased the characteristic Greek ebullience, and were hanging loosely at the sides, more reminiscent of Americans. She read this as signifying impenetrable matters, the stuff of Greek tragedy. She was correct in this assessment, for the Prime Minister was being presented with the most difficult conundrum he, or any of his recent predecessors, had faced in that high office.

Helena had noticed a woman keeping an eye on her, something anybody with her background automatically picked up, even if all the action was behind the back. It was a ninth sense, without which one didn't live long in that game. Helena contrived to disappear and come around behind her without being seen. The woman was scanning the crowd, trying to pick up sight of Helena, after inexplicably losing sight of her. This was the fifth skill of her trade, to disappear in full view, and reappear a moment later somewhere else, often as not, as in this case, *behind* the target.

Helena was trying to place the woman in Greek intelligence. She might well be an agent without Helena knowing it, because her service, like most others, was organized in cells, often of three, such that a member knows at most one person in any other cell. This security precaution was essential to limit the damage to the whole organization if one or only a few members of it are captured, and juiced (or worse) until they talk. And the first demand was always, "Give me names."

Helena was flipping the pages of her memory for faces – no luck. Then she noticed that Charon was eyeing them with surreptitious glances. Helena surmised that this woman was probably on Charon's leash, perhaps her replacement as his top female field agent. She wouldn't have bet her career on it, but the odds were not too bad either.

"Hello. I am trying to place you. Have we met?" This ancient opening couldn't be bettered, so Helena used it, watching every scintilla of body language, facial expression, and flash of eyes. Her target was naturally startled, yet only for a millisecond, and instantly recovered her demeanour. Helena tentatively confirmed her diagnosis, "professional".

"No, we haven't met, but we have a common col ... acquaintance." The woman's face screamed, "damn" for she had erred; Helena had caught it, and the other noted she had. So, Charon was a mutual colleague – sure, her presumption was definitely confirmed, and she was satisfied that her skills had not deteriorated in a year or so out of the field.

The woman's body was slender-medium with extremely well toned muscles, fully tanned skin with no tan-line under the serious gold necklace worn around her long neck. She was wearing the same hairstyle as Helena, regarding her out of deep-pool black eyes set in a strong, square, younger, unmistakably Greek face.

"Cassandra."

Helena couldn't tell if this was her real name, or codename, so she smiled enigmatically, and gave her own.

"Pandora."

The silent nod of Cassandra's acknowledgement, without the slightest hint of surprise, proved that this was her codename, now disclosed with Helena's. It was a familiar game, the exchange of the most vital information by way of the subtlest nonverbal indications.

Cassandra tipped her head in Charon's direction. "What do you find in him?"

"Great strengths."

"And weaknesses." Cassandra winked. To Helena's questioning gaze, she elaborated. "For women. And they for him."

The unspoken question hung in the air, speaking volumes. Helena shook her head to confirm it.

"Never?" Cassandra was now transformed into more of a gossip, than experienced professional. Apparently she couldn't help herself when it came to Charon. This was a weakness that Helena had never shared with some others she had known, including herself in her own relationship with Spiros. With her, as for him, professional needs always came first, and both of them knew it. That had been confirmed as recently as this afternoon.

"Quite frankly, I don't understand what women see in him." This admission had slipped out from under Helena's barriers. She shouldn't have said it. Maybe Cassandra was cleverer than she had at first imagined – the old enemy of underestimating opponents – perhaps the deadliest of all. Helena gave a wry smile; both knew it was now an even one point each.

Then Cassandra conceded the game. Perhaps she felt her parting comment was worth it. "Well," she winked, her tongue flicking repeatedly in and out. "We don't call him *The Lizard* for nothing, my dear. *Byeee!*"

Chapter 4

Ulysses at Sea

With their minds fixed on the distant shore, they pulled on the oars with resolution.

Spiros had awakened early as usual. They could be late-night people, but there was a difference. Helena could sleep eight hours or more afterwards into the morning, Spiros couldn't. He normally slept precisely six hours. If he went to bed at his normal 11PM, he would be awake at 5AM, and be sitting with his coffee in plenty of time for the sunrise, summer or winter. If an evening such as yesterday's delayed his bedtime, he still awoke for the sun. If it were lovemaking the hour didn't matter, and thirty minutes of shuteye was sufficient.

He regretted that yesterday had been the full double day, yet Helena's project was top priority, easily worth his life if he had expired over the hot keyboard. It was the old days again, the young days, when every sunrise brought magic, and he knew that the day's labour had been worth a week. He had broken the back of the full Project Plan, complete with 80 pages of detailed text. He also made several telephone calls, and contacts in person to set it up.

Helena was waking up very slowly as usual, dreams gradually being replaced by surrealistic images of her surroundings. She was concerned about the youthful team she had left behind in London. Contact was a critical part of building up a team. On reflection though, she decided she could indulge herself in a little more time with Spiros, and offered herself the not unreasonable excuse that there was still work to do on the planning this end. In any case, she knew he would insist.

She could hear him downstairs hammering the keys, so she took a quick shower, padded down the stairs barefoot, and slipped by the library-study to the kitchen. He had eleven different blends of coffee, all unground beans. She selected his morning favourite and busied herself setting up a breakfast of fresh sliced pineapple, with the imported mango and papaya just turning ripe in the basket, halves of lime to squeeze on the fruit, croissants, honey of Attica, and unsalted butter. She backed herself through the swinging door, and ferried the heaped-up tray towards the breakfast nook under the grand windows in the far corner of the sejour. As she passed the open door of the

42

library, unseen by Spiros hunched over his keyboard, she blew warm kisses of morning across the coffee towards the door. She had learned a long time ago that this was the only way to draw him away from work without making him grumpy at being forced to take a break. Calling out to him was a no-no – not punishable by death – for a first offence. The same applied to afternoon naps, where it could be capital, even if the call was from the Prime Minister.

His normal riposte was, "God himself can wait for my nap."

"Perfect timing, my love, my life – I have just finished." Spiros took her head in his hands from behind, and kissed her ear. She shuddered from the ticklishness, turned her head and welcomed a deep and lingering kiss.

He sat down opposite and cast her a meaningful look straight in the eyes. She answered with a slow series of nods and a coquettish smile. Spiros relaxed into his chair, a broad smile of desire spreading across his face.

"I can afford three days, and not an hour more." She didn't have to apologize, or say she was sorry it could not be more.

"So, my sleek, loving Kat, we will just have to make it count, won't we?"

"Yes, Spiro, we will."

"I make it two hours here to go over the plans. You read, I'll make some more calls, and then we will talk." He began wolfing down a croissant.

Helena touched his lips with a firm index finger. "Easy does it. We have nearly ten months ahead of us. You've already broken the back of it, haven't you?"

"Yes – you're right on both counts. I'll change down a gear."

"Or two, or three?"

"Agreed. And we'll efface the normal definitions of time. Let every minute be an hour, every hour a day, and every day a month.

"So," he concluded, "a little of both worlds, I think." Helena didn't understand what he meant, but was more than content to put herself in his strong hands, literally and figuratively.

"You know, I have *two* cats now?"

"*Ti?*"

"You and my new boat!"

He chuckled, "So my golden one, we have time for a little *volta*, eh?"

"Yes, yes, we have time for a short run on your new boat."

Piraeus was just as shabby and wonderful as it had always been for her. Spiros drove slowly past all the ferryboat docks, ships plying to and fro between there and a score and more of Greek islands. Tourists in their multicoloured T-shirts and shorts mingled with hoary old Greeks and local families, bound for these paradises large and small, scattered like smoky amethysts across the darkly, dappled Aegean.

At the yacht harbour Spiros turned his car over to a sun-baked ancient Greek and his Adonisian grandson for safekeeping. The young man illuminated a smile for Helena's benefit, and she couldn't help smiling back at this typical, yet always surprising wonder of male Greek beauty; yes she repeated to herself, "beauty" was the right word. Spiros didn't miss a beat, and waggled a warning finger at him to good-naturedly stake out his prior claim to this woman.

Helena had been on long trips with Spiros in his previous yacht, all over most of the Eastern Mediterranean, and to virtually every major island in the Aegean Sea. The new boat was quite different, much more rectangular than sleek, and then she caught his earlier joke, for it was a catamaran. The superstructure, looking more like a squarish house than a traditional boat, was perched on two separate, narrow hulls. The boat was named *Helena*, and she felt a thrill of pleasure. Then her practiced eye noticed that the paint job was recent, and heaven only knew how many other names lay beneath. She knew better than to let this bother her, in fact, quite the opposite. She loved Spiros, and so his happiness was more important than anything else to her, for only with those feelings would she receive full measure in return. She had an ironic thought: men needed the practice to stay in practice. She would no doubt receive the full benefit of that experience.

It was another motor-sailboat, the single mast towering above them as they stepped aboard. The grand tour revealed at least double the living space of the earlier boat in less length at the waterline. The salon would have done justice to a large villa, with plenty of room below inside the two hulls for six bedrooms, four of them doubles, plus spacious cabin-space for crew, storage, and the flying bridge.

"May I introduce our Giorgio?"

"Charmed, madame." He bowed low, and kissed her hand. "Welcome aboard the Helena." There hadn't been the slightest hesitation over the name, so he was either extremely practiced at this deception, or maybe that was the actual name. Again, she decided she didn't care one way or the other.

"Giorgio, just a little *volta* as we discussed."

"Yessir."

They motored out of the harbour onto a smoky glass tabletop of ocean, the smoothest she had ever seen it. The long coast stretched to the southern horizon, lined with a broad band of the traditional, brilliant white Greek homes backed by brown hills behind, the whole doubled by a perfect reflection on the water. The image rippled behind them as their wake split the world in two, seeming to leave their hopes and fears back there somewhere in another universe.

An hour later they were sharing drinks on the top deck as the sun set, burning the reflected images of the departing coast into the smoothly undulating sea. It was perfect for them, just what they needed to come down from the high of their labours of the last two days for him, and some six months of Herculean preparation for her.

"An early dinner, then repair to our nest below?"

She met the cook, the galley boy, another beautiful lad no more than eighteen, the steward, whom she knew from earlier cruises, and both deck hands at dinner. At first, Helena had felt a twinge of disappointment. The image beforehand in her mind had been the obvious one of tête-à-tête, with the staff remaining discretely in the background.

As usual, his judgment had been vindicated. This was his seafaring family, and within a short time of the introductions, they were bantering and teasing each other, Helena's colloquial Greek coming back to her in great gobbets as she struggled to keep up with the flow. She was drawn out of herself into this fresh world, as old as Greek history. It was fun; it was more than that, it was a coming together. She vowed to make this happen with her new family. Then a dark shadow clouded her eyes; she hadn't had one like this for too long. Maybe it was time to move this part of her life on, as she was trying, apparently with little success so far, to move on in her professional one.

Finally, they were alone in the lounge at the bow end of the grand salon, with the sea darkening, and the crescent moon low in the west leading Venus, signalling the hour of playful rest to lovers everywhere as the earth turned and the tides inexorably followed.

They heeded this call to the bedroom below, for an endless hour or three, and an imperceptible transition to deep and dreamless sleep.

It was the millennium – Helena was up before Spiros! She was delighted, for she had always believed, her mothering side anyway, that he needed more sleep. Perhaps this was, in all fairness, to some degree a need to compensate for her own dilatory, morning ways. No matter, the sunrise was magnificent as she looked to the east. If she wasn't mistaken, they were anchored in the harbour of Chania, Crete. There was the charming town she knew so well set out before her to the south, and to the right, the long isthmus of Akra Spatha stretching back towards Athens. That was impossible; they couldn't have made such a distance in the time.

Spiros came silently up behind her, and covered her eyes with his hands. He was too late, but made the most of it. "Surprise!" He removed his hands, and kissed her behind the ear, blowing kisses into it.

"So how did we get here?" Helena giggled in response to the extra ticklishness of Spiros' as yet unshaved cheeks.

"Both my cats are fast, dear one."

"Not that way, I'm not." She gave him a coquettish frown, "Maybe I'll turn over a new leaf in that department."

"Lunch over there," he indicated the town, "and then the Island?"

They walked hand in hand along the quayside of Chania town, past a score of restaurants well known to them. Spiros waved to the odd passer-by, and they entered a cool, dark *kaphenion*, eyes completely blinded by the contrast with the dazzling light outside. A group of darkly dressed older Greeks sat around their table as they had done, or so it seemed, forever, playing *tavli*.

"Spiros!" they chorused. Several jumped up, and embraced him warmly, one after the other. He drew up two more chairs, and the routine was repeated, with warm handshakes, touched with a hint of deference, from each for Helena. Then they got down to the serious business of swapping stories, embellished as only the riper, amateur Greek sages can.

Helena suspected that Spiros' pig bombing episode would join several other stories and they could be there for hours; it had happened before. She tugged on his elbow and said, "You promised me lunch, darling, and time is precious." Spiros raised his eyes heavenward in mock helplessness, saluted his friends as one sailor to another, and swept out of the *kaphenion*.

They took lunch in a small, agreeable restaurant at the western end of the docks, where tables ran down to the edge of the quayside. The waves slapped delightedly against it, carrying the sweet tang of the sea mingled with smoky aromas of fried squid, and the slightly stale whiff of octopus drying in the sun.

She ordered the lamb *souvlaki* without seeing the menu, having detected the faint perfume of the dish emanating from the restaurant. It came with brightly coloured rice and an overflowing portion of Greek salad, topped with the always delightful, sea-salt enhanced pieces of feta cheese. The olive oil surrounding the salad caught the warmth of the sun, releasing its unmistakable fragrance distilled from the scorched olive groves high above the town. It was all washed down with a bottle of the light, tangy, greenish-white, Cretan wine, fine with lamb, and a perfect accompaniment for Spiros' selection of grilled prawns.

After lunch they walked in the narrow, almost claustrophobic, whitewashed streets behind the waterfront, rekindling deep memories of previous visits. After an hour or so of exploration, Helena caught a flash of a blue she had seen a few times reflected in the sea, but not before this moment anywhere on land. She was drawn towards a window that the post-meridian sun was just reaching. The full glory previously concealed in the small shop's windows was revealed in a blinding revelation. It was nothing more, nor less, than stacks of the most wonderfully blue pots, plates, cups, and bowls she had ever seen.

"Spiro, that's superb, isn't it? What a colour. Unique!"

The shop was closed, but a discreet little sign in the window gave the usual early-evening hours when presumably one could do business.

"The owner must be working in the potter's shed. I must meet him, or her."

The colour was most definitely not the typical dark cobalt blue of 95% or more of similar products produced in thousands of potteries around the world. This one was slightly less dense, yet a fully saturated deep blue, with only the slightest trace of green, no relationship either with the common turquoises or other similar possibilities. Helena knew something of the glazes used throughout the ages, and this was new in her experience. She wondered which combination of metallic salts had been used to produce it. The prices were also about double what she would have expected to pay, no doubt reflecting the added cost of the miracle formula. She resolved to learn more, and hopefully obtain some for – for what?

She realized, as if seeing it for the first time, that she didn't have a home of her own. Her life had been one rented flat after another, so she had no place in her memory to set these objects and see in her mind's eye how they might complement a kitchen or dining room.

These were disturbing thoughts, but she welcomed them, for they forced her to begin feeling her way through other aspects of her life that were crying out for resolution.

The yacht glided easily across the straits to the northwest, and approached what Helena knew was Spiros' own island. An advantage of the catamaran was made apparent in the ease with which the captain docked the boat. The two engines were widely separated at the stern, so he could almost turn the ship around its own mast. The deck hands she had met at dinner the night before made fast, and Spiros handed her to the gangway, and so they entered his private domain.

She had been here before. He had a sprawling villa, not without charm, on the hill above the tiny village. Everyone in the short main street greeted him warmly; many with Greek bear hugs and shook hands with Helena. She remembered a few of the more memorable characters, and perhaps they her, as they made their way slowly up the street.

Spiros then did something quite out of character by entering the only market shop, and after greeting the proprietor, "*Costaki mou*", began shopping with an air of concentration. He filled one basket, then a second, and staggered out of the shop, setting the heavy load down next to their overnight bags, which he had separated from their other luggage that had already been ferried up to the Villa.

The fish market was next, and he bought all that was left, a bit of mullet and some scraps of squid. She felt they had been lucky to get that so late in the day.

Curiouser and curiouser, said the donkey to the herdsman, Helena thought to herself as she trailed along behind, totally mystified.

She picked up her share, one bag of groceries, and her overnight, and followed her man down the dusty road, around the headland, and then along the deserted beach beyond. They passed the sign that said in several languages, "Private Beach Please No Entry" in its English version. She knew there was a single tourist hotel and resort in the opposite direction, individual cabanas tastefully built of stone and masonry, in the local Greek style, complete with the odd cupola in shining blue paint to contrast with the eggshell white walls and bougainvillea bushes the size of trees. Both it and the villa shared a superb beach, better and larger than this, so where were they going, and why?

The pleasant little beach of rough sand curved around in a hollow, crescent moon shape towards the final headland before the island took its turn to the north. As they approached that outcropping of cinder-black rock, Spiros turned inland a few metres, and in between two large olive trees, seemed to discover a modest hut in the local fisherman's style, as it no doubt had once been.

"Whew. Thanks for carrying your share of the load." Spiros dropped his bag of groceries on the wood-plank counter in the kitchen corner of the single room, and Helena followed suit. The overnight bags went on the single bed against the opposite wall. Helena thought to herself that she did like togetherness, but this was ridiculous if it was his intention that they spend the night in that bed. Spiros alone would easily overflow it, and noting the spindly legs and rusting nails holding it together, might easily destroy it on first sitting.

It was as if he had entered a different world, and perhaps he had. Spiros rapidly unpacked the groceries, pulled down three or four items of canned and bottled goods standing forlornly on sagging little shelves nailed on simple supports.

He gestured to Helena, setting out onions, garlic, tomatoes and cucumber. She took up the only serrated knife to begin trimming and dicing the vegetables. He sliced open the red mullet and pressed garlic and onion into grooves he had cut in the fish. He dusted on the salt, some pepper, and a touch of hot sauce from an old bottle; the label so blackened with age and spilled sauce as to be unreadable.

He trimmed the pieces of squid, placed them in a simple plastic bowl, and added further slices of garlic as she diced them out on the boards. There was no need for a cutting block, the counter itself served perfectly well.

Helena scooped up a bucket of water from the water butt under the sink, fed by a pipe from the roof, washed her hands, and prepared the Greek salad in a suitable wooden bowl that had been set upside down on the end of the counter, together with a small pile of other kitchen utensils and dining equipment. She crumbled the Feta cheese between her fingers, and licked off her hands. "Sous chef's privilege," she grinned, seeing now at last where this might be going. The bed remained her only major concern.

One of the few concessions to post World War 2 technology was the aluminium foil in which Spiros wrapped the fish, and squid separately, with their garnishes. He pulled an ordinary fisherman's catch-box out from under the counter, and arranged everything in it, tossing in some matches, fire-starting sticks, another concession, salt-shaker and a few other small items for good measure.

Nodding at the door, he led the way out of the hut, and then turned left to the modest headland where the beach appeared to end. He continued into the mouth of a wide and shallow cave, and then put down the box on one of four flat rocks of a height on which one could sit with some degree of comfort. It had a clean floor of rough sand, and smelled freshly of the sea, for it was not deep enough to have acquired the less pleasant odours of many such places in Helena's experience.

Spiros sat down on the largest stone, and dragged a makeshift barbecue from behind it, together with a sack of charcoal, and in a flash, had it loaded, with the starters smoking merrily in fulfilment of their brief destiny. After a momentary burst of slightly unpleasant smokiness, the fire caught, and a bed of coals began to form, glowing softly. He laid the foil-wrapped fish and squid upon the grill, placed a terra cotta pot upside down over them, and slapped his hands together with satisfaction no less than the head chef of a world-class restaurant.

Spiros took off his shoes, and Helena did the same.

"Let's take a walk while the fish cooks." He took her hand, and they retraced their steps along the beach, dancing in and out of the cool water, heading towards the setting sun.

They came to a place where the sand in a small dune-like outcropping, extended a few metres out into the sea, sculpted by the currents and winds. A bed of lilies had made their home along the ridge, sharing it with a few tufts of grass, and Helena stopped to admire them. She caressed several in turn, marvelling at the wonder of such a simple truth.

"They toil not, neither do they spin..." she said, mainly to herself, but Spiros heard her, and whispered the second line she was trying to remember.

"But Solomon in all his glory was not arrayed like one of these!"

They stood on the little beach with the lilies swaying slightly in the welcome of a cooling breeze, and watched the sun set, split into orange and red bands, behind the low hill in the centre of the island.

Back in the cave, Spiros performed a few more examples of legerdemain. A bottle of chilled ouzo was produced, and served in seashell cups. *"Stin ygieia mas"*.

"To my wonderful *Prospero.*" she replied, with a touch of irony in her voice.

Taking the mood and her meaning, he rose, and bowed, drawing an imaginary, Shakespearean cloak around himself. "Always at your service."

She knew that he preferred his native ouzo, to the best whiskeys, cognac, or any of the others, at any price.

He then produced the *meze* of baked squid with garlic, and uncovered the Greek salad, dousing it with olive oil, and pressing halved limes strongly between his thumb and forefinger until they popped to give up their last drop of succulent, aromatic juice. He broke the bread, and began eating in the time-tested way with bare hands. Helena hesitated for just a moment, shrugged to herself, and dug in, literally, first scooping out the middles of the small halved loaves, eating the soft insides, then taking up and dropping in the delicacies set out before her, eating plate and serving together. Though she had spent most of her life in Greece, she had never before eaten in this way, perfectly acceptable in many parts of the country.

When Spiros unwrapped the whole fish, the cave was filled with a complex mixture of aromas that fully justified a tall toque, with the coveted French title, *Chef de Cuisine*. Helena shook her head in wonder. The whole day had been so different from expectations, that her points of reference had been erased, a *tabula rasa* created instead, not unlike the large flat stone that was serving as the table set between them, without a single eating implement upon it. He had also produced by magic, from behind his rock, a bottle of cave-chilled retsina wine.

Their fingers were just able to stand the heat long enough to separate the sections of fish between the cuts Spiros had made, and transfer them intact to more hollowed-out fresh small loaves. It was thirsty work, and a second bottle of wine appeared, opened with a flourish, Spiros showing off again. Then fate intervened and the cork broke off inside the bottle, so the wine tended to splash and gurgle as he filled the seashell cups. He laughed, chiding himself for being so clumsy.

It was magic of another kind that overtook them as the meal wound down to the sopping up of miraculous sauces with the last shards of bread. He kissed her only once, fully, and it was as if they had never before existed, created on the spot by a benevolent god of life and love.

Spiros hastily tidied up, and repacked the fisherman's box. Helena expected him to lead the way back to the hut, and so to discover by what trick of magic he intended to make a workable bed for them.

He got up, a bit heavily she thought, partly the wine, and the quantity of food, which had been more than adequate, and once again rummaged about in the back of the cave behind the magician's stone.

He came out with a full double mattress tucked lightly under his arm, and motioned towards the cave's mouth. "We wouldn't want to get any sand in the wrong places, would we, my golden Helena. Come with me, and help me launch our thousand ships of pleasure."

Shaking her head again – it was getting to be a habit this day – she most willingly followed him outside. He unrolled the mattress outside the cave, on a flat area of sand framed on three sides by smooth, clean rocks. The waterside lay down a shoulder of small, well-rounded pebbles, soft waves caressing these slopes a few metres away. The profile of Crete's western range was visible across the sound to the south, cutting jagged edges in the starry sky.

He began to undress, laying his clothes out on the rocks, setting aside also the two beach towels that had been wrapped up inside the mattress. Helena followed, and he led her down to the sea. "It is all sandy bottom here, we can swim or go wading, nothing to worry about." He again led, and they breaststroked their way out into the cove.

They stood on the sandy bottom and embraced, the cool water just right to erase the afternoon's sometimes almost oppressive heat, and for the moment to hold their ardour in check. When this was no longer working, Helena led Spiros up the pebbled beach to their bed, and they towelled off, letting the warm rocks behind them and the light breeze finish the job.

Neither of them retained the slightest vestige of perfume or cologne, save those of the sea. Spiros' skin was slightly sticky from the salt water, and his lips tasted of the same sea salt with which he had seasoned the meal.

"Strosse Toh Stroma Sou" Spiros crooned softly, and she followed his instruction from their song, laying down on the mattress for two, so that they could embrace.

"Helena, please hear me on something. I value my possessions, and my life, especially as you have rejuvenated it. Nothing pleases me, and I think most of us, more than sharing whatever we have with someone special."

"You're not possessed by your possessions, are you?"

"I try not to be." He waved his hand towards the hut. "If I had to start over maybe I'd be a painter, or sculptor, right here."

"And I would come to you."

"I say again, if I had to start over, from this rude hut, everything else erased, I would be content, and doubly so, if you were here with me." Spiros looked deeply into her star-speckled eyes, and kissed her, the fluttering of soft, fuzzy moths.

It was their first time, again, the most powerful magic of all. This circle was complete for her, and ready to open again in a new direction. She resolved to begin closing several others in her life that had been revealed to her most poignantly this day.

They spent the full three days in the hut, shopping together, collecting shells, running on the beach, swimming, and in general, having what Helena later described to Irini as, "An Idyll."

She thought several times how endearing it was that he organized almost everything, and took the lead. Was this something else to be opened out in her next life? Had she spent too much of her own organizing things for others, and a sovereign nation?

To preserve the last moment on the island, Spiros whistled up the charter helicopter from Chania Airport, and skimming just above the waves, they were ferried across the sea, finally bouncing up into the air over the olive groves, landing next to the Olympic Airways jet, already warming up for the run to Athens, with connections to London on the same afternoon.

She waved goodbye to him through the narrow, oval window, wiping tears away as she tried to come to terms with this second Greek drama in which she had become enmeshed.

Chapter 5

A Dragon Appears

Count the heads – it may have more than one.

The next day, 06:00 hours, Helena's flat in London

"Bleep – ... – Bleedlebeep – ... – BEEP. BEEP. BEEP...

CHARON TO HELENA – <u>MOST SECRET</u> –
   COMPANY BUSINESS – **CODE RED**
   MAJOR LEAK THIS END **INSIDE THE SERVICE**. DEALT WITH.
   ORDERS ALREADY GIVEN. 2 X 2 CELLS ON THE LOOSE.
   I HAVE NO WAY TO RECALL THEM.
HELENA TO CHARON
   WILL IT SPREAD?
CHARON TO HELENA:
   DON'T THINK SO. NO TIME BEYOND SETTING UP A 2X2.
   ALSO SECURITY FOR THEM IS AS IMPORTANT AS FOR US.
   AND THERE MAY BE A VENDETTA ANGLE.
HELENA TO CHARON:
   IF VENDETTA, LIKELY CONTAINABLE.
   IF NOT, ANYBODY'S GUESS.
CHARON TO HELENA:
   YES. TAKE ALL PRECAUTIONS
   <u>DOUBLE-OH</u> RESOLUTIONS IF NECESSARY.
HELENA TO CHARON:
   THE TEAM?
CHARON TO HELENA:
   NO I REPEAT <u>NO</u> DISCLOSURE. BACKUP ARRIVES TONIGHT.
HELENA TO CHARON:
   THAT VIOLATES MY COMMITMENTS HERE.
CHARON TO HELENA:
   I KNOW BUT THIS IS A COMPANY MATTER AT THE HIGHEST
   LEVELS. <u>NO DISCLOSURE</u>. COVER IT ANOTHER WAY.

Needless to say, Helena was wide-awake, and had dressed between messages. She always laid her quick-change clothes across a chair back, Velcro-strap shoes neatly between the legs, weapons on the seat; she had several, all semi-legal in the UK but nonetheless extremely effective. Old habits die hard.

She was certain that nobody knew where her personal safe house was, because only she did. There was the remote possibility that she had been followed from Heathrow airport last evening, yet out of strong habits again, she had double-dropped tails, and hadn't sensed anything. Well-honed spy-senses were no guarantee – another truth painfully learned on a few occasions in the past. She was not the only first-class operative in the world.

It was an internal service matter, which meant that the leak was from within the company itself. That disclosure had sent her heart and brain into overdrive. In her 20 years this had happened only twice, not a bad record for any intelligence service, and neither had been high up. This smacked of the worst, and the other cases had each cost two lives, one innocent, and one guilty. Something like this could wipe her and a dozen others off the face of the earth in an afternoon.

She reviewed the possibilities as she sipped her coffee. As Charon had mentioned "vendetta", she wondered if it was personal or professional. She had certainly made enemies, unavoidably including one or two in the service. Her most dangerous assignment had been to short-circuit a rogue agent who had a strong grudge based on his mistaken belief that another agent had stolen his lover. It was unfounded, but the danger was in the mind of the beholder, and facts meant little.

The second possibility was far more dangerous. If the motivation was to stop or punish the project itself, then they were all at risk. That would be a first for her, as the other team members were amateurs. The earlier cases had involved only experienced professionals, even if some were a bit green; nevertheless they were fully trained and informed pro ... *informed* ... "Dammit". She swallowed the last of the coffee, choking on it and her emotions, "amateurs and *uninformed*. Shit!"

She could tell them, but it would be impossible to keep that secret from Charon. He would know almost before she did it. Her own service, ex-service, would be watching one way or another. And the project could not continue without that support. Spiros himself might be taken out of the game.

This was the worst of all possible worlds, the conflict between loyalties and duties. Her loyalties and obligations to her young associates, voluntarily taken upon herself, were of the highest kind. The duties imposed on her by others, in this case Charon, without her consent, were merely orders, a lower ranking commitment. Then she saw Charon's point. She could easily be endangering others unknown to her by disclosing. There was little choice but to follow his directive, but that didn't make it less than the hardest decision she had ever made.

There seemed only one option left to her, to go out there and nip it in the bud. Do it in person, dirty and personal if it came to it, face to face, the long knife slippery with blood on her hand, looking the loser straight in the eyes as the life drained away. She had been there before.

On this enterprise she hadn't anticipated casualties. She wondered how she could have been so naïve. It seemed they had already taken at least one back in Greece, probably the guilty party, but she well knew that once this sort of thing started it was as difficult to stop as a war.

Helena went down the stairs, stepped out the back door, and made her way along the alley, turning into Commercial Street. It was a shadow of its old times, when the street was filled with markets, and every warehouse was an emporium *to the trade*. Yet, this was a market morning, and a few survivors still set out their misty-eyed fish on heaps of ice, and early bird hawkers were already haranguing small groups of punters with the ageless words: "Look 'ere, what could be fairer than that?"

She had intentionally set up her own safe house in one of the few remaining truly undeveloped, seedy parts of London. She often dressed down, at least in her overcoat, and maintained changes of clothes in the project safe house, not to mention disguise kits. She would soon introduce her team to that part of the game.

She reassured herself that she had not been aware of anything untoward at Heathrow airport, or on the way home, yet she sensed something now. If true, that was a deep problem, because they could only be nearby at this moment if her safe house had been found. She could also expect them to be top-graders, and the standard double-backs, shop windows, and all the other tools wouldn't be likely to work. Nevertheless, she very discretely exercised them all with such care that the followers would not detect that she was checking it out. As expected, nothing was seen. Maybe she was imagining it, but in the end, she trusted her instincts instead of favouring hope above experience.

It was too dangerous to go to the project safe house. The leak had only happened the day before, and the earliest anybody could have taken up the chase was yesterday evening on her return from Greece. She pushed through the door of her local coffee shop, and took a seat in the back corner against the last front window, affording her an unobstructed view of the street and all passers-by. In the colder months, condensation on the windows would make such surveillance impossible; at this time of year it was still difficult because Darley, the proprietress of the café, didn't believe in washing windows.

"Usual double coffee, neat, Luv?"

Helena smiled and beckoned Darley closer with the slightest tilt of her head. "Any strangers in this morning?" Or, she added as an afterthought, "late last night?"

Helena, able to view her at a close proximity, suddenly realised that Darley probably wasn't as old as she had previously thought. She wasn't stooped, nor overweight, and Helena could see that she didn't dye her hair, unless a professional had done it within the last 48 hours. She couldn't picture Darley in a hair salon, or being able to do that good a job herself, or taking the time to do so. Her face was lined, but not deeply, yet she gave the impression of greater age. Helena concluded that thirty years of hard work and long hours, starting at age 14 or so could have done the job.

"No, all reglers."

"Hey, darlin', how's about them Danish?" Everyone just naturally called her that.

Darley had turned to answer her customer, and then twisted around, rubbing her back at a flash of discomfort from the unexpected movement. "Now ya mention, two men, as I was a closin' up, one-ish." Helena waited for more, reaching into her handbag for encouragement. They had played this game before. It always paid to have an outside man or two, and with her local newsagent across the street, Darley was the second of these vital watchdogs. "Wanted the street name; one fiftyish, dyed blond hair, medium, strong woman; other late twenties, tall, square-head, butch black hair, male muscle."

"Thanks." Helena slid a ten-pound note across the table under her hand, and Darley retrieved it over the edge of the table. Even somebody standing next to them would have had difficulty in seeing the transaction, a form of magic many in her line had mastered, and everyone in Helena's.

There was no definite suspicion from two non-locals happening into the café at closing time, she thought, yet it bore consideration. The fact that their ages differed, and were unlikely to be closely related, was a significant point. Another thought winkled its way up Helena's spine, a rare one-off she had been warned about in the service when she was still green herself.

She went to the miniscule, ancient, and yet spotlessly clean loo just to her right. This was another reason for making this her table whenever possible. She could watch everyone and all movements within the café, including visits to the facilities.

She locked the door behind her, and sat on the toilet with the cover down, a tiny hand basin within reach in front of her. Helena pushed the chromium drain plug tight down, and dumped the contents of her handbag into it. She fingered her way through each item, setting them out, one by one, on the narrow shelf above. Nothing seemed out of the ordinary. Next came the change purse, including all the coins, all carefully examined. Then she pulled out the keys in the side pocket. She was about to push them back; the empty purse was not quite right. She flexed the thin layers of soft leather, and then slipped her index finger in. There was something stuck to the inside, and she freed it with some difficulty using her fingernail.

It was a postage-stamp sized chip of plastic about the thickness of the cardboard backing from a writing pad. She knew instantly what it was, why it was there, and how it had got there. It was first-class tradecraft, and the latest kit. She had never seen a tracking transmitter and battery in such a small package.

Somebody aboard the same plane had probably tagged her on the flight to London. The agent only had to open the overhead compartment, reach in, open her handbag, then the change purse, peel off the unit's protective plastic cover, and stick it in. No need to see it, going by feel alone would certainly be easy enough even for an amateur. She always used to keep her handbag over her shoulder and across her neck at all times or used the belt-bag and all the other tricks, but being out of the game had lulled her into a false sense of security in some of the small things. She now realized that the new game was far more serious and deadly than the old one. She vowed that nothing would ever be left to chance again.

She knew she had probably lost him, her or them on the way back from the airport. A range of 50 metres, certainly achievable in such a device, would have refreshed the trail, and nailed her to the safe house. That also meant they could lay-back on the following, and stay well off her radar screen. She carefully replaced the device, swept everything back into her handbag, and returned to her table.

She flipped open her digital telephone with determination, keying the number of her flat and a series of text messages:

SEND: COMMAND STATUS PIN 24266442.
REPLY: ENTRY SECURE. NO ENTRY SINCE LAST RESET.
SEND: SELF DESTRUCT CODE: 67aK92bqDE.
REPLY: ACKNOWLEDGED. REPEAT CODE.
SEND: 67aK92bqDE.
REPLY: COUNTDOWN BEGINS. 30 … 29 … 28 … ."

Helena then fast-keyed for the emergency services. "I want to report a fire at Number 82A, Commercial Close, off Commercial Road. It's the penthouse flat."

Adam and Peter met as agreed at 8AM in the safe house. Adam had a long list of computer tasks, and Peter was installing several convenience items including a heat pump for warmth in winter and air conditioning in summer. The latter was not strictly necessary, or common in the UK, but the insulation of the basement was effective, and the equipment produced considerable heat. Their comfort and the computers' were justification enough as he saw it, Adam agreeing wholeheartedly. In any case, it would make a nice surprise for everyone.

Peter hummed softly as he unrolled extension cords for the electrical wiring, and Adam fired up the computers, which produced a music of their own from spinning disks, and the sliding to and fro of the mice.

"Some New Age okay, Peter?"

"Sure, why not."

Adam slipped an audio CD into the main server, and a creditable sound spoke softly from two pretty decent loudspeakers. The music was reminiscent of warm seas and tropical jungles.

Peter brought in coffee and hot chocolate on a tray. "What'cha up to, ole buddy?"

"The usual housekeeping, then check out the new software I got that stores our local UK digital text-phone messaging. Helena insisted we keep a secure copy; it's part of our documentation."

"I thought 'secure' meant that nobody but the receiver could..."

"Sure, that's right, but it all passes through here, and Helena wants a record. This system is top security, several fail-safes, remote and intruder self-destruct, all those goodies, no significant risk. So let's see if it's working." Adam's fingers flew, the mouse scurrying back and forth. The screen scrolled the latest messages first:

```
HELENA TO CHARON
    WILL IT SPREAD?
HELENA TO CHARON:
    IF VENDETTA, LIKELY CONTAINABLE.
    IF NOT, ANYBODY'S GUESS.
HELENA TO CHARON:
    THE TEAM?
HELENA TO CHARON:
    THAT VIOLATES MY COMMITMENTS HERE.
```

Adam keyed the music player software to pause, and the room fell silent.

Peter shook his head and frowned. "Are you thinking what I'm thinking?"

"Doesn't look good."

"It's obviously a two-way with Charon, where's the other half?"

"We only have access to our encryption. If Charon had used ours, we'd have it. He was obviously using a higher level. I think..."

"We've got trouble here, real trouble." Peter was tapping hard on the screen.

"And Helena's caught in the middle."

"Okay, start from the top, will what 'spread'?"

"Well, the 'trouble', whatever it is." Adam mused quietly to himself for a moment. "What danger can spread, though??"

"Based on my old warehouse crowd, who were usually pretty tight-lipped, especially when something was on the make ... I'd guess it's a 'blab' – but what would our spy-craft partners call it?"

"A leak."

"Shee-ite, Adam, not their end, surely?"

"Helena said it's hot, and I think she was worried about the number of people we might need. How many have we got, here and in Greece?"

"Don't know, probably several besides us. We always tried to keep it below a half dozen, and *no birds*, at least none with any attachments to the team, get me drift?"

Adam nodded.

"What does she mean by a 'vendetta' anyway?"

"Well, something along the lines of 'getting even' and 'personal'."

"Like a grudge or a blood-feud? Sure, we had 'em, always nasty."

"I think so."

"Surely not *their* end?"

Adam paused. "I can't see through the last two lines. 'Team' and 'violates commitments', any ideas?"

"Oh, that's easy. Charon is telling her she can't tell us, and she is telling him that she has promised to keep us square."

Adam patted Peter on the back; he knew he wouldn't have been able to figure it out that quickly by himself. He was rapidly becoming aware of the value of being street smart.

"So, what are we goin' to do about it?

"What can we do? She's on her own, and so are we. They don't want us in the game. Probably think we're amateurs, likely to gum up the works."

"We are, but she's got four against her, two by two, and maybe the long knives are out for us too, did you think of that?"

"You're probably right, and I was beginning to feel a bit jumpy."

" But what do *we* do about it?"

"We'd better warn Irini."

ADAM TO IRINI: POSSIBLE PROBLEMS, WATCH YOURSELF.

"Shouldn't we give her the whole story?

"Sure, but what? We have ideas, no confirmation. Why worry her? She's sharp; she'll take it seriously. What more can she do?"

"Okay, okay, just a thought." Peter grabbed the phone. "Trev, glad I caught you. Need two of your best bloodhounds, the type wot can take care of themselves, get me drift?"

"When?"

"Yesterday."

"Okay, call it ten AM, where?"

"Garfunkels Restaurant, Tottenham Court Road station, white carnation."

"If I can get the two I want, they know you."

"I'll wear it anyway."

"For luck, yes, I remember. On a no-show, call me back, mobile."

Helena finished her coffee, chatted casually with Darley at the cash register, then went out and walked down the street towards Liverpool Street station. She bought a *Guardian* at the newsagents. She hoped that the transmitter still had some juice left so that she could play out act two her way. It was a long walk, but a pleasant morning, and no doubt they all would benefit from the exercise.

The restaurant was not crowded at this hour, and it was easy for Adam to spot the two men Trev had sent. Peter happened to be in the loos when they arrived, so their scan of the place gave rise to frowns. Adam waved to them, and they came over, glancing around cautiously. "Peter will be back in a flash with the cash. I'm Adam, his associate. He'll verify that when he comes out. Please sit down."

They did so with obvious hesitations of body language. Their identical plaid cloth jackets, same light brown crew cut, facial resemblances, plus a perceptible age difference, marked them as brothers. They were both in their twenties, lithe, whip-strong, tanned from an early holiday together he reckoned, and probably warehousemen given their body conditioning and connection with Peter's background.

"Thanks lads." Peter slid into the booth on Adam's side. "He's okay. Here's the gig." Peter handed a picture across. "Name not important. She's a, uh, friend." Peter cleverly put the emphasis on the words so that his colleagues would take it that this was personal, and emotional, rather than the dark business of their reality.

"You'll still have to watch yourselves." Peter felt it was morally necessary to warn them, even though they all knew the most dangerous situations were often of just this kind. It was all reasonably truthful; even they didn't know the depth of this particular problem.

"She's being followed, maybe two, maybe four or more, could be of either sex, any age. When I get more info, I'll pass it on *toute suite*." In response to their blank stares, Peter translated from his recently learned basic French, "Right away, lads."

"What do you think, Peter, distract them and get Helena clear?" Adam shrugged uncertainly.

"For my money," Peter offered, "track them to earth. Find out where they live. Report."

Adam agreed. They were both trying to answer the questions: "What would Helena do? How would an experienced intelligence agent deal with this?"

One of the men handed over a slip of paper. "Here's our mobiles' numbers. It's done. Where do we start?"

"That's one of our problems. I'll have instructions for you shortly."

Adam slid two envelopes across the table. Each contained a hundred pounds he had taken out of his own bank account, as Peter had requested.

"For expenses." Peter added, to curt nods, the envelopes seeming to disappear from the table without either man having touched them. "Hang around the Underground right here, it's central, and you can go in any direction."

"Okay. Best to yah." The two departed without further comment. Adam noted with some interest that names had not been used. Was this evidence of another similarity between life on the darker side south of the Thames, and the new game they were learning?

"We don't dare go to the safe house until we are sure the coast is clear, eh?" Peter spoke in a non-questioning voice, as though it answered itself, which as Adam confirmed with a nod, it did.

"But we need one in any case."

They went around the corner and took a room in the Jackson Hotel, Bloomsbury. The concierge gave them an extra once-over, and they had to smile at that in the ancient, iron-grilled lift. "He thinks we're a couple of gay brothers, I think." Peter offered, to Adam's bashful nod.

"No luggage, midday, uncertain how long we are staying. I'd have been curious myself." Adam feigned a hug, and Peter copied him.

"If we were in to that, and I have some mates who are," Peter admitted without the slightest discomfort, "we could have a lot more fun than we are going to this afternoon."

"Safer too." Then Adam thought again. Maybe all of life was one big risk, and if it wasn't, wouldn't be worthwhile.

Peter keyed in Helena's number and the access codes.

Helena had bought a day return to Cambridge. She wanted to be on a train, one on the empty side. At this hour, the stopping train to Cambridge was ideal. After buying the tickets she took a seat in the waiting room with a clear view of the ticket windows and awaited developments.

This posed a challenge for her pursuers, whom she knew were there. What she didn't know was whether they were the same two as at the café last night, two or more others, or what, and that information was vital.

When it was three minutes to departure, and they had still not appeared to buy tickets, Helena was forced to trot across and through the doors to the platform. A young boy was coming back from the train that was loading up for Cambridge. He was about to pass her by, when suddenly she put out a friendly arm, and caught him. "How many tickets did the lady ask you to buy?"

The astonished boy could not help but blurt out the answer: "Four." Then, "Who are you? … How did you know?" He looked guilty now, and quite right too, Helena thought to herself. Probably pocketed at least a quid or two (actually, it was a generous fiver).

She answered his question, though, "I saw you buy them." She reached into her handbag, and folded a tenner in her fist. The boy's eyes glowed. "Describe them and it's yours."

"Well," he looked back over his shoulder, "two old men…"

Helena interrupted in the interest of time. "How old? Think. At your age, all older people look old, do they not?"

"Yes, well, about the same as my mother, so thirty or so – my dad's ten years older – a 'tall and small' pair (he was thinking of a new TV series, yet that was nevertheless helpful), suits, dark, striped, light raincoats."

"Do you know a Burberry?"

"Yes, like that, but cheaper I think, tan coloured."

"And the other two?

"Well, older lady, blond, dark jumper. Big, young man, younger than the others, strong…"

The whistle was blowing, and Helena had to run, but she had what she needed. The boy ran off with the ten-pound note, the first he had ever earned.

Helena should have caught on the moment she saw a youngster no more than eight years old buying a handful of tickets, but it had not registered until she saw him again, coming *back* from a departure platform. She put down one mark in her favour, and two against, for the effort. With that kind of scoring, she wouldn't live out the day, if their intent were termination.

As the platform was then clear, except for three last-minute runners, herself now joining with them, she could hope that her encounter with the lad had not been seen. Another question: how did they know she was going to Cambridge? There were several answers, but the most likely, she told herself as she stepped aboard, was that one of them had been standing right behind her when she bought her ticket. Had she lost it all, every cat's whisker of intuition?

At this rate she wouldn't last the hour! Just another broken body tossed off the train, as simple as that. The thought of such a fate was not what was causing goose bumps to rise on her forearms, any more than one of them with a naked knife standing right in front of her would. It was the loss of her sharpness that rankled, and cut as deep as such a weapon might. She scanned a nearly empty car near the back, no likely occupants on the descriptions she had, and sat down at an end window seat facing forward with a full view of the car and the other carriages beyond. There was also enough space between her and the blind corner at the exit so that she would have a fair shot at any attack from that quarter.

Much of her disquiet was because her team was at risk, perhaps under attack, and she was helpless to do anything about it for the moment. Her first duty had to be to employ herself in the gathering of as much intelligence as possible – for that read identifications. Only armed with that would she, and they, have a chance. Her opponents would see it on the reverse side of the coin – that she was the professional – and had to be dealt with first. This realization eased her spirits somewhat, and she settled in to wait.

Might some professional muscle lunge around the blind corner, silenced gun or blade at the ready? That was possible, but unlikely. A dark alley tonight, or whatever hotel room she was forced to repair to, were far more likely, and safe for them. Or perhaps they were counting on her flat, unless they had put it together when the fire engines howled past as they walked down to Liverpool Street.

Half an hour later, as the train approached Duxford, its last stop before Cambridge, her secure digital phone vibrated (she had turned off the chimes). With her right hand in her light overcoat pocket, aimed up at the blind spot between her and the rear door, she keyed the phone with her left hand.

"Peter here. Where are you?"

"Where I need to be. Any problems? Why the call?"

"Hold a sec."

Adam had tugged on Peter's arm. "What are you going to say?"

"Lie, I suppose, tell her Charon has sent a message. She'll put it together."

"Not a bad idea, but why not the truth? That we have her half of the conversation, and figured it out, mostly you did, anyway."

Peter handed the phone to Adam. "Adam here. I was working the computers this morning, as you know, and when I tested the phone text messaging storage option, your half of the conversation with Charon popped up, first thing."

Helena painfully rapped her left fist against her head with the phone still clutched in it. She had automatically replied using their own fully secure encoding, but should have used the Agency's.

"Hello, still there?"

"Yes lads. So you put it together?"

"Yes, well, mostly Peter; we didn't have much to go on."

Helena had already concluded that by recollection, and she marked Peter up more points than she had lost that day.

"Helena, Peter has a couple of sharp guys, really, maybe not quite in your league, but solid, know what I mean?"

"Okay."

"Well, what are we going to do about it? What's the play, Helena?"

"Give me a tick." She had intended the old reliable of sticking the transmitter under the seat, and switching trains at the next stop. She knew from the schedule that the southbound stopped there only a couple of minutes after this train arrived, and they were on time (for once). With luck, her pursuers would be dropped for a while. Backup was on the way, and waiting for it was by the book. On the other hand it could be a long battle that way.

Now she had other options, and saw that her plan was weak. Her first thought of the morning was the correct one, to bring them along, *not* lose them, identify, find some way to turn the game around, and track them. It was personnel for this last step that had defeated her. She realized that she should have called the boys herself, amateurs and Charon notwithstanding, exactly as she would have done when in the service. Local backup would have been her first call, not her last.

"Okay Peter, Adam, I want to turn the tables. You were right to hire some help. It's far too dangerous for you two to expose yourselves. Here's the play. I'll be back, with, I hope, all four tails, Liverpool Street, at, let's see, 13:40 hours, from Cambridge. Track them if you can spot them, don't touch, don't be seen. I think this round may be for keeps."

"Following was our half-baked idea too, Helena."

"It was not half-baked, it's spot on. One female, fifties, dyed blond hair, medium, strong, may be in dark jumper, partner, male, late twenties, tall, square-head, butch cut, black hair, muscle. Two men, thirty, 'tall and small' like the TV series, dark striped suits, imitation Burberry tan raincoats."

Peter whistled. "Got a good look at them did you?"

"No, haven't seen any of them. Look, lads, I'll try to have them in tow at Liverpool Street. I'll drop them, right out in plain sight, so that should help with the ID. Just look for them, and don't worry about me, okay?"

"Right."

"Out."

The train was pulling into Duxford station. Helena moved forward in the car, and exited at the front. She was enjoying life again, and felt that the pages before her were not blank anymore. The southbound was just coming along the platform, and she took the opportunity to board at once rather than scanning the platform to spot her pursuers. A series of possibilities crossed her mind. Yes, that's probably what they would be expecting. Yet maybe they would feel that this was too easy. Were they being sucked in? Or was she simply trying to double-drop tails? The latter was more likely, and sure enough, the four followed dutifully without a qualm.

Helena was able to spot them all towards the front of the north-bound, boarding at the rear of her train. She watched them by looking through her window and along the reflections in the windows of the other train. It was a lucky coincidence that both trains were at the platform together.

Who were they working for? What was their intent? What was in it for them, or their masters? It was difficult for Helena to speculate on these questions. If British MI5 were involved, she would understand, and know what to do. Indeed, she would be surprised if they didn't come out of the woodwork at some point.

Nevertheless, these people had been ordered to do something, by someone high in the Greek intelligence services. That was difficult enough to take in, but she had to accept it. The "why" and "what" completely escaped her. Perhaps she would eventually be told, but "eventually" was the operable word, and not much comfort.

She needed to figure it out right now. Helena had taken a seat among other people, with a rear view back through the carriages. At each stop she tried to see if any of them got off the train, but this had proved to be difficult, and she couldn't be sure.

Her thoughts turned again to the motivation. She had scuppered the plans of more than one criminal gang, but she also knew that they rarely attacked those who officially worked against them. There was too much danger and risk of exposure from a governmental backlash. Economic interests, personal motives? She hadn't stolen anybody's lover, killed or injured anybody for whom revenge might follow.

The timing was certainly suspicious, coming within three days of her disclosure to Spiros, and the involvement of Charon. Whatever happened, she was determined to get to the bottom of it, even if that must wait until after the Lift.

The train squeaked to a halt, and Helena was first off, striding forward ahead of the pack. She didn't look back, and instead made directly for the *Pret a Manger*. She took a table at the rear with a clear view across the café through to the exits by courtesy of wall-to-wall windows. After a much-needed cup of coffee and an apricot croissant for lunch, she stuck the radio transmitter under her table, got up, and performed her standard disappearing act. No need to go to the loos and through a window, or anything like that. She simply put on her light overcoat, reversed, flipping it inside out while lifting it from the seat back, took a floppy hat out of its pocket, dropped her chignon with a shake of the head, and went out concealed behind her own hair and a gaggle of students.

They all left the station together. Just at the main door, Helena stepped aside, and trotted around the corner to another coffee shop, ducked in, and watched the exit. Sometimes the simplest tricks are the best.

Back in the station, the two agents had been watching from a stand-up café across the concourse from *Pret a Manger*. Helena was there, and then gone, when they looked up a few seconds later. Their radio direction finder remained on target, and so they continued to eat their lunch snack. After ten minutes they finally tumbled to the truth. Madame walked across, sat down at Helena's table, and retrieved the tracker, using her fingernail as the only necessary tool.

She let her partner follow at a distance, leaving the restaurant and the station. They thought they could pick up Helena later at her flat, and so called it a day. They knew that her professional reinforcements wouldn't be in London for at least another two or three hours, so they didn't double-drop tails. It would be by the book like everyone else had to do after they arrived. Their information was sound, and sufficiently up-to-date for their purposes, but they had underestimated their opposition.

HELENA TO PETER AND ADAM:
CLEAR. DON'T GO TO SAFE HOUSE. WHERE ARE YOU?
PETER AND ADAM:
ROOM 16, JACKSON HOTEL, BLOOMSBURY.
HELENA:
THAT WILL DO NICELY. ETA THIRTY MINUTES.

Three knocks. "Okay lads, it's me."
"Thank God you're safe, Helena."
"Any news from your operatives?"
Peter smiled with satisfaction, "On the scent."
"They spotted them?"
"The couple – the others didn't get off the train."
"Are you going to lie low for a while then?" Adam questioned.
"No, need a new place."
"What? Why? We'll pick them up eventually, won't we?" Adam was visibly worried, and not just for Helena. His thoughts had turned uncomfortably to Irini.
"Burned down," was all that Helena said.

"What?" The lads chorused.

"By self-destruct. I phoned it in and then called 999. That's one reason I had a penthouse, if you could describe that dump as such. No danger to others."

"Well I never!" Peter gasped, shaking his head. "You're starting over from scratch?"

"Well, I needed a new wardrobe anyway!"

Helena's phone chimed the text music.

CHARON TO HELENA:
BACKUP IS HERE, HEATHROW.
HELENA TO CHARON:
COME ON IN. KEEP IN TOUCH. MAY HAVE WORD SHORTLY.

Peter's phone spoke. "Two gone to ground, 227B, Park Close, apartment 5."

Helena sent this as text to Charon with the descriptions. She added the comment, "Courtesy of Peter's operatives."

CHARON TO HELENA:
GOOD, FAST WORK. WE'LL TAKE IT FROM HERE.
WORD IS CONFIRMED, 2X2. ANY INFO ON OTHERS?
HELENA TO CHARON:
DESCRIPTION FOLLOWS.
LEFT CAMBRIDGE TO LONDON TRAIN
AT INTERMEDIATE STATION 13:00 ISH.
WHEREABOUTS UNKNOWN AT THIS TIME.
CHARON TO HELENA:
WE'LL HOLD THE PAIR & WATCH THEIR UNSAFE HOUSE FOR
OTHERS. SMART TO BE MILES APART,
BUT YOU NEVER KNOW.
HELENA TO CHARON:
PETER TUGGING SLEEVE. TRAIN TO LIVERPOOL STREET,
NOT KINGS X. IS THIS A DOUBLE OH TAKEOUT?
CHARON TO HELENA:
NOT IF WE CAN GRAB THEM CLEAN.
STRONGER ALTERNATIVE (FOR US) HAS BEEN ARRANGED.

They had pizza delivered to the hotel room for dinner, and then Adam went back to his dorm. Peter was held behind by Helena, and in the end, they fell asleep in the separate beds. For a moment Peter thought that maybe something he had in mind might happen, out of the blue, swinger-style. He had decided to make a play for Helena, and certainly realized it was both unlikely, and would demand great delicacy. He was looking forward to the challenge.

Instead Helena had told him quite pointedly how well he had done, and that she would feel safer doing it by the book this night, with a partner. Truthfully, she was feeling professional loneliness, yet tinged with respect and a degree of affection for Peter.

When he thought about it the next day, Peter put it down as a good start. They had bonded that night, always a good thing when "on the game", and by that he meant the project, not "chasing the birds", yet it applied to both if it came to that.

CHARON TO HELENA:
    3AM REPORT: TWO IN HAND AND OFF TO POKEY.
    WILL KNOW MUCH MORE LATER.
    NO SIGN OF OTHER TWO. ONE STAYS HERE,
        TWO TO FAN OUT. I DON'T EXPECT PEOPLE
    OF THIS CALIBER TO SHOW UP HERE.
HELENA TO CHARON:
    THANK YOU. GET SOME REST YOURSELVES.

Helena showed Peter the messages, and translated the first line to his questioning frown. "They'll get the juice, Peter, and then we'll know what they know."

"God, can you do that?"

"Sure, we can do it, but I didn't imply it was legal!"

Chapter 6

In the Shadows of the British Museum

Sometimes the Copies are better than the Originals.

Irini's flat, a converted loft, lay down a narrow cul-de-sac off Museum Street, from which the British Museum's imposing outline could be seen. At times she felt she was sailing above the tops of the brave plane trees that graced the hidden courtyard below. It was an unexpectedly quiet corner, seemingly far from the hubbub of Bloomsbury Way's incessant traffic.

Irini counted herself so lucky to have found it. Although modest in size, she had the third floor to herself, and its limitations were outweighed by convenience and the surrounding ambiance. Its mixture of exotic antique bookshops, delis, pubs, and ethnic restaurants, all on an intimate scale, were exactly what she felt she needed to sustain her. It was only a short walk from the Courtauld and Senate House libraries, almost within the protective shadows of the British Museum.

Here, one space encompassed all: kitchen, dining room, and behind a delicately carved wooden screen from Thailand, the bedroom. Her private bathroom was across the landing. All was a harmonious miniature.

She smiled to herself as she imagined Adam's reaction to the flat's dimensions. "Hardly enough room to swing a cat round." She'd warned him. As if she would use her precious *Achilles* for such a pointless demonstration. Neither, she was quite sure, would Achilles have cooperated. He had an innate sense of his own feline gravitas, both in personality and his six kilograms of robust form. Nevertheless, he generally favoured graceful postures, which showed off his white elegance, and startling blue-green eyes.

It was the quality of light that filtered through the skylights that had clinched the deal for her. This never failed to lift her spirits, even in the darkest days of a London winter. It also encouraged her to sketch, among other things, the sculptures that had become the focus of her life. It also drew from her the expressions of the spirit embodied in them, a quality that had eluded her when she had the originals in front of her at the British Museum. She fully appreciated the irony, in that she was working here with small copies purchased in the museum shop.

Although not obsessive in her tidiness, and suspicious of those who were, circumstances forced her compliance to a reasonable discipline.

She thought, as she prepared the nibbles, pre-dinner drinks, and light meal, that she must remember to warn Adam to duck his head where the beams bent low, especially over the bed. She giggled to herself as a scene that had not before entered her mind flooded into her consciousness. First of all, where did this come from? Second, was she serious, ready, willing, or unable?

The entry speaker buzzed, and Irini took the two steps from the kitchen alcove to the door, and pressed the release button. She flitted around the room, setting out the glasses, and the ice bucket. Then came the discreet knock at the door. She took a deep breath, counted to three to ease the rhythm of her heart's palpitations, and slipped the latch.

Adam smiled, and it came across as intended, sweetly modest. He probably did not intend to reveal vulnerability, yet it was clearly expressed there by both whether either of them saw it in the other or not. He thrust forward a generous bouquet of her favourite flowers, striped Tiger lilies. It was the gesture of an amateur, of course, but she didn't mind, and accepted them with a slight curtsey. She welcomed him across the threshold by sweeping the flowers behind her, and moving slightly to the side behind the half-open door. There wasn't room to comfortably step back in the usual way because the dining table and living room furniture filled the room.

She closed the door behind him, and he reached forward to draw her to him, and delivered a light, cheek-to-cheek kiss on each side. This was a new gesture, picked up from his European associates. They were both nervous, yet this was right for them at that moment, and helped to dissipate the adrenaline.

Irini sniffed the bouquet with eyes closed in rapture, taking in the opulent fragrance. She beamed, "You remembered." She had only mentioned her favourite flower to him once. In her experience of men – limited though it was, as she had to admit to herself yet again – one usually had to take a full page in the *Times* to have any effect.

Achilles jumped down from his normal position at the end of the couch, where the curve of the padded armrest provided ideal back support, and observed the proceedings from a discreet distance. His posture was the same as that of a shy person waiting to be introduced in circumstances that were not yet quite resolved.

Irini knelt down, and the cat minced over to her, accepting a stroke of the back, but remained on the opposite side from Adam. "This is *Achilles*."

"Why the name?" Adam asked, having been introduced to the half-compliant cat.

"He's my *Achilles` Heel*," she said with a dry smile, "one of the few distractions that can release me from the ... mundane."

Achilles, now formally introduced, felt able to come around behind Irini. Adam made the right moves, and presented the back of his hand kneeling on one knee. The cat sniffed it delicately, and cocked its head, so that Adam could rub the top of it. He then risked a half stroke of the back, and the cat raised it in response. The formal introduction completed courteously by all concerned, Achilles turned away, and returned to his couch. He lost no time rotating the statutory three times, before settling into precisely the same position he habitually occupied, little warmth having been lost during his brief absence, the minimum that feline courtesy required. It was also clear that he would pay little further attention to Adam, unless he should intrude on his personal space.

Adam impressed her as handsome enough, and seemed to improve with time as she came to know him, through the combination of his physical appearance and his emerging personality. She knew that for her the physical side of a relationship was less important than finding a reason for an attachment, but had seen hopeful signs in his adventurousness and in the fact that he didn't take his good looks seriously or try to trade on them. She hoped that this evening would begin to lay the foundations for something more profound.

Irini was stunning, the most physically perfect woman Adam had ever seen up-close, never mind on a serious date. She was of above average height but not willowy, with medium arms and legs, smooth kneecaps and narrower than average hips like a boy's. Her blemish free, satin skin was lightly dusted here and there with the finest fuzz of soft hair, naturally auburn. Adam would have described her short, straight hairdo as a "crew cut plus". Her personality was delightfully up beat, but he also saw a slightly butch edge to it, without being intrusive, perhaps part of her defensive mechanisms. Each of these characteristics struck Adam as ideally attractive, both individually and in ensemble.

In his experience, most beautiful women were unapproachable. He certainly understood the reasons and sympathized, but wasn't that the easy way out? Did it not render them ultimately lonely? He remembered reading a book with that theme based on interviews of fifty of the world's most beautiful models. He smiled to himself. The plainer examples of the species were still attractive to the right man, and really did have an easier run, though few would have agreed with him. He would have been deeply shocked if Irini had confessed her feelings of insecurity on the subject of frigidity.

Adam felt more than a little bashful about moves, body language, and to what degree he should take control. It was Irini's turf, so he felt his way through it step by step. How many times had he been alone with a woman? How many dates had he really been on? He decided, this time relying on his analytical side, that he didn't have a statistically significant sample, so there was no guide. It was "wing it time", a rarity in his life. He decided to savour this emotion, and roll with the waves, rocking him physically and emotionally.

These thoughts forced a smile from Adam over the dessert that Irini completely misinterpreted as simple satisfaction, unaware of the conundrums of life that were whipsawing Adam at this moment.

Irini got up from the table sat down on the opposite end of the couch to her cat, and Adam followed to sit between them. Achilles cast a baleful eye at him, then shrugged. Perhaps this rare newcomer in their lives would keep his distance. In a moment he was snoring softly, front paws twitching to the rhythm of some daydream, perhaps running in a cat's version of Elysian Fields.

There was an awkward silence that Irini broke with the old ploy of asking him more about himself. "So, what was all that about the bank vault in New York?" Adam had mentioned this in passing when giving his verbal Curriculum Vitae to the group, and Irini had pulled some newspaper articles off the Internet from the time, to follow up out of personal interest.

"Aw, just a gig for some fun." Adam shook his head in self-deprecation, as though it happened every day to someone, somewhere. Irini knew better, so he was forced to fill the pregnant pause with more details.

"Well, it always frosts me when some so-called expert pontificates on an obvious fallacy. This guy had a new design for an all-electronic vault, patent in-hand, and everything. The bank was making a big deal out of it, so I went to the New York Public Library and got a photocopy of the patent. I guess there was some sort of deal going on between them; maybe the bank was investing in his new idea, or something. I never found out about that. The design was laughable, and full of holes."

"So what did you do?"

"Well, the right thing, I thought. I wrote a letter to the inventor care of the bank, pointing out one of the obvious problems."

"And?"

"And, well, this attorney shows up at my house and serves me with papers. They were suing me! Well, I couldn't believe it, and neither could my dad, and for once in his life he stood up for me." This last admission was covered with a strained smile of hidden pain. If Adam had realized how transparent his facial language had been, he would have done something about it. But endearingly, to her, he wore all of this on his open face without shame or worry that somebody might use such insights to hurt him. She suspected, correctly, that he had been taken advantage of in this way, and to his cost.

"For what?" Irini's incredulity surfaced with a sharp intake of breath.

"Trumped up – they wanted to silence me – but they miscalculated. They didn't know me, and they didn't know my dad. He hired a real sharpie, and we counter-sued for harassment. They hadn't expected that, still I saw it was going to cost my dad a lot of money, and hassle he couldn't afford. So I cut it all off at the pass."

"How did you manage that; seems like a tall order for a, what, sixteen year old?"

"Mayhaps, but you know me, I'll go for it, if I can. So I called a press conference."

"Did anybody come?"

"Oh sure, a stringer from the *New York Times* and the local advertiser. It was a bit of a no-no, like our attorney told me afterwards, but he was smiling. I remembered that scene in the old film with Paul Newman, *Cool Hand Luke*, where he says he can eat fifty eggs."

"I remember. It was one of the rare Hollywood films with a tragic ending, but uplifting. An almost European feel to it."

"That's the one. Well, anyway, I said I could open the vault any time they wanted. I said that I had written a letter to the inventor trying to be helpful, but all we had gotten was a nasty lawsuit, and I hadn't done anything wrong. You know how you feel at that age when you're blamed for something you haven't done.

"Well, the *New York Times* jumped on the bank, and they were embarrassed. After that they tried to back off, but my dad wouldn't let them without the bank paying our legal costs and a hundred grand on top! Imagine that." Now his expression was one of open admiration for his father.

"So the bank said that if I could open the safe, I could pick up a briefcase inside the vault door with the hundred grand, and they'd settle with our lawyers. But if I failed, we had to pay the costs both sides."

"How much was that?"

"Hell, I don't know, maybe twenty grand."

"That's a hefty sum, Adam. What if you had failed?"

"I didn't, did I?"

"No doubt they were getting their money's worth on the publicity either way." Irini offered.

"Uh, sure, I guess. Hadn't really thought of it that way."

"So how did you do it?"

"As I had thought, their computer-based system was too complicated, and didn't have a mechanical backup. Most electronic safes have both. That was my point. So I knew the way in was using a worm, up an open trapdoor."

Irini didn't ask; she simply waited, and was delivered of the answers.

"Well, in software, like any complex system, the programmers need to test, and to do that efficiently they need entry points, like doors in a large building. It's no good having to go through all the program's operations to reach and find and fix some error. So at major crossroads in the logic, special entry points are programmed in. Usually they forget to close all of them off.

"The Bank's system used an electronic key. The manager would insert it into a slot making connection with the computer inside. This black box had a little computer in it that would provide the necessary codes to open the safe. The only problem was the fact that the thumb-print of the manager had to be pressed on a small glass window in the door."

"Quite a problem, I should think?"

"Naw, bit of hassle hacking into the New York Driver's License Bureau – piece of cake compared with the DOD." He had inadvertently let a darker corner of his past slip in.

"Yes, I remember – that's something, the Department of Defence isn't it?"

"Yes, but I was only following the lead of a very famous Brit – famous in our circles anyway – who did yours a year or so before me. As usual our people paid no attention to anything or anybody anywhere else, left it wide open and I couldn't resist. They would have thrown me in the can, and dropped the key down a well, but I wasn't fourteen by a few days, and they couldn't."

"You were put in a special school, weren't you?"

"Yep, youth custody for two years."

"That's awful!"

"Actually it wasn't so bad. They relied a lot on education by computer, the latest *in* thing. I learned to fix system software problems, and sometimes the hardware. They rewarded me for helping out, so after a while I had my own computer, and then it was the sixteen hours a day of a true addict."

"What about school?"

"Got it there, by computer. I can see now that I was learning a lot in many fields – that kind of surfing is irresistible and it just soaks in, like that." Adam snapped his fingers. "I'm a bit weak on history and art, the sort of things you and the others love so much, but I got a taste – virtual tours of the Louvre on the Internet, that sort of thing."

"So, going back to the bank, let me get this straight. You got his fingerprint from the State records?"

"Exactly, and I made a copy on my thumb with *NuSkin*; you use it to cover wounds. It was a bit of work. I had to make a photographic copy in the negative, transfer that to glass, which I etched with hydrofluoric acid in the usual way. I put mould release on that, and painted on the NuSkin, and pressed my finger down on it. So I was him for the day, thumb-wise at least."

"And the small matter of the black box computer-key?"

"I had what is called an industrial process control unit, long since obsolete, picked up in a second hand computer shop. I used it to turn my lights on and off on verbal commands, that sort of thing. Played a trick or two on my younger brother, and dad, too. I had been working in software with worms and trap doors all my adult life – if that's the right expression for a teenager – so the rest was easy. I loaded it with a program that would find any trap door left open, and then push code through it that completely disabled the software, so the safe had to open."

"So, tell me, what is a worm?"

Adam laughed throatily, "Just a bit of code, but neat name, eh? It is called a worm because it worms its way through another piece of software, and eats it up, just like us, after we die – pretty soon, no more us – pretty soon, no more program. Then 'click' and open sesame."

"You actually said that, and waved your hand, didn't you?"

"I guess. I mean hell, Irini, might as well enjoy the moment. Like the man said, we only get fifteen minutes worth of them in one lifetime. I learned that one too, but it was fun while it lasted."

"Was the briefcase there as promised?"

"Oh sure, and I made a big deal out of picking it up, and holding it out in front of the TV cameras. Just like I've seen your Chancellor of the Exchequer do when he tells everyone how much more tax we'll be paying. It was a laugh and a half."

"And a bit for the bank account?"

"Yes, and I opened mine right then and there in that very same bank!"

Irini laughed, and laughed, until she had to wipe her eyes. This last of the several ironies in his tale was one too many and she couldn't help herself.

He stopped laughing before she did and turned serious. "There was something else, much more important than my fleeting fame and fortune. The bullies at school were silenced forever – worth more to me than all the rest."

His account gave Irini much to feel her way through. Quite a lot of it she respected and admired, but much of it she did not yet fully understand or identify with. Her life at that age had been so different.

She had only herself to blame for throwing the floodgates open. In a sense she had created a temporary six-foot-two Frankenstein of volubility she could not control. His energy could be used in so many other directions, and she began to blame herself for her own mounting physical frustration. She had been attracted to him as a person, and now wanted him to shut up.

The pleasurable yet sharply disquieting inner yearnings and squirmings, that were delicate yet undeniable, were a new experience at this level for her. She wondered sardonically if a lower-cut top, more attention to perfume, or extra candles here and there around the room, incense burning, a lamp hidden behind the bed casting a softer light, might have given Adam more clues. Then she debated with herself, what were her feelings? Was she ready? She finally decided that in spite of his decisive manner, sometimes bordering on the brash, that it was she who must take the lead in the subtleties of intimacy.

They had been caressing and lightly fondling each other throughout the evening. If things were to move forward he knew that it was his turn to take some initiative. He began by drawing Irini towards him more strongly, almost into a bear hug, limited by the fact that they were sitting down. His head came to rest on her shoulder, and she wrapped her arm around his neck and cuddled, of necessity, somewhat awkwardly. There was just the hint of nervous vibration in her embrace, and he paused. Not to think this time, but to feel. His inner voice then spoke through him as though vocalized by another person.

"I wonder if we are ready for this just now?"

Irini was captured by his gesture, obviously generous, against all that she had been led to believe that motivated men. It was, she later realized, the moment when she came to love him. And for what most of all? – For his sensitivity, a trait she had hoped for, but not expected to find in him.

She now knew that this was not the time, and was certain that Adam had come to the same conclusion. It had been the best of evenings. Irini needed to say much about herself that had not yet come out, but there would be time, and it had been her own fault as she ruefully admitted to herself.

She hugged him again, the twanging in the nerves and muscles now mercifully absent. "Thank you," was all she said.

He understood that this was a dismissal, but not a rejection, and truth to tell, felt relieved. He was sure there would be another time, and the right moment would come. It would be better for this decision, as hard as it was.

Later, she was lying in bed, watching the last inch of candle light flicker. It animated the movements of the Thai dancers on the screen. She suddenly saw that her previous interpretation of this art as simply stylised beauty was now revealed in a fresh dimension. The formerly static postures of bodies and hands had been transformed, energized into sensual expression and movements. Perhaps this was in keeping with her newly awakened self. Was this how to see inside Thai eroticism? How, she now reproved herself, could have possibly thought she could interpret anything in that genre before she herself had been awakened to it? Could this also unlock for her some of the Greek enigmas?

Chapter 7

A Man and a Woman

Is it ever wise to ask a friend's advice?

The next day

Adam and Peter were having lunch in the refectory of the London School of Economics. The food was pretty good, the price was right, and it was a microcosm of the world. The future leaders of nations, heads of great companies, teachers and other potential influentials, milled about in the large, antiseptically modern, airy room. Nobody really noticed the deficit of architecture, or the plastic tabletops and chairs.

Adam temporised by raising a peripheral subject, forcing Peter to talk about himself. "I'm hearing strange rumours about missing lorry loads of Army shoes, and a half dozen other capers, from your, shall we say, somewhat chequered past?"

"Where'd you hear that?"

"Well, let's just say a couple of the birds you introduced me to at your old haunt. Your connections sure paid off yesterday, in Spades. By the way, thanks for trusting me to share a drink with your friends."

"Maybe in view of the gen you picked up on me from me ex-birds, it might have been a mistake. No, seriously mate, you may've grown up on another planet, but a straight shooter's a straight shooter, north or south of the river, and you'll always be welcome down there. Besides I've got a feeling we might be doing a bit more business with that lot in the not too distant future."

"Okay, so give."

"Nothing much, a bit off the back, now and then."

"Two truck, uh, lorry loads of Army shoes – that's the big time, especially if you get caught."

Peter smiled thinly, "Yeah, guess so, but bloody hell, you only live once."

"What did you do with all the money?"

"A few readies, me boy. Always wanted to travel, so that's what I did. Went trekking in Nepal, and wandered for a fortnight round the temples of Angkor Wat in Cambodia." Peter's eyes misted over in serene recollection. "You could drop *all* the castles of England in the moat of the Great Angkor Temple with acres to spare."

Peter had been surprised at what he found there, and was deeply moved by his experiences. A burgeoning interest in ancient monuments, history, and the unfathomable mysteries of our human past and progress, was the last thing he would have bet on in himself. He found that foreign travel activated his mind, and he now felt untrammelled by his own limited past, revelling in the fresh history of ancient times and places.

Peter also realized that his new friends and associates at the LSE were challenging him to reach out to new horizons, this time intellectual and personal. Most of the people he met were open, all different ages, nationalities, and free of the stereotypical British, class-oriented limitations he had experienced in his earlier years.

Raised in a single parent home by his mother, he had spent a large part of his life on the street with his mates.

Adam knew that this was how Peter had honed his abilities in dealing with people. Adam was trying to open up in this area, but realized that this was still a long reach for him at present.

Conversely, Peter knew that Adam was his opposite, the loner who deals more comfortably with things, rather than people. He wondered if they could bridge the gap, and if simply liking each other was enough of a bond to enable them to become true friends.

Each knew that the other was deep in his individual personal transformation, the outcomes at this time quite impossible to predict.

"I don't know if I can make it with you lot, Adam."

"What makes you think that?"

"I'm not in this league, eh? Really? Am I?" He glanced around the large room.

"Peter, I know you didn't like school much, or the Army. The only things you liked about your warehousing and trucking jobs were your mates. Have I got that right?"

"Spot on. People I understand."

"Do you know why you didn't like your other lives?"

"Just didn't make sense. Most of 'em are a bit dim."

"I thought you *liked* people, Peter."

This forced him to think behind a deep, face-wrinkling grimace. He shook his head. "I want to like them – stupid – eh?" He was immersed in the dark agony of an ancient conflict. Then Adam thought he saw it – a pretty fundamental revelation to him that said as much about his naïveté as Peter's.

"Do you want me to answer for you?"

"That would make a change." Peter did not entirely trust Adam's ability to judge the situation; it was like asking a plumber to do a bit of brain surgery.

"What did you think of your school teachers, your Army bosses, and their brethren in the warehouses?"

"I told you, dim."

"You know what I think?" To Peter's slight nod, Adam dropped the bomb that cauterises, and then resurrects. "You are, you were, smarter than any of them, but didn't believe it, and were afraid to admit it to yourself."

Peter visibly shook at the blow, and then took it on board. He grinned at the thought that maybe plumbers could do psychology, if not brain surgery.

"You know, Adam, it's not easy for me over here, this side of the river, in the LSE and all the rest."

"Who said it was *easy*? I know how hard it is to hit it off naturally with people like you do. I think I've had it soft on the intellectual side by starting young, so I take my hat off to you for dealing with all this as a latecomer. It's tough enough for me, or anybody, make no mistake."

They played with their food for a time in silence.

Suddenly, Peter looked up with a wide grin. "So, mate, how did it go with Irini last night?"

Adam experienced a momentary regret from having told Peter that he had a date with her. Why did he do it? Was it partly to brag just that little, harmless bit? To stake out a claim, to give notice to another man who might himself be wanting to circle round? Whatever the reasons he had to pay the price in the currency of feedback, and do so carefully to protect everyone's feelings, his own definitely included.

"We had a great evening, Peetie."

Peter did not approve of the diminutive, but let is pass with a tight smile. "That's not what I meant, and you know it."

Adam sidestepped once again. "What percentage of first dates have you converted, my dear friend, the amateur rake?"

Peter grinned widely, and winked. "Nuff said, nuff said."

"Exactly. Nuff said."

"Ah, so you didn't. What did happen?" Peter had turned genuinely solicitous, perhaps looking for a way to help.

"Well, we had our drinks, and talked a lot, the usual."

"Gave her your life story, then, did we?"

Adam sensed the trap, and responded warily. "Well, ah…"

"Common mistake, me friend, common mistake."

"It went great. And she did ask for it." Adam continued, defensively.

"But did you ask her? I withdraw the question." Now he sounded like a seedy solicitor from his side of town. "Did you come up for breath?"

Silence was consent here, as surely as in the law, and both knew it.

"How long exactly did you spend on your autobiography? Straight, now."

"Uh, well, gosh, a couple of hours I guess."

"Non-stop?" If true this was certainly the early summer, indoor English record, if not for the Commonwealth.

Adam hung his head, in mock shame, nodding silently.

Peter reached across the table and patted him on the arm. "Sorry, mate, didn't mean to rub it in. We've all been there. Don't take it so hard."

"Okay, thanks." When Adam said these simple words, Peter knew that he meant it a hundred percent, enough said for sure.

"So, how did the evening go from there?"

"Well, when I finally wound down," Adam shook his head at his own stupidity, "I felt it was time to make a move."

"High time old chap." Peter beckoned for more with eager hands.

"We had a wonderful hug on the couch."

"Whose head was on whose shoulder?"

"Mine on hers, I think, yes, then she embraced my head with her arm."

"Bit awkward that?"

"No, not uncomfortable, it was okay, it was sweet, it was close."

Peter concealed his anguish at everything being absolutely backward, and wondered how he could help his new friend. A friend who could have been a rival, save for a decision he had made a day or two earlier. He admitted to himself that the bigger game he had in his sights was probably unattainable, but he was certain of one thing, he would learn a lot about life and women by trying.

"How did it end?"

Adam was reluctant to admit that he had called it off, yet he might as well have said it out loud, for Peter had read every scintilla of the rest of the evening in his face. This gave him pause for thoughts similar to those that Irini must have had. While his new friend had not run the evening the way he would have done at this later point in his life, Peter was well aware of the differences in age and experience, and had acquired a reasonable grasp of the world from the woman's eye. He concluded that this might have been the best for them after all, and he wanted that for both of them.

"So, there'll be another date?"

Let off the hook, as he saw it, Adam nodded vigorously, "Yep, and soon, perhaps tomorrow. Irini said something about cooking me a Greek dinner."

"That's all right then." Peter clapped Adam on the shoulders, and smiled encouragement.

"Really? So I didn't blow it?"

Peter smiled to himself at the double entendre. Adam interpreted this as simple camaraderie.

"No, you were right to be yourself, and go with your feelings. "

"And maybe, my limitations?" Adam finally admitted.

"Everyone has 'em, mate, just make sure you turn them into strengths."

"So, what do I do next?"

"Play it straight. I do ... these days." He didn't elaborate on his earlier mistakes of another kind.

"Adam, two bits of advice, for what they're worth."

"Sure, what are they?"

"First, the obvious one. Just be yourself, and follow your gut feeling."

"I surprised myself last night. I've got real, strong feelings."

"That goes with the territory. Listen lad, like my old drill Sergeant always used to say. 'Peter, remember one thing, when the moon is right, their feelings are stronger than ours!'"

"Naw, they're cool, and calm, so we have to press our suit."

"The difference is that men think about sex every nine minutes – didn't some American say that? Anyway, the point is we are usually ready, always have those feelings, and maybe the women only have them from time to time. So we wait, and then we pounce, like a 'jagular' from the tree." This reference to *Winnie the Pooh* made them both chuckle at a shared literary experience. This was the only book Peter's mother had ever read to him as a child; and the memory of it was so strong that his eyes stung with emotion.

"So watch for the slightest sign. The tiniest gesture can mean open sesame, right?"

"Okay, I guess." This indicated a fairly strong agreement from Adam.

"One for the road?"

Adam glanced at him and nodded slightly.

"Next time, ask *her* for her life story, and then listen for as long as it takes. You think your two hours was long? For a bloke it was much too long, remember that. For the women, well, it could take until the small hours, but in the end, you'll score, if that is what you want, and either way, she's yours for the duration."

Helena determined to continue her personal life and the project as separate entities so far as was practical, partly due to, and partly despite the fact that there were still two nemeses at large with unknown motives. Were they personal, professional, anti-project or the residuum of a long-forgotten need for retribution? She still didn't know, and that was a dangerous form of ignorance.

So she met Irini as agreed for lunch at the Spaghetti House Restaurant, in the Sicilian Arcade, off Bloomsbury Way. It was showing its age, but the local university and professional crowds placed it high on their list of desirable restaurants. The staff were particularly well managed, always with a smile and crisp, not overly attentive service, and the prices were reasonable for London.

They were sitting on high stools at the bar, waiting for a table, talking about everything except Adam, the subject uppermost on their minds. Irini sipped her drink, and asked softly, "So how was the break with your mysterious 'S. A.' in Athens?"

"We did important business."

"Both for the team, and yourselves, I hope."

Helena smiled sweetly in fond recollection. "I miss him already. His name is Spiros Anguelopoulos, and everyone will hear about him at the meeting later today, along with a few other bits and pieces. So let's wait on that subject, okay?"

"Certainly, but your mystery man has definitely been on our minds for the last week."

"Understandable."

"Peter's cryptic message of yesterday was a bit frightening."

"A yellow light, a warning. Keep an eye out, that's all."

The waiter announced that their table was ready.

When they were in their seats, Helena broached the subject of Adam. "So, what happened with Adam?"

Irini leaned forward towards Helena across the table, and smiled uncertainly.

"I'm not really sure. It was going really well and then we sort of backed off from taking it any further."

"What did he say?"

"He said he didn't think the time was right and I agreed with him. Maybe we both thought it was happening too quickly."

They had decided to share the lasagne al forno, and a large mixed salad between them. Their good judgment was amply confirmed when the huge slab of lasagne was plumped down in the middle of the table. The rich perfume of ripening tomatoes from the south of Italy wafted across the table, tinged with the aromatic flavours of oregano. "Parmesan?" The waiter sprinkled generously until each said to stop, Irini waving her hand for more until Helena thought that her half would disappear under a cloud of the cream-coloured powder.

"Yes, I like my parmesan with lasagne!"

Helena laughed richly, and dismissed the waiter with his smile intact. "Why not. We only live once."

"You were going to start a new life, Helena, and now after a short break, you are back on the old trail." Irini saw that this had struck a raw nerve, so she changed the subject back to Adam. "He was the one who backed off really – I just agreed with him."

"Well, it could mean one of two things. The second is a non-starter."

"And the first?'

"Perhaps he sensed your reluctance." Irini had been looking down at her uneaten lasagne, but grasped Helena's eyes intently.

"When I went to Athens to see Spiros I didn't really know what to expect, and there were moments when I was afraid that things might go wrong between us, but that didn't stop me from going."

"You mean Adam picked up on my uncertainties?"

"Maybe. That's probably why he put the brakes on even though he knew it was what you both wanted.

"He didn't say he wasn't ready, he said he was unsure. No, that's wrong. What he actually said was, 'I wonder if we are ready for this just now.'"

"Oh well, that's different," Helena relaxed, and smiled gently. "He stopped because he thought that was what you wanted, not because he wanted to."

Irini smiled, looked down and began eating the lunch that she no longer wanted. She suddenly had another hunger, and it wouldn't be satisfied in this restaurant, or any other.

Helena continued, "Does that make sense?"

"Yes, of course, and that's what I felt at the time."

"You've got to think about putting your doubts behind you."

"So what does the last virgin over 21 east of Cornwall on this green and pleasant isle do about it?"

"Cook the man dinner, and then see how you feel."

"I know what I will feel, Helena. I will be scared to death."

"It's the same for all of us, men included."

"I think maybe it can be harder for them than for us."

"So take control – without seeming to of course. Even if he knew you were a bit unsure the last time, he'll sense that you're ready now." Helena knew that once they had overcome their insecurities it would only be a question of lighting the touch paper and standing back.

As Irini returned to the museum across the courtyard, a breathless young man in a dark, striped suit, ran up to her. "Miss Baynes? I'm Jamie Peters, *Sunday Times*." He flashed his press card, and pushed it back into the top pocket of his tan raincoat. "Spare me a moment?"

"I'm late. Could we make it another time?"

"Just a quickie. It's a nice day. I can do the interview right here while we walk. Okay?" He was what Irini had always imagined a young, eager reporter would be. Impeccably dressed, nevertheless somehow dishevelled, his clothes looked clean but it was obvious that he had not bothered to iron them. His straight, uncombed hair bounced around his forehead as he kept pace with her. His skin had the pallor of a subterranean creature that had never seen the sun, and his face, punctuated by two jet-black, close-set raisin-eyes, would certainly have impressed a casting director as a natural for the local troglodyte in a C-class horror flick. His grin was further proof of her firm view that many Britons would have done better to embrace orthodontia more widely than they had.

"Why the interest in me, I'm a new employee, bottom rung of a tall ladder?"

"We report in detail on the museums and galleries. You may have noticed that we mention all significant appointments in the monthly column." She hadn't, but tried to conceal the fact with a half-genuine smile. It was difficult to resist media interest, as Adam had admitted to her in his own case, "Before I wised up, that is."

He noted that Irini's body language had turned negative, and tried another direction. "You're Greek, aren't you? The only one in the museum? And with all the recent noise about your Elgins, well, we are interested in your views."

"Half Greek by heritage, UK citizen by choice." Something decidedly disquieting was niggling at the nape of her neck, but she couldn't quite place it. "Look, you have my name, and position, there really isn't anything more I can say that will help."

"There certainly is. You lecture on them, guide visitors…"

She interrupted curtly, which took a conscious effort against her normal desire to achieve courteous dismissals. This man was not interested in her; there was something else. "I'm sorry, but I have nothing further to say. I'm late. Goodbye."

Going up the steps she contrived to look back, but he had already turned, and was hurrying out the great iron gates behind her that guarded the treasures of the world.

The team was seated once again at the round table in Safe House One. Helena had laid out the four o'clock tea, with a tray of sweets. It had worked with Spiros, and couldn't do any harm here either.

"I have a lot to report from Athens, so let's get right on it. This first slide shows the full list of team members. It can be argued that we should limit our knowledge of names and positions to the bare minimum, so that if one of us is compromised, at least there remains a core of personnel that you cannot betray under drugs or worse."

"Surely, Helena," Irini interjected, "it won't come to that?"

Adam shook his head so vigorously that his circlets of wavy hair bounced around his forehead. "Governments are above the law, and always have been, only we have only just recently realized it."

Helena continued, "They will juice you in an instant, demand the names, and you'll sing like a canary, first time, every time." To Irini's questioning stare, she added, "Drugs".

"So, we'll just have to make sure that none of us get nabbed before our time. It's one for all, and all for one, the chain forged, and limited by the weakest link. There isn't a weak link in this room, or back in Athens.

"You are all risking your lives – probably not literally – but certainly you are risking the whole of your future, as Irini said the other day, win or lose. So I believe that it should all be on the table, and everyone on the next slide has agreed, and I emphasize *everyone*." She then keyed the computer.

Cognizant persons:

Greek Prime Minister
    Authorizations, cover-up if necessary
Spiros Anguelopoulos
    Finance, political coordination, transport, logistics
    Command and control (East), security (East), backup
Helena
    Command and control West and overall command
Peter
    Logistics, Lift Team command, security West
Adam
    Entry, exit, museum security, technical oversight
Irini
    Museum espionage, diversions, mission oversight
Charon
    Heads a cell of three, two operatives, backup

Note: ten persons: max. to keep the lid on something this big

File: OpEl Ver1.5 NoHD-Save Encrypted: GammaBlix-3.27
Page 18 of 86

"This goes all the way to the top?" Peter questioned, incredulously.

"Yes." Helena replied. She then debriefed her time with Spiros, leaving out any personal intimacies. Many items had been carefully debated before decisions were reached, then to be included in this and many additional slides in what was now a Project Plan.

"Initially I didn't want Charon. In fact, I didn't want anyone on that list other than us, and Spiros. Obviously the Prime Minister has to be in on it, *alone*, with his only contact through Spiros."

Peter offered, "If I understand anything about such things, it would be the P-M's head if anybody got a copy of even this one page."

"It probably isn't that desperate, but we take all, and I repeat *all* precautions. You do not need to know who 'Charon' is precisely, and that lack of specific knowledge neither compromises our mission, nor in any way adds to our risks. I therefore ask you to voluntarily agree to this condition. If there is any objection, let us discuss it openly. I initially opposed this idea, but have been convinced on hard reasoning that we are much better off with him and his two colleagues, and that indeed, the mission could not be completed at least on the Eastern Front without them. I will tell you that I have the utmost confidence in Charon." There was no dissent.

In fact, the three others in the room had each of them figured out that he was a Greek espionage officer, and if they had been forced to guess, would have placed him as Helena's Spymaster. She had made no secret of the basic structure of the service she had risen in during her twenty year career to become a senior member.

"He also answers directly only to the Prime Minister, and on an equal basis, to Spiros. I have accepted this organizational structure, and ask that you consider doing so here this afternoon. We will hear discussion openly on any subject relating to this." There was none.

A few key matters remain to be finalized, but I will summarize the current plan. A special exhibition is coming to the British Museum from Greece early in the new year, and will stay for just over three months. The present schedule is that it will close on Friday evening, 28 April. The lorry load of art works and some items in marble is scheduled to return to Greece that same evening. We will have an authorization for that, and it is the plan at the moment to use it to release the Elgin originals, take them to a major airport, probably Heathrow, and fly them to Greece, arriving hopefully before the sun rises over Athens on that Saturday. It is a holiday weekend here, with the first of May falling on the Monday, so if there are problems we may have extra time to resolve them, and we can hope for a more relaxed security situation, especially after hours.

"The next slide is self explanatory." Helena laughed thinly with everyone. "It is significant that the next 66 pages of the document relate to specifics. You are welcome to go over any or all of it at any time, and to add (as we must) additional pages as issues are resolved, or raised without immediate resolution. This does allow us to make the obvious assignments to each of us here, and the job begins in earnest tomorrow.

Summary Plan

Infiltrate the British Museum and defeat security
Lift the Marbles (check numbers and weights)
Fly them out? Other methods? Aircraft, pilot, logistics
Get staff clear. Legal problems? Staff, P-M, others?

Note (Spiros): I know this looks simple, but it isn't.

File: OpEl Ver1.5 NoHD-Save Encrypted: GammaBlix-3.27
Page 20 of 86

"Your individual assignments are on the sheets in front of you, and we will certainly entertain any questions at any time. However, from this moment forward, you are not to discuss, joke about, or in any other way mention any aspect of this operation to anyone, including among yourselves, except when you are in a facility designated by me as a safe house. We have this one for now, and I will be creating one or two more at least. It doesn't show, except perhaps to Adam's practiced eyes, but this place is radio proof, and we have the most sophisticated available bug monitors comparable to any security agency including MI5 and the CIA among others. They have been specially modified by Greek intelligence, and so are also invisible to these and all other established agencies. I have asked Adam to give a brief rundown on these precautions and security of communications.

"This miserable little basement flat cost over 300,000 pounds – quid – to secure. The glass in the windows is transparent, yet conducts electricity, and all the walls have been clad in metal, painted in simulated wood. Pretty ugly, but it does the job. Radio transmissions into and out of this room are quite simply, impossible. That's why our portable telephones must be plugged into a special connector right here. These are specially modified, digitally encrypted devices, so that we can communicate via the normal citywide mobile networks, but nobody can listen in (except where we are talking) so bear that in mind. Secure text messaging is also possible, and encouraged.

"The windows have been mounted in shock proof rubber, and they are vibrated by a voice coil that prevents anyone listening in by bouncing laser light off the window, and recording the physical vibrations. Yes, that's possible, so when you make love to your sweethearts, remember; anybody can listen in with fifty quid's worth of electronic equipment, and do so from a quarter of a mile away.

"Bug detection is by way of permanent monitors both inside and outside the building, so that the latest transmit on command types would be detected. There are other precautions I need not bore you with; you can read about all of this in notebook seven, on this shelf. The specifications are all there, and I don't need to say that no documents ever leave this room, including your own notes. You will memorize all relevant data, and leave all written material here.

"We back up all computer files on a minute-by-minute basis, on secure network lines, fully encrypted. For that reason, the operation has rented and sealed the whole structure. The excuse is renovation. Peter has more to say on this in a moment. Are there any questions?

"Peter."

"Okay, boys and girls, over here. Anybody who burgles us is toast! "The self destruct uses flame throwers. They shoot oil for a few seconds as another warning before igniting. Adam has put flash bombs in the drawers and computer equipment. Buildings on the sides'll be okay, but I can see Granny Smith knocked flat next door.

"Anybody tries to force entry when we're here, we come to this spot and pull the blue handle up, on what looks like an ordinary fridge door. A countdown begins. It lasts thirty seconds: *Time to Self Destruct, thirty, twenty-nine, twenty-eight*, like that. You can stop it by closing the door, and pressing the handle down. Just closing the door will not work, so an intruder has thirty seconds to get out. For normal use we turn the handle, so, instead of pulling it.

"Okay, we go. Pull up on the handle. Open the door. Grab a metal shelf, fingers go through them, and pull out smartish." With a crash, the bottles of beer and soft drinks tumbled across the floor.

The back of the fridge came out with the shelves, revealing what looked like a large laundry chute. "When you dive through there – head-first is good – you'll be goin' down a long child's slide, and fetch up on soft foam rubber. Last one down pulls another blue lever at the bottom, and the chute bangs shut up here with a blast-proof door."

Helena took over. "Thank you, Peter. You will find yourselves in a small room with some light. You can open a panel on the far side that lets out onto a line-side working platform of the Circle Line Underground, about 50 metres west of Euston Square Station, which is to your right. There are suitcases with a change of clothes, suitably marked, plus one spare. Put on the Underground uniforms, open the panel, step out on the walkway, and close it behind. You can then walk to the station, and catch any train as an employee free of charge. You know better than to step down on the rails, but this isn't necessary; it's a clear run. Any questions?"

Helena continued. "There is just one other item which is on the agenda of every meeting: security. In addition to keeping eyes open, watching for tails, and all the rest, you are to report anything that so much as twitches a cat's whisker. Don't be bashful. Anything, and I repeat *anything*, the slightest bit out of the ordinary, report it. Let the team and our backups deal with it. You will not be thought silly. I can tell you from experience that most of these inklings come to nothing. Well and good, perhaps expected. I can also tell you that if we are aware and follow our instincts, almost every serious eventuality can be spotted early in this way.

"Any questions?" She looked from one to the next around the room, holding eye contact just that extra beat each time. All faces were clear – all body language normal – except – maybe – Irini. Helena came back to her a second time with a smile.

Irini suddenly recalled her encounter with Jamie Peter's that afternoon. She had thought it was meaningless but now that Helena was looking at her again, she knew that there was something about it that at this moment seemed odd.

"There is something – it's probably unimportant but..." She began to describe the meeting, and as she filled in the details she was surprised that she had managed to remember not only every word that he had said to her but also managed to provide a good description of him and everything about him.

"I did feel *at the time* that there was something just a bit *off*."

"Irini, and all of you, no mark against her, indeed, on the contrary for a most observant report, but do you see what I mean? Probably nothing, but it will be checked out.

"Any further comments? I declare this meeting adjourned until your next call on the mobiles." She scanned once again the three overloaded faces of her comrades. They had a lot to take in, but she was sure they had done so. She felt as comfortable with them as she had been with any group of high-level intelligence officers and others of similar rank she had ever met (or opposed) in the old life. If a problem were to arise, it would not be an internal one, Station West. Then there was always the Expected, Unexpected. Well, that was another story entirely. One dose already from Charon, and she was certain that it wouldn't be the last.

Chapter 8

Forget Chemistry: It's the Electric Company

Nothing so distracts the mind, or frees the spirit, as the presence of your lover.

Irini left the British Museum at lunchtime to visit Andreas Hadjis who ran a deli and Greek grocery store nearby. He had become a good friend and she took any excuse to pop in to his aromatic domain. The narrow shop was tucked contentedly in between the Chinese antiquary bookshop and the Happy Thai restaurant.

As she walked in, Andreas boomed, *"Ti kaneis, paithi mou."* She loved the shop for many reasons, speaking Greek being one of them. Andreas had one of those resonant Greek voices that was guaranteed to be heard across a harbour, rising as it did from his ample belly. At least it wasn't the more typical strident shout. Nevertheless, she felt that he had never learned to adjust its volume to fit within the limited confines of his shop.

She returned his greeting "how are you", with *"Poli kala"*, and the customary cheek-to-cheek embrace. He could see that she was bubbling over, and it didn't take a man of his experience long to guess what it probably meant. He was as delighted for her as if he had been her father.

Andreas was round, from head to toe. His round, brown eyes were centred in a round head, topped with an immense bush of Greek curls. She always smiled at this, for she had countless images of the same gracing almost every statue of a Greek man, but fair to say, most of them named Adonis, not Andreas.

"Andreas, I'm going to cook a moussaka. I'm out of your best Kalamata olive oil, and if you have it, I need the olives to go with it."

His eyes glowed in anticipation as they discussed the finer points of the preparation. It was necessary for him to manoeuvre with some care between the overloaded shelves, mini earthquakes in his wake rattling the odd bottle as the floor eased under his weight.

"Achilles sends his purry greetings." She thanked Andreas warmly, promising to return another time for a longer chat, and hurried off clutching two heavy bags of shopping. She intended to visit him as soon as possible, in a mid afternoon when the shop would be quiet, to consult him in his role as her friendly, local father confessor.

She turned left out of the shop, crossed Museum Street diagonally and entered her cul-de-sac. The sky was a sparkling sapphire, and the air was fresh with a light early summer breeze that had found its way through the labyrinthine streets of Bloomsbury, to caress the leaves on the plane trees still glistening with the patina of spring.

Irini struggled up the three flights. Puffing gently as she unlocked the door was a reminder that she had missed out on regular exercise for the last few days. It had been a hard week, with at least three jobs to do: the museum, the last research tasks, and the pressures of the looming enterprise.

The prospect of allowing herself a half afternoon for a fresh creative endeavour brought great pleasure. She enjoyed cooking, yet felt that the results of her labours often disappeared far too quickly. An image of Adam floated past, the omnivorous American demolishing the meal in the twinkling of an eager eye.

He must be told the proper pronunciation of "moussaka", with emphasis on the last syllable, instead of the penultimate. As she layered the kaseri cheese with the minced lamb her thoughts turned to the evening in prospect.

After Adam's previous visit her intent had been clear, and she had been secure in herself. Now a disturbing loss of confidence was rising. She wondered whether it was this way for everyone on the brink of a new relationship, and whether it was always a question, instead of a decision?

This was overtaken by irresistible thrills of excitement, and a physical sensation of longing that was new to her. Then she relaxed, and told herself sternly this was a natural progression that almost everyone survived. She continued her preparations in a light trance, immersed in a miasma of agreeable expectation.

She knew a little about Adam, and it was obvious that he was not the archetypical nerd. He had an openness to new experiences, enjoyed long walks in both the city and countryside, and toned his body by regular swims in the University pool, a habit carried forward from his days on the high school swimming team.

Unlike her own, his face was photogenic. He had, in fact, modelled briefly for a men's wear catalogue. He had told her he felt it was boring, "Not my thing. Give me fresh air on a long walk in the park, or my computer for a stroll in cyberspace."

A fresh thought came as she crushed the garlic and wiped her eyes. Perhaps his nonchalance might be his strongest tool in the end, just as soon as he realized it, without then deciding to exploit it.

Irini had arranged the half-afternoon break by exchanging the shift with a colleague, so after setting the tiny microwave on "fan oven" for the necessary time, she left the flat, and walked out the cul-de-sac for the return to work. There was little foot traffic at this time of day, and she glanced contentedly back at Andreas' shop. And there he was, not Andreas, but Jamie Peters! She tried hard to disguise any hint of body language that might reveal she had recognized him, and apparently succeeded, because he started to follow her. She used a trick that Helena had taught them during a walkabout after the first meeting. "Look in the shop-front glass across the street, head straight ahead, averting only the eyes, which is invisible from behind."

Irini snapped her fingers, pretending that she had forgotten something, crossed the street, and headed straight back for Andreas' store. She could hardly help but smile to herself as her pursuer awkwardly stopped to look in a window on his side, then reverse his walk up the street. She slipped casually into the shop.

"Irini, good thing you came back. I think there's a man following you. He hung around the street after you went up to your flat, then –"

"Shsst. Here he comes. Thank you, Andreas, I spotted him too. May I do some business in the back?"

"Need you ask?" He patted her on the backside like a father, and pushed her lovingly towards the rear.

IRINI: TEXT TO HELENA, ENCRYPTED SECURE: <u>CODE YELLOW</u>.
    FOLLOWED BY JAMIE OF TIMES.
    AT ANDREAS' SHOP. ADVISE.

HELENA TO IRINI:
    WE LEFT FIVE MINUTES AGO. WAS ABOUT TO TEXT YOU
    MYSELF. HE'S NOT WITH THE TIMES, I JUST CHECKED.
    SHOULD HAVE DONE IT FIRST THING THIS MORNING.
    WELL SPOTTED. WE'LL MAKE A SPY OF YOU YET!
    CODE YELLOW, RIGHT CALL. STAY THERE OUT OF SIGHT.
LOVE, HELENA.

Irini had to smile at the salutation. It was definitely not out of the spy book.

A few endless minutes later, a stooped, old lady entered the shop and Andreas greeted her warmly. "Welcome. What can I do for you?" He had immediately noticed that she was new in the neighbourhood, always a prime moment for any shopkeeper.

Then, unexpectedly, the woman put her index finger forcefully to his lips, and whispered, "Please go about your business as usual. I'm with Irini!"

"She's in the back." Andreas knew from that moment that something serious was afoot, and not just the lover he suspected had entered her life. He resolved to keep a father's wary eye out for her. His vigilance was to prove vital.

Irini licked dry lips. A momentary horror flew through her mind, raising goose bumps. She feared that she was about to be literally bagged by the bag lady and dragged off to give up the names.

"Shsst, it's me, Helena. Under the circumstances we must not be recognized together. There might be two of them out there, but don't worry, we're on top of all possibilities."

Andreas shortly came back to them. "Strange thing, but two coppers picked up that fellow, then one of them waved to me like we were old friends, yet I've never seen him before."

"Thanks, Andreas.

"Irini, we'll just wait a few more minutes. I know you need to get back to work, and we don't want to raise any suspicion there either." Helena's phone chimed.

BACKUP ALL CLEAR. END CODE YELLOW.

The museum at this time was crowded with people going about their business; some were catching a quick hour in their favourite gallery, others were professional artists engaged in drawing and painting copies of the originals. Mercifully, the school groups had long since departed. Irini enjoyed dealing with eager, animated children with inquiring minds, and was finding a useful challenge in making presentations to these groups. Yet, late afternoon at the museum was of a different quality, with a measure of poise and calm, which was for her the best part of the day.

At five she had the difficult job of explaining to a group of Chinese tourists the cultural heritage represented by the Parthenon Marbles. Their civilization was far older and no less significant than her own, and as different as wine and bourbon. To compound the difficulties, the reality of the gallery was, for her, overlaid with transparent, surrealistic images relating to actually lifting these massive sculptures and sending them back to their birthplace. It was phantasmagorical, the room filled with ghostly presences, from the ancient sculptors chipping away at the marble, to themselves scurrying around, filling boxes, then freezing as the security alarms went off. Finally there were the sensual thrills running up and down her back, overflowing and erasing the other levels of her consciousness.

Then the spell was broken by a question from the oldest and most venerable member of the group, a deeply hunched man with mottled parchment for skin. She welcomed the shattering of her reveries, and paid close attention to answering his question, an observant one. "Why did the sculptors work the backs that would never be seen against the walls behind them, set as they were, so high above their heads?"

At last, she was flying like a bird across the museum courtyard, which seemed a mile wide – waited impatiently for traffic to pause at the zebra crossing, and struggled against the high tide of crowds on the narrow pavements.

Irini finally reached her cul-de-sac, and breathlessly ran up the stairs to her flat. She was not in such a hurry as to forget to check behind, which she did cleverly by twice crossing the street between cars in the heavy traffic, window-gazing.

It was 7:15 already, the momentous hour of 8:00 looming with so much to do. Only twenty minutes was available for a shower and make up, cut short at less than half what she had planned.

Irini tugged on the skirt, and impatiently pulled the matching blue and green Thai silk blouse over her head, thrusting arms through the sleeveless – blast – backwards. She spoke sternly to herself, calmly took off the offending garment, righted it, and settled comfortably into the fabric which caressed her bare skin and tickled – blast again – she hadn't put on her bra, either the standard, or the frilly, sexy one. She laughed out loud to herself, flopping down on the couch as much from exhaustion as simple dizziness. This was deep, for she had been debating all day over which one to use. So in the end, her other self had made the decision. "Can't decide? Okay, then forget them both!" She stood up and looked down at herself. It was true, she didn't need it, and so why worry? Yet there were many such reasons bubbling away in her internal cauldron.

She set the table carefully, arranging, and rearranging each item, from wine glasses to candles. At least the moussaka smelled right, and the Greek salad came out of the refrigerator still looking fresh and inviting as she crumbled the Feta cheese over it. She always made it with lettuce, green onions, and a hint of basil, the king of herbs, in addition to the official ingredients.

Salad on the table, then, some ice in the bucket, white wine in the fridge ready to be opened, blast, where is the corkscrew, ah, yes, right there on the table in front of me.

"Buzz!" It can't be, but it was, already a few minutes after eight.
"It's me."
"Buzz."
Just time to light the candles, but then the matches wouldn't strike, and the knock on the door put an end to these plans, on the scrap heap with so many other small things she had planned to do. It was the moment, and Irini took her customary three deep breaths, stepped to the door, and then behind it, to admit her guest.

He stepped forward as the door closed behind, her hand unintentionally brushing his.

Skin burned.

Lips parted.

The contact was cool, the tips of tongues scorching.

Their embrace crushed his offering of lilies, petals floating casually to the floor. Then they were out of themselves, desperately seeking to merge into one.

It didn't take any time at all.

Achilles had slept through the first act on the couch, while these antics of the strange furless creatures from another universe, who lived with him, had played themselves out in the bedroom. He stretched, yawned as wide as a circus tiger, and jumped down. He walked purposefully to the door, and went through the interior cat flap to use his part of the facilities in the hallway.

He came back in a few minutes, and after enjoyably nosing the flower petals scattered just inside the door, prepared to settle down for a meditative wash with brush-up and contemplation of life. Instead, he noticed, and followed a trail of discarded clothing. A silk blouse first, he recognized as that of his mistress, and then a shirt he didn't place, yet his nose had suspicions from an earlier brief introduction. Then came a skirt and panties well known to him. He didn't appreciate the meaning of this ordering, for it implied that Irini had been the first to stand fully revealed to her lover-to-be. These were followed by trousers, under pants, and finally, shoes and socks at the side of the bed.

Soft snores welcomed him, so he jumped up to occupy the last morsel of space, which was just enough for him. He turned and formed himself into the curve of her middle as he had done so often before. This was different however, because behind her there was this other person, who had not yet obtained his permission to be there, and until it was granted, he would be ignored.

Adam stirred from sleeping in spoons behind Irini. "I'm sorry."

"What?" She replied in a voice drugged by departing mists of sleep.

"I'm sorry."

"For what?"

"That, it, I, couldn't make it last longer." His voice was that of a child confessing his darkest sin.

Irini flipped onto her back, knocking the unseen and unfelt Achilles off the bed, flat on the floor. "Meow-row?"

"Sorry."

"You too?"

"Sorry, I was talking to the cat, knocked him off the bed." She reached down to rub Achilles' ears in consolation. He accepted the down payment, and then staggered off, quite disoriented.

"I doubt if any other woman's first time was any better."

Adam smiled down at her, and kissed the turned-up tip of her nose. "Thank you." Then he registered the full meaning of her comment. "Truly, your first time? That's amazing, unbelievable."

"No it isn't."

"A woman of such beauty, intelligence, intensity…"

"Hush, my love." She pressed a finger on his lips. The aftertaste of her touch began to burn, with a delayed action like certain hot chillies used in eastern dishes.

"The truth?" She offered with knitted brows.

"Okay."

"I was afraid of it, for years, and centuries, and eons."

He managed to croak out, "Me too." Then: "My first time." The feelings that flooded his heart were so intense that he thought it had missed several beats, and well it might have.

"Did it hurt?" He asked solicitously.

"Truthfully? A bit, but that was washed away in waves of pleasurc."

These feelings could only be relieved by another kiss, yet instead of devouring, as he thought he intended, it came out as soft. He teased her lower lip between his two; then she did the same to his upper lip. Tongues flicked ends to ends, this time feeling warm, instead of either hot or cool. Everything felt warm. Two or three kisses were enough to fully rouse them both, but instead of rushing forward, they danced to a different orchestration, one more likely to have been penned in the forties of the last century, than the beat of the new one they had followed earlier.

The room was dark except for city light stealing in through the windows, yet he could see her miraculous form clearly enough, soft shadows under her perfect breasts, standing proud, the pert confections on each filling out under his light, circular touches. Irini moaned softly, and arched her head back on the pillow.

He ran fingers hither and yon, taking the time to examine every square centimetre as though this was the map of his lifetime's happiness laid out before him. Her chin was perfection, and he massaged it lightly with the ends of his fingers, then her forehead, eyes, and that wonderful nose that was so much part of her personality. Their nervous systems were one, the conduits each point of contact, he feeling her every vibration, and contrariwise.

There was the hollow in the front of her neck, now yielding a few beads of her sweet perfume, the carotid channels with the fingernails, yes, that was sending a rush up and down her body – he could feel it directly in his own as if she had been working his most sensitive places. He followed there with tongue and kisses, his amorata now arching her back with every touch, and then a sharp shout flew from her to the ends of the earth. Irini was panting, legs scissoring side to side, opening and closing, in what he now decided were raptures of some kind. He hadn't been sure at first, for her cry had been totally unexpected.

He tried to comfort her, and pressed down with his hands on her belly, but they slipped, and at the first touch of her centre, she cried out again, and he could feel the vibrations as though they were his own orgasms, and so made his discovery, one of many to follow, yet perhaps the most important of all. He continued to massage and press lightly, finding that a circular motion seemed to work the best. Irini was hyperventilating, breathing at a rate he had never witnessed before, including colleagues on the swim team after an exhausting competition.

Was this safe? He stopped for a moment, but Irini almost screamed at him, "Don't stop! Don't stop *ever*."

It was obvious that she was no longer physically present, to herself, but for him it was a sight he would never forget. It was a most extraordinary performance, far beyond anything he could have imagined.

Achilles chose this moment to jump up on the bed and have a look for himself, but it didn't seem to have much effect on him. He appeared to shrug, and lay down next to Irini, his nose not far from her right ear, his right paw on her right arm. She was gripping the headboard with both hands, writhing to and fro, Achilles seeming to purr further encouragement into her ear.

Adam couldn't stand it any more, and jumped aboard, her welcome the most sublime and all encompassing feeling, beyond fantasy. Now his weight was upon her, and he had no choice but to follow her rhythm. Again, it didn't take him long, and with a shout, his body flew upward, and after a loud "thwack", he fell forward.

She had hyperventilated herself to unconsciousness, and slowly came back, the dizziness and orgasmic tingling all over her body gradually dissipating like another world half-remembered on waking. She felt his weight upon her, and his fulsome presence in her, and this forced a final orgasm, one she experienced in full consciousness, each squeeze sending softer shudders, until at last, she exhaled, as though for the last time in a long life.

"Adam?"

"ADAM?"

With some difficulty, she managed to roll him off her, and he sprawled out on the bed, a body in complete repose.

"God!" She felt for his pulse, panicked by her worst nightmare. She felt nothing! Finally fumbling her index finger into the right place, she could feel his heartbeat, hammering away, at least two beats per second. "Thank God."

He groaned, and raised his hand to the top of his head. "What happened?"

"I don't know, my love; you certainly gave me a fright."

"What?"

"You were out cold, me lad, stone cold." She immediately regretted the choice of words, but it didn't seem to matter.

Then a dreadful thought surfaced. She had forgotten to warn him about the low ceiling above the bed!

She pushed his hand away, and felt the back of his head for herself. Sure enough, a large and quite firm bump was rising under her fingers.

"I'm so sorry, Adam."

"What?" He was still groggy, and didn't really yet understand what had happened.

"I forgot to warn you about..." She tapped her knuckles smartly on the beam that crossed above the centre of the bed.

Achilles had watched all this, and certainly understood the last part of it, but he simply yawned, turned around three times, set his back to the headboard, and in a moment was purring contentedly in sleep.

Chapter 9

Adam the Improbable Sculptor

Love Conquers All: Amor Vincit Omnia

Next day

DUTY ROSTER:
    PETER: CONTINUE SEARCH FOR SAFE HOUSE TWO
    IRINI: SETTLE IN. GET LIST OF ELGINS
        BY NAMES WITH PHOTOS
    ADAM: GET AHEAD AT IMPERIAL.
        YOU HAVE A WEEK OF WORK WITH US.
HELENA: MEETING TONIGHT, S. H. ONE, 8PM

The digital mobile phones of each team member displayed these text messages, chiming a wake up call at 8AM. "Helena's certainly back in the saddle." Adam said as he busied himself with a light breakfast, set on a lap tray, and delivered to his lover in bed.

"That means work, I'll wager." Irini issued a wan little smile.

"Right on, lover, and it looks like I'll be on overtime at Imperial today." He showed her the glowing screen of the mobile. "Timing's okay for me there; today is just enough to clear my desk for a week."

"What are you doing?"

"Finishing the specifications for some memory interface chips, super high speed, if you must know, dear heart, and once they are sent off, there's not a lot for me to do for a while. Anyway, as you know, it's on again, off again, over at the Quantum Lab.

"So," he looked at her meaningfully, "we should be able to cadge some quality time for us without too much difficulty."

"If Helena can keep her demands in check."

"Yep, and that's a bit of an *if* isn't it?"

"Helena is pushing us too hard, too soon, I think."

"The word is sacrifice, and ours is not to reason why, ours is but to do, and do, and do."

He set the empty tray aside. "I've got fifteen minutes." So they filled it with hugs.

Peter met Adam at the Imperial College canteen for a quick lunch of cheeseburgers, hot off the grill, and fast. Adam liked them because the chef used *liquid smoke* seasoning, the grill area exuding the ersatz yet delightful aroma of a nonexistent mesquite charcoal fire. He also did *not* squash the meat down when the order was for "well done" as so many cooks were wont to do. Adam had, on a number of occasions, disingenuously lectured unimpressed chefs he had never met before on this finer point of burger cuisine. The humour in these encounters would not have been apparent to him before coming to Europe.

The place had a different hustle and bustle than the LSE equivalent. Adam knew the reasons, a central part of his life. He was sure it was partly the freedom implied by the more informal clothes of his techno-type colleagues, and their ebullient personalities when freed from the sterile laboratories and computers in which they worked their long and often solitary hours.

Adam squished on a triple helping of *French's* American mustard, and then added a bit more for good measure. Peter winced, and applied his preference, Colman's English, in a thin coating.

"So, Adam, how did it go last night?"

"I don't tell tales out of school, buddy."

"You're not in school any more, so give!"

"Well..." Adam smiled sheepishly, and didn't look Peter in the eye. It was all the answer Peter needed. He reached across the table, and patted Adam smartly on the shoulders. "Good on you mate! I'm delighted for you both. So tell me, how was the big moment?"

"I don't..."

"Relax, I won't tell anybody, honest. Just between you and me."

"Well, I was unconscious at the time." His sheepishness increased.

Peter was puzzled at first and then his face lit up in understanding. "Oh, right. That's happened to me a couple of times. Bloody amazing."

"Well, uh ... it wasn't quite like that!" Adam bent forward and tapped the back of his head. Peter reached over and touched the sizeable bump there.

It took him a moment, and then he understood. "Ah, so she forgot to warn you about the beam over the bed?"

"Hey, how did you know about that?"

"Steady on, I went to her place once, and I do have an eye for architecture, okay? I haven't touched her, honest."

"Sure, okay. I believe you, but I wonder how many wouldn't?"

"The odd girl friend, I think – yes just the odd, old girl friend."

A similar scene was being played out in the LSE Refectory between Irini and Helena. They were having a more refined lunch of the Indian Special Grill with rice and a side salad. The tandoori aromas were tangy, conditioning their choice as they moved along the counter.

Helena simply looked at Irini inquiringly. Irini gazed back with bright eyes and pink cheeks. Helena nodded and said nothing directly.

After some initial small talk, Irini finally broke her silence. "I made a wonderful moussaka, Helena, with a lot of help from Andreas, you know, in the deli."

"Oh yes, I remember."

She smiled. "We didn't eat it."

"Something go wrong with the oven? Oh what a shame."

"No, it was perfect. We just didn't eat…"

"Oh, I get it." Helena sighed, sharing in Irini's pleasure. "Say no more, eh?"

"Exactly."

"I'm really happy for both of you."

"He was very patient, and I was over the top several times."

"You're very lucky."

"Yes, I know. There was just one teensy, weensy, little problem."

"And what was that?"

"I forgot to tell him about the beam over the bed, and, well…"

Helena slapped the back of her head. "Knockout?"

"Yes, in the eleventh round."

They took each other's hands, squeezed happiness through them, and laughed uproariously, catching the attention of everyone in their half of the hall. It was a delicious moment.

A new hot-or-cold heat-pump air conditioning unit purred softly in the back corner. This latest addition to the safe house had been suggested by Peter, obtained and installed by him. It was certainly

Helena's rule, and common sense, that no ordinary tradesman could now or at any time be admitted to this room.

Fortunately, Adam could fix any computer or electronics, and Peter was a bob-tailed, jack-of-all-trades, to use his own words.

Peter had been surveying possible estate agent opportunities for a second safe house.

When he finished his report, Helena said to general surprise, "We will probably need at least three. So, Peter, keep looking for that penthouse unit with the flat, obstruction-free roof."

"We've got possibilities. Must we own it, or is a lease okay?"

"Either is fine. We won't be making anything like the same number of modifications as were necessary here."

"Irini?"

"I've got the list and photos of the Elgins, no problem with that, but there doesn't seem to be any information on sizes and weights. I'm reluctant to ask that kind of question too widely around the shop."

"Quite right. Let's turn to Adam now, and see if perhaps that problem can be addressed in a different way. I feel sure he will be overjoyed to learn that he now has a fourth job!"

"What?" Adam, on the verge of dozing off, awoke with a surprised look on his face. Helena was struggling with duty overload herself and made no comment. Also, she had stolen an afternoon's kip, and knew he had not.

Helena handed over a piece of paper headed "Consulting Contract". It seemed that one Adam Blix would be consulting for the Albertson Foundation, assigned to the team at the British Museum that was engaged in copying to marble the full set of sculptures. They all knew that this was going on, and that these copies were shortly going to be sent to Greece as substitutes for the originals the museum and the British government had refused to repatriate.

"Wow!" Adam whistled as his eye caught the fees line. "Is this right? Five Hundred Quid a *day*?"

"Hey," Peter almost shouted, "great! So where's mine?"

"Purely nominal," Helena commented.

"So it's all a fake?" Adam's face fell in an agony of disappointment.

"No, they'll issue real checks, and you will have to pay your taxes on it, and the net is yours to keep."

"Good. Wonderful." Suddenly Adam was unsure, whipsawed between the two extremes of joy and guilt, for he empathized with Peter.

"So what about me?" Peter whined, reverting to type for a brief moment. A man from Southwark and points south didn't take kindly to unequal distribution of the spoils, and that was how he saw it. Then he realized his mistake. "Yeah, okay, I know, don't tell me Helena, or anybody else. The word is 'sacrifice'."

It was not an auspicious moment, one she had failed to anticipate, and that was her fault. Adam came to the rescue.

"Okay, everyone, this isn't right. It's like the waiters and waitresses, bus boys, and bottle washers in a restaurant. Most of them have the policy that tips go in the box and are shared out fairly to everyone. So how about we all put any extras into the box? Then use them as we all agree, either by equal distributions, or for comfort or whatever, that fall outside the project."

"That's extremely generous of you, Adam." So Helena's mistake had come out all right in the end. This was additional most welcome evidence for her that they had a team, all of whom cared about each other both personally and professionally.

"I see there's a real job for me, with some meat in it." Adam had finished scanning the documentation, and with a flourish, he signed it.

Next morning, Adam replayed the breakfast in bed for Irini, and she paid with soft kisses. They had overslept, and it was a rush for her to reach the museum on time at 9AM. There was one unexpected and most welcome benefit from Adam's new assignment, the fact that they could go to work together. Neither had really appreciated that boon the night before.

They walked the short blocks to the museum, hand in hand, the world seen now through different emotions. Adam no longer envied the other couples on the pavements. It was the other way around now, heads snapping about to catch a longer look at Irini. He sympathized, for he had himself been a prisoner of those empty longings for more years than he chose to count.

It was the dawn of a new age in every corner of their lives. The professional side had turned into a bizarre, kaleidoscopic inversion of what anyone else would have defined with that word. The world tilted and turned as they crossed the courtyard to walk up the steps under the classical Greek portico of the world's premier museum.

"I've got to check in with security, Irini, and then I'll be wherever they are doing the carving."

"I know where you'll be. I have the children's shifts today, so I'll be free about three. Would you like a tour of the museum with me?"

"An honour, my lady." Adam bowed, and kissed her hand, to the delectation of several passers by, none of them sensing the agonies that lay behind the gesture. Adam and Irini knew they would feel the misery of every minute of separation, though it was within the same building.

Adam was given a map of the museum intended for insiders, showing every office, corridor and storeroom. That was in itself a valuable item, but Irini had already provided hers to the project a few days earlier. He easily found his way to the right door, and inserted what he had immediately recognized as an ordinary, push-in, magnetic-stripe, credit-card type of security pass. The small screen replied:

Enter Personal Identification Number

He keyed his in from memory, having already torn up and destroyed the original he had been given in the security office. There was no real reason for his act, no matter of project security that suggested it; he was merely following Helena's "First Rule for Spies". Memorize everything you need, and destroy all copies, whether or not you can foresee a problem, or believe there isn't one.

The screen replied:

This is your First Use. You may Change your Passkey PIN now Key Y for Yes to change the assigned PIN, or N for No.

He pressed "Y", and then to the prompt, entered: "1248163264128256512 1024" at which point the system responded:

20 Numbers Maximum

The last three he had keyed were deleted, and he now had a 20-digit codeword he could always easily remember because it was not a random number, but one obtained from a simple arithmetical formula. He remembered the formula, not the number. Had he needed a secure code against a determined adversary he would have chosen something quite different, for anyone seeing this particular sequence of numbers, and looking at it the right way, could find the rule. "Double, double, toil and trouble," he hummed to himself, from a recent hit record.

The door clicked open to a short passageway, more like an airlock in a space station, than a hallway. He could already hear a cacophony seeping through the next door. He was forced to repeat the security at the second door, and was impressed that the computer already knew his new number. That may seem obvious, given the speed of modern computers. Yet he had experienced stranger gaps in such procedures, because programmers in his experience didn't frequently think about practicalities such as delay times or user convenience. It was just such sloppiness that had opened a new life for him as a certain bank vault door swung open to his touch.

The room was a chaotic, horrendously noisy enclave, completely out of character compared with the quietude of the museum left behind him. Huge fans drew dust up underneath cavernous hoods, as machinery ground its way across slabs of marble. Everyone wore surgical masks, curved full-face helmets, ear protection, and hard hats. His entry had started a red light spinning madly next to a dusty table on his right, and a young man came over. "You must be Adam Blitz?"

The noise was so intense that Adam didn't know whether his new colleague had made the classic error with his name, but this time he didn't care. He handed over the papers from the Foundation, and the man bent forward to read them, dust falling off of his bright yellow hard hat. He opened a large metal cabinet behind the table, and handed Adam a smock, his hard hat with Adam Blix already stencilled on it, the transparent hood and faceplate that resembled the space suit helmet from a low budget Hollywood science fiction movie, a box of disposable facemasks, and a personalized pair of sound-deadening headphones. He felt they were unusually efficient to be so well prepared for him.

The man motioned him to follow, and gave him an introductory tour. Adam paid close attention to the industrial, computer-controlled pantographs. He had never seen anything quite like them, though he certainly knew that such machines existed.

The process was simple enough in principle. A typical Elgin consisted of a slab of marble slightly less than a metre square, an English yard or so, and a hand's span in thickness. On its face was the bas-relief dating back how far he was embarrassed in himself for not knowing. It was clipped to the steel worktable with a cloth underneath to protect the back despite lacking any particular value, but he understood that such protection would be expected.

To its right was an equal slab of fresh marble, already cut to match the edge profile of the original. The machine was working its face into an exact replica of the original.

As a child he had been given a pencil-pantograph, then really an antique design, but one that had seen a fresh vogue for a time as a toy. A drawing was placed in a tray on the left side, and a blank piece of paper on the right. An articulated pair of joints allowed the user to trace the original drawing with a pointer, while the apparatus moved a soft lead pencil attached to the right side across the fresh paper. Each movement of the pointer on the left was reproduced on the right, and a copy, with or without extra embellishments by the artist, could be created.

Many industrial machines existed using the same principle, a template on one side, traced by a stylus, a lathe or milling machine on the other, joined together by a mechanism which reproduced, amplified, or reduced, the corresponding motion so that a physical copy could be created in solid material.

The modern version substituted a computer to control motors driving the cutter, but the principle was the same, just more flexible. In this case, the computer guided a stylus across the surface of the original, and computed positions for the cutter. This solved the very real problem involved in objects of art, in that there were interstices, angles, undercuts and overhangs necessary to a faithful copy.

The sensing side was lifting the stylus up, angling it as required, to find the next direction, vertical, or at an angle, or up inside under an overhang, at which the next cut would be made on the copy. So unlike the direct mechanical versions, this one was not necessarily synchronized.

The computer could first move the stylus over, around, and into the original, and then when the program was satisfied that it could guide the cutter appropriately, it would then command the cuts. A

115

movable head on the cutter allowed the computer to select many different styles of cutting head, from extraordinarily delicate through the gamut to heavy conical ones, rather like a larger version of the selection a dental surgeon has available. This included articulated styli, and matching cutter-heads, for those hard to reach, interior spaces.

Its sensing side was quite a subtle process, in stark contrast to the sheer hard work, noise, and flying chips of stone blasted from the copy each time the system decided that it could safely cut.

Because of the delay between the sensing and cutting, Adam had the impression that the delicate touch of the original sculptor was actually being carefully considered, and only then implemented with sound and fury signifying much. Adam had tried to picture this in his mind beforehand, but had totally failed to appreciate either aspect, the subtleties in detecting the shapes, or the sheer power of the physical process. He then wondered if the same dichotomy had existed in the ancient sculptor's workshop?

He followed his new partner across the room, and they entered what was intended to be a quiet corner, soundproofed. And so it seemed, when the door thumped shut, and was latched. The windows were double-glazed, the walls at least six inches thick, no doubt stuffed with insulation. They took off their helmets and headphones.

"Paul Alberts, pleased to meet you. I'm the foreman here."

"Blix, Adam Blix."

Paul smiled, "As in Bond, James Bond. I like it. More important, we need you."

The project design had overlooked one critical detail. How the obvious could be missed was something that used to bemuse Adam when he was younger. The experience of making a few similar blunders himself, and not just over the chessboard, had answered the conundrum; being human, it was easy.

The machines he had seen were perfectly capable of dealing with the flat slabs that made up the majority of the Elgin marbles. The stylus and cutter worked into areas under overhangs, cut in any direction, in tight corners, and what on first inspection looked to be impossible for either sculptor or machine. What the former could do, the latter could also, with the right tools.

The problem was that there was more to the Elgin Marbles than these relatively flat and moderate sized bas-relief pieces. There were about fifteen, large, three-dimensional sculptures, of a couple of metres in extent. He had seen some photographs in his assignment dossier, and would ask Irini to show him the originals that very afternoon, to personally gauge the scale, and literally, the depth of the problem.

It was theoretically possible to obtain larger versions of the machines he had just seen, but there were two difficulties. First, they had to be made to order, definitely not a stock item. The delivery time was minimum three months, and they didn't have three months plus the production time. The copy marbles were out of there in less than that time. The second issue was cost, not insurmountable for Spiros could write the check tomorrow; it would nevertheless be quite substantial. Adam smiled to himself. If he could solve the problem, his fees would be modest in the extreme compared to the savings. He then understood why consultants could sometimes command a hundred times the astronomical rate, from his point-of-view, that he had been offered for this assignment.

The problem was clearly set out before him, and he said as much. "I didn't see any accuracy specifications in my brief, Paul, do you have any feeling for that?"

"Sure!" His American accent was now readily apparent, and Adam warmed to him on that basis, for no particularly good reason – professional was professional, but that's how he felt anyway. It turned out that the feeling was mutual on this and other grounds, and they were destined to become fast friends. Adam couldn't be sure about his hair colour, for it was overlaid with the dust of Greek marble, but decided it was probably the natural dark blond it appeared to be. Paul was a lithe, strong man, obviously accustomed to a mix of mental and physical work.

"Locally, over an area like so," Paul made a circle with his thumb and forefinger, "we work to less than a half millimetre, about the thickness of five sheets of paper. It is my understanding that for the bigger objects, we need not hold that tolerance over larger distances. For example, it does not matter if the raised arm of Hercules is here, or here." Paul had held up a well-muscled arm, bicep swelling as he clenched his fist to hold the imaginary spear, then moved his fist a few millimetres to illustrate the point.

"So let me get this straight. We want the local surfaces to be smooth, and continuous – no good having edges and ridges on smooth skin, eh? But if the arm is slightly askew, nobody will notice, and the copy is adequate to the purpose."

"Exactly. It's the old problem of the tight tolerance locally for smoothness, and a looser one over distance, providing the two can join seamlessly together."

Adam already had an idea that might work in these circumstances. If the tight tolerance had been demanded over a distance of metres, he could not see an alternative to the precision, large-scale pantograph. It would be a huge version of what he had seen, and it would have extra arbours to hold the sensor and cutter in any position within several cubic metres of space. No wonder they were expensive, and a custom job, with long delivery lead-times.

"Okay, Paul, I've got the story. Thanks for the tour."

"They have given you a small, and the operable word is 'small', office through there. I believe it used to be a broom closet."

"I've had worse; one time a converted loo, or as you and I say, bathroom."

"That's life on the cutting-edge of technology, eh?" Paul gave a rich guffaw, and rose to don his gear once more. "One more time up the Eiger, my boys, one more time." With that he opened the door, deafening Adam until it closed again, before he could go through to check out his office.

He found it immediately, and was impressed again. The fresh, incised plastic plaque attached to it, read "Adam Blix: Consultant". The inside was less than impressive, yet there was just room for the drafting table, a Computer Aided Design workstation computer on the museum's network, one chair, and a coat hook on the back of the door. He could still smell the residual perfumes, if that was the right word, of the recently departed cleaning fluids.

Adam set to work at once, first checking out the computer's repertoire of software. Then eschewing all modern technology, he unscrewed the cap of a real-ink drafting pen from the drawer under the table, and began to make some preliminary sketches on the top sheet of paper.

Adam's computer chimed, *NetMessenger* popping up on the screen.

"You're late, my Champion of Cyberspace. Irini."

"Cripes." Adam shut down the computer, waiting impatiently for the all clear, then dashed out the door. He was forced to don his protective gear to go back through the cutting room. He hung up his things in the long cabinet, and went back through the airlock.

When he spotted her, threading her way through the school parties, her startling beauty again struck him. "How lucky I am to have found her," he thought. "And what have I done to deserve her?" The intoxications of first love, despite such a short separation, were almost unbearable.

They embraced, and she led him towards the Duveen Gallery, and his first physical sight of the Elgins, in person.

His hand did not leave hers during the tour. Her knowledge of so many civilizations, for example, Hittite and Babylonian, some of which Adam had never heard of, impressed him and revealed new horizons. Yet it was her sensitivity to artistic sculpted forms that was such a revelation to him. Through her eyes he began to see fresh relationships. It was like taking a psychedelic drug, and then seeing shapes and colours for the first time, in an altered consciousness. These insights were intensified by his realization that he faced much more than the task of merely reproducing the sculptor's touch, but the depth of feeling as well.

After a tour lasting much longer than either of them had realized, the closing bell sounded, and visitors were forced to leave. "Well, we could withdraw to my little cupboard of an office," Irini suggested, then smiled almost shyly. "It would be different..."

Passing through the security doors at several levels, which Adam noted with great interest, they penetrated the entrails of the museum itself. Her supervisor Doctor Denis Potterton had given her a tiny workspace. He had made it abundantly clear, that she had him to thank personally for the fact that she had anything at all. She opened the door to Adam, with the pride and joy of sharing this small part of her working life with him.

The effect of his physical proximity, for the length of their tour, had radically changed her mental set. Gone was the need to explain the Centaurs, or the procession of historical events necessary to illuminate the diverse relationships between the objects they had seen. Much as she loved the cold sculptures of the master's perfection, she wanted *him*! So pushing her precious books aside, many of them tumbling to the floor, she cleared her desk.

"Well," he said afterwards, "that was *quite* different." He had been swept up by her urgency, in surroundings one might otherwise have felt were unromantic.

Adam realized that Irini's interpretations, given during the tour, of the subtle relationships between feelings, form, history, and eroticism, had imbued him with a powerful emotional sense of the ageless, human sprit. This had been unexpectedly transferred into their lovemaking, creating an other-worldly experience of such intensity that they both felt quite shaky on leaving the museum.

They made a brief visit to Andreas' deli on the way home, and bought groceries, randomly at first as if in a trance. Andreas noticing this solicitously asked if anything was wrong. Irini replied with a crisp laugh, "No." Yet Andreas had known better from the moment they entered his shop. He offered his best Feta cheese to taste, thinking a little food would help. It did. They ended up buying half a kilo. Andreas, who had met Adam only fleetingly before, tentatively decided that he might be almost good enough for his flawless Irini.

Adam tapped meaningfully on the display case, and Andreas began withdrawing large prawns one by one, until Adam held up his hand. Andreas smiled, "So, enough for you two *and* the cat, I think."

Adam knew that there remained one furry obstacle that might block easy access to her and her domain. Irini had told him about Achilles' fondness for prawns, bordering on mania. Indeed he had spotted the custom-cut plaque on the wall beside the cat flap, which read, "*Amor 'Prawn' Vincit Omnia*".

Thus armed, Adam produced his powerfully odoriferous package for Achilles. All resistance was instantly overcome. He leapt eagerly on Adam's lap; strategically placed to intercept his rightful, lion's share of Adam's hand peeled prawns on their way to a bowl on the table in front of them. Achilles sometimes proffered a tentative paw, no claws, just a timely reminder, often punctuated with an ecstatic head-rub against his hand.

Later, when Adam appeared without the offering, he was just as welcome. Achilles knew it had been a symbolic one, and now Adam was an accepted part of his domain, under his influence and protection.

A prawn salad and French bread made up for the lunch Adam had never bothered to eat, interspersed with sips of an ice cold *vin blanc ordinaire*. They laughed, not for the first time, over the dinner of two nights ago, a casualty of their explosive passion. There was less urgency this time, and light touches carried their own nuances of pleasure, until they were safely ensconced under the protective influence of the god Morpheus.

HELENA TO SPIROS:
    PLEASE DEBRIEF ME ON THE LEAK AND CONSEQUENCES.
    EVERYONE WANTS TO KNOW.
SPIROS TO HELENA:
    THEY DON'T HAVE A NEED TO KNOW. RATHER NOT.
HELENA TO SPIROS:
    THEN HOW ABOUT ME?

There was a sensible pause. Helena waited patiently because her request was a *forcing* one.

SPIROS TO HELENA:
    OKAY, BUT YOU WON'T LIKE IT. CHARON IS EMBARRASSED,
        NUFF SAID? HE CHOSE TWO OPERATIVES
        FOR HIS CELL ON YOUR PROJECT. TOP PEOPLE.
    WE KNEW WE HAD A LEAK HIGH IN THE SERVICE.
    BY BAD LUCK SHE WAS IT, and PICKED.
    GOOD NEWS IS WE PLUGGED THAT LEAK FOR GOOD.
    NEW PAIR, PLUTON AND CASSANDRA.
        YOU KNOW HER I THINK.

Helena suspected that there was a lot more to it than this. She had to request the report – it should have come without prompting. Also the details were not quite credible, unless it really was just dumb bad luck. Then anger rose, for there was another possibility.

HELENA TO SPIROS:
    SO, WE WERE THE BAIT!
    HOW DARE ANYBODY USE ME AND MY PLAN LIKE THAT!
SPIROS TO HELENA:
    I CAN SEE HOW YOU MIGHT THINK THAT.
    IT DIDN'T HAPPEN THAT WAY. TRUST ME.
HELENA TO SPIROS:
    HOW DID IT COME DOWN, THEN?
    AND HOW DO YOU KNOW IT WASN'T LIKE THAT?

121

SPIROS TO HELENA:
YOU KNOW MY METHODS. NO DOUBT IT WAS ACCIDENTAL.
SHE WAS THE NUMBER ONE CHOICE.
HELENA TO SPIROS:
GOD! I KNOW WHO. AT LEAST SHE WASN'T OUR
SPYMISTRESS.
THE HEAD OF BRITISH MI5 AT ONE TIME WAS A SPY,
FOR THE RUSSIANS.
HE LIVED OUT HIS LIFE RIGHT HERE IN BRITAIN!
SPIROS TO HELENA:
SURE, I REMEMBER, UNDERLING WROTE A BANNED BOOK.
NOT OUR WAY – TERMINATED WITH EXTREME PREJUDICE.

HELENA TO SPIROS:
…! …? … ONE OF YOUR STORIES IN A YEAR OR TWO?
SPIROS TO HELENA:
NOT THIS TIME. U NO WHO DOESN'T FARM IT OUT WHEN
HIS DOG MUST BE KILLED.
HELENA TO SPIROS:
POOR MAN.
SPIROS TO HELENA:
TOUGH CALL. ROUGH JOB.
HELENA TO SPIROS:
YES, THAT'S WHY I DIDN'T WANT IT.
SPIROS TO HELENA:
HE ASKED? YOU NEVER TOLD ME. THAT CHANGES A LOT.
HELENA TO SPIROS:
NO, SPIRAKI MOU, IT DOESN'T CHANGE ANYTHING.
SPIROS TO HELENA:
LOOSE ENDS TIDIED UP. BIG JOB. TAKE CARE. LOVE.

HELENA TO SPIROS:
THE BIG QUESTION THEN, IS WHY?
SPIROS TO HELENA:
WE STILL DON'T KNOW FOR SURE.
HELENA TO SPIROS:
WAIT, I REMEMBER. SHE WAS THE LOVER OF AJAX. DAMN.
SPIROS TO HELENA:
THOUGHT OF THAT.
SHE NEVER BELIEVED YOU WERE HIS LOVER.
HELENA TO SPIROS:
HE WAS MY PARTNER; SHE BLAMED ME FOR HIS DEATH.

SPIROS TO HELENA:
　　CLEARLY IN THE LINE OF DUTY. IT WASN'T YOUR FAULT.
HELENA TO SPIROS:
　　IT'S <u>ALWAYS</u> THE PARTNER'S FAULT WHEN THAT HAPPENS.
SPIROS TO HELENA:
　　DON'T KNOW IF I SHOULD PASS THIS ON,
　　BUT PERHAPS I MUST. HER LAST WORDS
　　WHEN SHE KNEW SHE WAS FOR THE CHOP:
　　　　"ASK HELENA TO FORGIVE ME."

It offered another conundrum, a final unanswerable question, now beyond the grave. There was a lot to think about, enough for years perhaps – nothing more to say for now – except:

LOVE AND HUGS.
LOVE … AND HUGS.

Chapter 10

Just A Few More Loose Ends

Well Begun is Half Done. (B Franklin)

The next few days

HELENA TO ADAM:

PROVIDE <u>DETAILED</u> LIST WITH <u>FULL</u> DIMENSIONS FOR ALL PACKING BOXES FOR ELGIN COPIES TOGETHER WITH NAMES OR LABELS SPECIFIC TO EACH, DRAWINGS FOR INTERIOR INSERTS WHERE NECESSARY FOR SUPPORT, ABSOLUTELY <u>ASAP</u>. THIS MUST AGREE EXACTLY WITH THE FORTHCOMING SHIPMENT. I NEED TO SEND THESE SPECIFICATIONS IN ADVANCE TO SPIROS IN ATHENS.

Adam rolled over in Irini's bed, and set the mobile phone down on the bedside table. "Now I have five jobs, which is about three too many."

"What is it, darling?" Irini squinted at the bedside clock. "Helena, I'll bet, and she's sending her missives out earlier, and earlier. It's only 7AM."

Adam yawned, "She could at least put a delayed alarm on them, but she usually forgets."

"I don't think *that* lady ever forgets *anything*. I can help with some of it, so let's get at it. Maybe we can have more than a furtive half hour together tonight."

"Irini, you are off at 3PM today, and so – am – I – and tonight will be different, I promise."

ADAM TO HELENA:

SUMMARY LIST OF ELGINS, DETAILS IN APPENDIX ATTACHED
    TO BE UPDATED AS NECESSARY
    FINAL DETAILS IN SOME CASES UNAVAILABLE
MUSEUM IS PRETTY CAGEY ABOUT THESE SPECIFICATIONS
    ESPECIALLY SIZE AND WEIGHT
THE COPY-TEAM HAS SOME OF THE BASICS, SO HERE GOES:

56 FRIEZE SLABS (METOPES) MOST 1M SQUARE (BOXED)
    ESTIMATED WEIGHT 300 KG EACH (15-20 TONS TOTAL)
    SOME WERE CUT IN HALF BY ELGIN
WE ARE COPYING THESE FULL SIZE TO REPAIR THE CUTS
    THESE WILL BE 1X2 METRES AND WEIGH DOUBLE
15 PEDIMENTAL STATUES OF PHEIDIAS
    VARIABLE: LIST ATTACHED 200 KG TO 2 TONS
    NOT COPYING YET, SO EXACT WEIGHTS UNAVAILABLE.
SHOCKINGLY SOME OF THESE WERE ALSO CUT!
    WE FIX FOR COPIES.
    IMAGINE SLICING THE MONA LISA IN HALF.
1 CARYATID (1X1X2 M) 4 TONS (ESTIMATE NOT WEIGHED)
    DETAILED DRAWINGS ARE NOT EASY TO DO
    FOR SUCH IRREGULAR OBJECTS.
1 DORIC COLUMN FROM THE ERECHTHEUM
    (COPY UNDECIDED – MAY BE IMPRACTICAL)
    IF SENT IT WILL BE 60X60 CM BY ABOUT 3 METRES, 2 TONS.
THERE ARE SEVERAL MISCELLANEOUS "ELGIN" SCULPTURES
    MOST ARE NOT FROM THE PARTHENON
    FINAL DECISION ON NUMBER TO BE COPIED IS PENDING
PLEASE INSTRUCT FURTHER ON THESE UNRESOLVED DETAILS
    ADAM

Irini received permission from her boss, Denis Potterton, to take a day or two in support of Adam's consultancy. She was certain that if he had tumbled to their new relationship, he would have refused out of jealous pique. Irini was not the most experienced woman of her age in these matters, yet his unwelcome approaches, including the occasional brushing-touch, had been laced with obvious intent. She knew she would eventually have to do something about his advances, but she was just too busy at the moment.

They were standing in front of the fifteen pedimental sculptures of Pheidias, which had originally been set in the triangular pediment at the west end of the Parthenon. As a consequence of the triangular space, they ranged in size from less than a metre in height, to the towering figures of Athena and Poseidon that stood in the centre. These were the objects that his consultancy was dealing with: how to copy them with the machinery they had, or perhaps augment with some additional equipment that was readily available.

Their reason for being here today was the problem of boxing them up, first the copies as Helena had rather peremptorily, and mysteriously demanded ASAP, and later for the originals themselves. Why she appeared to need two separate sets of shipping crates, in *advance* of sending the copies to Athens, was a mystery, one which Adam was determined to get to the bottom of. The original idea had been to surreptitiously send back the cases used in shipping the copies to Athens, and simply reuse them for the originals. It would have been a relatively easy job to build containers for the copies of these irregular objects in the copy-room when supports and stays could be cut and fit by trial and error. It was going to be a major engineering and drafting job to prepare detailed specifications in advance, so that a box built at a distance would accurately fit them.

The pedimental end of the Duveen gallery was crowded on this morning. Several students from the Slade School of Art, probably would-be sculptors, were sitting with easels and doing pencil sketches of the tableau. One of Irini's museum colleagues, looking every inch the bespectacled English Professor, was giving the spiel, which Irini also knew by heart.

"The eastern pediment of the Parthenon is lost, except for a few fragments. The western pediment here in the British Museum is centred on a quarrel between Athena and Poseidon. The trunk of Poseidon shown here is a recent copy from the original in the Acropolis Museum in Athens, the only original piece held there. All the remaining fifteen sculptures are to be seen here before us, in the original marble as worked by Pheidias' school in the 5th century BC.

"The far corner of the pediment depicts the river god, himself representing the Ilissus River in human form. As you can see he is supporting himself on his left arm, raising himself from the narrow confines imposed by the low ceiling height in the corner, apparently to watch the proceedings in the centre.

"The anatomical detail of the muscles, sinews, and bone structure carved out of the marble on this statue is nothing less than astounding. As you can see in the opposite, southern gable, there is a horse's head that appears to spring from the soil after Poseidon has pierced the earth with his trident. He is quarrelling with Athena over the patronage of the city.

"It is not apparent in a display here at eye-level, but the horse's head was so placed by the sculptor, that those looking up at it from below to the pediment on which it rested high above their heads, gave the impression that it was rising from the abyss, foaming and struggling to free itself. For me, the movement is as real in this frozen statue as if this was a motion picture, and no Hollywood special effects could equal it.

"This principle of viewing from below applies to everything you see here. Do try to visualize the deliberate choices made by the sculptor, so as to transmit the strength and impression of the composition, through judicious selection of perspective and optical angle which Pheidias himself had calculated and produced so brilliantly in the stone. Thank you. If anyone has a question, I will be pleased to do my best to help."

Adam had brought one of the museum's collapsible staff chairs into the gallery, and was beginning to sketch the river god. On the way in to work this morning he had purchased a retractable, 3-metre tape measure from the tiny hardware shop three doors down from Andreas' deli. Irini was making measurements between the extremities and other vulnerable parts of the sculptures and the floor underneath each. She came over from time to time, patted Adam on the head, and handed him the dimensions, which he then transferred to the drawing.

After a few rounds of this, Adam caught her hand, and pulled her down to a kneeling position beside him. He threw down the pencil, and it did end-to-end somersaults on the floor. "This isn't going to work, you know; it's not accurate enough."

A young woman from among the artists who were also working the tableau was standing behind him. She laughed richly, "You're right, *that* will never do." Adam was somewhat taken aback, but held his work out in front of them, turning it this way and that.

"I don't know," he grinned, "there's hope, no?"

"Not a sausage." The visiting artist patted him on the back, "Keep at it, sunshine."

"Hey wait a minute," Adam called out as she turned. She came back uncertainly, by no means sure how her remark had gone down.

Adam smiled and she relaxed. She was Adam's archetype of the *serious art student*: medium in every dimension, classically nondescript. Her straight black hair hung in disarray over her shoulders, high forehead peaking like the profile of a volcanic hill, opposed by a receding chin, black eyes set too widely apart even for her moon-round face, probably her best feature in a catalogue of "not quites". Her smile was genuine, and she obviously had a sense of humour.

Adam stood up. "Adam Blix, and this is Irini Baynes."

"Naomi Marks, pleased to meet you."

Irini asked, "Are you from the Slade?"

"Yes we are." Naomi introduced the five others, who now gathered in a semicircle around them.

Adam cocked his head, "The Slade School of Art, at London University?"

"Indeed."

"I'm at Imperial."

"So, we're all of the brotherhood." Naomi concluded, as the handshakes were completed. "I understand; obviously you're not directly into art."

"That's right, yet I find myself immersed in it, a wondrous new part of my life, thanks to my Irini, here." He hugged her, oblivious to the others present for that instant of intimacy.

The art students were interested in why Adam had been sketching. "If that's the word for it," as Naomi put it with a smile.

"Yeah," he said disarmingly, "I knew it wasn't even good enough for the drafting table."

This thought mystified the others, and Adam explained that he needed to produce accurate drawings, with precise measurements in all three dimensions, so that boxes could be built *in advance* to ship the copies to be made later of these sculptures.

"I'm Steve Walters." The only man in the group shook hands again and replied, "I've heard of that project. So you're on it, Adam?"

"Sure, and I'm up to here in work, and I don't know a quick way to get this part of it done."

"Well," Naomi suggested doubtfully, "can we help? Perhaps we could make the drawings, ah, more efficiently." She chose her words carefully; she had earlier assumed he had some experience in art.

"Well, I don't know, the real problem is that we need dimensioned drawings."

Steve brightened, "I know a bit about that. Maybe we could work together on it."

"He is too modest by half," Naomi winked, "got his degree in engineering, but he has turned to art – come into the *real* world."

He laughed, "Okay, I had that coming, and it's true. I can't get into buildings, and bridges, and things like that. They probably won't last my lifetime, nor a century, never mind millennia. And they don't have the soul that an artist puts into their work."

A few days ago, Adam would not have had the slightest clue about where Steve was coming from. A week, in love, is a long time in life, and today, he *felt* precisely what had transformed the man. Adam was pretty sure he wouldn't be trading his computers for a hammer, chisel, and block of marble any time soon, but his life would never be the same again. Paul Albert, back in the cutting room, was on his mind, and he could imagine him doing exactly that.

"Hey," Adam enthused, "that's not a bad idea, Steve. It's a lot of work, and we need accurate results, fast. I've got a contract here, and there could be some ready money in it."

That was irresistible, and the six students edged forward as if to make sure that none of them were left out.

Adam furnished them with the details, and it was agreed that the new team from the Slade would prepare the full drawings, with designated supports, so that the treasures could be safely transported. They would determine the shape and size of each of the fifteen sculptures, plus the caryatid, compute the interior dimensions, and place the supports within the smallest rectangular space necessary to containment. This would include precision draftsman's drawings from the CAD program Adam was using, which was the same one Steve was already familiar with.

The total contractual fixed-fee of six thousand pounds was suggested by Adam, and instantly agreed to by the others. So Adam, who two days earlier had never had a consulting contract, now had his first subcontract to manage, from specification, through costing, to final result. It felt to him that it was all in a day's work, and he marvelled at how easily he had adapted to the situation. He had always felt that life should have an element of adventure to it, but a few weeks earlier he had begun to despair that this had gone out of his life. Despite interesting work and challenges including the Quantum Lab, everything had begun to taste of dust. However, it had been the dust of antiquity reborn that had transformed his life. It also helped him to better understand Peter's ongoing transformations.

Back in the game again, old boy, out of the doldrums, sails up, and away.

Consultant's Report

Copying the Larger Parthenon Sculptures
An Inexpensive and Adequate Solution
By: Adam Blix

Executive Summary:

The equipment originally purchased to effect the physical copying of the Elgin Marbles is more than adequate for the Parthenon Frieze bas-relief pieces (metopes), numbering 56 roughly one metre square sculptures. This work is progressing satisfactorily and will be completed on schedule.

These machines, Howell P-Graph Mark IV with Interior Sculpting Option, are not capable of cutting to a depth of greater than 40 centimetres, nor a span of more than 1 by 2 metres. This consultancy proposes a timely, inexpensive method for adapting this class of equipment to the more demanding task of copying the other full three-dimensional sculptures with extents in the required range of 2-3 metres in all three dimensions.

The consultancy proposes the purchase of two Howell P-Graph Mark V units capable of operating over a range of 1 metre in vertical and horizontal movement, in addition to the full 1 metre in depth instead of the 40 centimetres of the Mark IV. The incremental cost is under 15%. We will also purchase their Step-bridging Software Option SBSO Beta Test Version. This has the capability of smoothly bridging between sections of a large object after the Mark V unit has been moved. The Howell Company recently completed this extension of their programs, for precisely the reason we have encountered, to deal with larger complex objects.

It is up to the customer to build the necessary apparatus, suitable to the specific application, which permits the sensing and cutting systems to be accurately mounted and demounted as needed to complete the scan and copy operations on a large object. The accuracy both in local smoothness and long-range is adequate, see later sections.

Appendix A provides detailed engineering drawings for a sturdy, simple set of arbours. These will be bolted to the floor, and the sculpture to be copied is securely mounted underneath on a pedestal of at least 1-metre thickness above the floor (so as to be able to undercut). The blank marble is mounted under a matching set of arbours and pedestal.

The process is easy to understand and implement. The arbours are drilled with reasonably accurate mounting holes so that the Mark V sensor and cutter units can be suspended in space near the source sculpture and copy. Next, a portion of the source is scanned, and cut on the target. When that is complete, we demount, and remount the sensor-cutter units at the next, *overlapping* position.

The referenced software allows for the fact that the job is incomplete at each stage, and that a move is necessary. It therefore stores the regions near the overlaps in memory, and we move the units a maximum of 0.8 metres, so that the software can smooth the joins between the sequential positionings necessary to complete the job. It can also compensate for significant errors in mounting positions by the device of fitting mathematically to the surfaces previously scanned and cut.

Appendix B provides the operations bulletin, as modified by the consultant. It is necessary for a human operator to provide special inputs to the software in any case where a tunnel (interior gap) extends between two or more of the sequential positions. This was not catered for in the beta-version software, and will happen frequently in this application. It is impossible for the software to know what lies on the other side, which will not be scanned and cut until later. The consultant recommends that personnel (*i.e.* artists) experienced in sculpting, who are also computer literate, be retained for this task.

Appendix C provides the Curriculum Vitae of three students in advanced studies at the Slade School of Art, London University, who in the consultant's opinion would admirably meet these requirements. They, with three other colleagues, were instrumental in solving a difficult problem relating to the secure boxing and packing of these copies under the consultant's supervision.

Coda

HELENA TO SPIROS:
    HERE IS ADAM'S FULL LIST WITH ATTACHMENTS.
    PLEASE, NO EXPLANATIONS FOR NOW.
    PLEASE DO WHAT I HAVE ASKED TO THE LETTER.
    ADD FULL ELGIN COPIES BOXES TO MT ATHOS TREASURES
    ON ALL DOCS., EXHIBITION LISTS, and MANIFESTS.
    USE THE FICTITIOUS NAMES I HAVE PROVIDED.
    IT IS ESSENTIAL THAT THERE ARE NO DISCREPANCIES
    ON NUMBERS, COUNTS, and SIZES.
SPIROS TO HELENA: CHECK TO SEE THAT I UNDERSTAND:
    1. MOUNT ATHOS SHIPMENT INCLUDES ELGIN COPY BOXES
    2. FICTITIOUSLY LABELED YET COMPLETE ONE TO ONE.
    3. WHAT DO WE PUT IN THEM, IF ANYTHING?
    4. I DON'T UNDERSTAND, BUT WILL COMPLY.
HELENA TO SPIROS:
    1. CORRECT
    2. CORRECT
    3. THAT IS FOR ME ALONE. YOUR PART IS COMPLETE.
    4. NOT SURE EITHER, JUST TRYING TO BUY INSURANCE.
SPIROS TO HELENA:
    I UNDERSTAND. WE'VE BEEN THERE BEFORE. GOOD LUCK
    LOVE AND HUGS AND LOVE AND HUGS. YOUR SPIRO

As Adam drifted off to sleep in Irini's arms, lulled by her soft snores, he thought once again about the conundrum of the boxes. Why was it necessary to have two sets, specified in advance, when those used for shipping the copies to Athens could simply be returned secretly to London as in the original plan as he understood it? He fully intended to get to the bottom of the mystery.

But it would drop off of his radar screen, unable to compete with the distractions of work and his love life. He should have considered it again if he really wanted to second-guess Helena's plan, one that went much deeper, and was more labyrinthine than the original caves of Ariadne, under the ancient city of Knossos on Crete, which predated the Parthenon Sculptures by another thousand years.

END OF PART ONE

PART TWO

Chapter 11

All Security is Relative

You can break most security systems by insinuating yourself between a user and the system.

London, three months later, late September

Adam and Irini had taken their first holiday together, a delightful long weekend in Brighton. The weather had cooperated for three brilliant days in a row, the tail end of a summer heat wave. It had amused them both when one of the tabloids headlined on the third day:

Heat Wave Continues
No Relief in Sight

"You know, Adam, the weather headlines are always so dismal in this country, week after week. Then when we get a couple of good days, it's always the same. 'No Relief in Sight.' Why not something cheerful, but I suppose that's beyond them."

"Maybe it's their journalist's way of getting even with those of us able to take advantage of it, when they are cooped up in their dingy, green-walled, windowless offices."

"Sounds like a good theory to me. So how do I take advantage of you again, now that we're back in dark, rainy, London?"

"Seems like the perfect day for it." Adam kissed Irini with fond recollections of their best moments from the holiday.

"Like hell it is; it's pissing down with rain out there, and we have to go to work."

When they had shaken out the umbrellas, and stashed them in Irini's pocket-sized office, Adam took her arm. "Let's crack the British Museum security systems this morning."

Adam led the way up the back stairs until he came to a door labelled:

Secure Storage Area
Senior Curators Only

There was a standard-issue entry box on a panel to the left of the door. The personal security card was inserted in the slot, and then the Personal Identification Number (PIN) was entered in the same way as at a bank's cash dispenser.

Adam had recognized on his first day that the system at the British Museum was quite basic and practically out of date. He also knew that the weakness of the system lay in the fact that all security rested with the card and the PIN, and there was no fail-safe check elsewhere in the system.

The little box beside the door had a very basic computer inside. It did two simple jobs only. First it checked to see if the PIN entered was the one that matched the number on the magnetic stripe. This proved that the holder of the card was the authorized one unless the PIN had been stolen.

Second, the little computer had a list, sent by its connection to a phone line just like surfing the Internet on a home computer. If you were on the list for that door in the museum's database, you got in, if not, even the card and PIN would not let you through.

"Your card and PIN won't work here, will it Irini?"

"No, I'm not authorized at this level. This is a secure area for storing artefacts not on display. I don't usually go in there, unless I have to get an item to put in the display cases downstairs and then I'm always escorted by a senior curator."

"Well, let's see." Adam hummed a tune to himself as he took a small black box out of his pocket. He inserted a blank magnetic stripe-card into a slot on the side of the box. It zipped in, and then out. A numeric display came to life on the top of the box, reading: "210963".

Adam then slipped the fresh card he had just made into the door's security box, and keyed "210963" into the numeric keypad. The green light came on, and the door released with a click. "Voila, Irini, the hand has many fingers." He waggled five of them under her nose, and triumphantly withdrew the card. "Nothing to it."

He opened the door, looked inside, and then closed it. "We don't really want to take any of these priceless treasures, do we? Not today, anyway."

Irini was frankly astonished. "How did you get the card, and the code?"

"Let's go to the coffee shop, and treat ourselves to a second breakfast. I'm hungry."

"I should think so after all that."

Adam sipped his hot chocolate pensively. "As you know, we are going to need to break the security system here."

Irini replied, "We've all been wondering for a long time just how you're going to do that."

"Sure, that's understandable. Do you really want the insider's story on these cards, your credit card, and bank security? It takes a bit of chalk-talk, fascinating for me to be sure, but I have had doubts about trying to push all this down possibly unwelcoming throats."

Irini tapped the table, "Try it out on me."

"That's what I'd hoped you'd say. Right. Standard security is based on two things. First, something you physically have, and can hold in your hand, like a bank credit card, or one of these." He waved his own personal British Museum security card as if conjuring a magic trick. "Hopefully it is not easy to copy, but in fact they often are. Second, something that you know, in your head, that matches up with the physical object.

"A house key is the first level of security, something that you have, period. That's all you need to get in. If somebody steals it, or can make a copy, they can get in your house.

"Something you know, by itself, is another single level of security, as with electronic door codes for entry to apartment houses.

"Put the two together, and one has a reasonable level of security. You have a key, this card, but it is useless unless you also know the PIN that goes with it. So, if the card is stolen, it cannot be used, same as your bank card. Drop it in the street, no problem; your account cannot be accessed. Somebody would have to look over your shoulder, say, and see you key in your PIN code, and then get your card."

Irini summarized. "So, let me get this straight. My PIN number is on the magnetic stripe, and the little security box checks to see that the number I enter is the same."

"That's it, basically, with one very important little extra." Adam turned his card over. "This is a magnetic strip on the back, just the same as a bit of tape from a music cassette, or the floppy disk in your computer. It can be read with a very simple, cheap device. You can buy magnetic card reader-writers for about fifty quid, quite legally. There's one of them in my magic black box.

"So, if that was all there was to it, your bank card in the street would be a doddle. The thief would simply buy one of those, read your card, and he'd have your PIN, and all your money."

Irini brightened with understanding. "I think I understand; let me say?"

"Sure, go for it."

"The PIN is on the back, all right, but it's in a secret code."

"I'm impressed, and I'm not being condescending. That's exactly right."

"Easy – you get a card, read the back, and break the code." Irini flashed an enigmatic smile as though she had just done it herself.

"That's okay in principle, yet codes can be made as hard to break as one chooses, and there is plenty of room on this stripe to use a code that cannot be broken. And, in some cases, the PIN is stored in the bank's remote computer."

"I read somewhere that *any* code is vulnerable, given a big enough computer, like the *Enigma* project during World War Two."

"Sure, but only if you have enough time. If the code is deep, all the computers in the world running since the year zero wouldn't be able to crack one, never mind the millions of these little beauties that are running around. That won't quite do it, Irini, so one has to find another way."

There obviously was another way, because Adam had just done it before her eyes. "So, you are telling me that you didn't look over anybody's shoulder to see their PIN number, and you didn't steal the card, and yet you were able to produce one and its PIN right in front of me? Adam, you are a magician!"

"Magic isn't necessary, as we will see. I didn't have to peek, or steal cards or files with the numbers in them, or do any other risky business."

"Am I right, the physical card you actually used was not an official one?"

"Yes. The card I used is a standard blank that Peter got for me. They are not available to the general public, so he goes underground for it. It's just a piece of plastic the right size and thickness, with a blank, magnetic stripe on the back, just like an unrecorded tape cassette."

She knew Adam was posing the puzzle for her to solve, but Irini didn't think it was likely she would succeed. This wasn't her meat, and Adam was one of the world's most successful security experts. Peter was taking lessons, and had told her that Adam could open standard safes, as well as the more challenging electronic types, as he had done in New York.

Adam knew what she had been thinking. "Okay, Irini, let's see if an intelligent, if not brilliant…"

"Thanks, Adam," she interrupted, dryly.

"… Non-expert in security can figure out how it is done. If you can, well, the sky's the limit. Say I can borrow your bank card for half a minute. Can I read the information off of it?"

"I guess, it's just numbers recorded on the magnetic stripe."

"Can I then make a copy?"

"Of course, I just saw you make one from scratch."

"I didn't have access to anybody's physical card, yet I was able to obtain the coded information from its stripe anyway. And I didn't peek at a PIN, over a shoulder or with binoculars, but I got the PIN. So what's the general principle? Where's the weak link – actually in almost any security system? Think about it. The card goes down through a slot, a card reader inside reads it, and then the numbers are manually punched in on a keypad. The computer inside checks it out, releasing access if all is correct."

Irini was thinking but it wasn't making much sense. How could Adam get the information off the card without having it, and the PIN without seeing it? "A question?" Adam nodded. "Did you somehow get inside the box beside the door and steal the information from its little computer?"

"Not quite, because I can't get inside their black box this time. But, is there some place I can put myself, or *some cute little piece of equipment* so that at one swipe, we get both the card's data, and the PIN?"

They finished their coffee and hot chocolate, two croissants with jam and butter, and a refill on the coffee, all the while Irini was thinking hard. Finally, she gave up, and relaxed as she held Adam's hand. Then, like lightning had struck, she had the answer to beating all systems of this kind. You have to put something *in between* the user and the system. She had it, and then it was gone, for that seemed impossible.

"So, Irini, what's the answer?"

"I thought I had it when I relaxed and you stroked my hand, but it's gone now."

"What were you thinking?"

Somewhat embarrassed at what she now felt was a ridiculous idea, she whispered, "Okay, but it sounds stupid."

"Try me."

"Well, I thought of somehow getting something in between the user and the system that could pick up what's on the card, and get their PIN as they keyed it in."

Adam sat back, genuinely pleased with her. "That's right. First class, Irini. It took you, what, about ten minutes to work it out. It took me months the first time."

She basked in his praise, yet to be honest with herself, she still didn't have a clue what it all meant, and finally said so.

"Okay, now design the system I have in my other pocket."

She shrugged, helplessly. "I haven't a clue."

"You've figured out what you need to do, so just think it through like an engineer, do it in the real world step by step."

"I'll try. The cardholder approaches the machine, and slips the card into the slot. So what do we do there? Put something on the outside to read the card? No, that won't work, anybody would notice."

"Unless…" Adam prompted.

"Unless, yes! Unless it was invisible, or, *disguised* somehow. So how would you do that?"

"There's only one way in this kind of situation, think about it."

"Unless, unless," she struggled, "unless it looked the same as the box. A little bit extra on the front that does the job, maybe?"

Adam reached into his other pocket, and took out what looked exactly like one of the museum's door security boxes. It was thinner, and she then saw that it was designed to fit over the face, with a slot, and pushbuttons on it. He slipped it back into his pocket.

"You can do all that in something so thin and small?"

"Well, I didn't say it was easy, but it's all in there. The card is read as it slides through, but the card reader to do that costs a lot more than fifty quid. It's no thicker than a coat of paint, really just a surface on the lip of my thin slot. Capturing the PIN is easy, because the user presses my keys on the outside. They physically push through to the keys on the inside, so there is no difference in feel, and the data is easily recorded. The computer is on a chip, but without its usual leggy not-so-little box – you've seen them – I use a raw chip, micro-wires soldered to it, and so on, just basic engineering after that. To pick up the data I simply clip it on, leave it until at least one authorised user has come by to use it, then pluck it off and take it back to my computer.

"Come on. Let's perform the acid test."

Adam led the way past the Duveen Gallery, through the separate area devoted to the Caryatid and a short gallery containing other Greek treasures, to a double-door marked: "Secure Exit to Garage".

He took out his trusty black box, keyed the door number into its keypad, and inserted the same card he had used before. It disappeared, and then came back out again. The number "151161" appeared in the window. He slipped the card into the security box, the number worked, and the green light came on. He took the card out, and the light went out after a few seconds. "I won't risk opening the door, yet as you can see, the way is clear for us."

He tapped on the box. "Just noticed something about those two numbers. The first was 210963, and this one was 151161. These are special numbers we all use, every day, and each one of us has our very own. Very bad form to use them for top-security PINs. You spot it?"

Irini adored puzzles, and Adam's way of presenting them. She was sure he would be a good teacher if he chose that profession. Yet she was exhausted, and it wasn't lunchtime yet, her active floor shift due to start in a few minutes. "Sorry, Adam, I'm a bit tired. Don't see it."

"Birth dates, my love, they are almost certainly both birth dates. So anybody with access to personnel files has half what they need to break the system."

Safe House Two, the same evening

This one was the opposite of the other, buried as it was in a dismal, dark basement, but with the advantage of instant emergency egress to the London Underground. Number Two would do for a luxury flat. It was a glass-surround penthouse on the twelfth floor of the King Richard Mansions, a short walk from King's Cross Station and within a few minutes of their own flats.

It had two bedrooms, and Peter had arranged for one to be converted into a safe room, with all available anti eavesdropping devices, similar to the first. All meetings discussing any aspect of the plot were held in that room.

The roof had been open, but after a hassle with the authorities, it now sported an inflated, grey rubberised plastic dome. They had a variance permit good for only one year, but that was more than enough for their purposes. The cover story was to make tests of a new mobile telephone system, and satellite link, out of the weather.

Helena had insisted on the usual master control panel, with micro-miniature cameras covering the entrance twelve floors below, corridors, and all relevant access points, including the fire escapes.

The cameras had been mounted inside the walls at the necessary points, with lenses no bigger than a letter "o". Peter had offered to repaint the halls and stairs, which had been in desperate need of it. The landlord was naturally delighted. After the cameras and wires were in place, a crew was hired to redecorate. Peter then carefully removed the small spots of silicone he had put on each lens to protect it. With some technical help from Adam, Peter had done all the work by himself, and had learned a lot about electronics and computer interfacing.

After a pleasant hour of relaxed chat, Helena got up, led them into the safe room, and brought the meeting to order.

"First, I think we should thank Peter for all his hard work on this safe house. He has not only dealt most subtly with the security arrangements, but has taken the time and trouble to make it something of a home for us." Everyone applauded sincerely.

"He will brief us now on the security and other technical systems."

Peter fired up the computer, and for the first time in his life gave a formal presentation, projected on the screen from the computer. Helena could see that with a bit more training, he would be perfectly capable of running his own company.

"I will save the *pièce de résistance* for the end of the meeting." With this cryptic promise, he turned the chair back to Helena.

"Adam has his report on museum security."

Adam covered the nature of security systems on a series of slides, presenting the technicalities without abridgement, in much the same way as he had done with Irini that morning.

"In conclusion, I must say we are fortunate that the systems are really, by today's standards, quite crude, and as we have seen, can be circumvented in several ways, at least one of which does not require any espionage such as nicking files and bribing people. We don't need Helena to tell us that those alternatives are strictly a last resort, or a backup. Irini and I are working on ideas for that, and we will probably find a way to have more than one method in hand on the day. She has a few words to say on that subject. Thank you."

"As Adam has said, some of these people are careless with passwords, and we may be able to use that nearer the time. We will run tests from time to time with Adam's black box system, and keep track of things, like how often people change their PINs. Meanwhile, I have reconnoitred the facility, and made fully detailed maps virtually down to the cracks in the walls, and Adam will be making a three-dimensional model on the computer. That will take us several more weeks, but as we have over seven months to Lift Day, we don't anticipate any time-pressure on that.

"I have made disappointing progress on full organizational charts, and employment histories of both existing staff, and for those who have left in the last three years. Helena has shown us how valuable such contacts can be, for example, if disgruntled ex-staff can be identified, and cultivated ... nice word that, in this context.

"Helena has said that we will be using consultants to trace all of these people, set up dossiers on their contacts, associates, friends, and lovers. I'm glad that I already know all that about myself; I would rather hate to be some poor secretary with something illicit in her background that we might be forced to use. I hope we won't use anyone in that sense, and if we have to, we will find some way –"

Helena interrupted, "That is being taken care of, and rest assured, we will minimize the need for blackmail and compensate anyone as best we can, if we do. That's straight from headquarters in Athens."

"Thanks Helena, I'll sleep a little better ... that's all I have."

There were tasks to assign, and Helena did this in her usual businesslike manner, complete with more computer slides. They also went over the plans, identified loose ends, made further assignments, and updated the Project Plan. It now consisted of 368 pages in the computer, and Adam would be adding the huge file dealing with the whole building complete with all relevant wiring, plumbing, access routes, and the security connections.

She indicated that Peter's forthcoming work would include some initial contacts in his south London underworld, to begin checking out possible candidates for his hit team, the group that would physically lift, box, and load the spoils of this cultural war.

Helena concluded, "This is the most dangerous aspect of the plan. We will be working together on that from now on. Peter has something in mind for after the meeting, and if nobody has anything more to report, however trivial, we are now adjourned."

Peter led them out of the safe room, and around to the rear of the flat, where there was a pull-down, loft-access type of staircase. It slid smoothly out of its box in the ceiling, and was clearly of good manufacture. "Most are flimsy, won't come down when you need them to. We've got the best."

They easily ascended to the roof, and emerged under the dome, which was just beginning to deflate slightly because of the open hatch. Peter kicked it shut behind them, and in a moment the fan had stiffened it up again. "If you must leave the hatch open, pull this red handle, and compressed air will keep the dome up.

"If we've gotta get away in a hurry, pull this lever here." He did so, and the shroud in the middle of the room was released and rapidly retracted to one side. A helicopter was revealed standing in the middle of the room!

"Wow! Straight out of James Bond." Adam enthused, trotting over to pass his hand lovingly across its sleek hull. He had secretly dreamed of learning to fly, and had always been particularly fond of the helicopter, although he knew they were notoriously difficult to fly.

Peter continued, proudly. "It is a five-seater, pilot, co-pilot, and three passengers. There's enough lift for at least two more people, so if we stack'em like firewood on the back seat, six or seven could get clear.

"The 'copter will fire up to full lift in fifteen seconds. Remember to duck under the blades if the pilot hits the revs before you're aboard, word to the wise, eh?"

"So how does it take off ... the dome and all?" Irini asked.

"The dome's tied to the roof at eight spots round the outside, gas bottle rockets at each one." He was enjoying the mystery and its effects on the faces of Irini and Adam.

"Release is by radio control, here," Peter opened the left, pilot's door, "this red lever marked 'Dome Release'. Depending on wind direction, six of the rockets throw it over our heads and it fetches up on the opposite side. The roof is clear for takeoff. Questions?"

Adam scrunched his face, "Okay, so we are all here, and the baddies are coming up the stairs, we run up here, jump in the plane, pull the levers, and then what? Who in hell flies it?"

Helena laughed expansively, "We do!"

"What?"

"Howzat?"

Helena continued unperturbed. "Peter is already licensed, got his ticket last week in fact. Seems he has a talent for flying. You have to get your fixed-wing cert first, and then you train on one like this. I don't have his natural talent, but expect to have mine in a month or so. And we *all* need to be able to do it, so Adam, Irini, you are scheduled Saturdays and Sundays, at the Redhill airfield, starting weekend after next."

Reading the manuals that evening, Adam learned that it was a new design, partly computer controlled, like the Airbus Industry's big jets, so it was much easier to fly than conventional 'copters.

Adam was frankly astonished, and then it sunk in, that another one of his desires was going to come true if he could pass the test. First Irini, and now this – it was almost too much to take in over ten or twenty years, never mind in a single summer.

He was sure there would now be two loves in his life, and he hoped he could handle them.

Chapter 12

A Trial

Trials are sent to test us.

Geoffrey Hayward had hand-picked Denis Potterton. At the interview five years ago, Hayward, in his role as director of the British Museum, had spotted in him those qualities he was looking for – the lean and hungry look of ambition.

Potterton was no longer well known for his dedication to research in his fields of Byzantine manuscripts and numismatics. This had been put to one side of late in pursuit of his ambitions.

When Irini appeared in his life, he saw her as a beautiful accoutrement to his grand scenario. He still thought of most women as fundamentally malleable, as indeed his own mother had been to his domineering father. With a woman like Irini at his side, her beauty and erudition a pleasing adjunct, he would be a powerful contender for advancement.

He knew that his physical attributes were negligible, and this gave rise to a perpetual inner conflict. He had never learned to like himself, never mind love, or even come to terms with himself.

He hated his thin, weasel-like face every time it confronted him in the shaving mirror, often reflecting that his considerable talents deserved a much more pleasing outer shell. It also didn't help that he was soft-spoken and nervous in mannerisms, words tumbling out of his mouth, albeit in a highly articulate torrent.

He decided that the conquest of Irini must now assume a priority, and he resolved to undertake it immediately. He reassured himself, as he looked in the mirror: "After all, I have position and influence, both in the academic world and in the museum hierarchy. She's only on the bottom rung of the ladder, and could easily be dislodged." He laughed at the image. "Yes, perhaps a timely reminder might strip the scales from her eyes, and bring her to heel."

First thing Monday morning he picked up his office phone.

Irini was startled by the call from her immediate supervisor; he had always left her to her own devices.

Hoping the meeting would be brief, she reluctantly climbed the stairs, thinking of the joys of Adam. She knocked and entered, stepping across the not inconsiderable office space that he had aggrandized to himself. She noted the empty, sterile desk, save for a dossier labelled "Miss Baynes".

"Ah, *there* you are, Irini," he said, as if by implication, she'd been hiding from him.

Instinctively, she returned his greeting formally, "Yes, Doctor Potterton, you sent for me?"

Her terse businesslike reply was not what he had been fantasizing about. "Well, yes – do sit down Irini, my dear."

She recoiled at the unsolicited endearment.

"As you know, we do like to look after staff here at the British Museum, especially the more junior members."

He decided to shift the ground, got up from his desk, and made a gesture to Irini that she should sit at the low coffee table in one of two comfortable leather chairs.

"Sherry, time, I think. Sweet or dry?"

He took her hand before she had realized what was happening, and guided her to the chair; his other hand lightly propelled her on her shoulder blades, and then slid sensually down her back.

His audacity took her breath away and she tried to avoid sitting down, but found herself in the chair before she could readjust her balance. "Neither thank you. I really am very busy and unless there was something specific… I should get back to work."

"Of course, my dear," he purred, "but not before I have told you about the reception for senior staff organized as one of the events associated with the museum's anniversary. I hardly need to tell you that it would be an excellent opportunity for you to meet and be seen by people of influence." He paused, "I must represent our division, and we have been allocated two invitations. I shall take you as my personal assistant and escort. As you know, Emily Stone would normally take priority as your superior."

Astonished at his arrogance, and without thinking, she gulped, "No, I can't. Emily Stone would be much more – suitable for you."

His face clouded over, the muscles working in his cheeks. Emily Stone was in her late forties, amiable in an emaciated sort of way, but indistinguishable from the dry parchments she poured over day after day.

"I mean, more suitably qualified than I am," she blurted out, then reflected on the pattern – one she had been aware of for some time, and now keenly regretted not having dealt with earlier. She owed it to herself, and to him as she saw it, to settle the matter now, as sympathetically as possible. Fairness was always important to her, and to be honest with herself she harboured a faint feeling of sympathy for him because of his obvious lack of physical charm.

"Perhaps, but I expect you to come. It is an opportunity you…"

"There is something I must tell you. I am secretly engaged." She inadvertently looked down at her bare third finger. She wondered how Adam would react to this news.

Irini looked directly at him, but contact eluded her as his eyes flitted nervously around the room. "I trust your first report is well underway for the director's meeting in two days' time."

She gasped inwardly. She knew that he was being malicious, because this was the first time he had mentioned it since her arrival, and then no specific time limit had been given. She had naturally assumed that the report would not be called for until after the customary six-month probationary period.

"So," he asked in an insistent voice, "what is your subject?"

She extemporized: "The Elgin Marbles Interpreted for Children."

"Well, ah, we don't call them by that name."

"You are quite right, sorry, 'The Parthenon Marbles Interpreted for Children'. Thank you for that correction."

It upset her that she could only feel irritation and mounting anger. She rose to go, sighing inwardly, and reached the door before Potterton had recovered himself. "Goodbye, Doctor Potterton," she said angrily. Slamming the door gave her great satisfaction.

The thought of Emily Stone stuck in his gullet. He saw it as oblique reference to his own personal unattractiveness. He spent the evening scheming other ways of ensnaring his precious Miss Baynes.

That evening, Adam noticed immediately that Irini was upset, and trying hard to conceal her feelings. She had suggested a rare visit to Adam's miniscule student flat in the University precincts west of Russell Square. As a junior member of staff with the Quantum Computer Research Project, he had qualified for slightly better accommodation, but even that was far from adequate.

He hadn't spent much time at his own digs since their romance had begun so dramatically three months ago, but had been happy to take her there if that was what she wanted.

Adam had recently found an interest in cooking, and they had been experimenting at Irini's flat. He had frequently benefited from advice on the QT from Andreas, often passed to him secretly behind the canned goods section in deep whispers. But his room only had a single cooking ring, no oven or microwave and was unsuitable for anything interesting. So they had brought in an *Andreas special*, and Adam eagerly opened the box to see what he had in store for them this time.

Irini picked over her *mezethes*, including her favourite *humus* with Andreas' special hand-made *dolmades*, stuffed with rice and minced lamb that made a meal in itself.

Suddenly, she burst into open sobs. "Blast *Potty*, Bastard!"

Not surprisingly, Adam had no idea what she was talking about, but her pain was obvious, and he embraced her again.

"If it will help, what you can, when you can."

Then it all burst out in angry, broken thoughts, but it didn't take Adam long to figure out the basics. Though the details were by no means clear at this stage, he understood enough to realise that she had been subjected to blatant sexual harassment and his initial indignation quickly turned to rage. However, he controlled his anger realising that her need to be comforted was greater than his desire to kill someone.

"Irini, look, it wasn't your fault. We'll deal with it together, okay?"

She nodded like a child being comforted by her mother. Adam didn't see this as a weakness, she needed help and he was pleased she wanted it from him.

He took her hand. "Whatever it is, we'll work it out, together. No pressure, okay? What you can, when you can, will be the watchword, agreed?"

Tears welled in her eyes, arising equally from the endearment of Adam's sensitivity, and the rough emotions from the encounter at work. She had naturally assumed that her first real job would be an exciting new world, and that the problems would only be those of the challenges in the assignment and responsibilities. Irini felt deeply betrayed by her supervisor. She had not expected to suffer the slings and arrows of disturbed personalities in those set above her in the hierarchy. Then she understood what many before her must also have learned the hard way, that the worst problems on the job are often precisely of this kind.

Adam had been deep in thought for a moment. "How about we knock that report on the head, right here, tonight if you feel up to it, or as soon as you feel able to tackle it."

He came around the tiny table dragging his chair behind him, sat down, and gave her a proper hug. She rested her head on his shoulder, and wiped away the last of the tears.

They were replaced with hot, dry anger, "Stupid bastard." A beat, then, "No, he's not stupid, he's a brilliant schemer. He had me going, that's for sure. Dammit, he won't get to me, I – won't – let him."

It was clear to him that Irini was now much more composed. She had an excellent memory, and was able to recount every moment of her meeting with Potterton, including full quotations. Adam typed up her version of events onto his computer verbatim. It beggared credibility. He saw clearly that this man had some serious problems, and that this didn't bode well for the future.

Irini agreed that they should assuage all this nastiness in a bout of work. Adam fired up his grey box, it was electric blue in fact, and was soon whipping his mouse back and forth, Irini at his side offering suggestions as they surfed the net for background information on child psychology, and bibliographic references in the scientific literature. In a half hour, they had more than enough, changed places, and Irini began keying at her blistering, touch-typing pace, the thoughts flowing as they had only rarely done, powered in this case by anger discharged through burying Potterton in a report of substance.

By midnight, Adam was shaking his head in wonder, equally hyped-up, sleep a distant future hope. This was outside his field, but the report read well, and they were sure it compared favourably with examples they had read for background written by established professionals in child psychology. They were confident that it had worked out well, because one *always* knows when it has not. They pushed back from the computer desk with a satisfied sigh, as the printer discharged the fifty-six-page document into its hopper. True, about half was paraphrased background information taken from references, as most substantive reports of this kind are. The bibliography, limited to papers they had read in their entirety rather than listing anything to make it look good, ran to a full page.

"Wow," Adam grinned, "congratulations; good show, Irini."

"Well, I had a little help from my partner. Thanks."

Sleep was impossible so they made love well into the small hours, on Adam's totally unsatisfactory single bed with the mattress he laughingly described as "Best grade Afghani cardboard." It could have been up in the heavens on the softest clouds imaginable.

Irini knocked on the door, and when "Potty Potterton" – as the staff referred to him more often than not – opened it, she pushed past him, tossed her report on his empty desk, then turned and left, before he was able to summon a word to his astonished lips.

She had taken the trouble to drop by the neighbourhood Instaprint shop to have five copies made and professionally bound with an attractive cover page in colour cadged from the museum's website. She made further distribution to selected colleagues, and passed one up to the director's secretary for good measure, just to make sure her boss couldn't play any more of his nasty games.

The next day her assignment sheet called for the usual mix of minor duties before moving out onto the floor to deal with the public. On this occasion she had received three keys to display cabinets in the Sumerian and Early Greek Artefacts area, together with a rubber-banded bundle of fresh description-cards. The task, one she had performed several times in the past, was to replace the old cards, yellowing with age, and rearrange the exhibits in as pleasing a manner as possible. The new cards had been made up in several European and Asiatic languages, part of a new policy she heartily agreed with.

She closed the last case, and checked that it was locked. Just as she did so, George, one of the guards, whom she knew in passing, grabbed her arm, and jerked her along after him. "Doctor Potterton wants to see you, right now."

Deeply shocked and totally mystified, Irini stumbled along behind him, embarrassed and actually hurting from his grip. He was strong, as were many of the security guards, and he was bruising her arm.

The door to Potterton's office slammed shut behind them. George pushed her forward so sharply, that she banged up against the front of the desk. Potterton grabbed her handbag as it flipped on top of his desk. She was so astonished that it was her turn to be speechless.

"George, you will witness."

"Yessir."

Potterton held her handbag in his left hand from the bottom, with the top completely exposed, and then motioning with his head to George that he should come closer, slipped the catch with his right hand. It snapped open.

"George, I am now going to empty it in plain view on the top of my desk, so." He tipped her handbag over, and its contents spilled out. Everything remained on the desk except for her compact, which rolled across it, and fell on the floor. "Leave it for now."

Potterton stirred his index finger through the pile to spread the items out. "Aha!" He exclaimed, like a poorly acted Sherlock Holmes, "What have we here?"

Irini gaped, transfixed. Standing out like a fried egg flat on the table, with several of her personal items overlapping sections of it, was what she instantly recognized as the *Necklace of Agamemnon*. This small but important and featured object had been in her hands only a few minutes before, as she had tastefully draped it partly across its card. Holding such ancient objects in her own hand, as she did from time to time, provided some of the most emotionally powerful moments on the job. She had *not* put it in her handbag, and had no idea how it had come to be there.

"George, you stand as my witness that Miss Baynes has apparently stolen this priceless object."

"Yessir."

Potterton lifted it up from under the other items, turned it over in his hands, and carefully examined it. "I say before this witness, that this is the original, not the copy we sell in the gift shop, either the base-metal version, or the reproduction in gold."

Irini had to support herself on the edge of his desk, her world spinning out of control. She felt lucky not to have fainted. She did not realize it, but had she done so, and been tended medically by someone else, all of Potterton's carefully laid plans would have failed. However, she managed to remain standing, and so would have to face the music.

Potterton glared at her with a triumphant expression. "Do you fully understand what is happening, Miss Baynes?"

"No, I don't. I didn't take that necklace, and have no idea how it got in my bag." Then an horrific thought buckled her legs. She defiantly threw back, "*If* it did, *Doctor* Potty Potterton!"

He fumed at the name, but rapidly recovered himself, and coolly slipped the knife in. "George, could you please leave the room now."

When the guard had left, he continued with an obsequious grimace. "I don't say that all this cannot be, ah, *squared!*"

Now it was clear as crystal. She was trapped as surely as a hare in the noose. Potterton had made her one of the classic offers one could not afford to refuse. Therefore there was only one thing to do, and that was to refuse it, damn the torpedoes.

Strength flowed back into her legs, and perfused through the rest of her body, finally reaching the top of her head, visibly raising her hackles.

"I know what you have done, and why you have done it. I deny absolutely any involvement in this sordid business…"

Potterton interrupted. "Are you prepared to go to prison? That necklace is a priceless treasure of this museum, and you are caught red handed. Denial will do you no good. Bear with me for a moment before you make your decision."

Potterton laid it out in shocking clarity. "The necklace on my desk here is the original. Examine it yourself if you like. The one in the case is the reproduction in gold that we sell in the gift shop. One of them was sold yesterday to a young man who bears a striking resemblance to your dear Adam, for cash. I hired him myself, and exchanged the copy for the original in that case last evening."

He paused menacingly. "You will drop Adam at once, and take up with me, and this whole business will disappear."

Irini was struck dumb. Her first thought was that she didn't understand how anyone could possibly believe such a scheme could work. Then she knew what she was up against. This man in front of her was insane, as much as the maniac who cut throats at midnight. Worse, at least in that case, it didn't hurt for long, and then one was at peace. She didn't know how the battle could be fought, but fight she would.

"I bloody well won't." She picked up the necklace. "You can shove this up your backside." She threw it in his face, turned and stalked to the door. As she opened it, George walked through, forcing her back inside.

"Is that your final word? Don't let a momentary anger destroy your life, my dear."

"Don't you *ever* call me that again, BASTARD. Filthy, bastard."

Potterton shrugged with regret, yet he was confident, and had been all along, that either Irini would be his, or nobody else's, the certain result of the shame that would attend her for the rest of her life. "As you wish, so be it."

"I was going out to call the police."

"That's not the way we do it here, Miss Baynes. We don't air our dirty laundry outside." He dismissed the world with a sweep of his spindly arm. "We will call the director here to this office now. He will witness the evidence. You will be discharged with prejudice, and the stains on your career and personal life will be permanent, Miss Baynes."

Irini was unable to look the director in the face. Geoffrey Hayward picked up the necklace from the desk, put a museum seal through a ring in the chain, and pressed the clasp shut. He initialled the small tag, and it was placed in Potterton's safe. Irini was dismissed on the spot.

She started to gather up her personal effects, but her hand was stayed. "This is evidence, Miss Baynes," Potterton smiled evilly, "and will be held until further notice."

"This is outrageous. You can't do that. I need my keys, money, and credit cards every day."

"Until further notice, I am afraid," the director decided, to be sure not certain whether Potterton was exceeding his lawful authority. Had he been a more experienced man of the world, or less of a dictator in his own realm, he would have known that they had no such right, and further, that the police should have been called at once. Yet this was his empire, as he saw it, his word law, as he felt it.

George escorted Irini from the museum, not permitting her to clear her desk. He informed the other guards that she was not to be readmitted, and he actually pushed her through the staff's side door, her head bumping painfully on the heavy glass.

With tears running down her face she ran across the courtyard, across the street, narrowly missed on the zebra crossing by a speeding delivery bike, and not having a key to her own flat, continued to Andreas' shop, and burst in, openly sobbing, welcomed into his arms.

After consoling her, and placing a call to Adam, he closed the shop, escorted her to her flat, and opened the door with the spare key he held for her. She collapsed on the couch. Despite being disturbed in his slumbers, and sensing something was wrong, Achilles eased himself onto her lap. At that moment, Adam burst in, to kneel at her feet, and take her shaking body into his arms. With these three comforters at her side, she gradually found her sea legs against a world that had become a coracle foundering in the Roaring Forties.

It was some long minutes before Irini could give a half-cogent account of the bizarre events of the morning, but she did finally manage to do so. Adam was aware, as they all were from the first moment, that this was serious business. So he asked Irini to begin again, which also helped her relax into the narrative, and he transcribed a remarkable history for the second time in three days.

At the end Adam concluded that the museum was well over the line, but didn't know quite what to do on his own, so he bumped it upstairs.

He did a first class job of summarizing the facts to Helena on the phone. She called Spiros at once. She had also said that while this did appear to be a matter unrelated to the project, anything involving any member of the team, or the museum, demanded strong, accurate, and well considered action. As this involved *both*, that went double.

As it happened, Helena had pulled Spiros out of yet another meeting with the Prime Minister of Greece. A few minutes later, the Prime Minister made a call to the London law firm of Pearson, Fitz, and Johnson, and immediately had the ear of the senior partner.

Within fifteen minutes Helena had rung back, and told them that the number one International Attorney in London would be on the line, a Mister Benjamin Pearson, and they were to do exactly as he said. She explained that he was a close friend of the Prime Minister of Greece from their days at the University of Chicago Law School.

Their phone chimed again, and Benjamin Pearson himself was on the line. He asked if she would be more comfortable talking to him at her flat, and the great man himself came over without a quibble.

While they waited, Adam dashed back to his flat to get a copy of Irini's first transcription, which he then brought over to her computer so the two could be printed out in sequence.

Benjamin Pearson loomed in the doorway, a little out of breath, filling it with his ample, large-boned frame. His warm handshake and reassuring smile, immediately touched Irini's heart, and she was just able to blink back her tears.

"Control yourself," she told herself fiercely, "and thank your lucky stars that you are surrounded by so much loving support."

She introduced him to Adam, Andreas, and Achilles, then led him to her sole armchair, thinking her dining chairs might not cope with his overflowing bulk. Benjamin Pearson's euphonious nasal tones were different from Adam's, yet to Irini's ears, equally caressing.

He was introducing himself as succinctly as possible, while Irini took in the slightly larger than life dimensions of her new ally. He was immaculately clad in a finely tailored Saville Row suit, which tempered his size and added a British sophistication to his physical persona. Though the acquaintance was short, she immediately felt safe in his redoubtable hands and tried hard to distance herself from the nightmarish events of that morning.

Adam spoke first, "Would it help to see a transcription of events leading up to this morning's confrontation, and details of what happened earlier today?"

"Good thinking, Adam. It may surprise you to learn that such records are admissible in court, and can carry a lot of weight – though," he added, sensing Irini's nervousness, "I am confident this will be resolved without resorting to such a blunt instrument."

The lawyer read Adam's transcriptions with growing dismay. They could not tell whether this was a good sign, a response to the ridiculousness of the charges, or because he was concluding that it was the hopeless, open and shut case they all feared.

"Miss Irini, so it is your testi, ah, statement, that this Potterton fellow actually told you that he had hired an impersonator who resembled Adam here, to buy the reproduction, and then he himself made the switch in the display cabinet?"

Irini didn't believe it herself when she confirmed the facts.

"Mister Pearson..."

"Benjamin, please. Perhaps it will help if I say a word or two along these lines. Irini, anyone coming to this history will instantly understand that there are two possibilities. First, that the museum's case is obviously factual, open and shut, end of story." He held up a deprecating hand. "Second, that the totally unbelievable, improbable, and incredible alternative is obviously right." He smiled. "One thing I have learned, and it is not a new idea, is that truth has nothing to do with credibility, and credibility nothing to do with truth. In fact, in my experience, it is the opposite. The incredible is more often the truth in this kind of case, than the obvious. I have no doubt that this is a set-up, so please accept my word on that, and that I will lift this cloud sooner rather than later."

The phone took that moment to chime, and Adam handed the portable to the lawyer. "Yes, that's right. ... Okay, two PM, good, his office. ... You have the order? Great, meet me in front of the museum a few minutes before two. Good work, thanks again.

"Okay, this is how we are going to play it, if you agree. The museum has no right to hold your handbag and its contents unless they are prepared to involve the police, and in that case, the police would hold all the evidence. They are not going to go down that road. We have an appointment to see the director at 2PM. I propose to force them to agree to an internal hearing, and to put up a defence."

Irini was shaking with the tension, so Adam unabashedly went across to the couch, and held her tightly. "Are you up for that, Irini, because if you aren't, we don't do it."

"That's right," Benjamin agreed, "only if you are up to it."

Her momentary weakness had passed. "I don't see how you can possibly win, but we have it on the highest authority that you are the best, and I'm not taking this lying down, so there!"

Everyone knew her decision was based on internal strength, usefully bolstered by anger and sharpened by fear. If the case depended on those strengths, it would be won in a flash.

Adam invited Irini, Benjamin and Andreas for a pub lunch, but Andreas excused himself due to the press of business.

Benjamin eased the tension by first answering their questions. "I have a pleasant flat in Chiswick, a bit far out for convenience to the theatre, which I adore, so I often work late, and go directly from the office. I love London, and would never want to go back to the USA, not even New York."

Benjamin had chosen London in preference to South Carolina as both he and his wife Pat enjoyed the seemingly limitless possibilities of London's theatre land, concerts, art galleries and exhibitions. He was a keen collector, with interests ranging from snuffboxes to original political cartoons. His favourite was Hogarth, and he would scour many a second-hand bookshop, not only in London, but countrywide. Pat had learned to make the best of this all-consuming passion by discovering some of the charming, secret byways in England, such as Hay on Wye, Chipping Camden, and Rye, which had revealed many unexpected charms.

During the lunch break, Irini had seemed to steel herself for the ordeal. The attorney was watching her closely to read his client to the same end. He had seen worse situations, but not many, and he knew that legal machinations could grind down the strongest personalities.

At the entrance to the museum, Benjamin met a female colleague who handed him several envelopes with a bright, "Good luck, happy wanderer." It was apparently an inside joke with his assistant, because he smiled, and thanked her cordially.

A guard came out to meet them as they walked up to the doors. "I'm sorry, but Miss Baynes is barred from entry."

"My name is Benjamin Pearson, attorney at law representing Irini Baynes, and this is Adam Blix whom you know is on assignment here in his own right. We have an appointment at 2PM with the director, Doctor Geoffrey Hayward. Could you please verify that fact, and admit us as soon as possible." Benjamin's manner was direct, forceful, and obsequiously courteous, and this only rarely failed to calm the most irate opposition, as here, or in the courtroom.

The guard flicked open his portable telephone, and after a brief exchange, invited the party inside, handed each a visitor's badge, and led them up to Hayward's office.

Introductions were effected as before, and Hayward spoke first. "This matter is closed so far as I am concerned, Mister Pearson. It is an internal matter, and has been dealt with here."

"Doctor Hayward, I am representing Miss Baynes."

"That's obvious," he snapped sharply, "but it is irrelevant."

"Do you deny, Doctor, that you are holding Miss Baynes possessions, including her handbag, personal effects, money and credit cards?"

"Again, that is an internal matter, Mister Pearson."

"Actually, it's *Doctor* Pearson, if we are going to get right down in the trenches, but I'm easy, as we ex-colonial Americans like to say." It was apparent that the director had caught the accent, and was perhaps one of the rare British birds who didn't suffer the breed lightly, classing them with other lower species. In Adam's view, Benjamin had cleverly cut that down to size.

"I must ask again, are you or are you not holding her possessions?"

"We are, if you must know, as evidence."

"As *you* must know, or can determine by merely picking up your phone to the museum's counsel … Andrew Sims, I believe? We're old drinking buddies down the Inns, though I suspect he is not back from lunch yet – likes his cognac after…"

"What's your point, *counsellor*?"

"You would do well to watch your manner, Doctor Hayward. You have already opened yourself to a substantial civil lawsuit, irrespective of the ultimate disposition of any case you may believe you have against my client. My point, as you put it, is that you are holding another person's property, without right or cause in law, and that is a *criminal* offence."

"But, it's evidence," he bleated, not knowing which way to turn, feeling the icy, creeping fingers of doubt.

"Fine, let's call the police. Only they can determine the status of evidence, and only they or a court of proper jurisdiction have the right to hold it, for cause, in any action at law."

"That's the point," seeing a possible escape, "there is *no* action at law, it is an inter…"

"No matter is inherently internal, director, for the *law pervades all*. And if you insist, it will be brought to bear." Though it was apparent that he positively enjoyed this sort of thrust and parry, he had tired of the exchange, and tore open one of the envelopes he had been given at the entrance.

"I have here an injunction, signed this morning by Lord Robert Benchley, mandating that you release all of Miss Baynes' property to her forthwith, or appear at 4PM this afternoon to show cause before the High Court as to why you should not be held in contempt."

Hayward did not bother to read the paper that was thrust under his nose, but instead, picked up the phone. "Bring Miss Baynes' personal effects to my office ... Yes, now, immediately!"

A sheepish and characteristically nervous Denis Potterton came in, and handed Irini her handbag, then turned to leave.

"One moment, please, Mister Potterton." Benjamin commanded, instantly halting his quarry in mid stride. "Miss Baynes, will you please carefully examine your bag, and verify that all of its contents are present and correct."

"Everything is there except the necklace she stole."

"Mister, or is it *Doctor* Potterton, my apologies if so, but that charge has not yet been proven, and we deny it absolutely."

"It has been proven to *my* satisfaction, and that *is* final within these walls at least." The director smiled knowingly, but Pearson effaced it.

"You are not above the law, Doctor Hayward, here or anywhere else, nor am I, nor the Prime Minister himself in Number Ten. You have made a charge against my client, that is all, a charge, nothing more. Can you take that on board, or do we need to go to your counsel or higher authority? The Trustees, for example?"

This last was the magic stop-all. Everyone has a boss, even the President of the United States, though in his case, perhaps not on this planet.

Suddenly the truth of this fact, which Hayward had failed to see through the thick fog of his own egocentric mind-set, well honed over the last few years, crashed into his consciousness. His world view had inexplicably vanished. He felt naked and helpless.

The shock was profound. Pearson had anticipated the crash – indeed had engineered and facilitated it, not for the first time in his life. He had cracked nuts far harder than those Hayward thought he possessed. Pearson smiled at his image, the pause to think a calculated one, to give his victim time to sense the steel in the trap now clamped tightly on ... enough of that, he chided himself; this was about an important and deserving client, not his own ego or harmless entertainment.

Irini spoke up, "Everything is fine."

Potterton turned to leave, and this time nobody stopped him.

"So, that's it then?" Hayward said, uncertainly, yet hopefully.

"Not by a long shot. If you have now determined on a more open-minded view, and I think you have, you will realize that a person's career and good name are valuable assets, litigable at law, and more important, fundamental to human morality. Your own Potterton has stated quite clearly to my client that he expects she will never be able to work again in her profession, and that her personal life, including the relationship with her partner here, Adam, will be irretrievably damaged."

Hayward was now really frightened, for he could imagine Potterton actually saying such stupid nonsense, and worse, his manipulative personality at work in this. Was it possible that this was a set-up? No, he thought, the evidence was incontrovertible, witnessed, and ironclad. He decided to tough it out.

"My decision stands." Hayward stated it flatly.

Undeterred, Pearson said with assurance, "I think not. You have two choices. The first is to attempt to stand on that ground. In that case, Miss Baynes will sue the British Museum, its Trustees, Potterton, and yourself personally."

"Perhaps we can negotiate a settlement," Hayward replied, the standard escape clause available to those in his position suddenly occurring to him. "I might be prepared to provide an appropriate letter of recommendation, and drop the matter."

"Miss Baynes," Pearson spoke openly, "as you must be aware, that is one of the standard ways out of this sort of situation. You need to think carefully about such an offer."

Irini's back had stiffened perceptibly throughout these few hours. The injustice of the accusation, and the poisonous intent of her accuser, were a revelation to her of the reality of the darker side of life. She shook her head. "This isn't just about me, any more, is it? Doctor Potterton is a dangerous man. I have only just now realized that he has been guilty of sexual harassment against me for months, subtle at first, and then more aggressively. Now he has hatched a plot to destroy not just my professional life, but my personal relationships as well. There's another truth too, the same one that confronts a witness to, or a victim of, a serious crime who takes risks in bringing the perpetrators to justice – that it is our duty to protect others from falling into this man's clutches if we don't stop him."

"Miss Baynes," her counsel spoke one further time in warning, "you understand that you risk losing any case that may arise, against the certainty that the director here now sees as in his interest, to quietly settle the matter at this point." It was the old inequity of plea bargain blackmail, as he had always seen it. You offer the murderer second degree if he cops a plea of guilty, but go for the maximum sentence if he takes the trial and loses. If the man charged is innocent, what of the offer then?

She looked her counsel straight in the eye, and then the director. "I am going to quote a good friend of mine, 'This will not stand!'"

"My client has spoken, if I may say so, eloquently. Director, our counter-offer is that you drop your charges, dismiss Potterton, put a suitable letter in her file here, pay six months wages in compensation, and retain her in your employment if she so chooses. I am certain that this was a set-up. I don't know how it was pulled off, but I think you yourself are now entertaining serious doubts. It's up to you."

There was only one way to win, and that was to gain judgment against Miss Baynes. Then the director had the only intelligent thought that had come to him during this whole sordid business. "Would you be satisfied with a hearing, here, in private?"

"In principle." Pearson replied without hesitation.

"With *me* as the sole judge?"

"In principle." Adam and Irini's eyes shot wide in abject surprise.

Hayward then added, "As the final and governing determination, without subsequent recourse to law?"

"We may call any witnesses of our choice, at our expense, and you will provide any and all witnesses from your domain in the museum as if we had the right of subpoena, free of cost?"

"In principle." The tables were reversed, and the director went along with the tide.

"I or anyone else may represent Miss Baynes as if in a court of law?"

"The museum, likewise?"

"And, Director, you will not unreasonably oppose any normal procedure of court, as would be customary in any of the major democratic states? That is, you will not appeal to restrictive practices of the English courts?"

"I frankly don't know what you mean, counsellor, but if it's an everyday thing, say, in the American courts for example, I don't have any objection."

"Miss Baynes, will you trust me in this?"

She set her jaw. Benjamin continued, "We have a deal, if that hearing can be held within, say, ten days. I expect the defence will require about one day to present our case, shall we allow two days?"

So, there was going to be a trial. Irini was feeling a gathering cold in her feet, and she hoped it would not spread any further.

Chapter 13

The Trial

Never ask the witness a question in Court unless you know the answer in advance.

The plot had been hatched, and the accusation made, on the previous Wednesday, and the trial had been set for Wednesday of the week following. It was an agony of a week for Irini and Adam, and everything else in their life had been put on hold.

The marbles' copying job was finished. The copies had left by road for Greece the previous week, and arrived without incident. Adam had made a further proposal to the Foundation, and the museum. The copies sent off to Athens had been exact replicas of the Parthenon Marbles, including all defects and weathering that had eroded the sculptures. His proposal was to use the profiles stored in the computer to make a few further copies, and to do them in such a way as to restore as faithfully as possible, the original pre-erosion and pre-damage surfaces.

This was possible in principle by using the stored images, cutting replicas in wax, then using sculptors from the Slade School of Art whom he involved in the proposal, to restore both the physical, and where possible the less tangible touch and feeling of Pheidias and his school who had created the masterpieces in the first place. The final stage would be to use the wax as masters, and cut perfect reproductions in marble.

A preliminary study had been agreed, and funded by the Foundation (Spiros by proxy), and so Adam was continuing work, along with his two friends from the Slade, Naomi Marks and Steve Walters, the foreman Paul Alberts, and two artisans drawn from the original project. The equipment had been cleaned up, serviced, and put into storage, ready for any further use that might be approved.

Adam busied himself with that, and Irini did her best to stay sane.

On the Friday, Adam received a *subpoena* from Andrew Sims, the chief legal officer for the British Museum, *prosecuting* in the case of the British Museum versus Irini Baynes. It required that he appear at the museum's local precinct police station, at 10AM on the Monday. He checked with Benjamin, who said he would be there.

They met Sims in the police station waiting room. "Counsellor."

"Nice to see you again, Andrew. Too bad it couldn't be under happier circumstances."

"What we have here this morning is a line-up for Adam."

"Whoa," Pearson said, holding up an ample hand. "This isn't a criminal matter."

"Of course not, but a key part of our case is that Adam, here, purchased the replica necklace…"

"The hell I did. What's all this crap?"

"Easy, Adam. Perhaps it would be best if you waited outside for a moment."

"Bloody cheek, as Peter would say." But he did as requested.

"Look, Andrew, this is getting out of hand. We both know that eyewitness identifications are the weakest form of evidence, and the most likely to be wrong. And it goes double here, doesn't it? If Adam had not been frequenting the museum, in his official capacities, well, maybe there'd be a case for checking out the recollection of the sales girl. He has been in and out for months. No, this won't do."

"Sorry, Benjamin, but you have agreed to any reasonable court procedure, and this is certainly one."

"It's a police procedure."

"Admissible in court. Let's not fall out over this. Think about how it will look to the Judge."

Benjamin grimaced, "I am wondering if I made a defensible deal for my client there. I've lost a bit of sleep over that one."

"It surprised me a bit, but I suspect you have some ideas. How about it, let's go ahead and do it, and see where the chips fall."

Adam was led onto the infamous stage with the black lines behind indicating height, the one-way mirror, and five other men who both attorneys had to agree had been well selected as similar in appearance.

The sales girl unhesitatingly selected Adam, and this fact was set down in an Affidavit, which Adam, the sales girl, the supervising police officer, and both attorneys signed.

The day before the trial, Peter and Adam were sharing a lunch at the LSE Refectory. Peter had tried to cheer Adam up. He was going over the whole mess for the nth time, Peter listening patiently. They had reviewed the details of the critical moments between Irini closing the display case, and the necklace appearing in her handbag as the contents spilled out on the desk.

"It's no good, Peter, I can't figure it, even given what Potterton admitted privately to Irini."

"So how did he do it?" Peter asked yet again.

"Maybe it was the simplest thing of all; he palmed the necklace and dropped it in her bag."

"Irini says he didn't, she had her eye on it, the guard likewise."

"Peter, you're right, that's a dry hole. Let's drop it." Having made the decision, Adam's mind was freed of the logjam that had stymied him for a week, and another idea was then free to insinuate itself into his thick skull, as he felt it had been all week. He hadn't done any creative work the whole time, and had taken the opportunity to shuffle the papers that were becoming a greater part of his job with every passing month. He didn't like the feeling.

"Aagh," Adam groaned, slapping his head. "Dumbo. Now if only the other is in the desk – sorry Peter. Hey, I may need your help. Meet me in the Museum Tavern at 3, can do?"

"Sure, mate, on the dot."

Adam left his lunch behind, and ran all the way to the museum. "Just gone 1PM; there's still a chance." He used his own badge where that worked, and when it didn't, he took out one of his special black boxes, and created the passkeys he needed to make progress through the higher reaches of the building's alimentary tract.

He rapped softly on the door. No answer, so he inserted his special card in the security lock, programmed at the door the previous day, just in case. He opened the door a crack, peering hesitantly inside.

At the Museum Tavern, Peter waited for Adam, who came breathlessly in the door, a few minutes late. "Peetie, the game's afoot, and we've no time to lose. Lots of things to buy, and I need your help on some of the special, underground bits. Please?"

"Sure, but call me Peter, or Doctor Watson, to your Sherlock. What's the play?"

"Insurance. Come on."

The night before the trial, Adam took Irini out to dinner at their favourite Italian, the Spaghetti House; they were both feeling the pressure of an eternally frustrating week.

"What's happening to us? To the world?" Irini was almost in tears, as she had been all week. "We haven't made love for ages?"

"I know, my darling, but I still love you."

"Me too. What a kick in the backside." Then: "Adam, I'm afraid."

"I am too, but that's healthy, it keeps us on our toes."

"Yes, I know, but it all seems so hopeless. Benjamin, lovely man though he is, has Hayward, the Judge of his own case, in his own court. Why didn't we see this before, and speak up?"

"Irini, I did think of it, and have thought of little else since. Yet, I am now *certain* that we will win."

"How can you be?"

"I just am," he said emphatically. "I just am."

Benjamin Pearson guided Irini through the door to Potterton's large office, which had been converted into an improvised courtroom. Geoffrey Hayward, acting as Judge, sat behind Potterton's desk, which annoyed him, but there was nothing he could do about it. Andrew Sims, prosecuting, Denis Potterton, George the guard, and Adam Blix were already in the room. The door closed softly behind them.

The introductions were made. The only person Irini didn't know was Andrew Sims. He was in stark contrast to his legal adversary, slim and ingenuous looking, with an appearance that made him seem much younger than his late forties. This was not necessarily an advantage in his professional life, but it worked well for him socially. He had refined features, fair hair, and roundish blue-grey eyes, which emphasized the youthful impression. His Aberdeen accent imparted an authoritative note to his speech. That was an advantage in his profession, supported by a gritty determination. Benjamin found him a pleasant adversary, and there was mutual respect between them.

Benjamin's big frame with his large head, was indeed a contrast, somehow appropriately topped by a crest of steely grey hair matching his prominent eyes overarched with massive eyebrows, softened by laugh-wrinkles, pink face, and full lips.

Hayward began, "This will be an informal hearing, but I will be guided by the professional counsel present in any procedural matters. With the exception of the accused, I suggest we use first names in the interest of time. Andrew."

Benjamin shrugged, and rose to dominate the room. "I am sorry, Judge, but I must object at the outset. Any distinction between the accused, as you put it, and anyone else here, creates a negative impression against her from the start. Can we either use last names throughout, or first, for everyone? I would also feel happier referring to you either as 'Judge', or 'sir', if that is okay with you."

Andrew rose, "No objection."

"I would not have let that influence me in any way, Benjamin, but as Andrew has agreed, there is no reason to argue. And gentlemen, there is no need to jump to your feet to address the court, thank you."

Andrew said, "I have no procedural matters, Judge."

"I do, sir, one or two. Would it not be prudent for witnesses to be sequestered out of earshot from the court, ah, this room, and be admonished not to discuss the case either before or after they testify?"

"That's a bit over the top, isn't it, Benjamin?" Sims looked into his opponent's steely eyes, then shrugged in acquiescence. "I will agree."

"And I request permission to have a stenographer take down the proceedings, verbatim."

This was a different matter entirely. Andrew tipped his head forward with raised eyebrows. "Is that really necessary?"

"It is only so my client can have the benefit of an accurate transcript." He spoke in a seemingly ingenuous tone, which covered much more than was immediately apparent.

"But –" Geoffrey the Judge interceded, feeling for the first time a sense of unease that he could not yet fathom. He therefore felt his way delicately, as if through a dark and dangerous jungle. "You have agreed that the decision of this court, uh of me, of the British Museum through the office I hold in it, will be the final judge in this case."

"And so we have, sir, but your point does not in any way diminish my client's right to a full transcript. For example, she may be faced with defending herself in further pursuit of her career, if, for example, your judgment should go against her." Benjamin was wearing one of his trademarked, Cheshire cat smiles. One would not have guessed that a face even as round and full as his could accommodate one so wide.

Andrew smiled to himself. He had expected something like this, and instantly appreciated the implications for the judge. He wondered how long it would take Geoffrey to pick up on it. It was truly brilliant. At a stroke, Benjamin had spun the table a full half turn. Instead of the boss being the judge of his own case, in his own court, he was now only the judge, because the case could be exhibited *after the fact* to anyone willing to read a transcript. Such likely people as the Trustees of the British Museum, potential employers of Irini, and the *Times*, came readily to mind.

Andrew gave a moment's thought to objecting, but didn't for two reasons. First, he was lawyer enough to want a fair trial, and that meant an unbiased judge. Second, he anticipated Benjamin's argument regarding what had been agreed as to court procedure, the very argument that had forced the line-up, one of the few strong pieces of evidence he had for the prosecution.

Geoffrey looked at Andrew several times, but his counsel remained silent. "Well, I take it, silence by the museum's attorney means consent. You may admit your stenographer."

Benjamin gave a sigh of relief. He knew the hard truth would soon dawn on Geoffrey, for he was certainly intelligent, and then, he thought, we'll see what we will see. He nodded professional thanks to Andrew, who winked back behind his hand.

The witnesses were excused, leaving only the two attorneys, the judge and defendant. At a knock on the door, an attractive, very well dressed woman in her mid thirties came in, wheeling a cart behind her. She brushed her half-length, straight black hair back out of her eyes, and allowed Geoffrey to guide her to a power point, and arrange for a chair. She never smiled. That was her chief claim to fame. In a way, her professional code demanded this, so the only question the judge could have asked her was answered when she slid her license across the desk to him. He glanced at it, and returned it with a cordial gesture inviting her to sit down.

"My name is Jane Fowler. I am a licensed stenographer to the High Court in London, and will make a fair transcript of this hearing. If I raise my hand, so, the judge will stop the proceedings until I can complete what I am keying, or make any other adjustments. This is only rarely necessary with these computerized models. It can sometimes happen in the case of extraordinarily thick accents, or with nonverbal material. I enter those only if the judge so orders."

Andrew: "I will open the case with a summary of the events, and provide a list of the evidentiary materials." He proceeded to do so fairly, in Benjamin's view. He would have expected nothing less, and with roles reversed would have done so himself in virtually the same terms.

"I call Denis Potterton." The judge made a brief internal call on his desk telephone, and his subordinate entered, showing due deference, yet also displaying nervousness. Andrew began by running him through the oath, name, rank, and serial number questions, where he lived, studied, the publication history in general, and was somewhat surprised that there hadn't been much in the last three years.

This relaxed the man, and he then proceeded to give a good account of himself, covering under the prompting of his counsel, every significant point on Benjamin's list of items he expected to be raised against his client, and thankfully, nothing unexpected.

"Your witness."

Benjamin started to stand up, then sat heavily down. He felt that he had lost one of his key tools in being denied his feet – feet that were so firmly planted in the law, dating back through the male line in his family to his great, great grandfather.

"Doctor, ah, Denis. Very sorry, Judge, but old habits are hard to break, especially for old dogs like us." Geoffrey nodded with a smile. Benjamin had suspected from mannerisms displayed during the direct testimony that their judge had come to the conclusion that he had to be a fair judge. He could face serious consequences himself should he give a verdict other than that called for clearly on the evidence. Indeed, this judge had to brief himself for the defence! What a wonderful turnaround. Benjamin allowed himself a momentary flush of pleasure. He regretted that he had not had an opportunity to explain this to Adam and Irini, but on the other hand, they had to stay sharp, and he knew there was nothing quite like raw fear with strong kids to keep them that way.

"The defence accepts the bulk of your testimony as clear, and unquestionable." Denis relaxed the anticipated notch or two. "Can I review with you carefully, however, two or three critical moments, and I respectfully ask the Court's leave for a brief demonstration dealing with the handling of Irini's handbag." There was no objection, so he reached into his capacious briefcase, and withdrew the bag. "I would ask the other side here to stipulate that this is hers, and that we have endeavoured to put into it this morning the same contents, as best we could, as applied before."

The judge and Andrew nodded. "Denis, would you please stand up, and if the judge will move over for a moment, show us where the bag was resting before you opened it, and stand in the same position you did before at your desk." Denis did so, and Benjamin continued seamlessly. "You testified that you took up the bag and held your left hand underneath it, just so. That you then invited George, the guard, and Irini to come closer, and when they were, where, about here?" Benjamin positively delighted in being able to stand up and dominate the room and those in it.

"Yes, about there, counsellor. Sorry, I have forgotten your name."

"Benjamin will do, or 'hey you', so just relax, we need to get this right. The other two are standing this close, which I make to be less than two feet from the bag, because you were holding it out as you are now, is that correct?"

"Yes."

"Now open it just as you did last week, then pause please."

Denis raised his right hand to the slip-clasp on the top of the handbag, and pressed on it. It sprung open with an audible "click". "Is that how it was that morning; did it open quickly just like this time."

"Yes."

"Now, if you please, will you tip the bag over and dump its contents out on the desk top as nearly as you can, to how it was."

Denis cradled the handbag between his left hand supporting the bottom, and the right on one side, and then tipped it back towards himself, spilling the contents on the desk. "Please pause there." Benjamin had stayed Denis' hands with his own ham-like right hand. "I would call the court's attention to the fact that the bag is not directly in line with either front or side of the desk, but at about a 45 degree angle. This is natural, and I think any of us would have done that in this way. Denis, is this a fair repetition of what happened?

"Yes, so far as I am aware."

"Well, if there is any doubt let us clear it up now. Your left hand is under the bag, and the right hand is holding the right side of the handbag as you view it, and it has spilled its contents out on the desk with the bag at about a 45-degree angle, with your right hand between you and the handbag. In other words, your right hand does not in any way conceal the view of the witnesses, would you agree with that?"

"I would."

"I ask the court to note, and the stenographer to deal with it as best she can, that Denis' right hand is supporting the side of the bag nearer to him, and *the hand* is out of sight of the witnesses. As he testified a moment ago, his right hand was not concealing the bag, as would be the honest intent of someone emptying a handbag for witnesses to watch, so far so good. Yet in so doing, he must inevitably conceal his right hand behind the bag.

"Thank you. Could we also look for a moment at the quantity of items in this, a typical woman's handbag?" He smiled, "They are multifarious, are they not? Now, Denis, is it not true that this compact, on that occasion, rolled off the desk?"

"Yes, it did."

"Did you do or say anything to prevent any lapse of attention on the part of the witnesses? That is, you were obviously concerned about doing this fairly, were you not?"

"Yes, that's right. I said, 'Don't pick it up now.'"

"Thank you again. Is it your testimony that both witnesses' attention remained on the bag and its contents as they spilled out and then came to rest on the desk?"

"It is."

"Now, when everything had spilled out on the desk, what did you do next?"

"I put the empty handbag on the left side of the desk, so."

"So these things were now open to view?"

"Yes."

"Was the necklace visible at that time?"

"I honestly don't remember."

"Perhaps if I ask the question another way. Did you stir the contents with your index finger to make a search?"

"Ah, yes, I see. I believe that the necklace was not visible until I stirred the contents."

"So, it is fair to say that it was underneath the pile, so you could hardly have dropped it there, please excuse me but I must clarify these points, *after* you had tipped the handbag over, should you have had it in your hand as you stirred."

"I didn't drop it, if that is what you are implying."

"I have tried to make it clear that I am not accusing you of anything. I merely want to have a precise history of what did happen, from your point-of-view as the principal witness."

"Yes, I'm sorry, Benjamin, I can see that. Yes, I agree that it would have been difficult if not impossible to drop it onto the pile, and then recover it from underneath other items."

"Thank you. You may sit down now." Benjamin swept the personal effects back into the handbag, snapped it shut, and replaced it in his briefcase. Sitting down, he continued.

"Just one or two small points. Where is the reproduction necklace now?"

"It is here in my desk, locked up."

"That is what we understood from the director. Is it correct that he ordered the case opened on that same morning, the reproduction to be taken up, and a card of apology placed in its stead?"

"Yes, and I did that personally, and brought it up here, and locked it in my bottom right-hand desk drawer."

"Do all your desk drawers have locks?"

"They do, and all are locked up as we speak."

"And was there anything else in that bottom drawer, between the time you locked up the necklace, and this moment."

"Nothing, it was empty save for that."

"And you have not opened it at any time during this last week of storage there."

"I have not."

"The judge is a potential witness in this case, with which I have no problem if it becomes necessary for you, sir, to testify, but perhaps the witness can deal with another question. When you discovered the necklace, you testified that you examined it, and determined it was the original, and not a copy."

"That is right."

"So it is your testimony both as a witness, and an expert in this field, that the necklace on the desk was the original."

"Yes."

"You have testified that without in any way changing anything else, with the necklace in plain sight at all times, you called the director, that he came here, heard your charges, and then to establish the continuity of evidence, as we like to put it, had the commendable foresight to mark the original necklace with a museum seal, and initial the small cardboard tag."

"That is correct."

"And that you then placed the original, marked necklace in your personal office safe, there in the wall, closed and assured that it was locked, in the full view of all parties then present."

"That is correct."

"So let us get this absolutely clear. The original is in the safe in such a form that it can be positively identified should we ask that it be produced. And that the reproduction from the gift shop, rests in your desk drawer, where you and nobody else put it, directly brought here from the locked display case downstairs in the museum, not long after the tragic events of that morning."

"Yes."

"So just to review. The timeline was this. One, George apparently sees something suspicious, and brings Irini to your office. Two, you openly, verifiably and with some care of the witnesses' line of vision, tipped the contents of her handbag onto your desk, discovered the original necklace *under* the other items, called the director, and so it came to be in your safe untouched for the week."

"That is correct."

"Afterwards, under orders from the director, you went down to the museum, retrieved the copy, and put it in your desk drawer, where it has remained locked up for the week."

"That is correct."

"Thank you."

Denis rose to leave.

"Oh, just one more question."

Denis awkwardly caught off balance, half sat down again on the edge of the chair.

When did you give your last magic show for children?"

The question left Denis completely flummoxed, his reaction clearly evident to everyone in the room.

"Uh, I don't know what you mean."

"You are, are you not, a licensed magician to the Magic Society of Great Britain," Benjamin consulted his notebook, "ticket number 1806, and dated, what, some eighteen years in the past, and renewed every three years as required, right up to last year."

Denis had no choice now but to tough it out. "Okay, but how did you find out?"

"Was it your intent to conceal this information? No, strike that. Denis, please answer my question. When, approximately will do, did you give your last professional performance?"

"About a month ago, in Hampstead, for a Sunday afternoon birthday party." He replied sullenly.

"I have interviewed the mother, and she is prepared to testify that you claimed, and demonstrated, a specialty in prestidigitation. Is that a fair characterization of at least one of your skills? The ability to perform slight of hand at short range?"

There was a sensible pause. "It is."

"I put it to you, Denis, that you dropped the necklace by slight of hand into the bag as you opened it."

"I did not. You have seen yourself that this was unlikely to work."

"I accept that." Denis' surprise was manifest. "I put it to you that you dropped it on the pile as you stirred the contents, in such a way that it appeared to have been on the bottom."

"No, we have seen that it was on the bottom, and impossible."

"I accept that. Now, if you were going to do it, is there another way?"

"I don't see it."

"Permission, sir, to make another brief demonstration. Thank you."

Once again, Benjamin had the luxury of standing up. It was good for his back as well, and he gave a slight stretch. He asked the judge to kindly move to the side as before. He took the bag, and placed it on the desk, and asked the others to pay close attention. He showed both his hands were empty, and wiggled his fingers, which drew a muted laugh, the first of the day.

"Okay, now we do it again. I grasp and support the handbag underneath with my left hand, so. Then click, it is open, and I then place my right hand, see it, in full view, against the right side of the bag, and tip it over slowly." The contents tumbled out as before, and this time the compact again decided to roll on the floor.

Benjamin stood back, and indicated the desktop with a sweep of his hands, inviting their attention to the heap of objects on it. "Judge, could I ask you most kindly to stir the pile with your index finger, and see what turns up."

He complied, and in a few seconds, lying flat and flush on the tabletop, a necklace began to be revealed, and as he swept again, it was exposed. "Please pick it up if you will, and examine it."

"It is," he held it close to his face, looked at the back, and then hefted it, "undoubtedly one of our reproductions of the *Necklace of Agamemnon*, in gold!"

"It could have been in the bag all along." Denis croaked. He had watched Benjamin do exactly what he had done, drop the necklace out of the right hand while it was concealed behind the handbag to cascade down ahead of the other contents.

"I assure the court that the handbag contained only Irini's personal items, exactly as it did on the morning in question. I slipped my copy of the necklace from under my sleeve, just as I put my hand behind the bag, and dropped it just as it tipped over. Doctor Potterton, I put it to you that this is *exactly* what you did on Wednesday morning last week."

He could only shake his head. "Let the record show that he has answered in the negative, with a shake of the head. Is that right, Judge?"

"It is. I confirm it for the record. We will now take a recess for lunch, and reconvene here at 1:30PM sharp. I intend to continue this hearing to a conclusion, regardless of the hour."

Andrew's soft Scottish brogue reopened the proceedings for the prosecution. "I present in evidence the Affidavit of one of our sales ladies in the gift shop, signed by all relevant parties here, including opposing counsel, to the effect that she picked Adam Blix out of a fair police line-up as the purchaser, on the day before the alleged theft, a gold reproduction of the necklace, for three hundred pounds in cash."

"The defence stipulates to the Affidavit and its contents."

"The museum rests." Andrew Sims sat back in his chair. He knew that in a court of the criminal law his case was already lost, because of the golden thread that runs through British justice, so that an acquittal must be given if there is a small but reasonable doubt about guilt. Since this was not a criminal matter it would be decided on the balance of probabilities. Simply, which was more likely, that the obvious case put by the prosecution was just that, an unshakable open and shut matter, or the extraordinary claims of the defence against it?

Benjamin intoned in his deep baritone, "I call Adam Blix."

He came in and took the witness chair beside the desk. Benjamin went through the preliminaries, and then got down to it. "Adam, did I ask you to read a document through this morning, every word on every page, and to initial each page as you did that?"

"You did."

"Is that the document in your hands as we speak?"

"It is."

"Please tell us what it is, and where it came from."

Adam explained in detail the history and timeline of Irini's coming to him on that Monday, and how when she told him what happened in the first meeting with Potterton, he had typed it all directly into the computer, verbatim. And furthermore, within an hour of the events of the necklace on Wednesday, he had done the same for that.

"Then it is your testimony, that the document you hold in your hand is a fair and exact copy of the computer files you created that Monday evening, together with that of Wednesday morning, and that you have made no changes to either since each was initially drafted."

"That is correct."

"Judge, I move that this be admitted into evidence." There was no objection.

"Did I ask you over lunchtime to make a few copies, and to verify that each was complete?"

"You did, and I gave them to you at lunch."

Benjamin reached into his briefcase. "Are these those copies, also initialled by you?"

"They are."

Benjamin distributed them around the table, and the judge invited everyone to read them.

"I have provided a copy to Denis outside, and he has had an opportunity to read it. I reserve the right to recall him if necessary."

"Granted."

"Adam, what was your impression of Irini's state of mind when you transcribed this."

"Well, on the Monday, she had been desperately upset all afternoon, but by the evening, she was angry, but I would say, otherwise normal."

"So her testimony as reflected in this document was therefore, in your view, competent?"

"Sure, I'm sure of it."

"After you finished this, what did you two do then, at least in so far as you feel comfortable about telling us here."

This drew the second good-natured chuckle of the day. "Well, Doctor Potterton had laid a heavy sexual harassment scene on Irini, and when she didn't go along, hit her hard about some report she should have done, but knew nothing about. She turned it out in about five hours that night, after we had finished the transcription."

"Did you help her?"

"Sure, but only with surfing the net, and getting references whipped into shape for outline, and bibliography. She did all the text."

"On the Wednesday morning, what was her state of mind?"

"Pretty desperate, as you can imagine, but she had calmed down, and I believe she gave a good account of the events of that morning. It was only an hour and a bit after."

Benjamin had anticipated all the potentially awkward questions that could be asked on the prosecution's cross-examination, so Andrew had few questions left to ask.

He began with, "Adam, you have been romantically involved with Irini for some months, is that correct?"

"It is. I love her." Adam had been warned, as all witnesses are by their attorneys, to give the minimum possible truthful answers to questions by opposing counsel, and never to volunteer anything. Benjamin certainly forgave Adam for his endearing supplemental answer in this case.

"You would do anything for her?"

"Sure, anything that was legal, moral, and didn't hurt anybody else. I would not procure for her, steal for her, or in any other way help her or anybody else to steal treasures from the British Museum." Benjamin did not forgive Adam this one, but was sure no damage had been done. Yet there was something about Adam's bashful, rueful look that caused him to pause and his nose to itch. In a cross examination he would have suspected a cover-up or worse. He hoped Andrew didn't see it – good – missed it – but then he was not a courtroom specialist. This was to rankle with Benjamin for several days, and not finally be resolved for some months.

"I put it to you that you purchased the necklace on or about last Monday week for three hundred pounds in cash from the gift shop here at the museum, and gave it over to Irini, or by some other means, aided and abetted her theft."

"I did not." That was better, thought Benjamin.

"No more questions."

"I call Irini Baynes." Benjamin asked the standard questions in the usual way. Then, "Irini, have you read the document I am now handing you."

"Yes, as you asked me to this morning."

"Is that a fair rendering of the events of Monday and Wednesday of last wcck?"

"It is."

"In every relevant detail?"

"Yes, so far as I can remember them now."

"The first part was dictated to Adam last Monday-week in the early evening, and the second part within an hour or two of the events of last Wednesday morning?"

"Yes."

"We have heard testimony that later on that Monday evening you completed a major report for you supervisor, at his request, one that surprised you with its urgency, and lack of appropriate notice?"

"That's right. The first I had heard of it was during our interview that morning."

"Could I ask the Court if you the judge have seen this report?"

"Yes, a copy was delivered to me through my secretary."

"Have you read it?"

"I have skimmed it."

"Did you form a preliminary opinion?"

"I decided it was worth reading in full, and I will do so, if, ah, Miss Baynes, Irini, is acquitted here today."

"Irini, you made serious charges in your transcript about sexual harassment, including threats relating to accompanying your supervisor to a forthcoming reception. Were those events accurately recorded in the transcript relating to Monday?"

"They were."

"On the Wednesday, at one point did he send the guard George, out of the room?"

"He did."

"And then did he made the most astonishing admissions to you about the necklace incident, including admitting that he had done it, but that it could still be, how did he put it, yes, could still be *squared*?"

"That's right."

"Do you stand by every word, every implication, of the transcript on these points?"

"I do."

"Did you have anything whatever to do, before, during, or after the necklace was revealed to you on this desk, anything at all to do with its theft, or any other foreknowledge or involvement of any kind whatsoever, however slight?"

"I most certainly did not."

"Thank you, your witness, but may I ask that the Court and opposing counsel take account of the accused's vulnerability. That is why, having the strong evidence of the transcript, made so soon after the events, I have relied on it as confirmed by Irini, rather than engaging in a long winded and potentially upsetting direct examination."

Andrew began carefully. "Irini, you had the job of placing new cards in the display case containing the necklace, did you not?"

"Yes."

"When you completed the job the necklace, or a necklace, was in the case."

"Yes, and it was the same one that was there when I opened the case." Okay, maybe, just, Benjamin thought, wiping his brow with his handkerchief.

"I put it to you that you replaced the original necklace with the copy, and were caught red handed by the guard."

"That's a lie. I did no such thing." That's good, Irini, leave it there. Good girl.

"I have no further questions."

There followed a significant pause, Benjamin thinking about something Adam had joked with him about over lunch, but nobody had laughed. It had been about more ways than one way to switch things around, without a magician to help. He was sure Adam had been trying to say something to him, that he couldn't openly – ah, he thought, "I wonder."

"Do you have anything more for the defence?"

Benjamin felt that he had proven his case against the sterner test based on balance of probabilities, and could expect an acquittal. Yet the niggle just wouldn't go away. Should he close the loop, and finish the evidentiary trail, as he would surely do if it were the Crown Jewels?

"Judge, may we have a twenty minute recess?"

"We will break for tea, and reconvene here at 4:30PM sharp."

"Thank you for the recess, Judge. I call Marie Cox." After the customary introductory questions, he continued. "You work in the museum gift shop, is that correct?"

"Yes."

"I am showing you an affidavit. Is that your signature, and did you in fact pick one Adam Blix in a line-up, as the person who purchased from you, last Monday week, a gold reproduction of the *Necklace of Agamemnon*, for three hundred pounds in cash?"

"Yes, that's all true."

"When did you sell the most recent copy in gold of this necklace?"

"Odd you should ask that; it was as recently as last night."

"For cash?"

"Yes, two in a week, and for cash, most unusual."

"Can you describe the purchaser of last evening?"

"Well, he was well dressed, Saville Row or some such, large man, no hat, beautiful gold ring on his right index finger."

"What about his face?"

"Oh, can't say much, roundish – big nose!"

"Do you think you would recognize him again if we repeated the experiment at the police station, with another line-up?"

"Certainly."

"Have you seen him again since last night?"

"No."

"I am really quite sorry to have to put this to you, Miss Cox, but as you are aware, this is an important matter, and I accept as does everyone here, your good intentions. Have you seen this ring before?" Benjamin then brought his right hand up out of his pocket.

"Oh, heavens, it's you, isn't it? Should have spotted the suit, or the nose, for certain."

"Thank you, I'm rather fond of him. Yes, it's me for sure. I purchased that necklace last evening. You notice the sorts of things

179

many women do, is that a fair statement: the hat, coat, clothes, tie clip, tie, rings, and so on, much more than the face?"

"Yes, that's right."

"Can you say now, that beyond a reasonable doubt, the man you identified in the line-up was the man who purchased the necklace, not the night before as in my case, but nearly a week earlier?"

"I'm sorry, so very sorry. You are right. And I should have known better."

"Why is that?"

"Well, we see it all the time on the telly, don't we, the eyewitness who got it wrong."

"Thank you for your candour. If it is any comfort to you, it really is that way in real life. Eyewitnesses are the least reliable major form of evidence. Thank you, no further questions."

The prosecution didn't have any for this witness.

"Judge, I feel that our case is proven, even on the balance of probabilities. We have shown that the accuser had a motive, the opportunity, and command of the method. I have had no magician's training, though I have been able to save a client or two with the proverbial rabbit out of the hat." He had earned the only three laughs of the day, a hat trick. "And I managed to do it without any difficulty, and little practice." Benjamin extended his right arm, and by simply closing his hand, was able to extract the necklace again from under his cuff. "Just a little bit of any hand lotion that dries slightly sticky is enough to hold it, just at the cuff.

"However, you will appreciate that I could not be sure that Miss Cox would be able to correct herself, as she most forthrightly did here today, a breath of fresh air in any courtroom. So I took the precaution of calling for an expert witness, who should be outside by now, and I ask leave to call him, and further, suggest that the court have Denis Potterton readmitted to this room for the duration of my final examination."

"Do you intend to question him in any way again?" Andrew asked.

"No, I will waive any further examination of him."

"Then I don't see an objection." Geoffrey agreed.

Denis was brought back in, and extracted the two necklaces, one from his desk drawer, the other from the safe, keeping them separate and in plain view before the judge.

"Judge, could you please be so kind as to place the necklace from the desk drawer, the alleged reproduction, on the desk, to the left of the witness chair, and place the original to the right. So we will have the original to the right hand of a witness, and the copy to the left."

Geoffrey, as was his right, sitting in judgment, asked Denis, "Does anybody else have the combination to your safe?"

"No, and there isn't the obvious paper under the drawer, either, because I memorized it, years ago."

Benjamin intoned portentously, "I call Doctor Rodger Artwright."

He was an active, strong man in his forties, suntanned head to toe so far as could be seen, with light hair bleached in the sun atop an oblong face with a hawk-like nose. Benjamin sympathized with him on that point. He ran through his qualifications as an archaeologist, and expert on early Greek artefacts. Andrew stipulated agreement as to his expertise.

"Doctor Artwright, if you don't mind a little joke, you have one of those names that fits your profession, eh? Would you please examine the two gold necklaces on the desk, one at a time, carefully replacing each in the same place after you finish the examinations."

He did so, beginning on the right side. After a short time he put it back down, turning to the left side. After a longer pause in the second case, he withdrew a magnifying monocle, and looked closely at every link in the Greek pattern chain. He finally put it down. "Yes."

"Will you please give us your opinion of these objects."

"Certainly. The one on the right is a superb copy, in gold from the weight of it, and on the left most probably an original, though I would want a gold assay to make certain. We do that with the tiniest shaving, in our mass spectroscope. This isn't the *Necklace of Agamemnon*, or another new find very much like it of the same era, is it?"

The room was deathly silent.

The Judge cleared his throat. "I'm sorry – Doctor Artwright – but could you please favour us with one more check."

"Certainly." It did him credit that he took the magnifier to both, and spent an equal time on each. He tapped lightly on the table with certainty, "No mistake, the original is on the left, and the copy on the right."

Denis was sitting with his mouth wide open in disbelief. "That's impossible. Somebody switched them, must have." Then he realized that somehow, the game had been turned against him.

Benjamin was surprised, but not shocked, and now put it together easily. Well, he thought to himself wryly, "in my nearly fifty years at the bar, it's the first time I've ever run across this particular" – he rose to address the court, forgetting that he shouldn't have, yet Geoffrey seemed to expect it, and made no objection.

"May the Court please. There is a fundamental truth about human affairs that we often miss. I am not talking about the Golden Thread that runs through British justice, and I do admire the Rumpole books – have even been known to quote that one in court. This case is to be decided on the balance of probabilities: which scenario, explanation, history, is the more probable, given the evidence.

"At the beginning it appeared to be open and shut against my client, but appearances can be deceiving as we have seen. My Golden Rule is somewhat different, and it is this. Credibility has nothing to do with truth, and truth has nothing to do with credibility. This is the silver lining in any case of this kind. Another version, more commonly subscribed to by the police, and to their credit, reads, 'If it is too good to be true, it probably isn't.' When the stitch-up is perfect, it is exactly that, or at least the possibility should be considered. It was on that basis that I ordered very substantial checks on all the principals in this case, and yes, including you, Judge. We have all seen the results of that here today.

"The accuser before this court had the motive, the opportunity, and his method has been demonstrated. Indeed, an *amateur* has demonstrated it, namely me. I suggest that it was his avocation that gave him the idea, rather than being critical to the act itself. It was, in fact, my discovery of this facet of his background that pointed our way in this defence. I submit that not only has this been proven to the balance of probabilities, but to the Gold Standard, of beyond a reasonable doubt, not against my client, but against her accuser.

"I therefore call not only for a verdict exonerating my client, but one providing for full compensation, and a sanction against this man who sits before us, his mouth still open in astonishment, so that he should never again be in a position of authority over others."

There was a pause, while Geoffrey made another of his short internal calls.

"Andrew, do you have anything to add? Denis?" The judge paused for a very long moment.

"Denis Potterton, you are sacked forthwith." There was a knock on the door, and George was admitted with two other guards. "George, please wait for me outside until I call for you."

"Doctor Potterton, these guards will escort you off the premises. You are banned from ever setting foot in the British Museum, for the duration of my tenure, and my successors' pleasure. You will not touch anything in this room. I will personally examine everything here and return to you all that is rightfully yours. Dismissed."

The door opened, closed, then opened again, and Adam was admitted.

"Miss Baynes, it is the finding of this hearing that you are exonerated entirely. I will personally see to it that you are fully compensated in every way possible, and apologize profusely for the personal agonies you must have suffered, for which there is no possible compensation, other than my good will and best offices in support of your future career. My door is always open to you, from now on, at any hour.

"Benjamin, Doctor Pearson, I thank you personally for preventing a gross and egregious miscarriage of justice, and I will meet with you at the earliest mutually convenient opportunity to negotiate a civil and professional settlement."

Chapter 14

Irini's Convalescence

An emotional trauma is often worse than a physical one and usually takes longer to heal.

The verdict did not, and could not be expected to relieve Irini of all that had happened as though it had not happened. It was clear that she had been emotionally injured, and that it would take time to heal. Geoffrey Hayward appreciated this, and readily agreed that four weeks paid leave should be part of the settlement negotiated with Benjamin Pearson.

Settlement
Between Miss Irini Baynes and the British Museum

Article One: A letter shall issue over the signature of Doctor Geoffrey Hayward that outlines the wrongful charges against Irini Baynes, indicating that she was entirely innocent of the slightest involvement. The full written transcript of the hearing shall be appended, including the judgment of the director with all particulars. This shall also be maintained indefinitely in her personnel file.

Article Two: The museum shall grant her one-month of paid leave effective immediately, leaving contractual sick leave and accumulated holiday days as they would have been had she worked that month. The museum shall pay her the tax-free, tax-prepaid in her name sum of Fifty Thousand Pounds Sterling in partial compensation for emotional trauma. The museum shall further pay all reasonable medical costs over a maximum period of three years for psychological, psychiatric, and any other support, either private or under the health services of Great Britain at her sole choice, deemed necessary in the finding of her personal physician (Doctor Irrawadee or his authorized replacement). If a licensed physician finds that she is unable to work *for any reason*, the museum shall pay her full salary plus such costs for a period not to exceed three years.

Article Three: If Miss Baynes decides to remain in the employ of the British Museum, said decision to be reached within the above three years, she shall be continued in employment there without prejudice either in her favour or against her.

Article Four: The British Museum shall pay its own costs, and within thirty days, the full legal costs of Miss Baynes, detailed invoice attached. The total is Sterling Pounds 56,844 (Fifty Six Thousand Eight Hundred Forty Four) inclusive of VAT.

Signed: Geoffrey Hayward, Irini Baynes
    Benjamin Pearson, Andrew Sims

"Wow!" Adam whistled. "Fifty Grand." Yet it was clear to him that Irini was not impressed.

"I would give it all back for it not to have happened." She snapped her fingers, "like that".

"Sure, my love, sure, I understand, and you're right."

Adam and Irini, truth be told, would have given that sum back, or paid it if they had it, for each time they had been denied mutual loving comfort during the episode. It was now a week after the trial, and they had still not been able to recover their balance.

They were in the Greek restaurant awaiting the arrival of Helena, Peter and Benjamin Pearson.

Adam and Irini stood up. "Benjamin. How nice you could come."

"I wouldn't have missed this dinner for one with the President. How are we getting on?" He lowered himself carefully onto yet another chair in which he lacked complete confidence. He fixed Irini with a look of questioning encouragement.

"Well, okay."

"But not quite right, ah, *inside yourself.* Am I right?"

"Yes," she brightened, "that's exactly right."

"Irini, I and my partners in crime," he smiled as his own joke, "deal with clients who have been acquitted after long trials, proceedings that may have taken years, yes *years* is not uncommon. We also deal with those who are convicted, and we see them in prison, perhaps during an appeal that can last ten years. Sometimes they are then released. We are happy, and the client tries to be delighted, but usually it takes about the same length of time as the experience itself before they are beginning to feel themselves again.

"Some say that it takes as long to get over a love affair as the affair itself. This is like that, I think. So my advice to you is to accept that fact of our frail humanity, roll with the seas of life, and wait patiently to come out the other side. You will, I assure you. I know that the pittance I was able to obtain for you is no compensation at all."

His last words broke through to Irini's inner self, and she felt at least twenty percent lighter, as if that part of her burden had been lifted. Yes, she thought to herself, perhaps she had just a touch of guilt about that money, and an unrequited belief that it should somehow help, when it hadn't. She said as much out loud.

Benjamin agreed, "That's why I said it. We also see clients win huge settlements, and feel miserable afterwards. They would have given it all back for the injury not to have happened. That's very human, understandable, as normal as a sunrise."

Five minutes with this man was better than the five hours she had spent with a kind and capable psychological therapist. Or, she thought, to be fair to her, maybe it was all just coming better thanks to everyone involved. It had been a week since the trial, the same length of time as the pre-trial purgatory she had endured. Adam had been patient and a rock of strength. She didn't know how she would have handled all this without him, and felt that the seasickness of these stormy seas was at last receding.

"Helena, nice to see you." Benjamin half-rose to greet her arrival, showing another mannerism forced by his physique.

"Benjamin, I would like you to meet Peter."

"Pleasure, Peter."

"Sorry we are late," Helena added, half out of breath, "but we got caught in traffic after our flight today."

"Everyone," Peter grinned widely, "congratulations are in order. Helena soloed today, and will now get her license."

"Great!" Adam enthused, "I can't wait for our first lesson tomorrow."

"So, flying lessons?" Benjamin asked, brows wrinkled.

"Yes, we're learning to fly."

"All of you?" His new group of friends was full of surprises.

"Yes," Adam confirmed, "all of us." He pressed Irini's hand under the table, and she turned to smile at him, in that way of their old times, and Adam instantly knew that she had turned the corner towards life, as opposed to the self-imposed death of depression that she had flirted with for these two weeks.

They ordered, and made small talk about life, the universe, everything, except for their own recent history together. In the end, Benjamin could not contain himself any more. He had been bubbling over all evening with something on his mind that had to come out.

He fixed Adam with a baleful eye, and a wink. "So, what can you tell me about the necklaces, Adam?"

"Not much, counsellor." He winked back.

"You remember I said that we spent a lot of time and money checking up on everyone, and it was *everyone!*"

"Ah, so you have ... figured me out?"

"Pretty much, and I just want to say that in nearly half a century in the law, if I include university, I have never before had this particular experience."

"What *are* you two talking about?" Helena flashed a mysterious half-smile, half-frown around the table.

Benjamin, regretting that perhaps too much had been said already, held up a strong restraining hand. "Just confirming a small detail about the case; better if it is left there. After all, one doesn't want to say too much to any attorney, eh?"

Adam had understood all along that it had to remain a secret. Conspiracy is a criminal offence, either before or after the fact, and he already had one partner in crime, reliable though Peter was. The hidden history was the following.

On the day before the trial, Adam used his security system to enter Potterton's office, and then met Peter at the Museum Tavern. After Adam briefed him on what he needed, Peter called ahead on his portable phone, then led the way across town and the river, to Southwark. The call assured that his very special contact would be in the shop when they arrived, for mid afternoon was most definitely not normal hours for this sort of business – more towards midnight was the witching hour.

"Peter, nice to see you. So what have you dragged me out of my afternoon kip for? I hope it's worthwhile."

The man was a true dwarf, but unusually slender, unlike most of his compatriots who were on the heavy-boned side, as though a normal body had been compressed without deflation. He had only a topknot of silver grey hair on an otherwise bald, oversized head. It nodded from its weight as he spoke, and when he led them down the back stairs to his special shop.

"My friend here has some requirements."

"Just so," the little man said, opening the combination lock on a steel door, to let them through into his inner sanctum.

"So, young man, what can I do for you?"

"I've got to open a Slade-Archer, model 3A."

"Some antique shop nearby, eh? That's an old model, shouldn't be too difficult."

"That was my hope, but I am unfamiliar with it, so any advice would…"

"Certainly. I cut my teeth on the 2B and 3A. You could do it with a stethoscope, if you've got all night, but I have just the thing to make it quick and easy." With this he opened a display case, and took out another version of the inevitable black box. It had a stethoscope-like extension leading to a round, flat rubber disk not unlike those on the ammunition for a child's dart gun, and to the same purpose; if moistened it would stick to any flat surface.

Adam turned the box in his hand, "A Micro-Digital eight or sixteen would just fit –"

"I see you know your process computers young man; it's the sixteen with the autocorrelation software."

"That will help. So what's the scoop on the 3A?"

"It was a bit of a dead-end in the old days of the mechanicals, the only *five* combination lock ever made in its class. It goes *left* first, spin it clear to the first number, and then alternately, past zero (not the previous number) each time to the next."

"Five, eh? That *would* take all night, even if one had practiced for a month beforehand, and I have neither the month, nor the night."

"Then you came to the right shop."

Adam frowned in concentration. "The computer will store the numbers, and show them in this LED display here, and if I remember correctly, the software and the microphone in the sucker will take care of everything else."

"Yes, but remember one thing. You must turn the dial *one number at a time* and wait at least the one-second dwell-time. If that's the next number in the combo, the display will flash that number, then freeze on it. You then reverse back to zero, and so beginning *with* zero, which in this model may be the next number, to continue the process. It should get you there within five or ten minutes. Be patient. If you mess it up, you can start over from the last correct number. The system will follow you through the combo up to that point, no need to begin from scratch."

The little man was looking at him with his head on one side in obvious concentration. "I have a memory for faces, and yours is familiar, yet I know we have not met in person before. May I ask you something about your background, or would you rather leave it for, perhaps, another time?"

Peter spoke, "He is reliable, Adam."

"I didn't think anything else. Sure."

"Might you be Adam Blitz, sorry, no, that's not quite right, but the famous, or perhaps you might agree with me, the *in*famous child prodigy safecracker from New York?"

"The same. Adam Blix." He shook hands for the second time.

"Ah, yes, 'Blix', unusual name. I am most pleased to have met a fellow professional. Your safe will be a doddle. I'll wish you good luck, but you won't need it. By the way, my name is Mikko, and I would always welcome you here at any hour."

With a smile, Adam paid over the three thousand pounds out of the five that he had taken from his London bank just before meeting Peter. It represented both his satisfaction at the transaction, and the fact that he had been recognized, out of the blue, by a fellow of the brotherhood. It didn't happen every day, but when it did, it was far more likely to be in a shop like this, south of the tracks as he thought of it from his American background – the tracks in the case of London being the river Thames.

"Okay, Peter, you stand lookout." Adam whipped out his black box, and set it for the codes of Potterton's office. He had obtained them not long after Potterton had set Irini up, just in case, by placing his false cover on the lock's panel, waiting for him to enter his office, and then removing it, exactly as he had shown her in the happier times before her world had crashed. He opened the door and entered it for the second time that day.

Adam took his skeleton key ring out of his pocket, and had the bottom door of Potterton's office desk open in fifteen seconds flat. He laid the reproduction necklace out on the desk. He then turned to the safe. The rubber sucker gave a little trouble because the paint was the corrugated kind. He had to take a piece of emery cloth out of his little black bag to smooth it before it would hold fast. Mikko's system worked perfectly the first time, taking about six minutes to go through all the numbers, one of which was zero. Without his careful instructions, Adam might not have been able to quickly figure that out for himself. It was not natural to stop on the pass-number, so he smiled in appreciation of his advisor. The safe slid open, revealing the priceless necklace inside.

Adam took it out in his gloved hand, and frowned. "Problem?" Peter said, glancing back, "We're still all clear here."

"Nothing we can't deal with," Adam whispered back, "but it will take me a few minutes, and I'll need good light. Forget the door, and come here please."

Peter held the penlight close, while Adam worked the museum seal open with a pair of small tweezers and a thin pointed probe from his kit. He repeatedly inserted the probe into the clasp, designed to be one-time-only, until he had it positioned just under the tiny ratchet buried inside the seal. He then slowly teased the thin band back through.

"Just a minute now, and we're home." Adam then reset the seal through the other necklace in exactly the same position, which happened to be the third link from the medallion itself, an image of the minotaur, half man and half bull, which he had recently learned from Irini was the mythical creature of Knossos in Crete, guardian of the labyrinth, and one of Agamemnon's personal symbols. Having transferred the seal to the reproduction, he placed it in the safe, dropped the original into the desk drawer, and re-locked it with his skeletons. That took a frustrating five minutes. The lock was sticky-tight to close, because the sliding latch was not perfectly aligned with its slot. So it had been a hundred times as hard to lock, than it had been to unlock.

"So what's this all about, Adam?" Peter whispered, as they closed the door behind them.

"Insurance." Was the only answer he received.

Peter flew the helicopter like he had been doing it for half a lifetime; he undeniably had a talent for it. The four of them held hands, Irini and Adam in the back seat, Helena and Peter in the front whenever Peter could free a hand from the controls to do so.

"Want to take over, Helena?"

"Sure." She had her own crisp new license tucked away in her handbag along with the obligatory Logbook all pilots carry to record every minute of flying time along with any other relevant comments. Irini's flight instructor had introduced this subject by passing a dog-eared copy of a real logbook around the class. It ended with a posthumous note, in another hand: "Made a fatal mistake and crashed. Last flight not successful."

Green and pleasant forests alternated with striated brown fields of the autumn harvest. "That's the M4." Peter pointed out the window. "We are right on course." He tapped on the compass, and Helena yawed the aircraft left to take the agreed course towards Devon and their destination of Dartmouth. She banked left and right to thread their way through the low hills, affording superb views to their passengers, soon themselves to be pilots.

They bounced unexpectedly over the last hill, and were suddenly flung out over the sea. Helena banked very sharply right to align with the coast, eliciting sharp gasps of pleasure, spiced with a slight edge of disquiet from the back seat. They swung up the river Dart, turned left, and Helena brought them in to a landing on a helipad marked "**H**" in the parking area of a large estate.

Adam and Irini had taken their first lesson in the little Cessna training plane just before the four had boarded the leased helicopter. Adam couldn't wait to fly on his own, and his Irini was beginning to feel the bug's bite after an initial bout of uncertainty.

"That was perfect, Helena. I'll jump out, and tie down." Peter was as good as his word, and as soon as the aircraft was securely held fast, he stepped back. Helena switched off the turbine engine, and the blades spun slowly to rest, drooping down towards the earth as they lost lift. Then all was tied down, and they could disembark.

The villa on a hill overlooking the Channel, the charming old town of Dartmouth and the river Dart, had been rented out of the "tips box". After paying the substantial cost of this week's holiday there was over seventy thousand pounds still in the kitty, because Irini had thrown in her fifty on top of Adam's consulting fees. Everyone said that this was her money, for pain and suffering, but she countered that it was their money, because her salvation had been a team effort. She knew the whole truth now from Adam, so this was for her a sharp understanding. Being rid of that blood money had lifted the last of her depressive feelings.

Adam and Irini walked the soft hills, and narrow, picturesque streets of Dartmouth, every day. Midweek, Helena led all four of them down for a lunch, and pointed out the bookshop that had been owned and run by the original Christopher Robin, son of the famous author of *Winnie the Pooh*. They agreed that any adult who hasn't made the acquaintance would be well advised to read it, or better yet, to their children.

Adam and Irini's relationship had recovered in all respects, yet it was not quite the same as it had been during the summer before the debacle at the museum, and it would never be the same again. This confused and upset both of them for a time, but they came to understand that this was the nature of love and realized that most people went through these transitions. The positive side was that they had become more attentive to the other dimensions of a long-term relationship, from a simple bouquet of flowers presented by *either* of them to the other, sharing together in the preparation of a meal, or cleaning Achilles' toilette box. Adam was surprised to discover that these chores could be done lovingly, that they were part of their physical life together, and nothing else mattered to him. Except flying.

Peter was in love with Helena. She knew it, but would have put it in a different way. "Peter is trying to be in love with me." Experience told both of them that this was different from the *agape* of stunning first love and its bedfellows. They easily followed the dance steps of this version as both foreseeable and well defined, and felt that it was a worthy affirmation of great satisfaction.

Peter was a man of increasing sensitivity, and had been around the track a few times. He had loved, and been loved, one-way, each way, so had a clear grasp of the phenomenon. He naturally tried hard to make it into a two-way proposition, yet deep down they knew that the chasms between them in age, experience, background and other commitments, both personal and professional, would never be bridged to that final, essential degree.

Yet it was deeply satisfying to try, and he was overjoyed at simply holding hands with this woman. This relationship was certainly the model for his next, which he sensed would be the last love in his life. So it was in some sense a trial run. It was a measure of their maturity that both were able to revel in this kind of romance, and receive a very great deal in return.

After a particularly pleasant evening together in Helena's room, holding hands, hugging, kissing, and talking it all out, Helena was faced with engineering another easy let-down. She held him close one last time and said, "You know, Peter, that sex only baits the trap. Sex is *not* love."

He embraced her strongly. "You know," he decided with a clear rational assurance that perhaps he did not yet quite feel, "maybe this is actually stronger than it would be if we fell into the trap."

"I think that is one of the great truths of all time, my love, and that's why we haven't let it happen." It had naturally fallen to her to be the one to keep it at arm's length, literally, so he loved her all the more for her generosity in partly crediting him.

Helena had not interrupted their holiday with any mention of business. They returned to London at Safe House Two before picking up where they had left off with the dreaded silver-cased machines.

The fan in the computer whirred softly, and the clicks of the mouse-key punctuated the images flashing past on the screen. The four were gathered closely around, the two couples holding hands when they could, and pointing something out on the screen when they had to.

She ticked off the major headings, jumping effortlessly between distant pages as needed, as though she had memorized them all *with* their page numbers, able to command the next thought's details on the screen as easily as if they had been directly from her own brain. These connections had indeed been memorized. Helena hadn't become number two in the Greek intelligence service for nothing.

"Security: Adam has this in hand, Peter and Irini fully trained and up to speed. Facilities and lift-team: Peter has finished Safe House Two, starting on the latter. Personnel: Irini tells us she will have no problems now that Geoffrey is her champion. If that's the right image, eh, Irini.

"Planning: I'm beginning to feel we are almost on top of that. Now, as for the Unexpected as Expected: well, we have just had a big dose of that at the museum. It is an ill consequence indeed that doesn't have an up-side, and Irini's new status can't hurt. So we were doubly right to jump from a dizzy height on them over that appalling, and I still find unbelievable, fiasco."

"My feelings exactly, Helena. I still wake up in the middle of the night with a silent scream on my lips. How can anyone be so awful?"

"More along the lines of 'crazy'." Adam thought out loud.

Helena: "One final item, and don't get upset, we're professionals. I was followed the day we left on holiday. The security cameras must have picked him up, so I forwarded those files by remote command from my computer while we were in Devon, and we'll see what Spiros or Charon can do with them. I won't do the checking myself, to keep it at least twice-removed, double blind. I also reviewed the safe house sites by download to Devon last week. No sign of anyone near either one. We've been here before – double-drops, first time, every time, just to make sure it stays that way, right?"

Chapter 15

Spiros in London

An unexpected visit is often sweeter than one anticipated.

Helena was sitting quietly in her new, modest flat in Bayswater, reading *Crime and Punishment* by Dostoyevsky. She had noticed it while browsing in the second-hand bookshop for no better reason than the title's relevance to her current life.

She had dreamed various scenarios, in some cases waking up in a cold sweat shaking from head to toe. Sometimes the headlines were favourable:

Marvel of the Marbles Heist.

At other times they screamed:

Twenty-to-Life for Marbles Thieves.

Spiros had become the strong brick in the wall of their plans, worth his weight in diamonds. Yet Helena would have swapped it all for ten minutes in his arms. The three months since they had been together on his island stretched back an eternity, and the worst of it was she was no closer to a resolution in her own mind and heart than she had been throwing him a tear-stained kiss as the plane took off from Chania.

Her reveries were interrupted by her secure mobile. She keyed the access codes, and the unscrambled signal cleared the screen, Spiros' face coming to life upon it.

"*Agape mou.*"

"Spiros!"

"No time. Don't speak. Read message. Out."

The screen blanked and then scanned out the following:

CODE <u>YELLOW</u>: MOSCOW RULES
BRING WHOLE TEAM
GREEK EMBASSY
LONDON ASAP

Helena immediately keyed in a text message, which she then relayed directly to the secure digital telephones of Adam, Irini, and Peter:

CODE YELLOW: MOSCOW RULES
USE DISGUISE KIT "A" AND DOUBLE DROPS
GREEK EMBASSY 1A HOLLAND PARK
NOTTING HILL GATE TUBE
ASAP RSVP 1 HOUR OR LESS IF POSSIBLE?

She sent a confirming message back to Spiros, went to her personal safe and removed a shoebox sized metal box labelled "KIT A" on the side. It had a combination lock as well, and she opened it. The dark, straight black hair wig went on first, followed by a rubber nose extension. She used a special cleaning fluid to cleanse the skin, peeled off the seal, pressed it on, and then adjusted carefully in the mirror. The special glue set by catalytic action in a couple of minutes. She marvelled at its quality, for it blended perfectly and was undetectable. The kind of prosthesis used in motion pictures would not have passed on the street at five metres, but this one would do in bed with a lover, unless he liked to bite off the ends of noses. There were three other attachments in the kit: a large mole for placement on the chin complete with hair, another for the side of her jaw, and last a birthmark for the back of the right hand in the shape of a flattened strawberry in a purplish colour as if it had gone off in the sun.

The mobile phone chimed once, then after a minute, a second time, and finally a third, so each member had reported in.

ADAM: 1 HOUR
IRINI: 50 MIN
PETER: 1 HOUR
ME: 45 MIN

She added her own, estimated at 45 minutes, sent on to Spiros. Her heart leaped. He must be in London, at the Embassy, in the flesh!

The magic kit then produced some makeup that in a few minutes transformed Helena into a 60 plus year-old woman, complete with dark scarf. The instructions read, "Remember to hunch over when you walk, and favour the right foot. If you speak, use the accent of any language other than Greek or English; decide now and stick with it." Helena went to her closet, and selected the least conspicuous, darker shades available. She pulled on a low-brimmed black hat, and wide-rimmed, thick yet optically neutral glasses of the kind that darken some in the sunlight, and opened her door. She slipped a single long black hair from the wig into the doorjamb, and then double-locked the flat behind her.

The late afternoon traffic was gathering, and a taxi was out of the question, so she limped her way to the tube, got out at Knightsbridge station, went up the escalator, and along the Brompton Road to Harrods Department Store. She worked her way across the ground floor to the eastern side exit, went up the stairs (not the open escalator), back across the first floor, down the escalator, and out the west side exit. There was no possibility that she had been followed. She was lucky to find a taxi, so she changed her plans and took it, directly requesting, in a thick Hindi accent, an address near the Greek Embassy.

Surprise number one, Charon himself was behind the reception desk instead of the regular personnel. Helena went up to him, and in her new Hindi accent, asked for help with her visa. Charon handed her a blank sheet of paper, and directed her to a door at the rear of the reception area. Three other people were seated on a marble bench filling out paperwork, but they paid no attention to her, or at least they didn't appear to do so, yet one of them was in the employ of MI5, the British secret service. Had she known, and Charon certainly would know, no aspect of the procedures so far would have been changed.

A narrow staircase led down behind the door. She didn't know that there was a basement in this building. At the bottom, the door opened for her, and she fell into the arms of Spiros.

It was an anteroom, and they were alone except for a half dozen cameras and computerized recording, so they embraced, kissed and embraced again, and did quite a few things that in other circumstances would have led within minutes to the couch or bed. Both knew that it had all been recorded, but that didn't matter one whit to either of them, nor to those monitoring the cameras, or the others who later discretely erased the records as they were of no possible security use and indeed could be the opposite. They were on home ground, the soil of their beloved Greece, where these things were understood.

"So, I'm first in the hole?"

"Yes."

A green light flashed over the door, and Spiros continued, "We had best go through now, the others seem to be arriving."

He entered a code, and the inner door swooshed open, revealing another room beyond, about the size of a normal corporate boardroom. At the far end there was a large desk with a distinguished looking man sitting behind it in the dim light, writing in a large notebook. In front there was a small boardroom table with eight chairs, three each side, and two on the ends. The left wall was festooned with TV and computer monitors displaying scenes from inside and outside the Embassy, as well as international news, and no doubt, Helena deduced, the capability of direct secure communication with any Greek office or authority of substance anywhere in the world. It was obviously a situation room and command centre.

Spiros guided Helena to a door on their immediate right. "You can remove the makeup in there. You will also find a shoulder bag with your initials on it, in which you can carry any items back home without them being seen."

It was a comfortable dressing room with all the necessary accoutrements. Helena removed the prostheses, carefully disposing them in the burn bag that was hanging underneath the marble hand basin. All items that had been in the kit followed them into the bag. She retained her own clothes, placing the hat and her dark silk shawl in the shoulder bag.

Just as she finished, a Thai princess opened the door and came in. Helena said, "I'm finished, so it's all yours." Only then did she notice that it was Irini. She might have actually passed her on the street without recognition. The disguise was superb, as were the clothes.

"Hello, Helena. My respects to whomever created this kit. It was wonderful to wear it." Irini began rubbing off the thick makeup, pulled off the eyelashes and eyebrows, and tossed them with the magnificent, piled-up wig, into the burn bag. She removed the iridescent Thai silks and started to stuff them in her initialled shoulder bag, but Helena stayed her hand.

"Sorry, Irini, they must all go in there."

"Oh, no, I want to wear them again!"

"Very sad, they are beautiful, but imagine what might happen if they were found in your flat, and matched up with, say, a picture taken of you arriving?"

"That's so improbable as to be ridiculous."

"I know it may seem that way, but the unexpected does not consider the improbabilities."

"Sounds like something your old Spymaster might have said." Irini reluctantly dropped each of the silks into the black bag.

"You're right, he did."

Adam and Peter emerged from a door opposite leading to the men's dressing room, and the team was united in a safe house of quite a different taste from theirs.

The main door opened, and Charon came in, shaking hands all around, as Helena introduced him, and Spiros, to her partners. Although they knew both by name from the Project Plan, this was the first meeting, discounting their welcome by Charon when they had no idea who he was.

Charon addressed them crisply. "This room is absolutely secure, and we may freely discuss any matter in complete safety."

Helena's attention returned to the seventh man, behind the desk, and then a warm feeling surged towards her. She recognized those elegant hands. He took this moment to make one of his eloquent gestures, towards Spiros, who ushered everyone forward.

"It is my great honour to introduce you all to our Prime Minister."

He stood up and came around the desk, a warm greeting colouring his face, a perfectly manicured hand being proffered.

"You already know Helena Katsis."

"Mister Prime Minister."

"My pleasure, Kat."

He smiled, and held her hand for just that little bit longer than required, signifying much on many levels. "A simple 'sir' will be more than enough from this assembly."

"Mister Adam Blix."

"An honour, sir."

"Miss Irini Baynes

"An honour, sir." She curtseyed.

"Well, I see you have learned the English way in that, Miss Baynes, but you will know that we don't do that for ordinary politicians, much as it enchanted me." He held her hand twice as long as he had Helena's with a resonant smile to match the voice.

"Mister Peter Ryan."

"An honour, sir."

Helena had long ago debriefed her team on his background as a member of the team, in one way at least, the most senior.

She noticed deeper lines, and the wear and tear of cares on his broad forehead and around his eyes. His olive skin also seemed pale, compared with how Helena remembered him from three months before. He retained his formal, yet open manner, charm as often as not expressed by his hands and body to augment the voice. His American accent in English occasionally showed in evidence of his University days spent there. He had studied law, first at Athens, and then for the JD at the University of Chicago.

He had fond memories of those days, and they had provided him with many life-long contacts through encounters with American and international students in residence there. He had appreciated its quality of free-ranging debate that had been so sadly lacking in his native Athens during his youth. Remembering first-hand the oppressive Colonel's regime, he had vowed like many other dispersed Greeks to return home and recreate democracy. It had seen its early beginnings in ancient Greece, had been maintained by Great Britain and others during the intervening centuries, and must now come back home to stay.

After a few years practicing international law in a shipping firm, he had stepped onto the lower rungs of political life. He put his success down to a very succinct expression of his personal philosophy, one that came from the Sybil at Delphi herself. He reasoned that if you don't know yourself, you couldn't know or understand others. A key to his abilities in public office, and the negotiations that are always central to the exercise of power, was his willingness to put himself in the place of his adversaries. This fostered a characteristically pragmatic approach. He was a tough man when it was needed, yet he always weighed the personal equations in any decision.

The Prime Minister pushed his gold-rimmed spectacles back, and sat down on their side of the desk in order to achieve the maximum degree of intimacy.

"The reason you have not heard about my visit is that it is unofficial. You know how that works, so I won't bore you with the details of protocol, save that your meeting with me here is to remain confidential." His hands spoke serious intent, "Not to mention the other matters that may come up, under the heading of Top Secret.

"It is my great regret to have to report to you that my negotiations with the British Prime Minister in respect of the Marbles have failed. He is adamant, and I am certain there is no way forward on this front for the foreseeable future. Putting myself in his position, in his political environment, even if he was willing to return them, I don't see how he could do so and survive politically. You don't need me to tell you that these are the most intractable positions.

"You know, that I know…" he smiled at Charon, "Charon, my dear friend and colleague, you see how you rub off on me."

"Apologies, sir."

"Not at all, it just amuses me. As I was saying, you know that I am cognizant of your proposal, plans and project in that regard. I have called you here for a number of reasons.

"First, I want you to know, that I know, what you are risking, including the dire consequences that would attend failure. More than that, I know that even if you succeed, you will be making substantial sacrifices of other personal kinds. These are difficult to weigh, but I always try to weigh them. Is my meaning clear?" He looked from one to the next, eye-to-eye, pausing a sensible time in each case. No gesture or use of language could have conveyed more serious intent, or concern.

"As my American friends say, and as I imagine Adam here might have, let's cut to the chase. By the way, Mister Blix, do you happen to know where that aphorism comes from?"

"No sir, I don't."

"No matter, but I am a collector of expressions, especially foreign ones. So, where are we in all this? You are all risking your lives, your treasure, and your honour, and perhaps your freedom as well. Two of you have no connection with my country, and one is a fifty-percenter, if you will allow me that liberty, Miss Baynes. I am immensely impressed by what I have heard about the reasons the non-Greeks are with us in this.

"But, and I repeat, *but* we mustn't let this thing run away with us emotionally, absent a useful discipline of hard thinking from the left brain." He tapped his head meaningfully.

"Helena, if you will permit the liberty of a first name, our dear and much honoured Helena, you have already given the best years of your life, risked it and more, in the service of our country. I know that you weigh the personal sides most carefully, and have been open and just with your colleagues. Nevertheless, I ask you, and you all, to consider most carefully one more time – thinking rather than feeling – are you absolutely certain that this plan is achievable at acceptable risk. So, before you answer in haste, and that, on the other hand, if it is successful, the heavy personal price you still face is one you can afford to willingly pay, I repeat, *willingly* pay."

Adam coughed, and looked around the room. He sensed that this was his moment, holding as he did the outsider's brief and perspective. "Mister Prime Minister, sorry – sir – let me answer the emotional question first. I detest, sir, detest and distrust, hypocrisy of any kind or flavour. The treatment of your national heritage in this reeks of it. I say it shall not stand!"

The last word cracked around the room, bouncing smartly off the walls.

Peter interjected, "Dammit, we can do it. I'm the pessimist in this gang, and I say we can do it! Uh, sorry sir, I didn't mean to use…"

The Prime Minister interrupted, "It's fine with me; been known to do it myself, eh?" Spiros and Charon nodded with a smile.

The Prime Minister's right hand made the "maybe yes, maybe no" flapping motions like a wounded bird trying to take flight. "Yes, a bit of the emotional part, and the practical opinion, a fair mix." He turned to Helena. "You are in command here, your first such, though you have certainly run some highly successful field operations involving others, so nobody can deny that your C-V fits. So this is it, the moment of truth. What is the risk versus return here? Give me an assessment."

Helena had seen Charon do this a few times, once before this same man. In that case, which she remembered clearly, the plan was risky, the benefits substantial, yet the Prime Minister had pointed out that Greece could survive without them. It wasn't a pretty sight when the Prime Minister had finished with Charon, and the plan was scrapped, over his figuratively battered body. Charon was tough, and knew the game, so he had survived to serve another day. He and Helena had been part of the planning for an alternative approach, which a year or so later succeeded, admittedly in changed circumstances.

Sometimes it paid to wait, but not this time, she was sure. The ducks were lined up, the date and cover story set, and they would not align again any more than an eclipse having taken place today, would be repeated the next day in case of cloudy weather. She said as much, and ran through the summaries from the Project Plan from memory.

After a time, the Prime Minister held up a courteous stop-hand. "You've done your homework, and I don't think Charon himself could have handled this any better."

"I certainly agree, sir."

"We have half the equation. Is it our consensus that the probability of success is better than even?"

Silence in *this* instance was *not* consent.

"Less?"

Charon broke the uncomfortable silence. "I have discussed this point with Helena, as we have done a few times in the past, and we agree it is about one-third we win, fifty percent we lose, and the rest an 'abort' or a 'no-game' result."

The Prime Minister repeated his eye-to-eye contact around the room. "So, gentlemen and ladies, it's odds on that you will be cooling your – ah, sorry, what is that one, I do think it is so expressive?"

Adam grinned, "I think it is 'cooling your heels' sir."

"Yes, so, listen to me carefully. Your project management is saying it's likely that you will be cooling your heels in prison for most of the rest of your lives, with two-to-one against success, when you will still have adjustments to make.

"Now, we are going to do this in such a way that nobody is under any pressure, one way or the other, from me, your leaders, or each other. Charon, the ballots please."

Charon came forward with slips of paper, and identical soft lead pencils. He handed them around. "This will be a secret ballot. There are seven of us here, each involved in one way or another. I am probably the least at risk in this room. You will agree with me that the Prime Minister carries a heavy burden of ultimate responsibility, and the penalties that entails for him if we fail. Yet I must tell you that he said to me that his future is a fleabite compared with what you would face. So we will ballot in secret. Each of us will mark these with a simple 'Y' for yes, we go ahead, and an 'N' if anyone has any doubts – please note carefully that this is not about the mission itself – but rather weighing if you can afford to pay your own personal price of failure, or success, at these odds."

"Thank you Charon, you put that last point far better than I would have. So, we cast our lives and futures into the hat."

Adam mumbled to himself, "If you can't do the time, don't do the crime."

Charon hadn't heard clearly. "Adam, did you say something?"

Adam said it again in a louder voice, yet one clearly under stress.

The Prime Minister spread his hands in agreement. "Yes, I remember that one now, and that is the point, isn't it, so pause before you mark your ballots, and reflect on it carefully."

The slips were passed around, the hat filled, and the Prime Minister read out the results. "I have seven in favour, and none opposed. The die is cast for us all."

Then he clenched his right hand into a fist, with only the index finger extended, and jabbed it pointedly around the room, visiting each person present. "Now I am free to give you my personal assurance, on my honour as a man, setting aside all matters of status and office, that I will do whatever is in my power to minimize all risks, and to ameliorate any penalties that may arise. Are there any questions?" As had so often happened on this mission at these points of determination, there were none.

Spiros rose from his chair, and went to a blank wood panel in the side wall, and pressed on it to open what was revealed as a bar. The Prime Minister became the waiter, and took orders, while Spiros stood barman. "Spiros, my friend, scored any coups lately?"

"Regrettably no, sir, but I have my eye on one or two amusing possibilities after our present mission is completed, as I have *no doubt it will be*."

Spiros handed the Prime Minister his drink, last as the host. It was a 21-year-old single-malt Scotch whisky, and woe betide anyone on the staff who forgot to have it handy. He did not by any means imbibe either to excess, or daily, but when he needed one, that was it, no substitutes. "*Stin ygieia mas.*"

Spiros spoke confidentially, "Sir, speaking of coups, I have yet to hear from you how you pulled off the deal with Athanassios over the Treasures of Mount Athos."

As the Prime Minister switched into his raconteur mode with a little sigh of relief, his body relaxed, and at least ten years dropped from his face. A broad smile glowed, and he winked at Spiros.

"Well, nothing would have been possible without my dear friend here, with his contacts, pressure points, and a bit of the readies to lubricate them." Naturally his fingers simulated the paying of money.

"You see my friends," waving a hand as if to embrace them all, "one of the joys of my job is the extraordinary mixture of people I meet and must deal with. Archimandrite Athanassios was certainly one of them." As if in answer to Peter's unspoken question, he continued, "An Archimandrite is the leader of a monastic group, in this case, he was elected by the Abbots of the twenty monasteries that comprise the Mount Athos community in northern Greece.

"As you may know, when in situ within the monasteries, only men can see their treasures, and then only under special circumstances." He waved a deprecating hand in deference to the women present. "I know, that's not the modern way, but I would never suggest that most of them are living in this century, or the last!

"I met this extraordinary man while he was on retreat in the Monastery of Panagia Chozoviotissa, on the Cycladic island of Amorgos. You must imagine, my friends, the remarkable setting. The building clings like a barnacle to the sheer, in fact overhanging cliffs, high above the sea. The rear walls are the original stone, painted white, sometimes carved with candle-lit niches or bas-reliefs. There was little electricity, and the aroma of beeswax candles perfused the whole building. It is nowhere more than a few metres thick, and one feels that the whole edifice is poised to crash down the cliff at any moment to the bottom of the sea. I can picture archaeologists centuries from now searching for the second lost Atlantis of Chozoviotissa.

"There is no airport on the island, so I was dropped by helicopter in the small parking area at the foot of the cliff. So, like any other pilgrim, I had to walk up the 300 steps, and traverse the 900 years that separated me from the monastery's foundation in 1088. Everyone who visits is in awe of this grand work, a memorial hymn to human faith.

"When one gets there, what turns out to be the main door is little more than a hatchway. I think the seven dwarfs would have to duck to get in. Archimandrite Athanassios had come to the bottom of that last staircase to welcome me with an embrace, and lead me up to the door, which I might not otherwise have recognized as such."

He warmed to his task. "He had agreed to meet me at the end of his annual retreat there. Picture in your mind's eye an Icon of Saint John the Baptist, with his flowing grey beard and fiery eyes. This was the man in front of me, his tall figure accentuated by an elongated black hat, and flowing robes." The Prime Minister indicated an improbably tall hat with the sweep of his raised hand.

"His voice," he continued, "had a deep, mellifluous timbre, and reminded me of the monastery bell near my home as a child, echoing down the mountains and out onto the plains of Meteora. It spoke with resonant assurance, in consonance, as I was to discover, with his true personality. He was simultaneously ascetic, compassionate and charismatic, an unforgettable and powerful combination.

"If you think that I was impressed, you are right. He went from strength to strength as we negotiated first, the necessary basic agreement, and then the devils that are always in the details.

"The treasures had been lovingly protected and jealously guarded for so long that it took all of his personal resources to persuade his more conservative brothers and fellow abbots. He averred that sometimes he would get so exasperated that he felt completely bereft of brotherly love. He would cry out, 'You know, God, how hard it is to break with tradition, as Jesus himself found, yet surely they must realize that it is our duty to share this art, wisdom and knowledge with all mankind.' You all know what I would have done, and I think perhaps this was in his mind as well – just bang all their heads together!" The Prime Minister amply demonstrated this, strong hands slapping with a "smack", garnished with a chuckle.

"It was natural for me to think of the obvious parallels between his colleagues' position, and that of the British Museum. I had hoped to be as persuasive here, as he was there, but it was not to be. Perhaps if I had sent him instead – he would certainly make a great ambassador.

"So we made our agreement along the financial and contractual lines set out by Spiros here, and funded in part by his foundation, together with the British Museum, and certain private and government sources in both countries.

"Among the details, on the question of transportation, he confessed to me a distrust of flying, which he related to his being a man of caution. He remarked whimsically that he did not believe in asking too much of the good Lord. Therefore it was necessary to agree that the treasures would be transported by ship and land. 'If it was good enough for our Lord, it should be good enough for our beloved treasures.' He knew air crashes were rare, but he still felt he could not take the risk or responsibility." The Prime Minister illustrated a series of further unspoken details with a circular, continuous "and so on" gesture with his right hand.

"I agreed to this condition without any difficulty." He shrugged in an ironic gesture, "And as we now know, this requirement has proven to be a useful one for us in our enterprise.

"I gather that he will be present here for at least a short time during the exhibition, and if he comes he will be a guest of this Embassy. I do hope that you will have the opportunity to meet him at that time."

The Prime Minister shook hands again all around. As they filed out the door he remembered something else he had intended to say, and with the handshakes, added, somewhat wistfully, "You know, behind that gaunt, grey bewhiskered face, there was much compassion and wisdom. As we parted, I felt refreshed, and found myself saying so personally to God, speaking to Him for the first time in that way in a long time."

Chapter 16

Better than a Page in the *Times*

It pays to Advertise.

Helena dove and dipped the helicopter over and around the hills of the South Downs, turned east over Brighton, then along the coast, skimming low over the waves, dodging around headlands and the odd fishing boat. It had taken Spiros a few breathless minutes at the beginning of the flight to come to terms with Helena's amazing idea and unexpected new talents.

They had lifted up and free of the private airfield near Redhill, and within sight of the great international airport at Gatwick. Air traffic control had directed her under the flight path of incoming jets, which screamed across their trajectory only a few hundred feet above. His white knuckles gradually relaxed as he decided that if their lives ended then and there, it would have been worth it for her priceless surprise of this bright morning. He still couldn't quite believe that Helena had learned to fly such a craft during a single late summer – this trip her repayment, as she put it to him, for his long weekend on the yacht and then in his fisherman's shack.

Helena giggled like a schoolgirl as she spun the craft in a dancer's pirouette around a large yacht making for sea, everyone on board waving delightedly. As she left the boat behind, she tightened the spiral to a spin. Only a helicopter could perform this aerobatic display. A pair of white knuckles reappeared, "Yippee!"

The penthouse suite on top of an apartment block overlooked the town of Hastings on Sea and the English Channel beyond. The sky was blue, the ocean grey, streaked with an endless series of incoming waves riding slowly shoreward over the gradually shallowing sands below. It wasn't the light of Greece, or their beloved wine dark sea, yet it was beautiful in its own, silvery way. Spiros hugged Helena to him, turned and kissed her long enough to make at least a down payment on their three month separation.

Later they walked on the beach with arms around each other, struggling awkwardly to keep their balance in the shifting shingle.

They selected a small seafood house on the shore. Helena ordered the crab special for two, and they spent the evening looking repeatedly into each other's eyes, while carefully cracking the shells and extracting the tiny morsels of edible food with the tweezers solicitously provided by the management. After this further exercise, Spiros came up with a fresh revelation. "I've bought fifteen minutes on Channel 4, and we're going to tell the story of the Elgins!"

He explained, "Well, the Prime Minister's negotiations have failed, and so, we're going ahead on the other front. Maybe we can influence public opinion. After all, we don't want to be hunted as criminals for the rest of our lives, do we? Neither do we want the Greek position, nor our motivations to be misunderstood."

"That must have cost a bundle."

"Not as much as you might think, and it beats a page in the *Times*."

"I suspect they wouldn't publish it. Did you read their recent editorial on the subject?"

"No, I didn't have that, I gather, dubious pleasure."

"The talk will be illustrated with film clips and photographs." Spiros was avidly keying his laptop computer. "I've got references from the Internet, together with that *Times* editorial you referred to last night. They make interesting background reading and source material."

"Are you going to talk like a Greek, or an Englishman?"

Spiros raised two bushy eyebrows. "Just be myself, I think. It all hinges on rapport; can I take them with me back to sunny Greece, the rightful home of the Parthenon Marbles."

"I can look over the draft, if you agree. I might spot something."

"Any time, my love and light, any time."

Helena had made only a few changes. The prompter roll that Spiros had framed up on the computer looked good, but much would depend on how he presented it. He agreed to make some dry runs with Helena as judge and jury, and it did improve. When she sensed it had been enough, she held up a decisive hand and said so. "Too much prep might spoil it. You were right, be yourself, and just *feel* it flow. When is this grand event?"

"This Sunday evening, prime time, after the 7PM news."

"Hmm," Helena considered, "could be a good time."

"I have booked four more repeats using the tape, at various times suggested by the program director. I think we have the waterfront covered, from a British viewpoint on the media impact."

Helena shook her head again. "Must have cost a bundle."

"Well, my love, they are priceless, are they not?"

"Yes." She spoke softly, nestling her head under Spiros' chin.

"So the *Return versus Risk* equation of our beloved and much respected Charon, is infinity over a big risk, and if I remember my mathematics class all those years ago, that's still infinite. Hell, what does it matter? Who will know who we were a thousand years from now, or a hundred?"

"Well, Spiro, we know the names of Pericles, and Pheidias, and they lived 2,500 years ago. We know Aristophanes, and Sophocles from that time, and Homer after three thousand. Who is to say they won't know our names as restorers of that tradition to Greece?"

Spiros had a distant look in his eyes, but it was not from the perhaps selfish thoughts he had right after Helena first made the proposal. At this moment he was picturing the beatific facial transformation that would come to their Prime Minister as The Marbles were trundled up the curving, cypress-lined road leading to the new Acropolis Museum.

Dear Britain: Please Restore our Pride

Spiros Anguelopoulos: Channel 4
Prompter Roll
Timing 15 Minutes

You may be unaware that the British Museum, supported by the government, is holding the bulk of the sculptures made nearly 2,500 years ago, to decorate the Parthenon in Athens, which stands high on a hill, the Acropolis, above Athens, and is refusing to negotiate their possible repatriation to their homeland, my country, Greece, the so-called Elgin, or Parthenon Marbles.

[Film Clip scanning the Parthenon and Acropolis of Athens]
They argue that if the Parthenon sculptures were returned, it would set an unacceptable precedent so that the great museums of the world would have to return all their treasures to their countries of origin.

[Computer Simulation of the Parthenon as it was in antiquity]

This argument does not apply, because these Marbles are an inseparable part of the Parthenon as a structure, and make up the other half of the existing decorative sculptures. It is as though the stained glass windows had been removed from St. Paul's Cathedral for display in Athens. I submit that the Parthenon Marbles are a special case, and cannot be equated to such things as Egyptian sarcophagi, mummies, tablets or Easter Island monoliths – and not even with such unique Greek masterpieces as the Winged Victory of Samothrace or the Venus of Milos, which are properly held in museums outside Greece.

[Show comparison of St. Paul's with and without stained glass.]
In all save a tiny handful of exceptions of which the Elgin Marbles are perhaps the premier example, museum holdings are small, separable displays of objects from large classes. It does not matter to Greece, nor should it matter to any other country, if examples of local artefacts are scattered around the world. On the contrary, the presentation of cultures other than our own is a principal task of any national museum, and benefits the source country and its cultural heritage.

[Thousands of mummies, rooms full of Egyptian sarcophagi]
I could speak for a long time about the architectural wonders of the Parthenon as a building. Suffice to say that it was decorated with 160 metres (500 feet) of bas-relief, cut by the greatest sculptor of ancient times, Pheidias, and his school of artists. Excepting perhaps Angkor Wat in Cambodia, this is the largest and longest sculpture of its kind ever executed, and it dates nearly 2,500 years in our past, whereas Angkor is less than 1,000. It can be argued, and I do assert that the Acropolis, or the High City of Athens was the first major example of what we refer to today as Western Architecture. The city it floated above on the clouds, as it seems to do on some mornings as I view it from my flat, was the inventor of what has evolved over the centuries into western culture and our democratic traditions. The United Kingdom guarded this tradition, with others, during our dark centuries in Greece under foreign domination. We should honour both, the foundation, and the perpetuation, and my country stands ready to hold and exhibit this unique testimony to these principles, in the sculpted stone of Greece, returned home to their birthplace.

[Repeat of Parthenon as it was showing pedimental sculptures]
The history is truly fascinating. The Parthenon with all of its artistic decorations, unequalled in the history of the world, was completed in

211

the fifth century BC. We know the monument and its sculptures survived intact until at least 1674 when the French artist Jacques Carrey spent two weeks drawing it all. Tragically, more than half of the Parthenon and its treasures were blasted to smithereens during the bombardment by the Venetian general Franscesco Morosini in 1687, which was all the more reprehensible because he knew the Turks were storing gunpowder inside.

[Painting of Elgin, Drawing of Treasures being carted off]

Thomas Bruce, seventh Earl of Elgin, was appointed British ambassador at Constantinople in 1799 after serving as envoy in Brussels and Berlin. Britain had fought to kick Napoleon out of Turkey, which then governed Greece, so relations were good and a *firman*, which simply means a permit, was issued to Lord Elgin, empowering him to remove as many treasures from Greece as his ships could carry. The Royal Navy sailors spent the next twenty years doing so, first under Elgin, and then a host of other British officials. Lord Elgin carried off not half, as we hear from authorities here, but *all* of the sculptures, and metopes, that he could find or bring down from the building. All of the original frieze blocks (metopes) currently in Athens were those that were buried under the rubble from the disaster of 1687, later recovered by the Greek authorities. Fortunately, he didn't have enough ships, and a part of the Greek heritage remained in Athens and elsewhere, but not because of any self-imposed limitation. As for the claims that Elgin was a conservationist, note that he visited Delos in 1802 and removed an exquisite altar from that sacred place. It can now be seen in the ancestral home of the Elgins in Scotland.

[Fantasized drawings of the Houses of Parliament looted]

It is as though, during a time when Britain was at war, and you have had them, some other country, say Elandria, had carried off all or most of the decorative and some of the structural elements of London, including half the windows of the Houses of Parliament, and all the significant items from Westminster Abbey, St Paul's and a dozen other buildings, throwing Stonehenge in for good measure – all of this now standing semi-naked for tourists to gawk at. "Look what is left of London after the Elandrians finished with it." And further imagine that the altar of Canterbury cathedral was now a side table in the family home of Lord Elandria. Our War of Independence that broke out in 1821, finally put an end to Elgin's depredations, which had filled a total of 253 cases dispatched to London.

[Show stacks of cases on a dockside]
The polemics have got out of hand. The British Museum claims that they have prevented the effects of weathering that have afflicted the sculptures that remained on the Parthenon. The British "conservation" can be seen as inferior by anyone who takes the time to look.

[Drawing of Elgins in coal shed dripping black water]
My countrymen have also made false claims, now withdrawn, including that Elgin lost 14 cases of objects in a shipwreck while transporting them to England. That is not true, for he salvaged them at his own expense. In London, however, he exhibited them in appalling conditions in a garden shed, and then later they were stored in a coal shed for years, suffering the rapacious British climate. In 1816 he finally persuaded the British Parliament to purchase them from him for today's equivalent of several million pounds, and they have rested in the British Museum since.

[Contemporary painting of the Sultan bidding Elgin goodbye
        on the dock in Greece with baubles in hand]
The British arguments against returning the Marbles include:

First: they were bought legitimately from the Turks on the basis of a legal document (the Sultan's firman). The purchase "price" was paid in baubles of no great value. In any case, it is not legal to purchase treasures from an occupying force and move them to a third country. This principle is today forcing the return of art objects looted during the Second World War, so there is ample legal precedent.

[Mona Lisa, Winged Victory, and Venus de Milo cut in two.]
[Photographs of the cut-damaged Elgins in the British Museum]
Second: that they were removed to save them from total destruction. We have seen that this is not a defensible position. Elgin was interested in them for himself, and only asked for the government to take them off his hands because he wanted to get his money back on them, and could see that they were deteriorating under his care. That is the only good thing I can bring myself to say about him in this connection. He also damaged many, and imagine this, he cut priceless sculptures in half to facilitate transport, and gave little heed to the stability of buildings from which he removed structural elements such as a statue supporting the roof of a building.

[Photograph of damaged Erechtheum with missing caryatid –
        looking like a mouth without a front tooth.]

[Close up of Spiros' face]
Third: that the Greeks didn't care about their ancient treasures. Documented reports from the time, made on the spot, flatly contradict that assertion, one that is self-serving in the extreme.

[Show contemporary drawing of Greeks wailing at the quayside]
Fourth: lately since air pollution has come to Athens, it is suggested that they are better off now in London. That is not a fair statement of the history, or the effects, as can be easily verified. Both countries now have excellent conditions in which to display them.

[Close up of Spiros' face]
I call here tonight for all parties to this acrimonious dispute to stop the diatribes, and talk sense. That is one purpose of my appearance here, and I hope that all of you in the audience will accept my good faith.

[Show pictures of politicians who promised the repatriation]
This has become a political football – I regret to say in my own country as well as here. Successive British governments, beginning in modern times during World War Two have promised, and then retracted promises, to repatriate the Parthenon Marbles to Greece. Some of you will remember Melina Mercouri, the noted Greek actress and singer, and for a time our minister of culture, who obtained a United Nations mandate for their return (ignored by Britain) and devoted much of her later life to this quest. I follow proudly and humbly in her footsteps. I, and our Prime Minister, have had both public and private discussions recently with the highest officials in the British government. The British position is presently adamant against repatriation. Will this change tomorrow? Can it be reversed in the future, as it has been several times in the past?

[Melina Mercouri singing, then her before UNESCO committee]
You can make your voice heard, by voting on your screen to this television network, by telephone, mobile messaging, e-mail, and the Internet via this station's site. All of this information is now on your screen. Let us have a democratic solution to an inequity that stains the links between ancient Greece, and the Modern Democratic principles enshrined in the United Kingdom, the EU, Greece, and many others.

[Show contact points on screen]
The British Museum authorities have in effect suggested that the copies they generously permitted us to make "should do for the Greeks." I suggest it is the other way around. The copies, exact

copies recently made, should do for the British Museum. We can now make further copies for other museums around the world, so shouldn't the originals be allowed to rejoin their brothers and sisters, under the warm sky and bright sun of their own country, the birthplace of Western Civilization and Democracy?

[Show clip of copies being made in British Museum workshop]
My words are weak and cannot begin to reflect the true feelings of us Greeks, or the deep significance of these treasures. Perhaps those of a few others can compensate, and I would like to close with them.

[Spiros' face alternating with his hands full of expression]
The noted British artist Benjamin Robert Haydon was so thrilled by his first encounter with them that he said: "The sight of the sculptures, together with the thought that the eyes of Socrates and Plato had seen them, fascinatcd mc. I felt I was conquered by a passion to understand the depth of the divine art of the Greeks."

The mature sculptor Canova exclaimed: "Oh that I had but to begin again! To unlearn all that I had learned – I now at last see what ought to form the real school of sculpture."

Alexander Rangavis, standing under the eastern pediment of the Parthenon, on May 12, 1842, put it far better than I: "What would Europe say, atremble, if one should find a drawing by Raphael or Apelles and, unable to carry it all away, should cut off the legs or the head of that work of art? If England, the friend of valiant deeds, cannot carry this entire temple to her soil and, with it, the deep blue sky under which this all-white monument stands, and cannot carry the transparent air which bathes the temple and the brilliant sun that gilds it – if England cannot carry all those things to her far-northern climate then, just as kings and commoners formerly sent humble tokens of worship to the Parthenon and the Acropolis, so should England send us, as a token of reverence to the cradle of civilization, the temple's jewels which were snatched from it and lie now, far away and of little value, while the temple itself remains truncated and formless."

And finally, as your own Lord Byron, a tower of strength in our War for Independence said: "The sea-ruling Britannia snatched the last spoils of Greece."

Thank you.

"Spiros, I'm convinced, and I wasn't beforehand. Great job, and I mean that sincerely." The program director slapped him on the back, shaking his hand warmly.

Truth to say, Spiros had enjoyed his performance, and it was both natural, and effective. His voice ranged across all of his registers, from whispers to draw the audience closer, in full attention to perhaps the less interesting yet vital details, through the softly spoken penultimate peroration of Alexander Rangevis, to a monumentally booming voice to drive home the emotional moments. He knew these were the most important in any debate. Forget the facts, after you have heard them, but then accept their impact on one, lone human being, to feel the personal punch that changes hearts, and when the heart moves the mind usually follows.

The team had watched intently, but didn't come to *feel* the full impact until they relaxed into viewing it a second, third, fourth, and fifth time. It was bittersweet for Helena, for again Spiros was not with her. Adam first admired the logical arguments, and then felt them in his heart. Peter saw himself as a crusader standing beside Spiros as they fought off the infidel hordes (all English Roundheads), and then carried their spoils of victory back up the Acropolis. Irini had fallen in love with Spiros, and on the last repetition, knelt down and kissed his fading image on the screen.

The reception of the first broadcast at large in the country was muted, if it was at all detectable. Yet the advertising director at Channel 4 had been right, and it had received a significant audience, few switching off, captured by the sheer presence of Spiros, the Greek. He had been introduced as a "Greek industrialist, and philanthropist." That didn't cut much ice with the masses, at least not on the first hearing.

Nevertheless, in pubs and coffee corners all over the realm, those who had seen it often asked their colleagues if they had also. The answer was usually in the negative, so they then continued with something like, "Well, I didn't know we had stolen the treasures of Greece, did you?"

"For the what did you say?"

"The British Museum."

"What's that, mate?"

"A place we keep stolen treasures, I guess."

"This Greek guy said all that, on telly?"

"Sure did, and he meant it, sincerely."

"He's on again tonight."

"When?"

"Just before the Monday Night film."

"Oh, yes, I'm up for that film. I'll try to catch this geezer."

"Salt of the earth if ever I met one, on the telly anyway."

The papers gave small notices at first, except the *Times*, annoyed that he had overcalled their thunder from a recent editorial. It was noticed on the front page, with a large spread at the bottom of page 12, with an unattractive picture of Spiros, and a cartoon in questionable taste. Almost everyone who read this diatribe against Spiros, the "mad Greek" as they put it, took the time to see for themselves, so it backfired. The cartoon appeared on office bulletin boards all over the country often noting his next appearance.

The Harris poll published weekly samples. The percentage who know what the Elgins were went from 17% before, to 87% after, and the percentage favouring return went from 13% to 72%.

Spiros had most certainly not claimed that they were stolen treasures being held in the museum. He had been at pains to tell something of both sides of the story, and to offer a real alternative in the form of the copies. His candour was one of the reasons why most believed him, yet he understood that people tend to simplify to an absurdity most of the arguments they are confronted with, whether political, or on the sports page. In this case it had worked a miracle, for nobody had expected any such avalanche of public interest, or this transformation in awareness and opinion.

All agreed that Spiros' investment had been well worth it, and the Greek Prime Minister and others were pleased that a little extra political insurance had been purchased so effectively by one of their own, speaking in a foreign country, to a potentially hostile audience.

Spiros was invited to speak before the Oxford Union. He fit it into a final weekend with Helena before returning to Greece, and then on *Hard Talk* with Tim Sebastian, who exceptionally came to him to conduct the interview inside the Parthenon itself, as the Athenian sun set to provide all the warm light the camera needed.

Geoffrey Hayward declined to be interviewed on a subsequent program, probably a wise decision. The British Prime Minister faced repeated questioning everywhere he went, and at Question Time in Parliament for good measure. The Minister of Culture was more forthcoming, and stated that Spiros was correct in his assertion that the British had vacillated back and forth a dozen times, and he hoped that the issue might be resolved peacefully in the foreseeable future.

The Prime Minister of Greece and his ministers held their counsel, feeling anything they might say would only serve to deflect attention from Spiros' grand success.

Chapter 17

Enter The Real Villains

The unseen enemy is potentially the most frightening.

The Prime Minister of Britain was beside himself with frustration. He had more important things on his mind than, "A lousy stack of marbles gathering dust in a museum that everyone was fighting over like schoolchildren."

His Culture Minister, Robert Goodwin, pointed out to him that they were, in fact important, to Greece at least, and had, "Ahem, caught the public imagination."

The Foreign Secretary added that though Greece was a co-member of the European Union, it was still necessary to curry favour whenever possible, or at least to avoid giving overt offence.

The Chancellor added, in the haughty manner demanded by his self-image as the most important mandarin in government, "It is also a matter of trade, as my esteemed colleagues are implying."

"So what do we do about it?"

"Nothing, Prime Minister, for the moment anyway." Robert Goodwin's advice was sound, yet the Prime Minister chose to override it – not in front of the cabinet – but by the back door.

Sir Robert Mansfield, head of MI5, the British intelligence service, entered the conference room of Number Ten Downing Street, and made the long walk to the Prime Minister at the centre of the table. "Prime Minister, good to see you. What can I do for you?"

Sir Robert was a natty man of medium stature, who moved with assurance in any situation. He was arguably the most athletic person in senior government circles, and this had well preserved his late-forties physique. Few knew he had had a hair *removal*, and his oblong, perfectly formed head was one of the rare ones that could sensibly wear a Yul Brenner. He felt that it added to his special brand of mysterious *gravitas*. Those who had crossed him in any way, and suffered his wrath, later spelled that last word with "ss" at the end, and a hyphen after the "t". He was not a man to be trifled with, and by equal token, could be relied on absolutely, in matters both open, and clandestine.

His fine, aquiline nose twitched in anticipation, a thin smile emphasizing the small dimple in his sharp chin. He held the Prime Minister with yellow-green eyes until his opposite number broke off eye contact.

"I am concerned about the Elgin Marbles, Sir Robert. They are becoming a thorn in my side. What can we do about that?"

Sir Robert and his predecessors stretching back to at least 1066 had been approached in exactly this way, several times in each reign, by the monarch or minister of the day. The translation was clear. "Do something, do it now, do it effectively, and don't tell me or anybody else any more than we need to know, preferably nothing at all." It had the same implication as the historical outburst of Henry II, "Who will rid me of this tiresome priest?" Thomas a Beckett didn't last the week.

"Priority?"

"High enough, Sir Robert. This has cost me ten points off my popularity rating," he replied petulantly, "all from nothing."

"It happens. Prime Minister." Sir Robert turned, and left the room.

Sir Robert *directly* instructed one of his younger agents to give the British Museum a twice over. "Find out if there are any Greek nationals working there, check them out, find their associates, and open a dossier with all the basics. Then we'll look it over and have a little chat. The codename is PMBM."

The young junior agent, John Fiske, knew that a direct instruction from the top man meant to keep it between them, on the severest penalties. Normally he would receive his instructions from his Section Chief or by simple memorandum. So this was special. It did strike him as odd, though, because the stuffy old British Museum was the last place in which he would have expected such a special assignment. He did understand why he had been selected for the task, holding as he did his first degree in archaeology, followed unusually with a master's in criminology. Fellow students, and his girl friend at the time, now his wife and MI5 colleague, had teased him: "So, what are you pointing for, a top-class career rooting-out crooks from the depths of archaeological digs?" It was through his wife's interviews in MI5 that he had been drawn into the net himself.

"So what's first," he asked himself, then shrugged, and decided that he would go and see the Elgin Marbles. They had been in the news recently, and were certainly part of the Greek question. It had been a long time, and he did remember having a fondness for them, despite preferring modern sculpture.

She, a vision of loveliness, was lecturing a gaggle of school children, and John couldn't take his eyes off of her. And no ring, he assured himself. He therefore determined to wait until she was free, and try to obtain her personal services as a private guide. Meanwhile, he circled the Duveen Gallery, with a side trip to see the pedimental statuary in the alcove. He missed the departure of the group, and so had to rush across the long room to catch up with her before she disappeared from his life forever through a door marked "staff only".

"Hello," he opened breathlessly, "I've been waiting for you, hoping you could answer a few questions for me about the Marbles. My name is John Fiske." He put out his hand to shake hers.

Irini instantly grasped the whole picture. She was a practiced master of the polite, eventual brush-off, and followed the well-worn pattern: first courtesy, then minimum contact without appearing to be brusque, finally the disengagement.

"Well, what questions do you have?" Her voice plucked at his heartstrings as though she were playing them with her fingers embedded in his chest. A horrible thought creased his face – she had noticed – but not understood – he hadn't prepared a question.

This was not the moment to stumble, so he made one up from his last thought before this lady had erased all the others with her smile. "I noticed that some of the, what do you call them, the square bas reliefs, were roughly cut in half, not broken, but cut. Why was that?"

"When they were taken from Greece by Lord Elgin, early in the nineteenth century, he felt he had to cut some of them in order to make them easier to move. Did you notice that most of the statuary in the far gallery had been cut to pieces?"

"Come to think of it, yes I did." In this he was being entirely truthful. "My name is John, and yours?"

"Irini Baynes," but she punctuated it with a shrug of indifference, enough that this fellow should begin to get the message. He did, but that had never stopped him before, married or not.

"Miss Baynes, you will join me for tea in the coffee shop, please?" This was his way, a command rather than a question, and the only approach that could have set her off balance.

"I'm sorry … Mister Fiske, was it, but among other things I am engaged." It was more than wearing thin, especially without a ring.

He glanced at her left hand, and raised his eyebrows. He was a very attractive man in manner and physique. His natural blond curly hair, sharp facial features, and whip-strong arms were clearly visible in his short-sleeved shirt, the biceps alternately tensioning and relaxing unconsciously as he held her eyes for an answer. He was impeccably dressed, the shirt freshly starched with a horizontal striped motif that emphasized his chest, deep blue creased slacks, and black leather shoes that reflected the statues they were standing next to.

"Uh, ah, yes, *secret* you see."

"Well, until you put his ring on, I'm in the game." He was a clever man in both this, and his profession. He realized that it was not on just now, so he retreated gracefully, avoiding her inevitable final *no* by not opening himself to it, thus surviving to fight for her another day. "I will hope for more next time. Miss Baynes, I am most deeply charmed." He bowed, and as her hand automatically moved out a fraction, he took it and kissed it, holding her long, sensual fingers between his thumb and forefinger ever so lightly, and then allowed them to slip through to freedom at her side.

CONFIDENTIAL MEMORANDUM PMBM 1.0 Encrypted

FROM John Fiske TO Sir Robert Mansfield

PERSONNEL DOSSIERS:

Irini Baynes, junior curator, 4 months there, mother Greek,
    father Welsh. Chose UK Nationality at age 18
    Recently cleared of spurious charges, tight with director
    and supervisor. No reason for suspicion.
No other permanent Greek connections on staff.
    Two readers visiting from Greece on two-week
    assignments. No reason to suspect
Trace on Irini Baynes' Friends and Associates:
    Adam Blix, USA national, consultant on copying Elgin
    Marbles. Assigned to museum. Friend (fiancé?)
        Imperial College, writing PhD thesis
        Member of Quantum Computer development team IC
        No reason for suspicion

Peter Ryan, UK national
    LSE in last year of Trade Union Studies.
    Apparent friend of above
Helena Katsis, Greek national
    No museum connection. Apparent friend of above.
    Reading Social Anthropology at the LSE for PhD
Note: They seem to meet often as a foursome.
    Romantic or illicit connection is possible
    I sense they are security conscious, e.g. "dropping tails".
Recommendation: Light surveillance of all four.
Conclusion: I don't see a way to compromise them,
    yet one never knows.

ATTACHMENTS

Doctor Geoffrey Hayward welcomed Irini into his office, and cordially invited her to sit down in a comfortable leather armchair, one of six in his office. It was panelled with what appeared to be old mahogany with some of the most beautiful bookcases Irini had ever seen. She passed her hand along one of them as she came around the antique boardroom table to take the proffered chair.

"Miss Baynes, I have read your report on communication with our younger visitors. To understand that you did most of the actual drafting in a single evening is impressive, and the report reads very well even had I thought you might have spent much longer on it."

"Thank you Doctor Hayward."

"'Geoffrey' will do between us."

Irini thought about this for a moment, then took another short pause before answering. She didn't want to make the same blunder as with Potterton. "I am sorry, but I think I would find that uncomfortable, in the sense that others senior to me do refer to you as 'Doctor Hayward'. Can we compromise on that? I do respect you, all the more so for your eminently fair hearing. A lesser man might have made an easier decision."

"Certainly, I understand. I was not trying in any way to establish an informal relationship."

"I appreciate, and accept that, Doctor Hayward, thank you."

"My point is that I would like to suggest, if you agree, that you expand your report into a full set of recommendations. If these seem workable, as I expect they will, we shall consider implementing them over a period of time. I feel that we could improve in that area. Your view that many children leave here with little more than a good time – nothing wrong with that as it opens the door to more – but we seem to have failed to show them out the door with at least one important *question* in their mind. I do so agree with you that these are far more important than facts. With a question niggling away in their little heads, many answers can follow."

"I am pleased that you share my views on using the discovery method in teaching, to answer a question more often with another, rather than a sterile or unconnected fact that will soon be forgotten."

"Exactly, and you put that so well in the report. Are you interested in this suggestion?"

"I am most certainly."

"Then you are authorized to devote two hours, one half of a floor-shift, to this every day, and your assignment register will reflect the fact. Any further thoughts?"

An idea suddenly surfaced, and Irini replied, "Yes, indeed. As I will be making suggestions that may ultimately relate to staff, some of whom I do not know well, or are unaware of, would it be permissible for me to have access to general personnel records? It might help me achieve perspective on what would work, and what might not."

He was impressed by this thought, one that a person ultimately destined for management might have at this stage in her career. "That is a splendid idea. I will arrange for you to have full access on your computer in the museum, to the professional half of our database."

Irini couldn't believe her luck, both in thinking of the idea, and the director's alacrity in granting it. It was obvious to the whole team that access to internal records could prove critical, and she determined to seize any such opportunities the moment they arose.

Irini literally danced her way back home that afternoon, the last dark shades of the past month receding into the distance. Stepping on all the cracks in the pavements, she delighted once again in a little game she had played from time to time following the debacle of Potty Potterton, singing to herself in time with her footfalls:

Pu-si-llani-mous Pot-ty Potter-ton Pissed Pro-fuse-ly, Pit-ter Pat-ter-ingly, Ping Pong, Prox-i-mate-ly Pre-po-sess-ing-ly, Per-func-torially Past-a Pot!

Irini did not notice that the object of her scorn was following along behind in a cheap disguise, growing angrier with every slap-slap of her musically cadenced footsteps.

Chapter 18

A Stone's Throw South of the River

Friends who are unseen are often the most useful.

Hayward wanted to keep Potterton's dismissal as hush-hush as possible, so decided on a quiet internal promotion. Thus he chose Miss Emily Stone, D. Phil Oxon without a shred of hesitation.

When Irini heard the good news about her new supervisor, she reported back cheerfully to Adam. He knew that this appointment would help Irini to regain her confidence.

Emily turned out to be far less parchment-like than at first sight, and distinctly less ascetic. Though shy on first contact, with eyes that often sought the walls or looked away when speaking, there was a definite humorous twinkle there. Her greying hair was tied in a bun, as if she were afraid that its unruly waves would get out of control.

Irini entered her office one day, surprised to find her new supervisor smiling broadly and uttering the occasional chuckle. "Dear me," she laughed to herself, "I don't blame you."

She reluctantly returned to this century, looked up and said to Irini, "You can't imagine what humour there is in some eighth century manuscripts. These monks," she tapped the parchment meaningfully, "were obviously fed up with Bishop Wilfred of Ripon's officious, intrusive visitations, so they passed secret messages to one another, sometimes erotic cartoons, interspersed with the traditional devices in this beautiful illuminated Gospel. I am wondering if I shouldn't write a short monograph for the *Gay Times* magazine! I would probably have done the same if I had lived under the good bishop's stern rule, and I cannot help but feel a certain camaraderie with one or two of the better cartoonists."

Irini had stood mute for a moment at this unexpected side to her supervisor's personality. "Was the good bishop himself possibly suspect, perhaps with one or two of the more comely monks?"

She replied pensively, tongue visibly in-cheek. "Well, I don't *yet* have enough evidence against him to take to court, but I always suspect the overly self righteous types."

"Well, as you know, that has been an experience of mine recently."

Irini and Adam had agreed to invite her for dinner at Irini's flat, and it had been arranged for the next evening, immediately after work because the round trip to Emily's Hounslow home was too long.

Emily appeared at the door, promptly at seven as invited, with a beautiful bunch of dahlias in vibrant, wild colours. "They are from my garden and I have managed to keep them fresh all day." She also produced two bottles of good Chilean wine, which she hoped would lubricate their tongues and promote a lively exchange of views, the kind of evening that she most enjoyed.

Emily looked quite different from work, rejuvenated in an elegant three-quarter length cream silk tunic over a slim skirt of turquoise blue. As Irini warmly welcomed her guest, and introduced her to Adam, her eyes were riveted on Emily's jewellery. The necklace was shown to great advantage against the cream silk, and the bracelet was in matching style. They were intricate, interlocking circular shapes that spoke of a different age and culture, one that Irini only dimly recognized.

"My jewellery, yes, I put it on tonight as I knew it would interest you, my dear. They are copies of eighth century Celtic originals, and were a present from the Trustees of the St Gallen library, for some voluntary work I performed there." She added by way of explanation, more to Adam than to her young colleague, "St Gallen is a library in Switzerland, where I spent a wonderful summer working on their eighth century monastic manuscripts, including a number carried there from Britain by Celtic missionaries."

From this, Irini foresaw an invigorating evening, with wave upon wave of enthusiastic erudition from all sides, each person eager to contribute his or her favourite anecdotes, and equally willing to listen.

Adam served the wine while Emily ensconced herself. She chose the red and stuck with it throughout the evening.

Emily also appreciated and practiced good cooking, and had immediately detected mouth-watering aromas of Mediterranean herbs emanating from the kitchen area. She smiled to herself as she had anticipated this choice of cuisine, and was a woman who, despite her slender build, could hold her food, and as it would transpire, her wine, perhaps slightly less well.

The dinner was served informally at the small table, the customary Greek *mezes*, with several small dishes crowding the

227

table. Each of them was able to choose whatever took their fancy. Emily had not had very many traditional Greek meals, and was fascinated by this custom, which she averred reminded her of the Indonesian. She promised them to return the favour with such a meal at her home. She always enjoyed the opportunity to escape from her parchments and immerse herself in preparing that favourite cuisine of hers for guests. Both agreed to this with genuine enthusiasm.

The wine loosened all tongues, and each of them could not resist making entertaining contributions from their different backgrounds.

Irini related how she had become interested in classical Greek sculpture, partly because of her parentage. Adam then took his turn, entering fulsomely into the mysterious world of Quantum Mechanics. He got so carried away that Irini finally felt she had to kick him under the table.

The two women smiled indulgently, knowing how easy it was to get over animated when talking about one's own subject.

Then Emily found herself, in answer to Adam's polite question, waxing lyrical on her own specialty. She thought to herself happily, "This is so much better than a bunch of academics – one can really let rip! And speak one's mind, because people really want to know."

"Yes," she began, "I am a Bede specialist, the Venerable Bede, as he is popularly known. He was such an innovator as an historian."

She warmed to her theme, shedding all of her usual mannerisms of shyness. "The *Mills and Boon* of his day – the popular hagiographies – were not his cup of tea at all – silly potboilers most of them, ascribing one incredible miracle after another to the most unlikely of pseudo saints.

"No, Bede wrote in the serious style of the great Greek historians, who quoted their sources, tried to verify their facts, and said so when they were not sure. He was perhaps the first of our academic historians. His life's work was *The Ecclesiastical History of England*, completed in manuscript shortly before his death in 735. This work was not equalled in the field for several centuries thereafter."

Adam blinked, trying manfully to assimilate this outpouring from the byways of the eighth century, so long before the founding of the American Republic as to be for him, on first acquaintance, prehistoric.

"So, Emily, you are saying this man was a class act, and ahead of his time."

"Indeed, Adam, and I like your Americanism cast in his direction. I certainly agree with you, that he was ahead of his time."

With glasses recharged, she continued indefatigably, with a toast, "To the Venerable Bede, a Class Act." And without missing a beat, continued, "My passion in the seventh and eighth centuries doesn't stop at Bede's history. Take the Lindisfarne Gospels, for example. Originating from a tiny tide-washed island off the coast of Northumberland, these are the most exquisite Celtic illuminated manuscripts of all time."

Without the slightest pause, she proffered her wrist. "In fact, my jewellery is an attempt to copy the same style, which frequently repeats itself in the margins and in the magnificent leading capital letters at the beginning of each section. As you know, most visitors to the museum have never heard of them. So," smiling at Adam, "you can be forgiven if as an American you do not know them. I would venture the opinion that they are the most important treasures from these British islands."

She continued, now in such full flood that she could sip the wine without interrupting herself. Irini and Adam exchanged wry glances. "There's something else I have very strong feelings about. You see the Lindisfarne Gospels have not been stolen or removed like the Parthenon Marbles that Irini loves so much. I believe every country should guard its own unique treasures, and in situ if possible. Accessibility is not the problem it was, given modern transport, for people fly everywhere these days."

She waved an eloquent hand as if she was personally transporting them on magic carpets.

Adam managed to slip in, "And those who can't travel can access them via the Internet these days; they've even got live cameras at some of the better venues."

Emily raised her eyebrows questioningly to Adam. "I have heard about the 'net', but really, it's a bit of a closed book to me."

"I hope you'll let me give you a guided tour one day. It's quite an effective research tool. But beyond that, it can be a good way to exchange ideas with colleagues, and for circulating work to the widest possible specialist audience."

"I guard an open mind, so yes, Adam, with pleasure. So, You see," she resumed somewhat breathlessly, "I *know*, that museums all over the world have storerooms chock-a-block with artefacts they will never show. I think it's such a pity that they were taken in the first place, wrenched away from their birthplace." Her shyness had long since been overcome by passion as her voice rose animatedly. "Of course," she added more calmly, "I know the counter arguments used by museums."

During this outburst, Adam and Irini hadn't dared to look at one another, fearing that they might give something away.

Emily went on, "I can't say these things in my official capacity," finishing with a rush, "yet this is where my real sympathies lie." She paused, looking around the room, as though anxious that she might have been overheard. There came a sudden noise, "clack – thump".

"What's that?" Emily cried out in alarm.

The muscular Achilles emerged triumphantly from his exterior cat flap, with the blooded body of a fat Bloomsbury pigeon swinging to and fro in his mouth. He walked purposefully to Irini, and laid it at her feet.

"Ugh," breathed Emily, "is it dead?"

Irini took the matter in hand, and deftly dealt with the offending corpse, dropping it on Achilles' bird mat outside the door in the corridor between the flat's bed sit section, and her bathroom across the landing. "He knows if I put it there, he must deal with it himself. If he brings it in a second time, I throw it out. You *can* train cats."

Irini then set about making after dinner coffee, and the conversation continued agreeably on less controversial subjects.

When Emily set to leave, Adam offered to escort her down the stairs. Pausing on the landing, Emily noticed that the pigeon had been reduced to a scattering of feathers, and two feet only. "Irini," she asked faintly, "where's the rest of the pigeon?"

"When my Achilles eats a pigeon, he finishes the lot, beak, head, bones, and body. He usually leaves just the feet, and sometimes a small pile of grain, the contents of the bird's gizzard."

Emily stood in amazement as Achilles cleaned up, having indulged himself rather freely about the chops.

"Irini, Adam, I have very much enjoyed myself this evening, and again, I hope that you will be my guests in the not too distant future."

Adam left Emily in the hall downstairs, walked in a light drizzle up to the head of Museum Street, caught a taxi, and brought it back to the door for her. She waved goodbye, and the black cab swung around the corner, to disappear in the flashing lights of traffic, glistening in reflection on the mirrored pavements.

On his return to the flat, Irini expostulated, "Well! What a surprise. What a find."

Helena had suggested that Peter sound out his old mates, to ultimately form a trustworthy band for the actual loading of the Marbles. Adam had recently added that they would need a half-dozen or so false guards to impersonate some of the real ones during the lift.

Peter had made occasional forays to his old haunts to maintain contact with his friends. He had found it increasingly difficult to find the usual banter to fill in the pauses. So the task before him was a daunting one, when two years earlier it would have been easy and natural. He also saw that many of his former friends had in reality just been hangers on, and he had now shaken them off like a dog rids himself of the extra drops of water from a drenched coat.

Yet the real friends had stuck, like Trev. Trevor Green was ten years older than Peter, a trim figure due to his football refereeing in the amateur leagues. He had a round owlish face with wide set eyes, and a chirpy manner. He was a football fanatic with an incredible memory. This had been so useful in the old days at the warehouse, as well as for certain other jobs on the side. Peter smiled at the recollection. Trevor could recite all the players on all the teams for the last fifty years. He was eidetic as well and could put a name to every face, not only in football but anyone he had ever met or seen once in the pub.

Peter's visit to the Green Jug and Bottle was timed carefully to coincide with the end of the Big Match at Trev's local. They liked to watch them on a big screen in company with their mates because the spectatorship added to the excitement.

As he entered, Peter looked around for the old crowd. A few acknowledged him almost warily, but Trev made a beeline in his direction. His pleasure was unmistakable as he guided his buddy towards their favourite corner. Peter felt immediately reassured.

"Good to see you, Pete! Long time no see." Trev got him his usual half pint of Newcastle Brown without prompting, coming back with his own full pint of Guinness.

"So, how are things?" Trev asked, wiping the light touch of a foam moustache from his lips. "Keep you at it, at this college?"

Peter instinctively waved a dismissive hand yet admitted, "Yes, more work than I'd thought, and more difficult." Then he added sincerely, "But it's great, and I've no regrets."

Trev smiled with genuine pleasure to see Peter's satisfaction in what he plainly saw was a new life, bringing many changes.

"So, what do you get up to in your off duty, eh?" Trev continued his good-natured interrogation. "Nice bit of skirt, blond secretary, a swinging nurse perhaps?"

Peter smiled, and then a little ruefully, shook his head.

"Nothing?" Trev replied, with raised eyebrows.

"Well, not quite, *nothing*. There's this older lady, very sharp, in body and mind, and well..."

Trev continued for him, "Just a bit out of your league, eh?"

Peter leaned forward, confidentially, "Trev, there's something I need to tell someone. This is strictly between you and me?"

Trev did the same so eagerly that their heads actually touched.

"Well, I've achieved something that I never thought could happen. I've been learning to fly, and have my helicopter pilot's license."

Surprise was written squarely on Trev's face, presenting a comical visage. "Get away!" He flicked his fingers expressively, "Made a bit of a windfall, did we?"

"It's part of a job I have on the side. They paid for it."

"Well, good on you lad, so you'll be leading the Royal flight?" He teased with a wink.

Peter shrugged, "I'm not sure where this will lead."

Trev chuckled, "Good for a quick getaway, if you've got the readies for the chopper."

Peter was startled by Trev's remark being so close to the truth. "Again, strictly between us, if a little job came our way, would you..."

Peter interrupted in the affirmative, a glint from the old life lighting his eyes. "You know you don't have to ask."

"Actually I might need a dozen or so reliable mates, like you, really solid, you know what I mean."

Trev realized that the conversation had taken a completely different turn. This was business. "Well, there's my Jim, not a squeak out of him, you can depend on it." Trev said proudly. "He's my son, a strapping nightclub bouncer, with the family smarts, if you credit me there, and I could pull a few more like him. When for?"

"There's time, no rush, about six months from now."

"One of your little removal jobs, is it?" Trev murmured ironically.

"It's on the large side this time. Your Jim sounds just the job for it. But," he cautioned, "not for little old ladies, nuff said?"

"Good to keep the old hand in; never minded a bit of risk, spice of life."

"The memory as good as ever?" Peter asked.

"Try me," he smiled. "I'm in my prime, Peter me lad. No flies on me, and fighting fit." He patted his trim waistline.

"Still sharp on faces, then?" Peter added by way of clarification.

"I could sketch the lads from school as if it were yesterday."

"Good. If I gave you some pictures in a few weeks' time, could you find doubles for each of them, under the rose, part of the team?"

"Try me."

"I've got the readies for training as well; the old gym still there?"

"Alive and well – too many pen pushers for my taste – but okay."

"Might be a good idea to put everyone on a six month weight training program."

"As heavy as that?" Trev's eyes blinked owlishly.

Peter nodded. "And the money will be good, cash the same day, no shares, no afters, no problems."

"Count me in, Peter. Want another of your Browns, to go with the rest of mine?" Trev reached across and shook Peter's hand strongly.

Peter was relieved that it had gone so well. The old chemistry was still working between him and Trev at least.

Irini had not succeeded in avoiding at least an afternoon tea with the most persistent John Fiske. She had dreaded it the moment she had agreed to meet him there, but it had not turned out as badly as feared.

He mentioned his degree in archaeology, and they went on from there. He was knowledgeable about her beloved Elgin Marbles, and many other general areas in the field. Yet he had not given evidence of any special knowledge during their discussions. His background was apparently limited to that of a graduate who had not continued to grow in the profession. Furthermore, he had been cagey about his present job, lending an air of mystery to the encounter.

Irini was chuffed by the attentions of an attractive and attentive man, married though she now suspected he was. No ring, but he had the narrow band of slightly lighter tone underneath it against his well-tanned hands that was sufficient in evidence. She decided he was slightly flawed, an *operator*.

Irini trotted down the long, curving stairs from the museum's restaurant in the brilliant rotunda. Adam met her at the museum exit door, as usual, but unusually had had to wait an extra ten minutes. He intended only to tease her, having no idea of what she had just been doing. "So how did your date go with the tall, handsome...?"

Irini's terrorized face stopped Adam cold, but fortunately he only concluded that it had been a bad joke, and that Irini was still a bit more nervous than usual.

It was raining with that all consuming, all wetting, light drizzle that *Lunduntown* had trademarked long before the Norman invasion of 1066. It was as if the still air itself was somehow suffused with water, and that one would get soaked standing motionless under a capacious umbrella.

They moved cautiously across the museum courtyard, slicked by the combination of misty rain and droppings from sea birds driven up the Thames by a storm they knew was coming, but which the Met office of England had yet to predict.

They waited at the zebra crossing, moving forward only when the light traffic had cleared to create a generous gap. Just as they crossed the centre line, Adam caught a flash out of the corner of his right eye, pushed Irini ahead of him towards the kerb, and himself stumbled forward as a rogue delivery bike driven by an apparition in black leathers, and matching helmet with smoked faceplate, clipped Adam, adding to his momentum as he stumbled and fell across the pavement. Irini kept her balance, and turning, saw the bike shimmying out of control down the street. Then it sideswiped another car just pulling out, the biker thrown to the ground to slide forward some metres along the road.

Irini turned to Adam who was favouring his right elbow as he struggled to his feet. "Damn bikers." He limped along to Irini's flat, grateful for her support, where she applied disinfectant, dressed his skinned elbow, and then fortified each other with strong brandies. They had been lucky, he said, but she knew that his quick action had probably saved them from a nasty accident.

John Fiske had just recovered his own motorbike from the locking racks in front of the museum when the delivery bike roared down the road, obviously with the intention of striking Irini and Adam. He was of several minds at once. First, there was the woman, already taking a disproportionate share of his dreamtime; second, the deep question of "why"; and third, the discipline of his profession. It was the last that took over. He leaped on his bike, and with no time available to stow his bag, threw it over his shoulder.

As he pulled forward, he saw the assailant hit the car, spilling the cyclist. He determined to follow him and learn more about his own personal plot line that was thickening by the minute.

Then he noticed that a man and a woman had jumped out of a blue Rolls Royce – perhaps a doctor in the pair? Once again, his guesses were dashed on the scrap heap of unfulfilled probabilities. The two inexplicably grabbed the cyclist, who struggled to get away, and threw him through the open door onto the back seat. This curious tableau finished with the two jumping in the back with their undoubted captive. A third person at the wheel pulled out and drove off.

It didn't take the MI5 training lodged in his bones to dictate that he should follow. He was careful to stay well back, something he was adept at. Around the shop he was known as "Invisible Fiske". It was child's play to track a car unobserved in London traffic on a bike.

The Rolls went north, onto the A1 motorway for three exits, then off across the countryside. John enjoyed the challenge of remaining unobserved on open roads, and his stealth was soon rewarded as the car left the country road to enter the *Great Northern Sanatorium*. He ditched the bike in the undergrowth, and rushed forward until he came to a manicured lawn about fifty metres from the main entrance.

He threw down his backpack-bag, grabbed the telephoto digital camera, and snapped dozens of rapid-fire shots. He silently caught the faces of all three passengers in several side and full frontals, plus the car, and its registration. He waited breathlessly for a shot of the driver, but he or she remained concealed behind the smoky windows.

After 42 minutes by his watch, John dictating from time to time into the camera's audio memory, the two came out and got back in the car. John hastily stowed the camera, and retraced his steps, but the Rolls had disappeared over the shallow hills that led up to the sanatorium.

He had not regained contact as he approached the A1. Guessing that they were most likely to go back towards London, he ran 100 plus mph, weaving in between the cars and along the hard shoulder until he spotted them ten or twelve cars ahead, slowing in the traffic. It was then easy to follow down through North London to West Hampstead, and then the turn east up towards Hampstead proper. The car pulled into a drive, and he drove past, around the corner to wait for dark.

He sent a full report to his own secure computer at headquarters, and called for backup, laboriously keying the tiny pad with the stylus the manufacturer had provided. He cursed at several design faults – no excuse for that in a unit costing two grand. The tiny keys needed a dimple in the middle to catch the stylus. He resolved to fix that problem in his model workshop. He whiled away the time planning the next addition to his garden railway, all the while cursing the rain.

When it was dark he joined with his team, went back to the house, switched to infrared lenses, and took several shots. They defeated the external security, slipped into the garage, and fingerprinted the car. It was clean, except for clear prints of the two back-seat people on the left rear door. He wondered why they hadn't worn gloves, but found out a few hours later when they turned up dry in the national database and Interpol. Then he checked with the Greek authorities, with the same result. "If they have been forthcoming."

CHARON TO SPIROS: <u>RED ALERT</u>
    TROUBLE IN RIVER CITY
    MISSION INCREDIBLE ON THE JOB

And, on the other side of the city:

PRIVATE AND CONFIDENTIAL MEMORANDUM
FROM John Fiske
TO Sir Robert Mansfield: Encrypted

SUMMARY
    Apparent attempt on life of Irini Baynes and/or Adam Blix
    Attacker kidnapped by an organization unknown.

Fingerprinted two kidnappers from motor car
Unknown to UK, Interpol, and the Greeks (so they say)
That link feels strong enough to follow (one of my hunches)
Victim's identity known to Sanatorium (see attachment)
Refuse to disclose; they have official papers to back this up.
I suspect they are bogus – doc. and gov. sections are on it
Car is registered to untraceable corporate entity in Belize.
You don't need names there for that. Suspicious, of course.

RECOMMENDATION:

Raise Baynes profile, extend to other connections.
Something significant is obviously going on at museum.
No firm idea yet what it might be.
Professionals are watching the youngsters' backs.
I also get the feeling that they don't know it. Curious.

END OF PART TWO

PART THREE

Chapter 19

Whipsaws

The Impossible may not be Possible after all.

London, Wednesday 11 January, the following year

British Museum Staff Notice: New Security System
The New Security System will be Operational on Monday 16 Jan.
Will all Employees Obtain & Test New Access Cards and Codes
Security Chief's Temporary Office is in the Main Concourse
Please Direct any Questions to that Office this Week if Possible

Headline and article, Friday 20 January:

Coup for British Museum

The opening of the Treasures of Mount Athos Exhibition at the British Museum has met with universal critical acclaim. It is the first time in a thousand years of their history that these Icons and other Treasures have been on view outside Greece, and only the second time that they have been seen in public. The director of the British Museum, Geoffrey Hayward, was quoted as saying, "It's a feather in our cap, and one up on the Louvre! Unique in the history of Europe."

Sources credit Doctor Hayward, and a certain Greek philanthropist, who achieved some notoriety late last year with his television program highlighting the plight of the Elgin Marbles. Others see the Exhibition as a means of putting political pressure on the UK government and museum officials for the repatriation of the Parthenon Marbles. However, the Prime Minister, in a press release dated yesterday, ruled that out for at least the duration of this Parliament.

Monday 23 January, cyberspace

MEMORANDUM SECRET CLASSIFICATION

FROM John Fiske

TO Sir Robert Mansfield: Encrypted

REFERENCE: MI5 Background Memorandum IOM10166
"Quantum Computer Development –
Raised Profile – National Security Priority"

SUMMARY
Reference calls attention to this project as vital to security
It is underway at Imperial College London
Staff list is appended

BODY
I call to your direct attention, director, the name Adam Blix.
His name appears on Quantum Computer (QC) staff list.
You will recall that he is one of the PMBM surveillees
with relationships to the Greek Group.
Reference my previous private memoranda.
Is it more about the Quantum Computer than the museum?
Museum connection has always bothered me.
What's the point?
The QC is another matter entirely.
Could be a military-intelligence breakthrough.

RECOMMENDATION
Insert Operative into the QC Project as our Inside Man.
I attach two CVs from our staff with related backgrounds.
END

SECURE MAIL REPLY Mansfield to Fiske
APPROVED, Implement.
Well Spotted, John. Your Project
Name: PMBMQC.
Security Classification: Top Secret.
Report Directly to This Office as needed any hour.
END

Safe House One, <u>three months later</u>: Friday, 21 April, L–7 days.

Irini had the floor. "I'm sorry, Helena, troops, but I haven't been able to get enough leverage in the computer systems inside the museum for Adam to break the new security."

Adam agreed. "Helena, we're going to have to face the fact that the new security systems installed in January may stymie us."

Helena asked for the second time, a rare admission by her of failure to understand any point, in anybody's specialty, including Adam's arcane worlds. "Sorry, but could you run me through this one more time."

"Sure. You will remember the ease with which we were able to defeat the old-fashioned, magnetic stripe card security systems last summer.

"We used the simple device of placing an appliqué simulacrum of the security box itself on the face of it. This had the ability to record the simple coded data from the magnetic strip on the back of any card inserted through it, and to record the PIN code of the user of that door as it was keyed in. Blank cards are readily available in the underground thanks to Peter, and the computer in my black box could write a fresh card *identical* to the original user, and provide the corresponding PIN code in a small display from its memory. I simply inserted such a card into any door that particular person has access to, entered the PIN, and we were in.

"The cutest fraud using this principle that I ever heard of was to put a fake cash dispenser in a market or mall somewhere, one made up by the criminals. All it did was record the cards, and the PINs, one after the other, and then gave the unsuspecting user a message like, "The Computer is Down, Please Try Later, or Another Cash-point". Our colleagues in crime could pick up this data at their leisure, then use a black box like mine to raid thousands of bank accounts.

Then Adam dropped the bomb:

"The new system is free of any and all such threats to its integrity!"

There was the hushed sound of breaths indrawn.

"The reason is a bit arcane, but I'll give it my best shot. Imagine that the bank has a mathematical formula, instead of a simple coded number for your card-identity. Imagine further that your credit or security card itself contains a *computer*! That's what the little, striated gold square you see embedded in your bank cards actually is. This computer can calculate according to the same formula that the bank holds. So here's the drift. The bank sends down its link a random number, any number at all. The mathematical formula in your card's little computer changes that into another number. Consider a simple example, to double the number. When the double of the original number comes back uplink to the bank, the transaction is authorized. Next time the bank sends a different number – one never knows what will be sent. The computer in your card dutifully doubles it, and sends it back. What is being checked is not the numbers themselves, but the *formula*, and that is a very great deal more powerful."

Irini interjected, "Why can't we just ask our little card to tell us the formula?"

"Because it is built and programmed to refuse to allow any peeking at the internal codes, and the formula is physically etched in the silicon itself."

"I thought you could sneak into any computer, disable or overcome such small obstacles." Irini smiled beatifically at Adam, but was only half kidding. They had come to believe that he could do anything in this line, the impossible only taking a *little* longer.

"If the programmers leave a trap or system's door open, it's literally child's play these days; anybody prepared to study a bit, and then be patient with the right software can do it. The trouble is that these computers inside the credit cards are simple, stupid little beasts that do one job, and one job only: reply to the interrogation as the interrogator expects. In effect this verifies that the formula, or if you wish, the subprogram, in each is performing the expected calculation, and no other. Needless to say, there are no trapdoors. The code is simple, no need for any, and it is physically created in the silicon itself and therefore cannot be either examined or copied."

Peter was frowning in concentration. "Then why not ask the computer in the card a million, a billion, a really *huge* number of questions, and *deduce* the hidden code?"

"Well, Peter, that's the only way it can be done."

Peter brightened, and so Adam let him down gently.

"That's correct thinking, but it won't work. There are hugely more possible equations than there are numbers. We could spend six months on the mathematics in that field, the so-called *transfinite* numbers. And before anybody says there is only one infinity, let me assure you that there are many. The number of mathematical formulas is two 'hugers', to the infinite power, huger than the ordinary infinity of counting numbers! If we could try out all numbers on a card, and store the results, we could easily build a black box to replace the little card, because we would know the answer in advance."

"But that's impossible," Helena responded, "because there are too many numbers, in fact, an infinite number."

"Exactly. Or at the least, it is too long a list to work for us within the practical limitations of computer technology."

"So that's *it*?" Peter cried out in real anguish. "A bit of electronics and mathematics that I don't really understand, and that's IT!"

"There are other ways," Helena said sadly, "but they are dirty."

"Let's just lock up all the guards, take over the building, dynamite the doors, and get on with it." Peter's understandable frustration boiled over, and the others were not far behind.

"Yes, that's theoretically possible, but the odds are long, very long. It is far better to slip in undetected, and as much as possible, let life go on as usual, except in the back room we are cleaning out. People always get hurt, Peter." Helena concluded in a soft voice.

Peter had learned that one first hand once or twice, and it wasn't comfortable to live with afterward, despite being nothing more in his experience than a couple of lumps on thick heads or a broken arm.

Helena gritted, "We can't delay this much longer. Our plan A has been in deep trouble for months. Perhaps we can work out an extension of Plan B – we need to deal with cameras and the guards. Adam and Peter have been handling that one."

Peter took the floor. "Adam will defeat the security system cameras, seven all together, using the old standard, a recording of the room made at another time, and substituted for the live camera. Fortunately, they haven't yet replaced the fixed units with scan-on-command versions; that's not coming until the autumn.

"We will eliminate the three guards in our section by altering their beats, on faked orders by Adam as if from the Security Chief. They'll be on a changed assignment, watching over the Mount Athos Exhibition as it is struck and loaded in its lorry. Then they are assigned to sit inside the empty exhibition hall until their midnight shift ends. They will welcome the change, won't know anything different, and on our plan, neither will the Security Chief.

"Now you know that guards walk their beats. What you may not know is that when they pass certain stations, or posts, they slip a simple key into a time clock, and turn it. The key identifies them, and their location in the building is noted on the master security panel, and a chief security officer watches these movements twenty-four hours a day. We already have copies of these keys.

"It is therefore necessary that we have guards that look like those on duty to walk the beats on the L-night, and key the boxes in synchronism with the video playbacks being fed through the security systems. This covers us, and the absence of the guards reassigned to the exhibition hall.

"We have made tests for several weeks now, and it works smooth as silk. The substitute guards, who my colleague Trevor has provided, know the drill. We have simulated all of it in a warehouse we have set up to be a copy of the museum rooms we are working.

"The final rehearsal for the Lift itself takes place tomorrow night, and you are all cordially invited to watch us at work. If we have problems, we will repeat, but I expect it will go well enough for me to certify the team for Lift."

"Can't anybody turn the guard's keys at the right times?" Irini questioned.

Adam answered, "In principle, yes. But the practicalities dictate that they look enough like who is on duty, so that if another guard sees them at a distance, it looks okay. Otherwise we would have to take over the whole building."

"What if the security chief, or someone he deputizes, checks up on the checkers?" Helena hadn't thought of that until this moment.

"Well, we either push him into a closet, or create a diversion. We have contingency plans, yet our experience is that this never happens. The guards walk their separate beats, and don't talk on duty. The shift begins at 6PM. The Treasures of Mt Athos will be on their truck by 9PM, three hours after the museum closes on Friday night. So long as we have lifted the lot, and are away by midnight, when the guards rotate and take breaks – then sure, sometimes getting together for a coffee and a moment's chat – we are solid.

"Given the holiday weekend, Friday the 28th of April, through Monday 1st of May, we can expect that there won't be extra-duty after-hour guards, or any surprises of that kind."

Adam elaborated, "We have substitutes for all seven guards, to cover those assigned duty in our area, including sick-leave and all contingencies. If something really desperately unlucky happens, we call it as we see it, and tough it out. We have rehearsed hundreds of scenarios, and are quite confident." He smiled, "We know where all the closets are."

Helena nodded, "I don't see a lot of risk there from the Expected Unexpected. But how are we going to get through the doors without kidnapping the director, grabbing his cards, and juicing him for his codes? Or some such nonsense."

Adam shook his head, defeat creasing his tired face. Irini vowed to loosen him up tonight, if it was the last thing she did.

Irini began the moment Adam came in the door, kicking it closed behind them, then pulling him down to her for a deep kiss.

He was not reluctant, yet at the same time, she clearly felt his tension as if it were her own. She would draw his like the physicians of old taking blood. This was an attack, something she had never done before to anything like the same degree. Irini took her turns as the instigator of lovemaking, but before it had always been easygoing. Tonight, she was a tiger, a desperate, hungry beast.

Adam was at first taken slightly aback, and never quite managed to catch up. He tried hard to turn the play over, but Irini refused him, remaining in full control.

She had long since learned how to sense his level of arousal, and used this to full effect, until Adam had gone softly off to sensuous oblivion. Irini then gradually slowed the pace, easing off to small motions, and finally stopped altogether as he slipped off to sleep.

That had happened a few times before, but never after such a powerful or lengthy encounter. She hoped that she had done the right thing, and Adam would not feel deprived of his finish when he woke in the morning. Her intuitive voice had taken control, and she had let it drive the whole time.

Adam had entered an altered state of consciousness as surely as if he had spent a hundred lifetimes in a celestial *ashram*, or been juiced with some sort of truth serum, or had chanced a whole jar of *magic mushrooms* from where? Yes, Arizona in the United States.

He was not lost in space, one of his favourite and most powerful dream worlds. This was as far beyond that, as flying through the universe of his imagination was beyond one of his fast walks across London. It was as real as the lovemaking had been with Irini in that other reality he had forever left behind. He was lost in a miasma – a soup of numbers.

He swam in three dimensions. There was no surface to make headway for in escape, and no depth to drown in. It simply existed, he was inside it, and it was part of him. Nothing like this had ever happened in him before.

A pattern began to emerge, one that he vaguely recognized. Sequences of binary numbers, each of them precisely 128 bits in length, were twisting together like a new kind of spaghetti:

0101000101001010111011010101010100101011010010101010101
0010010110101010001010101010111010101010101010011010011

He was teasing the strands apart, but there were too many, oh so many, so many. *Om Mani Padme Hum. Om Mani Padme Hum.* The chant from a recording he had from that self-same *ashram* rumbled through this hyperspace of his imagination.

Peter was there with him, trying to free himself from the entanglement of sticky numerical spaghetti and frowning in concentration. "Then why not ask the computer in the card a billion, a really *huge* number of questions, and *deduce* the hidden code?"

Adam smiled encouragement at him, "Well, Peter, that's the only way it can be done."

"Questions … deduce … questions … ques … de … duce…"

Adam awoke, writhing desperately to free himself … from what? … He had mostly forgotten. His arms were thrashing in the twisted sheets, and he spun off of the bed on the rear side, thudding to the floor. He was drenched with sweat, and dizzily disoriented. At first he thought he was ill with a high fever, then the nausea passed off as he lay on the floor panting, staring at the ribbed ceiling crisscrossed with beams, one of which he knew intimately. Achilles, who had been sleeping draped against Irini's legs, raised his head and peered over the edge of the bed to give Adam a toothy yawn. As the mist cleared he saw he was in Irini's flat, on his back, on the floor.

This dream had not quite vanished with the dawn, and he retained a haunting recollection, the strongest of its kind he had ever experienced.

245

Something was tickling the inside of his head, and then it grew unbidden into a thundering revelation. Peter was right! And he was right. Between them, they were right. There was only one way to do it, if it was possible at all. The book said it was impossible to break such a formulaic code; that there was no way to get inside to find it. Yet the book had said the same about all the other ciphers and codes at one time or another down through history, and the code-breakers had always caught up and run past. *That* he believed in, because he had done it more than once.

Adam slapped his fist into an open hand. His own knowledge had concealed the truth from him, because unlike Peter, he *believed* in the inaccessibility of the higher infinities. Nevertheless there were *other* infinities, the ineffable soup inside the subatomic world – the Quantum World. "Yes!" He yelled, and slapped his fist again.

Fortunately, Irini was so soundly asleep that she was not awakened. It was just after 6AM, Lift Day Minus Six. Perhaps there was just time, and maybe there was just the one way.

Chapter 20

Inside, Outside, Upside Down

Truth has nothing to do with Credibility, and vice-versa.

Saturday, 22 April, L–6 Days:

"Okay Peetie, the coast is *clear*. I'll go in now, you go back to the bike and get my toolkit, okay?"

Peter Ryan screwed up his face in mock pain at the nickname. "Sure, thing, *Blitz*. For God's sake, I hope you know what you are doing. You did clear this with Helena, didn't you?"

Adam Blix turned from his partner at the lift, and showed his ID to the security guard. "I will sign in for my colleague now; he'll be back with some equipment shortly." The guard shrugged without really seeing either of them, and went back to his book: *Breaking the Bank of England.*

Adam proceeded down a short, dimly lit, bile-green corridor of the Imperial College department of computer science, and then around a corner. At the end of the next short hall the lighting changed, dispersing the stygian gloom. The massive door of a safe stood open, welcoming him to a basement laboratory.

He knew that there were no security cameras in the halls, and only the one here in the secure laboratory itself. Earlier that morning, when alone in the room, he had momentarily unplugged the cable between the camera and nether regions, and added an adapter connector "two into one switchable splitter" and then restored the connection. To anyone viewing the video it would have seemed like a momentary interruption, not significant in itself, and might well have already been erased as the security computer's disk memory had a limited capacity.

He began his assault by going to his bench, and picking up a book, then went to the library corner, which was underneath the camera and out of view. He took a Sony miniature videodisk recorder out of his pocket, hung it with a wire to a hook in the ceiling, and connected its cable to the splitter, and keyed "Record". He then got down from the chair, and remained in the library area. The Sony therefore picked up ten-minutes of live action in the empty room, recording the same as the camera's signal, which continued

247

uninterrupted back to the security office. He made no sounds at all as though reading, and the room maintained the silence of a vault.

Despite being a Saturday, it was fortunate that nobody else came in. Had anyone come he intended to repeat the exercise another time. After the ten minutes of recording, he climbed up on the chair, reset the splitter to standard position, and hit "play" on the Sony. When its small screen showed a correct picture, he set the splitter to "source" and got down off of the chair. The Sony was now providing the signal, the recording of an empty room, back to the security systems.

Free of surveillance, he went immediately to the centre workbench, and slipping on a pair of film-handler's, thin cotton gloves, began unplugging cables attached between an aluminium container about the size of a cigar box festooned with electronic connectors, and arrays of equipment standing in black cabinets all around the table.

He whipped off his shirt, revealing a body-pouch, pressed flat into his abdomen, securely strapped to his midriff. He pulled the Velcro straps free, removed and tossed a simulated copy of the aluminium box on the table, and pushed the original into the pouch, pressing the straps home. He then put on his shirt again, and began reattaching the cables to the substitute.

"So what's all this, then?" Adam's knees buckled, and he had to momentarily support himself on the laboratory bench.

"Just reconnecting the cables, George." The Expected, Unexpected, as Helena always put it.

George Travers was one of the lower level researchers who had joined the group early in the new year. His specialty was in the field of high-speed data transfer between computers. This was a key problem area when dealing with the extremely high computation speed of the new technology. He was competent in Adam's view, but now something else began to insinuate itself into his mind. This fellow was often around when there was no good reason, and seemed to come and go at random.

"Haway there, that won't do no good, you know," George continued in his Geordie accent, muffled by a typical London fog cold. "I saw what'cha did." He was obviously thinking about how to deal with this as he leaned nonchalantly against the half-open safe door. He well knew that Adam, clearly engaged in espionage as he saw it, might have a weapon. Then he brightened. "I'm goin' fer em – uh the coppers." With this he stepped back out of the room, and as

Adam stood there agape, with no real idea what to do next, the safe door slowly, and then with gathering momentum, thudded shut!

Adam slumped to the floor, exhausted, discouraged, and certain that his on-the-fly, ad-hoc addition to their plan would be their last.

A chill ran up Adam's back. What had George said? "I'm goin' fer em – uh the coppers." Yes, "fer *em* – fer *em* – *fer em*" as in "em-eye-five", MI5. George had caught himself in a blunder, and corrected it.

"Damn." Everyone on the computer project knew that MI5 was discreetly involved in the security, and were providing funding. Adam now understood the why of this increased attention. He mentally kicked himself. He should have thought of it months ago cold sober, as the project leaders must have done, instead of in his sleep at this late date. It was obvious to him now that this new technology could make it possible to break previously unbreakable codes.

The hypothesis was confirmed, and it was the warrant for his arrest, or worse. Better the cops, Adam then thought ruefully, far better the cops.

A slight whirring seemed to fill the room. It was coming from the safe door. "That was fast," Adam thought in resignation. "Well, they will find me standing up, ready for the cuffs." He struggled shakily to his feet. There was a click, and the crossbars began to pull back out of the wall. The door slowly opened.

"Well, Adam, I see you got yourself in a spot of bother." It was Peter! This was far more of a shock than the entry of George had been, yet Adam was instantly aware, his mind running on overdrive, legs strengthening like a butterfly inflating its wings before the first flight. "Shsst. Hang on," he whispered, waving Peter back out the open door. Peter was naturally disappointed, hoping for a more triumphant welcome, but then saw that Adam had other problems on his mind. He could be patient, but he couldn't conceal the wide grin of triumph from being one-up on his partner.

Adam looked around the small laboratory, his eyes lighting on George's personal attaché case in its usual position below the man's computer workstation. He looked at the clock. Still two minutes on the disk. Perfect. He grabbed the case, opened it, disconnected the two cables he had previously attached to the simulated box, and dropped it into George's briefcase. He took one of George's handkerchiefs out of the case, snapped it shut and tossed it to Peter still standing obediently in the open door.

Adam mounted the chair again, and first draped the handkerchief over the lens. He then switched the splitter to "camera", disconnected the Sony, and pocketed it. He decided against removing the splitter. To do so would put a glitch in the tape, and *this* recording was going to be viewed, and viewed again by the authorities. He would have to take that chance, or come back later.

He quietly moved the chair back into the library corner, tiptoed out of the room, and whispered with a finger to his lips. "Peter, can you do a muffled Geordie accent for me, from outside?"

"Sure." Peter whispered back.

"When I give you the high-five, say 'What-the' and nothing else, okay? You've got a very bad cold, so stuff your fist in your mouth, or something. Then I will struggle with you here, just outside the camera's view, then you run down the hall, loudly, half way to the corner and wait for me."

Peter was totally mystified, but readied himself to comply to the letter. He knew as well as Adam that this was *on the wing*. No time for thinking, do what his partner ordered, and do it right.

Adam gave the sign. "Whatta!" Adam then "attacked" Peter, and they struggled noisily just outside the safe door. When Adam twisted away, Peter ran down the hall.

Adam cried out, "Stop, thief." Standing just out of sight in the safe's doorway, he blew air up under the handkerchief so that it fluttered down off the lens. "Gottit!" With this final comment, he threw George's attaché case back into the room onto a bench in full view of the camera. He then pushed the safe door closed with a thump, spinning the main wheel, then all three dials, and punched the electronic lock activation. The safe was now multiply secure.

Adam beckoned to Peter, who trotted back. "Take off your shirt." Peter complied, and Adam did the same. He transferred the abdominal pouch, cinching it up tight on Peter's only slightly larger midriff. "Now run to the guard, and holler for the police! Go downstairs and slip this in your bike's side-box so nobody sees what you are doing and lock it. Then at the callbox behind the parking, dial 999 and repeat the call to the police. Wait out of sight until you see some plain-clothes people enter the building in a hurry, and then come back here. Leave the toolbox with me. Okay?"

"Sure, but aren't the coppers on the way?"

"Worse, I'm afraid, but we'll deal with them. Your story is that you went down to get tools for me. When you came back you saw me sitting outside the safe, and I told you to go for the cops. Got it?"

"Sure, in a doddle."

Adam sat down with his back against the wall in the hallway, going over his ad-hoc scenario several times.

There was a commotion at the elevator – lift – he corrected his thought.

"Stand aside; we are MI5!"

Adam stood up in the most relaxed manner he could muster for the occasion. George was coming around the corner with three other men. "And I locked – him – in – – the – – – safe." He slowed down like an old-style kitchen timer that had run out of windup. The look on George's face was priceless. Surprise became shock, then uncertainty, and finally settled on a hastily concealed raw fear. He could not have been more astonished had Adam been replaced by an extraterrestrial with a long, thin body, exquisite, foot-long fingers and glowing bug-eyes.

"I see you brought your, what shall we call them – backup team with you this time. What do you hope to do? Overpower me, and cover this all up? That would be right in character for you CIA types."

"We're MI5 – and just who are you?" The speaker was obviously the boss, and George's superior. Adam almost burst out laughing, but concealed it, mostly. The residual smile was probably interpreted by this fellow as obsequious, which would do okay.

It was a scene from *Men in Black*, for all except George were dressed in that colour, in quite formal cuts of slacks, white shirts, black striped ties, and tailored coats.

The other two could have been twins. Both were tallish, medium muscular build, with a skin pallor of stretched, clear silk. They hadn't seen the sun in a while – probably spent most of their time in a basement like this somewhere nearby dealing with detainees. Adam winced involuntarily at the image. They had black hair, crew cut, identical wristwatches peeking out from under their starched shirts; it would have been hilarious, if it hadn't been serious.

Adam whipped out his ID. "A research associate on *this* project."

The leader glanced at his man, George, a quizzical expression attacking his previous badge-thrust-forward demeanour. It was a cue to speak, but George was unable to muster a syllable.

"May I see your ID, please? This is a secure area." Adam smiled condescendingly.

"What?" The man was having a real adjustment problem. From the start he had been an unaccustomed step or two behind both events and this youngster in front of him. Yet he was experienced enough to tread carefully until he could survey the lay of the land.

Adam drew himself up to his full six foot two inch height, and bent slightly forward with raised eyebrows that overcalled his opponent as surely as a trumped Ace in bridge. "Your ID? You could be anybody. And you admit your connection with this thief who I have just foiled."

The dam finally burst, and George spluttered, foam tingeing his thin lips, narrowed eyes a study in nervous saccades. "That's aagh, ridic ... stupid, bloody rubbish."

His senior colleague had missed none of this, and doubt had congealed on his face. Mechanically, he withdrew his warrant card, and waved it under Adam's nose. He used the time to think.

"I see, John Fiske," Adam replied, with a nod of acceptance, "and the others?" He decided against speaking his thought – that they struck him as muscle – certainly solid citizens in every way.

When the boss didn't shake his head in the negative, they produced them, one by one.

Adam now smiled sweetly, "Thank you. Now tell me what you are going to do about him?" A wave of his hand embraced the space occupied by the hapless George. He visibly recoiled from this gesture, as if Adam had intended to cast a spell or strike a stout blow.

The MI5 leader made up his mind in a flash of intuition, and decided to go for broke. "Mister Blix, is it, I am placing you under arrest. Jack, cuff him!"

The wheel turned momentarily, then came around again. "Is this a citizen's arrest?"

"What?"

"You have no more right of arrest than an ordinary citizen. George, I place you under arrest. I don't have any cuffs, but will accept your good word that you won't resist."

Now there were five perplexed men standing in the circle. Adam knew that the cavalry was on the way, but would they get there before he disappeared into some dank cellar? Fortunately, the three MI5 colleagues, and especially their boss, knew they were fishing on a fogbound lake.

Peter took this moment to come around the corner, whistling a tune from Verdi's *Aida*. He approached the group with a quizzical look on his face, and then offered his hand to Adam. "Coppers on the way. Who's this lot? With George the thief?"

Then the scene changed into one of chaos as a half-dozen police officers came trotting up. "D-I Blake – Mister Blitz? You called?"

Peter shrugged with a casual smile to Adam's brief glance.

"Adam *Blix*. Yes, Detective Inspector, I did." He handed over his ID card. "I am a research associate on this project."

The three MI5 officers produced their cards, and started to back away as if to leave, George making to follow.

"Detective Inspector, I called because that man there, name of George Travers, if I remember the last name correctly, attempted to steal some equipment from the secure laboratory here. I stopped him, and locked up his briefcase in that room with the equipment I believe still inside it. He ran off, but now comes back with these self-identified MI5 gentlemen, one of them stating that I was under arrest."

The Detective Inspector of police motioned for the MI5 personnel to remain. "Is that true?"

"Is what true? That this *boy* accused one of my people of theft?"

"Later for all that. No, did you threaten to arrest Mister Blix?"

"Yes I did. We have a report that on the contrary, our Mister Travers prevented Blix from stealing equipment from this high-security laboratory."

"So, Mister Travers, what's your version?"

George summoned up a lot of strength, which Adam felt was much better than he would have managed in the circumstances. His version of the straight truth, unembellished, sounded so ridiculous as to be laughable. Adam felt more than just twinges of regret, but consoled himself as best he could with the soldier's rationalization that the war was more important than any individual, himself included, and with the fact that George was a snitch in the worst tradition of the East End of London.

The Detective Inspector of police was shaking his head as George ran down the clock once again. He was painfully aware of how it sounded in the circumstances. All the questions that one could ask had answers staring everyone in the face.

"For the record, Mister Blix?"

"Nothing complicated, Detective Inspector. I was coming into the facility. The safe door was half-open, as usual, and as I approached, George was coming out on the run, with our quantum computer in one hand and his briefcase in the other, trying to stuff it in. We literally collided in front of the door, here, and I wrested the case from him with the computer inside. He ran down the hall. I was unsure what to do, but protecting the equipment was my first duty, so I tossed the case back inside, shut the door to the safe, and waited outside. I knew that my colleague, Peter here, was coming back with my tools. When he arrived, I asked him to alert for the police with the guard, and then go downstairs and do the same on a '999', and wait for you to arrive."

This tissue of lies was immediately accepted as the simple truth.

The Detective Inspector carefully filled in the details. "This is your toolbox on the floor here?"

"It is."

"Can you open the safe?"

"I cannot do that alone. George, are you an 'A' or a 'B'?"

He shook his head.

"Detective Inspector, I am an 'A'. With a 'B' the safe can be opened. If George is a 'B' between us we have the necessary codes. That's the system here. It takes two on opposite teams to open it. The guard out front provides basic security, and senior team members can open up as necessary."

"George?" The Detective Inspector pleaded with open hands.

"Yeah, okay. I'm a 'B'."

Adam approached the safe and keyed the computer override, and when prompted, entered his PIN. George then put his in. A green light announced success. Adam spun the first of three dials fully clockwise, and stopped at 16. George spun the second counter clockwise to 32. Adam then turned the third dial clockwise one full turn past zero, and stopped at 8. The second green light came on. Adam then turned the large wheel, and the door was released. Two of the police officers helped pull it open.

"Don't touch anything, or enter the room. Sergeant, go out to where your phone works, and call forensics. Get them down here chop-chop. Call the Superintendent for me, and tell him to contact

MI5 liaison – who is probably out playing golf with some Pooh Bah or other, but the Super'll know." He pointed at another officer, "Get the suits from the car, and bring them up.

"I see a briefcase on the top of that lab table, there. Is that yours George?" The man nodded disconsolately.

"That's where I think it landed." Adam added.

Detective Inspector Blake's practiced eye scanned the room. He spotted the security camera at once. "We've got a security camera. Adam, do you know where all that is linked?"

"Not exactly, but this is a secure facility. They will certainly hold the recordings for at least a few hours."

"That's my thinking also, so no hurry. We'll pull them tonight as soon as the ducks line up here. Hold on a minute. That's a handkerchief on the floor." His gaze ran up to the camera, and down to the offending silk. "George, is that yours?"

Silence was his affirmation.

His eyes averted again. "Mister Blix, I see a pile of disconnected cables on that central table. Is that where you normally kept this special computer you have been talking about?"

"Yes, Detective Inspector, and it's obviously missing."

The second officer arrived with an armful of packages. D-I Blake broke one of them open. "I'm going to get the briefcase so we can look inside." The anti-contamination suit was made of a light yet strong paper-like material, reminiscent of the extra-strong mailing envelopes used for awkward items in the post. He pulled on the booties while standing on a mat of the same material, and then stepped gingerly into the safe room. He came back with the briefcase, and stood again on the mat in the vault doorway. It clicked open without a key or combination, and he opened it out under Adam's gaze.

"Is that the item?"

"Looks like it." Adam went to his toolbox, opened it, and took out a fresh pair of his film-handler's gloves.

"May I?"

"Don't smear the surface, but open it by all means."

Adam lifted the three black plastic tabs on the side of the lid, and it opened easily. The box was empty!

The Detective Inspector and George were as mystified as anybody else, so Adam feigned surprise and didn't do a bad job of it. "Wow! That's crazy?" Stay one step ahead.

"What should I see in this box?" Blake asked, carefully tasting each of the words.

"Well, first, there would be a motherboard, a small one, on insulators in the bottom. On that there would be a series of memory cards plugged in. They are about a half-inch by four inches, just like in any other computer if you have seen them. On this side there would be four large chips, about the size of matchbooks. These connectors are in about the right places, and are all present and correct. It's curiouser and curiouser, Detective Inspector."

"Yes, why not put something inside if it is a forgery? The perpetrator went to the trouble of the connectors. Why not go the whole way?" The Detective Inspector didn't bother to answer his own unanswerable question, and moved on. "Okay, I will put this back on the table where it was before."

He did that, and then came back out, taking off the suit, and stuffing it into its original package to throw away. "So where is the original?" This time he did answer his own question. "Three or four possibilities. One, maybe it wasn't here before any of this happened. Two, it was here, and George took it out with him, leaving Adam holding the empty bag, literally."

"I've got it!" George exulted, a man temporarily transformed. "Adam has it in his toolbox, that's the only explanation." From his point-of-view, this was completely logical, assuming Adam hadn't removed it another way.

"That's so ridiculous it isn't funny." Adam replied. "Either I would have taken it out some other way, or I wasn't involved." In this he was cleverly being both logical, and truthful, without admitting anything. As a final answer, he motioned towards his toolbox. One of the officers came forward, knelt down, and carefully examined the contents. There was not so much as a loose computer chip, just tools.

"Mister Travers, is it true that any hefty item carried past the guard must be examined?"

He nodded.

"Including briefcases?"

"Certainly."

"Were you counting on the guard missing a small box like that?"

"I wasn't counting on anything because I didn't steal it." The simple, incredible truth again, but it wasn't wearing any better than it had before.

The Detective Inspector adjourned to talk with the guard, and came back in a few minutes with his record book. "Sloppy fellow, let's you lot put down your own times in and out."

"That's not unusual, Detective Inspector, so please don't blame him." Adam smiled ingratiatingly.

The detective inspector read it off out loud. "It shows: Adam Blix in, Peter Ryan in, Peter Ryan out, George Travers in, Peter Ryan in, George Travers out, Peter Ryan out, MI5 in, Peter Ryan in, and then ourselves. Given the sloppy way the records are kept, this can accord with both stories." Still, he had the edge of a thought from two possible discrepancies. First, that Peter Ryan was in the hallway or laboratory *between* the entry and exit of George Travers. There could have been a *third man* involved. Second, there was the arrival of George *after* Adam, perhaps explained if Adam had been in the loos or elsewhere on the floor. He thought about questioning everyone on these points, and normally would have, but these alternatives to Adam's simple story were impossible to believe, and so no thought was given to them as rational possibilities.

"Mister Travers, I am afraid that I'm going to have to hold you for questioning. If you come voluntarily, it will not be necessary at this time to place you under arrest." This was his standard approach in such circumstances, because it gave the police the best of both worlds. He would not need to charge, or arrest him, and they could talk for weeks if he agreed. If he ever disagreed, the police could make the arrest, and then later bring him up before the magistrates within the statutory time.

George saw what was writ large on the wall, and shrugged.

The Detective Inspector was not a complete fool – indeed he was a successful, clear-thinking man of considerable experience. He couldn't see it now, and sensed he probably never would; yet there was at least one loose end standing out like a pikestaff. Where was the computer? There were the three alternatives he had enumerated earlier, plus one or two others, including at least the bizarre possibility that Adam had somehow pulled a double-whammy. Yet he couldn't get around the vault. If Adam had been inside, he would still be there if they hadn't opened it, unless at least two appropriately empowered members of the team had been outside, and willing to open it.

His sergeant came running up breathlessly. "The head of MI5, Sir Robert Mansfield, is upstairs as we speak. He says to send up all four of the MI5 people now, or he'll have your badge and your pension."

"And the Superintendent, *our superintendent*? What does he say?"

"He said it's your call, Detective Inspector."

Blake knew precisely what that meant. "Will you please escort them upstairs, with my compliments to Sir Robert."

Adam and Peter had agreed with the Detective Inspector that they would appear in his office the next day at 11AM to give their formal statements, and were then free to go. The guard searched Adam's toolbox by the book and would have done so in the absence of police swarming cheek by jowl in the short hallway.

Peter ran Adam pillion on the motorbike back to the new Safe Lab. Adam had passed the request to Helena that morning, getting her out of bed at an early hour as she had done so often to them. Peter had arranged the secure space, and Adam had already begun to load it with equipment before they went over to the Quantum Computer Lab.

Later they found themselves in a quiet back corner of their favourite pub, The Cock and Bull, and it was that kind of story to be debriefed. There were certainly some questions, mainly from Adam. "Okay, tell me how it came down."

"Well, when I came back with the toolbox, and rounded the corner, then jumped back, there was this fellow shutting the safe door in a hurry. I skipped into the loos, and peeked. I heard him say something about the coppers as the door closed. He spun the left-hand dial, and dashed up the hall, past me, signed out, and waited for the lift. When he had gone, I came down to the vault.

"We were surely in trouble. I had to get you out, but how? Then I saw your toolkit, and remembered some of what you had taught me. The one green light was still on, under the label "electronic interlock", and I felt he had touched only the one mechanical dial, the third in the set if this safe worked from right to left."

Adam grinned, and slapped the table. "So you assumed it was the leftmost, and third in the combo order?"

"Sure, I remembered your chat about mechanical dial safes. You mentioned two types, one where a dial is moved sequentially to three or more numbers, the classical case. The second is where there are three dials, each separate. Usually the first is clockwise, the second opposite, and so on."

"That's right."

"So I reasoned, and hoped, that this safe was right to left on the three wheels, in part because the computer side was on the right, and the hand would naturally move that way. As you taught me, mate, when the last dial is the only one remaining to be set, just turn to the final number in the right direction, and it will release."

"An Achilles heel of that design in my considered view," Adam replied in mock seriousness, as though addressing a seminar of experts. "Because actually, if the first two wheels are already resting on the correct number, turning the third in the right direction to the right number, will allow the bar that bridges all of them to drop because the three pins line up. If two or more are not aligned, each must be separately set and the stethoscope won't work."

"Thanks to your patience with me in explaining it all to a thickhead, I knew that George had been just that little bit careless."

"Peter, how many times do I, do we, do your tutors have to tell you that you're not a thickie, before you'll finally believe it?"

Peter paused a beat, the hint of a dry smile edging onto his lips. "So I made my first solo run with the stethoscope just like you showed me. If right wheel is clockwise, and centre dial is counter, the third is clockwise. So I turned it slowly, listening for the pin to drop. When I heard it, I left the wheel there for the, what did you call it, the dwell time, the second green light came on, and the lock released. It only remained to turn the big wheel, and pull the vault door open."

Peter whispered softly. "We were lucky, eh? Another touch by George, and you're in that dark cellar, and the Marbles stay in London."

"That's right, but we are lucky, you and I, are we not?"

Peter was for one of the first times in his life taking real personal and intellectual pleasure in working something out in his head, logically, and carefully. He was finding this to be an addictive pursuit, something new to him, and therefore fresh. He had spent most of his life on one semi-legal scam or another, more bent on figuring the chances, and the way around obstacles. These were valuable skills, and had a satisfaction of their own, but he was discovering something unexpected in himself. That he was far more turned on by this abstract kind of thinking, and it was irresistible when it actually produced a result – a result as he saw it – from nothing. He had never had that before, there always had to be the loaded truck with things falling off the back, something physical, simple, and obvious.

He reached across the table and offered his hand. "Adam, thanks for everything." Adam was surprised at this turn, for he himself had been ready to offer the thanks of the victim saved. He wasn't sure at first what had prompted this, but then he had an inkling of what Peter had been thinking, knowing these emotions intimately in himself.

Adam was coming to appreciate Peter's side of life, one that was equally central to their quest. He was enjoying dealing with frustrating, inexplicable, and erratic human beings, the uncertainties of doing demanding things in the real world instead of the sterile realms of cyberspace or the predictable ones within his own imagination.

He took the hand as offered. The days of a sometimes awkward relationship were now firmly in the past.

Chapter 21

Quantized Quanta Questioned

Any Sufficiently Advanced Technology
is Indistinguishable from Magic. (Sir Arthur Clarke)

The same evening, MI5 Headquarters

Sir Robert Mansfield, director of MI5, John Fiske, recently promoted senior agent, and George Travers, agent, were meeting in a secure conference room.

"I'm telling you, director, exactly what happened." George Travers was sweating profusely despite inadequate heating. The room was definitely on the chilly side in more ways than one.

"John," Sir Robert turned to him, "what is your assessment?"

"I'm faced with the same dilemma as you, Director. I cannot offer anything more." The problem was a simple one. Either George or Adam Blix was lying, and they couldn't be absolutely certain of their own man. They knew it, and he knew it. There was too much at stake.

The director turned back to George. "I'm sorry, but we're going to have to juice you!"

George's head fell chin on his chest. "Yeah, I guess it's the only way. Can I call my wife first?"

"I'm sorry, no, but we take care of our own, and everything will be done for you afterwards. How did you get on with it during your indoctrination into the service?"

"It lost me a weekend, sir, but I've seen worse, even from the smaller dose of the old formula we were given to try out. I had headaches for a week, and wasn't back to scratch for a fortnight. This will be worse, won't it?"

"Well, it all depends."

"Okay, let's do it before I change my mind, and bite down on my cyanide capsule." He was kidding for those days were long past, and since he knew he was innocent, he wouldn't have done it – probably not, anyway. He knew it was going to be a bad month.

After George was taken away to the private room in sickbay, Sir Robert turned to Fiske. "Good work, I say again. So we're pretty sure this is all about the Quantum Computer?"

"Word on the street is that there's a big bounty on it, stateside."

"The Americans and their sticky fingers again?"

"So it seems, Director."

"I was shocked at the minimal security in the lab. I'll have a word with the minister and somebody at Imperial College."

"If you don't mind my saying so, I think half our problems come from carelessness, often as not on the security front."

"If not three-quarters. Set it up to get Blix in here for the treatment."

"Yes, Sir Robert."

George was strapped down on a table to stop him hurting himself. The technician nurse came in with his tray. An IV hung on a pole, hospital-style, and a small needle was inserted into a vein in the back of his hand. This was the recommended way, because the hand could be restrained more securely than the arm and with greater safety for the subject.

These experts knew that the cattle prods and rubber hoses of the past were worse than useless because a weak person would soon say whatever they thought the interrogator wanted to hear. So it was generally accepted that the juice was best. It usually worked, and the results were reliable. The book said that it was theoretically possible for someone to be psychologically programmed, in advance, using similar drugs, so that they would at least try to cover up. These interrogators knew how to break through this in most cases, and where the victim's life was of no consequence, the process could be carried on until they had become a vegetable, or a corpse.

"Okay, George, here we go. I want you to count backwards from a hundred, okay?"

"Sure. 100, 99, 98, aagh."

"He's under the light anaesthetic now, so we wait a minute or two, and give the good stuff."

A tall, gaunt, ancient, and stooped man in a blue striped suit (he had given up the *whites* some years back so this was his trademark), slipped through a crack in the door. "I have the dossier and the director's instructions. Give him ten units."

The plunger pressed home. George's eyes snapped open alertly, but his mouth drooped and drooled, the expected response to this new combination of truth serums.

"Have you had the juice before, George?"

"Once." His voice was slurred, and limited by slackness in his lower face. He looked and sounded like someone who had suffered a stroke, and in a way he had, albeit a temporary one.

The nurse and interrogator, who nodded to each other, recognized all of these symptoms as entirely normal. Having experienced this themselves, they also knew that the brain's moral and inhibitory sections were turned off, and these often took some of the facial musculature controls with them.

George's subconscious had been opened, and all the dark insects that inhabited that region came fluttering up out of the depths. He was having to contend with a cacophony of these voices, all the bad things he had done, large and small, the latter in their hordes by far the worse – the bad days, experiences, and little horrors that had come into his life.

"Did you have anything to do with stealing the Quantum Computer?"

"No – aagh." He choked on a gob of his own saliva.

"When you arrived at the open door, was Adam Blix inside?"

"Yes."

"What was he doing?"

"Putting the Computer in some sort of bag. He had his shirt off."

"Did you lock the safe with him inside"

"Yes."

"Tell me exactly what you did, from when you began to push the door closed on him."

"I am pushing the door."

"Good, keep going."

"The door closes. I turn the handle to set the bars. I spin the dial."

"Dial? Singular, George? Did you spin only one George?"

"The left dial, I spun the left dial. Hurry. Get backup."

"The computer in the door, George, did you touch it?"

"No, green light, no."

"Thank you George."

"You're welcome."

"Give him the antidote, and rehydrate him, on the chop." With this the tall ghost left the room, and walked smartly to the director's office. He knocked and was instantly admitted.

"Robert, George is clean."

"Any clues?"

"Just one, he didn't properly reset the safe locks."

"I see it. Thank you."

"Any time."

SECURE MAIL Encrypted
  FROM Director to Fiske
George is Clean.
Didn't properly lock safe.
Possible Adam Blix's associate opened it.
  (the friend Peter – same man you listed before?)
Check Entry Records. Was Peter the Third Man?
Check Security Recordings.
  Report any inconsistencies.
Locate and Tab Blix for treatment.
END

Warehouse Southwark, same evening

Peter led Helena through the door into the large building. He spoke to a pair of guards on the door, "Nobody in or out without my okay."

"Yessir.

Helena stood still, amazed. They were in the British Museum's Duveen Gallery. True, the sculptures were all just jumbles of cemented concrete blocks, but they were located on the floor, or higher up on the walls, with matching partitions and paintwork, in uncanny agreement with the reality they would face in a week's time.

Peter led the way to the back, along the same path the Marbles would follow to the lorry, until they went through a double door that had been set in a larger opening, an exact copy of the final, secure door they needed to get through to the loading platform in the museum garage. There were two lorries at a loading dock, exactly as would be the case on the night. A group of about a dozen men were waiting on the dock.

"Helena, I would like you to meet the lads. Trev's the boss as you know." They went down the line, using first names only, but all were equally introduced and hands shaken.

Helena turned to face them, taking a step back. "Thank you, men. Peter and Trev will have given you the statutory warning."

Peter translated, "The scoop, boys, the warning, you know."

Helena continued, "This is a risky operation. If we're nicked, it's straight to jail, do not pass go, no second chance, no last minute reprieves. That's what the danger pay is all about."

Trev added, "Just like lorries by the motorway, lads, if the old bill comes along, it's the chop. Listen to the lady. The side door over there is the way out."

Nobody moved. "Once through this other door, it's for keeps."

Trev took out his referee's whistle, blew it, and hollered, "Let's show the lady that we're up for it." Oblivious to the double meaning, Trev ran down the line, through the loading doors into the *museum*.

"Hi, I'm baby Jim." A larger, heavier built version of Trev, was trotting by, and stopped to say hello to Peter, looking down to speak to him. "Course at the gym was a great idea; lost a bit of weight too, fat into muscle, and I'm damn sure I'm fitter." Off he dashed, flexing his muscles as if in living proof.

Helena wandered along behind, and then climbed up an open metal staircase on the side of the interior space. Peter made comments from time to time. She listened, and watched silently.

Trev was in his element, dashing from one end of the room to the other, uncannily like a referee on the field.

"By the way, he is in fact a respected referee in the amateur leagues; good training for this, I think – brought his whistle, and refreshments for halftime."

Helena smiled.

Trev shouted out, as if addressing teams on the pitch, "Now lads, this is the dress rehearsal. Remember, speed and efficiency."

"Helena, you can see the 56 identical boxes for the friezes. The lads have their ladders and portable scaffolding. They simply lift them down off the wall, two men on each, which is much faster than any other method. It can be 200 pounds a man, yet you can see they do it with nothing more than a grunt or two. Then they slide them down special ramps, directly into the crates on their mini low-loaders, all of which have high-impact polystyrene foam bottoms and siding."

"Thump, thump," they slid into their boxes, lids nailed down in a trice, then the four-wheeled low-loading carts were pulled out of the gallery and off to the lorry. Helena timed this operation for a moment, and found that a bit more than two per minute were disappearing around the corner. It would take less than a half-hour for all of them.

"That's the easy bit, and it's already a third finished in just a few minutes. All of the carts have rubber wheels, so it's quiet enough. We even have oil cans ready for any squeaks. I hope we have thought of everything; I have lists of equipment, spares, and all sorts as long as both my arms."

"The only way, Peter."

"We also have the awkward objects. 'Carrie' over there represents the caryatid, and the concrete simulation matches the support points in the box. It will simply be tipped over under the arbour the 'Carrie' crew are setting up, no need to lift her. We've rehearsed that one, and it goes well now, 15 minutes with the crew of four.

"The pedimental sculptures must be lifted into their boxes, and we use another two pair of arbours for that with chain tackles. We have timed it off to less than an hour twenty minutes for the lot. Each sculpture must be lifted, rotated, and eased down into the correct box. Again we have separately practiced this operation. We have two substitutes tonight, and they spell anybody who sprains himself, or cannot work on the night due to sickness. Everyone had their flu shots, and vitamin regimes for the last six months."

Helena said, "It was a lot of detailed work to make all the practice blocks fit the boxes, but I felt it was worth it. What do you think?"

"Yes, well, we hated the idea at the beginning, but now that we can practice the real thing, point-to-point, everything fitting perfectly, we can be sure there'll be no hitch on the night."

They descended to the floor, and walked around. As they passed Carrie, being lowered into her box, one of the lads laughed. "I hope the real one is prettier, eh lads?"

"We tried motorized equipment, but our hands worked better, so that's the way we do it."

A box labelled "Panagia Glykophiloussa", the one for "Carrie" the caryatid was being nailed shut, marked with one of the names from the Treasures of Mount Athos Exhibition that was never on exhibit. That illustrated the plan in a nutshell. The Exhibition lorry had come in with two sets of boxes. First, those actually containing the Mount Athos exhibits; second, a duplicate set of boxes to those here. Both sets had entered the museum with all items listed on the manifest under realistic names.

Their own lift-lorry had duplicates of the Mount Athos Exhibition pieces, plus the 90-odd marbles' boxes with matching labels. It was no problem to get a backup truck in to the museum. It didn't matter which one was examined because the two loads were identical, and would agree in every detail with the manifest that came in for the Exhibition three months earlier. Their lorry would go out under the pass for that exhibition. The Treasures lorry would be left behind until the Marbles were safely on Greek soil. It was unlikely that anybody would check to see if everything had actually gone on show, and that fact if discovered would not in itself be particularly suspicious.

Someone had written on Carrie's box with a spray paint scrawl, "Virgin giving sweet kiss", not a bad translation. If it kept the lads happy, Helena didn't have a problem. She recognized the names of the twenty monasteries of Mount Athos rolling by, stencilled on other cases, along with other suitable if phoney names.

The room hummed with panting, puffing, huffing, straining, heavy grunts and deep intakes of breath, murmured oaths, and large helpings of mutually supportive language: "good, got it, push it, lift your side, bit to your left" and so on.

Trev was everywhere, supporting, directing, praising, and reprimanding in good humour. It reminded Helena of an orchestrated dance, with the percussion section of grunts and scrapes, that developed its rhythm more surely as the ballet continued, getting smoother and more efficient as time passed. There were repeated patterns of shoving and heaving, edging and circling, followed by wiggling, the "thump", and then the patting in-place by strong, loving hands.

It all lent a unity to the operation. Then it was over, as the last of the heavy goods rolled out the door. "Hour and twenty, flat, Helena."

"That will do. Well done, Peter."

"Well, not bad that, guv." One said to Trev as he trotted up.

"Good workout".

Thumb up, "Organization, top on."

Trev, "Great job lads, it will be even better on the night."

Finally, Helena grasped it, the image that had been trying to rise in her mind. It had been a scene from *West Side Story*; truly both a ballet and a play, and it had been performed for her this night.

The crew gathered around, and Peter spoke gravely. "Mum's the word on all this lads – not to wives, lasses, or anybody. After it's over, you get tickets on Eurostar for a week in Paris, all expenses paid for two!"

"How come?"

Trev replied, "This is hot, men, so we need to cool off. We're sure nobody'll be able to mark any of you after, but better safe than sorry."

One football fan exclaimed, "I can see a Paris St Germain match."

Another, "Don't we have an English side in the Champion's league over there? I'll check it out."

"Been over for ciggies, and I kinda like the Froggies, specially some of their skirts, eh?"

Safe Laboratory, late the same evening

"Adam, clear me in please." Helena's face was on the screen of his portable.

Adam checked the computer monitors showing the outside camera views. "The street's clear, Helena, looks okay."

A moment later, the buzzer sounded on the door of the garage, Adam slipped the latch, and let Helena in.

She hugged Adam, which threw him a bit off balance, for this was not their normal greeting. "Peter's briefed me on all this," her hand swept around the small garage. "By the way, the Lift rehearsal went extremely well this evening."

"Great, so now we have just one little problem."

"That you're going to solve?"

"One can live in hope."

"So what's changed since yesterday? Must have been something pretty vital, for you to risk it all, on a throw of the dice – nicking the Quantum Computer – out from under the noses of MI5 – and *without* project clearance." It was obvious that Helena was more than uncomfortable with what Adam had done on the spur of the moment. Then she thought to herself, as a famous bridge player once put it of his partner, "Success washes away all sin."

"Well, it was Peter, you know, who broke the logjam."

"Peter? He didn't mention it to me."

"He's a bit bashful about that sort of thing, but it was him, for sure." Helena was motioning for more, as she turned on the kettle for a much needed coffee booster. "Well, you see, he didn't *believe* in the transfinite infinities. My block was that I did."

"So you were wrong? That would be a first, Adam, in your field anyway." Helena smiled, and unaccountably hugged him again.

"No, I was right on that, but what I was wrong about was believing that one couldn't get around infinity, just because it was infinite."

Helena continued beckoning impatiently for more as she poured out the coffee, and a tea for him. "Sounds pretty tough to me, Adam, so I suppose I believe in them, but most of all in you."

"Off I go giving a lecture again, but there's no other way. Here's what happens when you plug in one of these." He held up his British Museum pass that looked like a normal credit card. "This little gold square here, with the lines across it, is a tiny computer embedded in the card. It only does one thing. Give it a number, it applies the formula hard-wired in the circuits inside, and sends back the answer. If one tries to get at the internal program, you can't. Any tampering simply destroys the circuits. The formula and program is in the silicon itself, you see.

"Here's the way around it theoretically, and I emphasize, theoretically, because nobody's done it yet. Imagine the little equation inside, like my simple example of always doubling the input number. It receives, say, 224, and outputs 448; next time 504, outputs 1008, next 152, outputs 304, and so on. Now we can see that the function, the rule, is to double the number, just by looking at the sequence. Our brains figure out the equation buried in the chip, by looking at the results. It might feel to us that we didn't actually think about the problem. It just *occurs* to us.

"In the real device, the program or function or equation, whatever you want to call it, uses very long numbers, about 40 digit or 128 binary bit numbers, and the formula can be extremely complicated, perhaps bizarre, so we would never figure it out by looking at a few examples. Even with a top class computer, we couldn't do it, for at least two reasons. First, writing the program to discover the formula, the equivalent of what we did with our eye and brain before, is extraordinarily difficult. Indeed, it is impractical with our current computer equipment not to mention the limitations of our own brains in programming it for such a task. Second, we cannot begin to imagine what the formula might be like, so if we could program the system, we wouldn't know what we had, when we had it, or when we were finished.

"Now enter the Quantum Computer, the world's largest by far, an eight-thousand Qbit machine – the equivalent of just a hundred words of typing or so would fill its memory in a flash."

"Adam, do you have that right? Our latest home computers have thousands of millions of characters of memory."

"That's right, the spec sheet looks like something from the computer technology of the 1950s. Yet it does something that no other computer can do, and that is to *learn* from the dataflow through it *without having to program it*. And the speed is astronomically faster than anything else we have today, at least a billion times faster for certain operations.

"It happens that the task we have here is *ideally* suited to this little beauty. Here's what we need, as simple as pie. Imagine the doubling formula again, and that we are dealing with a security computer that is both sending us numbers, and receiving the answers, back and forth. What we want to do, eventually, is compute from the number received, a correct response. We don't require the formula; all we need is a black box that learns to get it right. Once in a while is fine, because we can wait for a hit, and then open the door.

"We don't need the security computer at all, just now. I have merely connected QC to my security pass. The QC has a simple program, yes we do program them, but in quite a different, far more general way than usual. It is sending the 128 bit numbers at an immense speed to the chip on the pass, which is sending back the answers. The QC pats itself on its back if it can calculate the next response, and when it succeeds, it stores that away in its infinite memory."

" I thought the QC's memory was extremely small."

"It is, but it is a pipeline to the Quantum World, where there is in effect another kind of memory, buried out of our sight, down in the subatomic realm. We just *push* the results in the top of that hopper, and the computer has learned that little bit, so that when the next comes along, it will be a little more likely to succeed. Hopefully there will be a second hit, a third, and so on, and if this works, a moment will come when it avalanches, and the QC *knows* what the next number will be, or gets enough hits to be practical for us."

"So, how does that actually work? I don't see it, Adam, sorry."

"Neither do I."

"What?"

"That's right, I don't understand *how* it works, but I do sort of understand *why* it does."

Helena replied with a frown, "I thought the *how* was always easier than the *why*."

"It always has been, until now, anyway. The Quantum World is different. Helena, how did you figure out the doubling rule from three or four numbers?"

"It just popped into my head, Adam. It's obvious."

"Well, there are those who put it like this. '*A deterministic computer cannot have consciousness, but a non deterministic one perhaps could.*' In other words, a machine that cannot do truly random things, can't think on its own, but one that can randomise, try things we haven't thought of, without thinking about it, is actually thinking."

"Riddles, enigmas, and more riddles. Are you suggesting that this little QC of yours can *think*, sort of like we do?"

"Well, I think," Adam smiled at the repetitions, "it will be a while before we can talk to QC, but she's sitting over there trying to think about my problem, exactly as you did a few minutes ago. We will know soon enough if she's interested in my problem, or something else. We can hope for the best."

"You give QC the feminine gender?"

"Well, I guess that falls to me, as the first to try her like this, and it seems appropriate, does it not? We men, as I did, tend to think deductively, give me A, and I will get to B, straight down the logical road. Women tend to come up with something like %^@ from A, a total surprise, yet when you have a look, it is a fresh insight. Ordinary computers are strictly deductive, A to B to C, and you have to tell them how to do it, every step of the way. Quantum Computers take in data as A then B, B then X, C then %, D then >*<, E then (something totally unexpected), and give the answer (next prediction) %^@ when no human would have thought it could go like that. An ordinary computer can only do one thing at a time. The QC can do a billion things *at the same time*. In fact, it cannot do anything else.

271

That's how a lot of people think our brain works, a billion synapses *sharing* in one thought. We feel that our thinking process is like a play going in a theatre somewhere specific inside our heads. Some sharpies say that's not how it is. Wow, sorry, that's a bit weird."

"It's okay, Adam." Helena patted him on the shoulder. "So how will we know when it is working?"

"We wait." Adam stepped over to the improvised lab bench, a plank across two smelly, empty oil drums. "Well, we've passed through something like a billion, billion, billion numbers already, and no hits. And yet, my little darling here," Adam patted QCs small box, "is going to come through."

"When?" Helena asked, uncertainty plainly written on her face.

"Eventually. She has no choice, really, and will get around to my problem, eventually."

"How *eventually* is that, Adam?"

"Well, I calculate that it should be something less than the present age of the universe! Unless, of course, I am right about what is going on in the Qbits and the subatomic structure of the other universe hiding in her tiny cells. Deep down in there, if I am right, lurks a model, a mirror of the largeness of space and time, her infinite inner world, and the one can shortcut the other, time-wise, and…"

"Ding!"

"Hey, Helena, that's our first hit! The first successful advance computation." Adam stroked the box, "That's it, my girl, give. Come to your lover, dear heart, and give!"

272

Chapter 22

Breakthrough

There is a theory that the Universe is mirrored in Quantum Space.

The next morning, Sunday, 23 April, Adam's Safe Lab, L–5 days

Adam had fallen asleep on the hard floor at the foot of his new beloved. Helena had taken the couch. A misty sun was just beginning to peek in through thin cracks around the garage door.

The most powerful alarm clock that anyone had so far created was trying to wake her sleepy lover.

"Ding!" … "Ding, Ding." … "Ding." … "Ding, ding, dinglinginginging." Adam finally awoke with a start.

He cast bleary eyes at the ordinary computer screen attached to QC, and in a box labelled "Percentage of Successful Predictions" he saw ".00000154, .00000162, .00000184…"

The bell was ringing continuously, so he shut it off, as Helena groggily slid her legs off the couch, and brushed the cobwebs, literally, from her hair, and then from her mind.

".00000962, .00001024, .00001164…"

Like Dorothy of Oz in her red shoes, this time Adam had believed. That did not banish doubts, but now they were evaporating, euphoria waiting in the wings to replace them. "Come on, baby, we need a bit more, just a bit."

".00002201, .00002354, .00003016…"

"Adam…"

"Shsst." Adam hushed her, fearing that it might break the spell.

Helena patted him on the shoulders, and went to make coffee, and look for some food. There was coffee, and fresh orange juice, but no food. "Just like men." She thought to herself.

She offered juice to Adam, who drank it automatically, clearly not realizing he had the cup in his hand, and as she sipped her coffee, she looked around the room. It was a mess, but that was to be expected. She wondered how many breakthroughs had come to mankind in such surroundings: Bell, Edison, Archimedes – no, she remembered, he was comfortably in his bath. Would this garage, or a reproduction of it someday grace a museum, to remember this moment, or was it just another flash in the pan of emerging technologies, to be forgotten before it had really been born? She had no doubt that something important was happening, and was comforted by the fact that none of them, the inventor, herself, or anyone else understood what was really happening. This was a very strange new world to her. She had been enchanted by the names Adam had mentioned for some of these arcane phenomena: "charm, colour, strange, spin..." She suspected that the physicists could not have known in the early days how appropriate these names would prove to be.

Adam sat back, seemingly discouraged, but it was only the exhaustion of success. He beckoned to her, and she came to stand beside him.

The screen gave the answer: ".00502261, .00502263, .00502264, .00502265, .00502265, .00502265..." then remained fixed on this number.

Adam smiled, and patted QC on the back. "It's just about good enough, Helena. QC is hitting about one in twenty thousand numbers, and that's the best she can do, but it is a triumph! Yes!" He then shouted, and stroked QC like he might have Irini in a quiet moment.

"You mean we have to stick the card in twenty thousand times before we can open the door?"

"No," Adam laughed deeply, "because they made a mistake. Don't we all, all the time, eh?

"Fortunately, as usual, we needed and got a little help from our enemies. In this case, it is that the designer of the system, you-know-where down the road, didn't shut off the interrogations after a certain number of *card* errors. You remember my report on all that work I did a month or two back, checking out the basics of the new system. They don't allow users to put in the wrong PIN number more than the customary three times, but if QC here is programmed to keep asking for more numbers, their computer will happily continue to try, at a rate of over one thousand times each second. So, we can expect a hit from QC substituting for a user's card in about three minutes on the average from this result. When it hits, QC will stop, and we will enter the PIN, which we got the same way as before. You remember, I had to make a fresh box-cover to match the new system, but that was just simple production. We have all the important PINs in hand. Now we have the black box to substitute for anybody's card."

"So how will it work?"

"I'll package QC here, and connect her to a thin flat cable, leading to a security card with the right contacts, you know, the little pads on that gold square on the credit cards, and QC will become the computer inside the card so far as the master security system is concerned."

"Hey, Adam, I understand that." Helena was satisfied, as the team captain, to at least grasp the mechanics, nothing more needed. As Adam himself didn't know how the damn thing worked, or how it could work, what more was there to know?

"Just one minor logistical problem."

"What's that, my King of Cyberspace?"

"I've got to have physical possession of the card of a person with access to the loading dock, and any others along the way. Given what we have done here, overnight should do."

"Hmm," Helena considered, "it is vital that they not know it has been missing, isn't it?" Then she answered her own question, "Otherwise they would change the card."

"Yes, and I think we had better have at least two or three, just in case they should lose their card just before we need it. Damn, that won't work."

Helena was suddenly afraid again. "What?"

"Well, Helena, we only have one QC."

"Yes, so now what?" She was a bit frustrated, and had uncharacteristically allowed it to show, but Adam went blithely on, oblivious at this moment to the subtle signs of body language.

"QC isn't like an ordinary computer, where we can read out the data, the whole contents of memory, and make as many copies of the system as we want. Just buy more computers, and copy in the software, fill a building with them, all identical, no problem.

"QC herself now has, as part of her substance you see, the answer to the impossible question of the hidden equation. It is buried inside her little window on Quantum Space." He paused. "Once again, more like our own brains than I like to admit, eh? Can't 'read out' that either, can we? Can't copy a brain, can we?

"We cannot copy her for two reasons. First we can't get another one in time; chips are special, and the security lid is surely on now. Second, even if we had a hundred on the bench here, each one would have to be separately developed by giving access to a physical card.

"Wait, maybe there is a way out. I'll test that with Irini's security card today. Maybe QC can learn both at the same time. Actually, now that I think about it, she probably can. I'll report tonight." Adam's mind was running at warp drive, as he had said, itself using the resources of the Quantum World, if the latest theories about our brains were to be believed. His hope that QC could learn more than one was not the shot in the dark that it appeared. He knew that everyone could learn many formulas, without getting a new brain, or copying the one we already have. His breakthrough, and most powerful contribution, was in believing that QC had a brain in some ways like our own, though it could not yet be seen or understood.

At the regular meeting that night, Adam made his presentation. He first covered the ground that Helena had already heard that morning, at the moment of triumph. Then he continued. "So I borrowed Irini's card, and started QC off again without changing anything, just plugged in the new card. She got confused for a time."

"Come off it, Adam," Peter interrupted, "you're making your new darling QC sound human again. How could you possibly know how she feels?"

"Tell me, Peter, say you know a fact as well as your own name, and then something happens, maybe you witness an accident or such like, and then when asked for it by the cop on the scene, have forgotten that familiar item along with others. What English words would you give to your state of mind?"

"Confused, frustrated – okay, I agree on the words."

"Well, I could test QC any time on this experiment, by the simple device of swapping the two security cards, and looking to see if she had forgotten about the first. So after a few minutes with Irini's card, I swapped mine back. And she had forgotten it. That scared me at first, because I was afraid it was back to square one. Just like I'd be worried about you, Peter, if you couldn't remember your address. I'd know something was wrong, whether you could tell me or not.

"That's what happened, and I thought I had made a terrible mistake, so I shoved Irini's card back in, and hoped for the best. After a couple of hours, QC converged – let's use that word, it is expressive – to Irini's hidden, secret formula, and surprise, it had taken less than half the time of my card, and the hit probability had doubled! Now when I put my card back in, the hit probability was extremely low again, but soon came back. After I had swapped the two cards a few times, QC converged to a hit percentage of .0112 percent for *both* cards. That is, I could put in either one, and get one hit out of ten-thousand, instead of half that."

"Seems like something for nothing," Peter came in again, "and where I come from, that's suspicious."

"Sure, and as the co-inventor of this process, Peter, I respect and accept your views. But look, what is happening is quite understandable. Think about us and how we learn. If we discuss some arithmetical, or historical fact, and learn it, isn't it easier to pick up the second, third, and others? Of course it is, because we already have an idea of how to go about the subject, how things relate. Well, QC does exactly the same.

"It is likely that the type of formula used for the cards follows a pattern – they are probably the same *sort* of equations. Like if they were using our example of the doubling formula: card two, the tripling formula, card three, the quadrupling formula, and so on. QC converged faster, and better, *because* QC had learned a bit about the general rules for the code, and applied them. I know that sounds too *human*, and yet there are smart people out there who think our brains are Quantum devices, and that we couldn't think without being able to reach that other infinite world deep inside our atoms.

"There is just one more possible problem. Will QC remember the third card after I have put in the fourth and fifth? I am hoping that the third and subsequent cards can be refreshed in the system, once they are in, if I use both Irini's and my card with each as the reference data. If that doesn't work, we will need all the cards at the same time."

Helena weighed in with the decision. "We will get, by whatever means is necessary, access to at least two, and preferably three cards for senior museum personnel, overnight, so that Adam can get them into QC, and we are bombproof against the, well, you know … any questions?" There were none, as usual, but there followed during the evening some rather cryptic text messages:

IRINI TO PETER AND ADAM
      MEET ME 9AM MUSEUM FORECOURT
      PETER, WE NEED A GOOD PICKPOCKET
    COPY: HELENA
HELENA TO ADAM:
      YOU'RE RED HOT, MINIMUM EXPOSURE.
      STAY IN THE LAB. THAT'S AN ORDER!

Irini was strolling around, feeding the pigeons with leftovers from her breakfast toast, as she had done from time to time. This morning there was a purpose, as she waited for her two colleagues.

Peter and Adam had met in the street outside, and came across to Irini together. She embraced first Peter, then Adam, and Adam again. "Helena told me that you are locked up in your lab, so you are forgiven, but I miss you."

"So do I, love. Not long now. What's up?"

Irini got straight down to business. "We need access to passes, so here's the drill. The Archimandrite Athanassios is giving a seminar this morning for VIPs, and Hayward is going. Last Week he invited me to come along because of my Greek. It is at the Press Club in Fleet Street. Here's a map. He keeps the pass in his outside lower right coat pocket, with his house keys. Peter, who's going to lift it?"

He looked down at his feet, and shuffled them on the pavement. "Uh, well, I am!"

"A talent you have kept well hidden from us." Adam shook his head with a sly smile.

"Well, you know how it is."

"Sure, Peter, we know." Irini was beaming. "But are you sure you're not rusty, or something, that you can do it?"

Peter grinned. "I thought you might want some proof, so…" He handed Adam his wallet, lifted from his *inside* coat pocket, while Irini was embracing him, his house keys taken from his outside left coat pocket, and Irini's wallet, slipped out of her handbag, he having opened it, lifted the goods, and closed it, all unfelt.

Irini shook her head. "I guess that's good enough, Peter.

"Peter, you don't know Hayward by sight, do you?"

"Nope."

"Adam, you'll need to ID him if it isn't obvious when we get out of the museum limo; I'm pretty sure we won't go by tube or taxi, but keep your eyes open. When we approach the door, I will try to be on his left side and stumble into him. Hopefully the timing will work for you, Peter.

"We are going to lunch afterwards, but I do not know where, so Peter, you will have to follow us. If coats are in the coat room, do you want to get it back in then, or later?"

"Whatever works. I'll get it back in his coat if I have to teleport it there."

"I believe you might just be able to do that, too, Peter." Irini laughed playfully, and lightly hit his shoulder with her fist.

The little lift went smoothly. Adam ran the pass back to the lab, through two department stores, and shifting hats twice, reversing the special coat Helena had given him after the Sunday safe house meeting. The followers who had tracked him from the museum to the Press Club were lost on the return to the lab, which advantageously was reached by an alternative route through a narrow walkway between two warehouses.

The meeting in the forecourt had been observed and photographed, but the efforts to use directional microphones to pick up what was being said, had failed.

FISKE TO TEAM:
    WE NEED A LIP READER OR TWO
    ADAM'S WHEREABOUTS UNKNOWN THIS HOUR

ADAM TO TEAM:
    ONE MORE IN QC, TWO TO GO
    SMOOTH AS SILK
    GREAT IDEA IRINI
THANKS PETER

"Irini, so very nice that you could meet me for tea." John Fiske was personally, as distinct from professionally, delighted that Irini had sent him the invitation as a text message via ordinary mobile phone. It was the first time she had contacted him for one of their occasional dates.

John had actually read the book on Greek sculpture Irini had recommended to him the last time they had met, and was able to discuss it with sensitivity. She had slowly warmed to him as a friend, verging on close friend. Her initial misgivings about him had gradually faded; she felt she had begun to understand him. He was obviously an operator when it came to women, but she felt he was doing it openly and so she happily forgave him.

He spluttered in his teacup when mid-sip, Irini suggested that they might share a drink at her flat. John had dreamed of this for all the months since he had first spotted her in the Duveen Gallery, enchanting a group of youngsters with her polished tales of ancient Greece. He had since eavesdropped two or three times, and quite genuinely respected her in this role.

The fact that she had taken the initiative took his breath away. He was a master at disguising body language, and he contrived to accept in an ingratiating way, without, he hoped, showing his surprise. Delight was okay, surprise, well a real man, he thought, is *never* surprised.

Irini took his coat as he came in through the door. She knew he had a master security pass to the museum, because they had compared their own the first week of the new system, and he had confided in her that his was a master. She knew he kept it in his left inside pocket, and removed it easily as she draped his coat over the back of one of the spindly, kitchen chairs. She invited him to the lone easy chair.

"I've got the glasses. Glenfiddich, neat?"

His mind spun, and then he remembered. She had happened on him in the Museum Tavern one afternoon after work early in the new year, and he had ordered it. John was impressed, and said so.

"Well, you're not easy to forget, John." Irini knew that she had to play the game just right. She realized she was using him, and that it was more than technically immoral. The thought that if it got out of control, the tables would be turned, and he would be using her, did not frighten her but she knew she must give it her full attention.

He was in the palm of her hand. As an experienced man he knew this, and that it could be turned. He resolved to try.

Irini moved to the second cat flap, which was positioned for access to the roof, just above a chest high bookshelf. "I think I hear Achilles." She pushed the flap outward, and passed the key into Adam's cold, wet hand. She was surprised when a drizzle-dampened Achilles shot through the flap into her arms. Irini staggered backward with this unexpected weighty arrival. Their plan could not have anticipated the cat actually being there; her comment had simply been the necessary cover.

Adam had waited patiently, lying on the roof, getting soaked. When Achilles had appeared to go through his flap, he curiously nuzzled Adam and he took the cat protectively under his coat. Adam's gesture was certainly appreciated, but when Irini made the pass,

Achilles decided that he had neither understood it, nor liked it very much, so when Adam released him, he shot through his door at speed.

John instinctively recoiled, doing his best to conceal the reaction. He was allergic to cats, and didn't like them, but he told himself sternly; this will have to be an exception. Irini lovingly towelled off her cat, and John found himself for the first time in his life wishing he were a cat. He took some comfort in the fact that the dampness might protect him from the worst ravages of his allergy. "Love her, love her cat," had to be his mantra for that evening.

Achilles had immediately read all of this from the open book of this new arrival in his home. Irini had noted John's reluctance to be forthcoming with the cat, and she had seen this before with others. After all, not every adult turned to putty in a cat's paws. So she moved to the couch and comforted Achilles on her lap.

John now had a wide chasm to bridge, the scant metre to the other half of Irini's couch. The way forward was first to talk, mainly listening to her, and then at an appropriate moment, jump across. Irini had worried about whether there would be enough to talk about, how to fill the awkward silences, and so on. They really did like, understand, and appreciate each other, and so, in the event, the time passed comfortably. It was apparent that he was playing the listen-to-the-lady game, so the rhythm was soon established, and she could remain in control.

Irini had set her secure digital mobile telephone on the bookshelf where she could see it, but John couldn't, and waited for Adam's message, with the ring turned off. She had feared an eternity, but the two and a half hours it took Adam to read the card passed quickly. When the message appeared, she stood up, stretched, and said, "Well, Achilles, another run on the roofs?"

He was more mystified by this than the earlier encounter with Adam, for Irini had never before pushed him through his flap. He was so surprised that his head was through, the rest following irresistibly, before he could put up any resistance.

"Hello again, old fellow," Adam whispered, "in here, under the coat." Adam handed the pass over to Irini, who stroked his hand before withdrawing inside. Achilles wanted to go straight back through the flap, but Adam thought it might seem suspicious, so he stroked him under the coat. Achilles changed his mind, and thought that this might be a nice new game after all. He was soon nuzzling Adam as he lay on the cold roof, once again getting soaked. After a suitable interval, Adam let Achilles go back in through the flap, slithered along the short roof to the fire escape, and back down the rear of the building.

Irini set out another round of drinks and took the sweet tray out of the fridge. John had taken the opportunity to move to the couch, but made the mistake of taking Achilles' space. The cat shortly came through the flap, landed on the bookshelf, and dropped like a jaguar into John's lap. It was to his great credit that he was able to sit still, and managed to stroke Achilles. Irini took that useful moment to bend over the chair and slip the security card back inside his coat pocket. The cat was not fooled, and after taking a cursory stroke, jumped down on the floor.

Irini had no choice but to set the tray down on the coffee table, and sit next to John on the couch. Anything else would have been discourteous in the extreme, and she was determined to remain cordial if possible.

John took her hand, and Irini did not withdraw it, but she did say, "John, I am fond of you, yet I do want to say that I…"

He interrupted what he knew she was going to say next, with a kiss. Irini could not draw back because John had pulled her smoothly forward, off balance, and she had no leverage with which to oppose him. His move was not unexpected, nor was it abrupt, or objectionable, in no way a grab. She had little choice but to go with the flow, and so decided if she was really still in control, to make the kiss a good one. She need not have worried. He saw to it that it was the best she had ever had, as far as a kiss goes, including Adam. It was always special in a different way with him, because that was first love, and a deep relationship, which they both knew would be permanent. This was different, and yet powerful, and that realization did shake her.

John Fiske was a senior master at this game, and only a junior master at the other. In a few minutes, Irini was lost in the sensations of his deep kisses, and subtle caresses. He did not make the mistake of attempting in any way to begin releasing her clothes. Instead, he made love to her with their clothes on, as she and Adam had done two or three times. Each time she thought of Adam, her passion skipped a beat, which he immediately sensed, and gave way briefly, only to begin again from a different direction.

It was not a passionate encounter in the sense that either was out of control, begging for more, groaning, and all the rest. They were both silent, and yet deeply involved. This was a strange, but vaguely familiar progression, delivering considerable, and not just superficial, pleasure. Their bodies were involved, but so were their thoughts. The moves were natural, yet planned in a sense, the responses a complex mixture of intellect and physical involvement. She likened it to an intimate dance, whirling on the lubricated hardwood, following a partner, both thinking and feeling about what came next in the music of love.

The world spun, as if they were in the dance that had filled her imagination, and exactly analogously to that *pas de deux* in her head, dizziness overtook her. Yet it was not that of a pirouette, but the deep rumbling of physical and emotional release, the final flood of sensations overflowing the dam, and sweeping all before it.

John held her shuddering body tightly in his arms, as she came down, and back into the present. Then she was crying, and blurted out, "Adam, forgive me."

John then showed his true mettle as a gentleman. "Irini, dear Irini, our woman in a million, there is nothing for him to forgive, and no apology needed. You noticed months ago that I am married, and I knew that you are equally committed. This was unsaid, but not ignored, by either of us." Look at me. He turned her tear-stained face to him. "This moment, and your tears, are but a dream, one that we may never share again, between us, or with another. It was a new kind of first love, and we turn aside from those at the peril of our regrets."

Irini knew that this was no line for the girls. She sensed that the whole experience had been, yes, exactly what he had said it was, "a new kind of first love", for both of them. She understood that he was far more experienced than she, and that made this first for him all the more powerful for both of them.

Irini nodded, and started to wipe away her tears, but he took her hand, and kissed them away with dry lips. They both knew that this was a one-off. Not because of guilt, or the existence for them both of their other partners, but for the ineffable reason that to attempt a repeat would destroy what they had experienced that night, and all value in any repetition.

ADAM TO TEAM:
    QC HOLDS GOOD PERCENTAGE OF HITS WITH NEW CARDS.
    PROCEED AS AGREED. SIMULTANEITY NOT NECESSSARY.

Tuesday morning, 25 April, L–3 days

Irini grabbed Emily Stone's arm as she was entering the museum.
Without ado, Irini broached the subject that was uppermost in her
mind. "Emily, you know you promised to show me the manuscript
room, and I'd love to see some of the invisible-ink cartoons. If
you've time this morning," she added. "I feel like a bit of light
relief."

Emily could see signs of stress around the corners of Irini's
usually tranquil eyes. She felt concerned for her young friend, and
sensed that while this request sprang from the heart, it was also more
than it seemed.

"Yes, with pleasure," Emily replied. "I could do with a bit of
light relief myself, and was planning to work there sometime this
week anyway."

They made their way there together, and Emily ushered Irini
through the door to the manuscript room, using her security pass, and
keying in her PIN number. In other circumstances Irini would have
been more enchanted by the proximity of so many of these rare
manuscripts, but now all she could think of was the card that lay in
Emily's jacket patch-pocket. The long room, dimly lit to protect the
manuscripts, reminded Irini of a medieval scriptorium, in which the
monks toiled industriously, and in some cases passionately, to
fashion their copies.

Emily led the way to her desk by the long display cases, and
drew up two chairs side by side, so they could pore over the bold
quill marks incised so many centuries before. After a little while,
Irini edged closer. Emily was preoccupied, squinting intently through
a loupe, her face creased with the effort required to hold it in place.
Emily's jacket had scrunched up, and Irini was able to easily extract
the card from the open folds.

Irini suddenly interrupted Emily's running translation, "I'm
sorry, Emily, I must dash to the loo." She made her way in the semi-
darkness to the security door, and let herself out. She found Adam
downstairs as by the prearrangement.

"Back in ninety minutes." He reconfirmed, reassuringly. "It goes faster each time, in about an hour of connection time."

She slipped the card surreptitiously into his hand.

Turning on her heel, she returned to Emily and the manuscript room. She tapped on the door for re-admittance. "Are you all right?" Emily asked. "Are you sure you want to stay? We can do this another morning if you like."

"Oh no," Irini assured her, "it's just one of those gastric bugs that catches you on the hop." She continued with emphasis, "No, it's the first time in my life I've ever seen such rare manuscripts." This was truthful, finding honesty a rare comfort in these painful times of deception. "I do so want to see more."

If Emily sensed a lack of concentration on Irini's part during their further explorations, she put it down to her physical discomfort. In spite of the extraordinary circumstances, Irini was impressed by the painstaking beauty of the illuminations, particularly those on the Celtic manuscripts, the subtle colours seemingly made more precious in the dim light.

The allotted time passed swiftly as Emily turned the pages, and at one point allowed Irini to hold one for herself, caressing it lightly between her fingers.

"Oh. Emily, sorry." Irini hurried to the door without further comment, wanting to keep her white lies to the minimum. She found Adam waiting right outside the door as agreed, and with only the briefest of encouraging smiles, wordlessly slipped the key back into Irini's hand.

She then waited three minutes by her watch, before knocking once again on the door. The reasons behind this were to fulfil Emily's expectations of a reasonable time for the necessary visit, and at this critical moment to make sure that Emily did not come out of the room unexpectedly. As Helena repeatedly warned them, *always* plan for all possibilities, and they had done so. There was no hitch, and Irini knocked softly on the door.

Irini murmured upon entering, "As I was saying, then," running a hand along the bookshelves, "extraordinary."

Emily was pleased that she could share her passion.

"Can we see a couple more before lunch?" Irini glided past Emily's jacket, now hanging conveniently on the back of her chair. Mission accomplished.

Irini gave a sigh of relief. She thought to herself, that this had been one of the most difficult things in the whole operation so far. She covered her sigh with a cough, "A touch of medieval dust, perhaps?"

Emily recommended that her young colleague take a good dose of a soothing herbal remedy, and solicitously offered to give her some of her own favourite from her office.

Emily then said, "It also does wonders for stress, my trusty panacea."

ADAM TO IRINI
    WE DON'T HAVE FISKE'S PIN. ANY IDEAS?
LOVE, ADAM

IRINI TO ADAM
    PUT YOUR BOX ON AND
    WATCH MY OFFICE AROUND 4PM
LOVE, IRINI

IRINI TO JOHN (UNENCRYPTED)
    COME TO MY OFFICE AROUND 4PM FOR TEA?
LOVE, IRINI

John Fiske's soft knock came on Irini's office door a few minutes before four.

"Who is it?"

"Me, John."

"Hands full, John."

"Just a minute, I'll use my card."

John entered to find Irini with a stack of books in her arms, and helped her lower them down to her desk. He embraced her, fully in his arms.

Irini bade him sit down in her guest chair, as she put a few more books on the shelves of her new office, a grand improvement on the previous closet. She arranged this and that, and then smiled endearingly. "Well, time for tea, my one-time-only, wonderful lover, who can do it all like a gentleman."

He bowed low, and took her hand.

"John, before we go, while we are still in private here, I want to say how much I admire and respect you. And to thank you for your maturity extended to me last night." She stilled his lips. "And for your wisdom. And for being the gentleman every woman hopes to meet, but we almost never do. Like Diogenes' search for the nonexistent honest man. I will never, ever forget you." She removed her fingers from his lips.

He had been ready to say many things, but was now lost for a response. It was plainly apparent to him that a very great deal lay behind her words, a deep lake of mystery.

An hour later, Irini was on her way home, and decided to pass by Andreas Hadjis' shop. She didn't know why, because she didn't really need to buy anything; they were all dining out that evening. As she entered the shop, her reasons for the visit came to her.

She toyed with canned goods and small packets of spices until the shop was empty of clients. He immediately came over to her with a strong hug for he sensed her disquiet. Before she could begin to assemble her thoughts on the romantic matters she wanted, and needed, to discuss with him, he inexplicably shushed her with a large index finger, and beckoned her to the window.

Andreas scanned the street. "They're not in view just now; were there when you came in."

"What? Who?"

"Two men, heavy-set, sharp dressers, look like twins. I think they have been stalking you, my dear."

All other thoughts were erased. "Thank you."

"It's not the first time, eh? Take care, Irini. Bad things have been happening lately."

Then, for the first time, Irini really frightened him. Without seeming to be either afraid or particularly concerned, she asked, "If anything does happen, if I don't contact you for a day or two, will you see to Achilles?"

He could not imagine what series of events in a young life could give rise to such coolness about a danger of this kind, together with an apparent acceptance of what he sensed were greater implied risks.

Chapter 23

Dinner with an Archimandrite

Our lives can turn on their heels in an instant.

That same evening, Tuesday L–3

Archimandrite Athanassios, the leader of the Mount Athos Communities, had arrived in London by Eurostar three days earlier with his retinue, as guests of the Greek Embassy, for the last week of the Exhibition. Although he was pleased to be in London, he found the first two days of official functions had left him drained, and disturbed his normally calm and tranquil regime of meditation on which so much of his inner peace depended.

It was with some reluctance that he accepted his new friend Spiros' invitation for dinner on his third evening. Then his mood brightened when he noticed Emily Stone's name on the guest list, for he shared her interests and had read several of her publications.

His day began with the celebration of the Liturgy, followed by some official visits in the morning at the Embassy.

"I'm going to have an uninterrupted afternoon of meditation." He said firmly to Brother Markos, his young assistant. With his inner harmony renewed, he drifted off to sleep, praising God for all his Blessings.

He was awakened by Markos' gentle tap on the door. "Father Athanassios, it is time for the dinner with Kyrios Anguelopoulos."

He arrived with the zest of refreshed spirits at a Greek restaurant in Bayswater, where Spiros had hired the private function room at the back.

Young Brother Markos accompanied him with an eager expression, but his Chaplain, the other member of his retinue, declined the invitation, preferring an evening of reminiscing with his old friend the Bishop.

"Well," beamed Spiros when the introductions had been made, and they were all seated appropriately at the table. "It's such a pleasure to see you here, Father Athanassios, for the last few days of the Exhibition. You who were so instrumental in facilitating it all."

Athanassios returned the courtesies, and then announced, "Brother Markos and I have a surprise for you that we have been practicing for this trip. If you will permit, we would like to sing a Grace. It's a late Byzantine Hymn of Thanks." His resonant bass, against the strong tenor of young Markos, vibrated around the private dining room.

Spiros and Helena loved the typical slow, modulating dissonances, which always stirred feelings of patriotism. For the others, it was simply moving to hear two voices sing with such eloquence.

Meditation was obviously good for Athanassios, as he positively sparkled that evening, on this, one of his rare outings from Mount Athos. He was well aware that he was surrounded by beauty. This didn't disconcert him; he simply enjoyed the sensation. The three women present represented that, for him, in three different aspects.

Irini, young, upright, and exquisite, wore a simple, modest, black sheath dress without jewellery. Helena, always self-assured, had selected a sea-blue long flowing gown, edged in gold with the Greek key pattern. Emily, intelligence radiating beauty of another kind yet equally unmistakable, was in her elegant, cream coloured, three-quarter length silk tunic over a deep blue contrasting slim skirt. She was wearing her uniquely expressive Celtic jewellery, the tasteful design instantly recognized by Athanassios. Among the young men, Adam was a good match for his comely Brother Markos, and Peter he recognized as a maturing, late starter, reminiscent of himself, for he also had found his calling later in life. Spiros added useful solidity, in the voice of a double bass.

Athanassios was most attentive to his guest's linguistic needs as he switched seamlessly between Greek and English. He had a long chat, tête-à-tête with Emily, who was seated next to him. They swapped candid thoughts about her eighth and ninth century manuscripts, and his tenth and eleventh century Greek and Latin texts.

The Archimandrite was extraordinarily sensitive to atmosphere. He revelled in this evening, such a contrast to the sterile official receptions of the last two days. This was so warm and spontaneous. When they smiled, or laughed, it was neither an automatic nor empty expression, but was from the heart, conveying inner joy.

He also felt emanations of something powerful operating here beneath the surface, unstated, but palpable. "Well," he thought, "whatever it is they have, they are united by some very strong bond, a profound unity of purpose." These feelings were reminiscent of his own, flowing from his commitment to a life in God.

He left the dinner in a perplexed state-of-mind. The emotions, which were binding together a remarkable group of people, remained just beyond his grasp. He was certain that there was an unresolved mystery here, something both moving and significant.

The next day, late Wednesday evening (L–2)
  And early hours of Thursday, 27 April, L–1

Irini was in her flat the day after the dinner with Athanassios, and she had a great deal on her mind. Her emotions were in turmoil, not so much because of John, though his name was high on the unresolved list, but the whole of her personal and professional life; a life she knew that one way or another was ending. She decided that she would pack tomorrow – then realised she couldn't do that either. Helena had specifically told them to leave all routines untouched. She swore silently, and knew she was going to miss all this.

Achilles was out being *le chat sur le toit*, prowling among the chimney pots, and peering in through high windows. He sometimes got an eyeful, and Irini an earful from neighbours thus affected. At least he would be taken care of through Andreas, and would presumably be able to go with her. She knew cats weren't allowed in jail, so she couldn't afford any thought of failure. "That's my girl," her inner voice chimed in, "chin up and no doubts."

She missed Adam desperately, but understood it was perhaps better, or at least safer, that he was locked up in his computer lab. Irini undressed for bed, all the way as was her custom year round. She had just pulled the sheets up when there came a tap on Achilles' cat flap. "I didn't lock it," Irini thought, but got up to push it open to make sure he could get in. Her hand was taken by Adam, who peeked in through the tiny portal.

"I can't quite fit through there. Can you slip the catch on the bathroom window?"

Adam was just able to slip in over the transom, lucky to avoid breaking the glass as he slid down on top of the loo, cracking the top of the seat, "sorry", and then to the floor. He shut and latched the small window. "I couldn't sleep." He stilled her lips. "I know I shouldn't be here, but I came in the back way. Nobody saw me."

Irini nodded and melted into Adam's arms, crossing the passage to the flat, embracing as they went.

They both knew that things were not quite right, yet managed to have a long session of low-key touching and pillow talk. Adam didn't ask about the night with John, and had decided that such things didn't matter, because he had confidence in their relationship. Confidence brings strength. He knew it was its absence that bred jealousy and all of the green devil's compatriots.

Irini wanted to tell him, but didn't know how.

They were shocked at the time, 3AM, with work to do in the morning, the Big Day a sunset away. "Water's boiling; I'll make tea."

Adam got out of bed, and wrapped the towel around himself that he had used earlier to take a much-needed shower as the garage didn't have one. He pulled the flat's door open, stepped around it, and closed it behind, intending to cross the hallway to the bathroom. The towel slipped, and he bent down to pick it up again.

"Thump!" The shadow of a large man fell across Adam, followed by the man himself, throwing Adam against the closed door of the flat while his assailant thudded to the floor, awkwardly propped up against the bathroom door on the other side.

Adam was confused, and tried to stand up. The man on the floor took aim for Adam's groin with his blackjack, but the blow landed on his thigh. "What?" Adam had struggled half way up to his feet again, braced against the flat's door for support.

Irini had heard the knock, and thought maybe Adam had locked himself out, and so stepped across, kettle in her right hand, and opened the door. It crashed inward, Adam following it to land on his hands and knees half way through.

"Twang!" Something hit hard and stuck in the door, narrowly missing Adam's backside. Irini instantly registered the tableau. A man in the hall to her left was taking aim at Adam with a gun. She instinctively threw the boiling kettle full of water straight into his face. The man screamed, and stumbled back along the short hall, fell backward over the balustrade at the end, and after a sickening, endless moment of silence, landed "thuck", head first on the concrete entrance hall three floors below.

The other man was struggling to get up from the floor, but he was wedged between Adam and the bathroom door. Still, he was trying to pull his man towards him, an alligator's grip on his leg. He took another swing at Adam's groin, striking him again on the leg. "OW!"

Irini almost stumbled turning around to go back the two steps to the kitchen sink, pulled open the door, and grabbed the first spray can that came to hand. Turning on her heels in a flash, she ran forward, aimed the spray at Adam's assailant, and jammed down the button. She hit him square in the face, and he slumped back with his head wedged tightly in the corner.

"Hissssssssssssss…" Irini was now flying on adrenaline and pure terror. "Hissssssssssssss!" The man tried to twist his head from side to side, but Irini stepped forward, and kept spraying, and spraying, and spraying.

The can finally ran down, spluttering its last in synchrony with the final gasps of their attacker. Adam kicked him in the head for good measure, but the man was already dead.

"Damn, Irini, what was all that about?" Then Adam knew. They had come for *him*. His stupid violation of orders had transformed Irini into the killer of two men. He knew she probably didn't realise this at that moment, but soon would.

Adam got up, leaving the towel on the floor, shrugged ruefully to himself at the picture – two nude youngsters had just dispatched two MI5 heavies. Adam had recognized the one on the floor, and had a fleeting memory of his look-alike in the hallway, aiming a gun at him. He had met them before. They were the same two who had accompanied John Fiske over at Imperial, the day he stole QC.

"Wait a minute," Adam turned back to the door. "Irini, that wasn't a gun, a regular gun anyway, it was a dart, see." Adam pulled it out, and handed it to her. "Be careful of the damn thing, it might go off yet."

Adam grabbed up his secure telephone, and keyed in the codes, first time. He congratulated himself, for his hands were vibrating like a loose tin roof in a hurricane.

"Helena! This is a Code Red. I repeat Code Red. Irini's flat. Two down. Send what help you can."

They had talked about what a "Code Red" meant, and that they were to use it only for events that directly threatened the mission. There was no doubt in Adam's mind that it was the right call.

Irini then realized what had happened, and ran to the balustrade. The obviously dead body of the second man lay broken on the floor below, crumpled in a fatal heap.

Adam had already checked number one, and had reported with a shake of his head.

She was sure she was going to cry – then a steely calm came over her. This was a war, and not of their making. She felt a huge hollow inside herself, and knew she was not going to cry. Then the more frightening thought: maybe she would never be able to cry again.

"Irini, what about the two flats below?"

"Spring holidays, fortnight together in the Algarve, just like last year."

"That's a break."

"What are we going to do about all this?" Her arm, still shaking, swept the hall and staircase beyond.

"I've bumped it upstairs. Helena's problem now."

It hadn't been five minutes, and the buzzer sounded. "Yes."

"Charon."

Irini pressed the release, and three figures came pounding up the stairs, Charon himself, in the flesh, followed by a man and a woman.

Adam's phone chimed. "Peter here; tell Charon, Helena and I, ETA five minutes, with vehicle." He passed the word, to a curt nod.

"Okay, where's the cat?" Charon questioned.

"Out."

"Call him. If you want him to go with you, get him in here. Quickly."

It was only later that Irini and the others realized the significance of Charon's first orders. His first thought had been for Irini's cat! They never were able to think of him as just the *mechanical spymaster* ever again.

Irini pushed open the cat flap, and whistled. She had trained Achilles to a special call, and was grateful for her foresight. She repeated the whistle twice more, and then let the flap close.

A squeal of tires announced further arrivals. Charon barked orders. "Adam, help them up with the tools. Irini, get anything of yours that's hidden or might be overlooked, and pile it all on the bed. Anything you don't care about, toss in the corner here next to the kitchen sink."

In a few minutes Adam, Peter, Helena, and Charon's two operatives returned, struggling up the stairs with piles of equipment. There were three Dyson micro vacuum cleaners, thick stacks of strong-sided cardboard boxes, a sack of cleaning solvents, tape, labels, marking pens, and many other items.

Charon made rapid-fire introductions: "Adam, Irini, this is Cassandra, and Pluton. Okay, we sterilize this place. I don't want a single hair follicle, DNA sample, or sign that anybody has lived here since antiquity. Got it?"

Pluton: "Paint it too, like last time?" His strong, square, Greek body, as close to professional muscle as any of them had seen in the Greek contingent, shrugged nonchalantly.

"That won't be necessary; just go over it all a third time instead."

Charon opened a large zip-lock bag and pulled out two thick, black, body bags. His impression of Adam went up a level when he helped bag the two corpses without having to be asked.

Adam couldn't help but smile at Peter's emergency vehicle. It was an ancient hearse, with long, curlicued windows, perfect for the job. The two bodies slid in easily, side by side on the floor. Irini later laid out her two hand-made single quilts on them. "Only fitting," she said, "as we don't have any coffins on short notice." Her attempt at graveyard humour was an elixir she and Adam needed several times that night before everything was wrapped up.

After about an hour, with Irini's things flying into boxes, carefully rolled up in bubble wrap when necessary, she and Adam paused for a five-minute break. As they stood in the hall, out of the way, the darkly comedic scene that they had played out in that very space suddenly came back to them, and they broke the tension by grinning at each other, then laughing, and finally howling in each other's arms, a few dry tears draining away the horrors.

Charon and Peter left with the bodies, and returned a half hour later with a van. The hearse and its contents were never seen again, and nobody ever mentioned the departed MI5 agents. The van was soon filled with Irini's life's possessions, in smartly packed, labelled and sealed boxes. Cassandra had taken charge of this operation, performing it with sensitivity and care.

Irini thought of Achilles again. Where was that silly cat? Time was short. It was obvious that Charon would soon give the marching orders, and that would be it. Then Irini had an idea, went in the bathroom, and climbed up on the cracked toilet seat to look out the window. "Yes!" She exclaimed, there he was, peering down through the side window. He was simply reluctant to come in, with all the activities he didn't understand. Irini went back around to the cat flap, and tried to coax him in, but he remained frustratingly just out of reach and wouldn't budge. Adam had to go up through the transom in a gathering light drizzle once again, back along the roof, and over to the cat.

"Playing this game again? Okay, but where's the coat, sunshine?" The props weren't right, but Achilles came to Adam, and he pushed him ignominiously through the flap into Irini's welcoming arms.

Safe House Three, a last-minute bolt-hole, was a separate unit in the back garden of a hotel near the Greek Embassy. It had been used many times before, and Charon helped Adam and Irini carry her bags up the steps. He gave them the fast tour. "Adam, your computer laboratory is through that door. Please check to see that everything is shipshape. You are to stay here until the Lift, and that's straight from Athens." He shook Adam's hand, hugged Irini, and scratched Achilles under his chin through the bars of his transport box.

Back in Irini's flat, Cassandra, and Pluton, with Peter and Helena under their direction, vacuumed, cleaned and scrubbed until the room was as sterile as a hospital operating room, and then they did it again. The door was left open behind them when they left at 8AM.

MI5 headquarters, later that morning, Thursday April 27, L–1

"That's right, Director, they were tracking Adam Blix and then just disappeared. Their last message was 'Blix in sight. Back with the goods shortly.' That was at just after 3AM this morning."

Sir Robert Mansfield shut off the speakerphone. "John, find out where they were, then where they are and what happened."

The phone buzzed again. "What? Irini Baynes isn't there? Scrubbed clean, nobody there for months? Son of a bitch, I'll bring that landlady in here and juice her! Miss Baynes has lived there for three years.

"John, find out why the cover up. This is big. Top priority. I'll hit my counterpart at the CIA, but if they're involved, I won't get a sausage. Damn Yanks. They always steal our best ideas."

And a later call: "She has walked into the museum, just like any other day? John, tab her, stick tight. I'll send you three agents. Double, triple tails. Find out where she goes after work."

Then in the mid afternoon: "Lost her? How could that be – I heard you were in her knickers. What happened? What are we, 'Morons Incorporated'? Shee-ite. And I am not referring to my respected Muslim brothers!"

Safe House Three 8PM the same evening

Adam continued briskly: "Irini tested QC on the main loading door, and all three codes worked a treat. We thought about doing a trial in the museum tonight, but that was too dangerous – and not so much because we might be seen. I proposed to use a guard's uniform, and that side of it is still pretty sleepy over there. The risk would be that the security chief might notice that these three eminent cardholders had been wandering around late, opening top security doors.

"No, we are safer to play it once, on the night, fingers crossed. I will keep QC warm in my bed tonight, and baby-sit her all day tomorrow. We'll be there with our bells on."

"That's what I was afraid of," Irini smiled thinly. "That other lady in your life is becoming tiresome to say the least."

Helena concluded, "That's how we always planned it. We get ready, rehearse, cover all the contingencies, and then do it once, do it right on the night, and walk away clean. That's how it's going to be. Irini calls in sick tomorrow, and we all stay here until the Lift. Good luck to us all.

Chapter 24

The Lift

Once upon a time the whole World rested on the shoulders of Atlas.

British Museum, Friday, 28 April, Lift day

John Fiske had staked out the British Museum all day, then left in disgust at 5 PM. Irini had not come in at all, and he had no report for his director. The man wouldn't be happy about that, but John didn't know what more he could do. He didn't suspect that the museum was the real nexus of the operation. Something big was certainly under way, for CIA types to sterilize an apartment, and *disappear* Irini, not to mention two missing MI5 agents. The agency believed that it was all about the Quantum Computer, so that laboratory and not the British Museum were under stakeout, and the assigned MI5 staff were all working aspects of that connection.

This was not a lucky accident. Ever since MI5 had been identified as sniffing around, the team's watchers had been watching their watchers. The first was the way their involvement was discovered. Potterton had been surveilled continuously after his debacle, just in case. When Charon, Cassandra, and Pluton had necessarily picked up Potterton after his aborted attempt to hit Adam and Irini, Charon and company arranged for him to be committed for a year for his own protection. It wasn't strictly legal, but the necessary hands had been greased. Two others, the only UK contacts of the traitor in Greek intelligence, had been similarly ensconced for the duration.

When Charon and company had parked their motorcar in the garage of their Hampstead safe house, they had taken the normal precautions. When MI5 thought they had broken in unobserved, they had in fact been observed, and Charon had taken pictures of the picture takers, then easily identified, and so the merry chase continued. The fingerprints intentionally planted on the car were those of a peasant woman and her charming husband, friends of Spiros, who had eagerly agreed to have their identities stolen in this way, *for a friend.* There was no chance that MI5, the CIA, and Greek authorities combined, would ever have been able to finger them from prints for the very good reason that theirs had never been taken, except by Spiros, to transfer to rubber, then to be used any time it was necessary. The spy game is 50% just these sorts of false scents, diversions, and indeed, games.

As soon as John Fiske of MI5 was personally identified, he was tracked from time to time, and as L-day approached, continuously, together with his associates, any time they came near the museum, Irini's flat, or any other sensitive location. Had he *not* voluntarily left the museum area that evening, or if any other colleagues had appeared, they would have been *disappeared* themselves, for the night. The team's favourite, shared by many agencies, was the drunk in the gutter ploy. In the event, they were delighted not to have to play that dirty trick on their British colleagues.

The guards coming on to the 6PM shift at the museum queued for the login. They turned their personal keys in the keyhole and inserted their security pass in the slot. The screen welcomed each with his or her assigned beat. Guards 2, 4, and 7 received unusual instructions. They were to patrol the Exhibition Hall and keep an eye on the packing and loading of the Treasures of Mount Athos, and then remain in the Hall until their shifts ended at midnight. They didn't question this, and it was in any case most welcome duty. They would be able to take regular breaks, and spend much of the evening sitting together socializing, instead of marching alone around the spooky, hallowed halls haunted with the remains and ghostly presences of ancient civilizations.

Adam grinned in satisfaction, and logged off his computer terminal in the back room of the workshop where the marbles had been copied almost a year ago. He had wound up his study of the improved copies a month previously, and had hopes that his project would be carried on by someone else in the future. It was a good idea, and the preliminary work had been encouraging. He set all of his computer accounts, and patches in the museum operating systems, including the one he had used to override the assignment of guards that evening, to self-destruct at 6AM on Saturday, April 29. All evidence of his tampering would disappear in a puff of cyber smoke.

He had come in an hour earlier with the personnel hired to strike the Mount Athos Exhibition. The intercontinental lorry with them aboard had backed carefully into bay number 2, next to the loading doors leading to the Exhibition Hall of the museum. The Elgins lorry had come in the previous day to occupy space number 1, which was near the second set of loading doors, those leading to a main hall in the museum. That was the door used to bring large objects into the museum proper, and the one through which the Elgin Marbles would pass this night if all went according to plan. He used his beloved QC to pass into the museum through that door, and a few minutes later, to test that he could open it from the inside. It was one of the few doors with security access controls in both directions.

Getting the two lorries, instead of one, into the loading area had proved to be easy. They simply used the same pass for *both*. It was unlikely that anybody would think it odd, either that they needed two, or that the same pass had been used both times. It was on exit that papers were carefully checked, and boxes counted.

The plan dealt with that difficulty by having two lorries with the same number of identically labelled boxes. The Mount Athos Treasures load coming in three months earlier from Greece had nearly 90 extra boxes at the front that were never unpacked, but shown on the manifest. They had been correct that nobody checked that *all* of them were actually used in the exhibition. These extra boxes were one for one with those used for the Elgin Marbles, and contained the Elgin copies. That is why Adam and his helpers from the Slade had been required to prepare the complete specifications for these boxes before the copies went forward to Athens from London. This made it possible to build them in advance, in Athens, so as to be part of the Mount Athos artefacts from the beginning, first for the exhibition at Thessalonica, and then, with the copies in the cases, for the subsequent shipment to London with the Treasures of Mount Athos.

Equally, the team's lorry came in with a set of Mount Athos boxes containing good copies of those treasures, plus their empty set for the Elgins from the rehearsal. Only one lorry would be able to leave, but it would be the one with the Elgins. After they had been flown to Greece, and the theft disclosed, the Mount Athos Treasures would leave the second time after the smoke had cleared.

With the museum guards diverted, they were free to begin making the other preparations. Three of their team, dressed as museum guards, took up the vacated posts in the Duveen Gallery and the areas they would be using or passing through. The three whom Adam had diverted determined which of their staff donned guard's uniforms, and took over as their doubles, so that from a distance they would physically fit the bill.

Each had a key matching the guards whom Adam had diverted. The team had obtained the full set over the past few months by taking quick impressions of the keys, one by one from each and every museum guard, when it became possible or could be arranged in each separate case. Some of the diversions had been humorous – a charming lady simply asking to hold his key in her hand had worked several times. Two guards kept their keys loose in their pockets, strictly against orders, and these were simply pickpocket-lifted, impressed in the wax, and returned in a matter of seconds, the diversion a collision with a pretty woman. This had been entertaining for the whole team; a pleasant diversion away from the more serious business that on occasion had threatened to get on top of them.

Adam started the camera game in the Duveen Gallery itself. He could walk freely around because if the senior security personnel in the control room saw him, he was a regular, no harm, no foul. He felt he could also get away with carrying tools, so he had arranged for a collapsible ladder to be built that fitted neatly in a large toolbox. He could then approach a camera, get underneath it out of view, pull his articulated ladder up out of the toolbox, ascend, and do his business.

It was similar to the Quantum Lab. He disconnected the video cable on the back of the camera, quickly inserted the splitter connecter, and reconnected the camera. If the control room was watching, the screen would go blank for a moment, and then the picture would come back. It was unlikely that anyone would investigate even if it were noticed. Adam then inserted a micro disk corresponding to the diverted guard into the Sony player, plugged its cable to the splitter, selected "play through", and "repeat on end" so that the control room would be watching reruns of a recording made a few days before with the same guard on duty, the instant replay disk rewinds occurring when the area was empty.

Tonight, Adam also hung a small, flat television screen under the camera. It showed the scene as it was transmitted to security control. The guard assigned to that station could then time his motions to roughly agree with that playback, and assure that he turned his key in the way stations in approximate synchrony with what he could see on the screen, or to do it at a reasonable time if off camera. The pattern began immediately, their guard saluting Adam as he passed by on the first round.

This was repeated for the other two cameras, lastly the one in the corridor leading to the loading door. As soon as it was bypassed, Adam went through that door, and returned to their lorry to wait.

Helena had really cracked the whip, and the Mount Athos Treasures were boxed and loaded in ninety minutes, a half hour early as she had hoped. Her team for that legitimate job was tired, and she had arranged for them to be served a buffet dinner and drinks in the empty Exhibition Hall. They were happy to be released, and joined the three displaced guards for a well-deserved break. It was necessary to hold them there incognito until the Elgins were loaded, so that all the outside hired help could be passed out at the same time. Having two different groups leave the museum would be suspicious, and they had to count on any guard outside the building not noticing, or not caring how many actually came out.

For the admission of such labour, it was only necessary to apply in advance to the museum, and get ordinary visitor clip-on badges. Irini had obtained enough of them for both crews. The Lift Team could have come in openly with the Mount Athos one, but they wanted to minimize the chances for identification later, and would risk only the late-night exit of the lift team, backs to the cameras, caps pulled low.

Helena closed the loading door from the Exhibition Hall, setting the security lock. She also set the latch from her side. She certainly didn't want any of them wandering back through. Even the guards with their passes and PINs could not now open the door number two from their side to the loading dock.

Adam had intentionally left his toolbox ladder against the wall next to this door. Helena was standing directly under the security camera that scanned the loading area. So far as the security control people upstairs were, or might be concerned, nothing untoward had yet occurred. Much that *was* would soon follow. It was now up to Helena to take care of the camera, following Adam's instructions.

This was trickier than the others, in that it scanned, but fortunately the security operators upstairs could not change its motion, and it continued automatically. Helena assembled the ladder, and climbed up with a pouch over her arm. She uncoupled the camera cable, substituted a switcher, and reattached the cable. The Sony came next. She connected it, and set "record mode pause". The small screen on the unit came to life with the scene below her in the empty garage. She waited for the camera to reach the extreme position, and then hit the "record" key. The scene in the unoccupied room was now being recorded.

Helena consulted her watch, and waited the agreed ten minutes, and then until the camera was in the extreme position ready to scan again across the room. The "replay" key was next to instantly rewind the disk and begin playing. She threw the switch on the splitter to "feed". Finally, she selected "replay on end" as the mode for the Sony, and snapped the case shut. This would continuously repeat the ten minutes of recording. Rewind on the disk was, unlike a tape, instantaneous, so there was no break in the action.

She walked along the loading dock to the other end with the Elgins lorry at door number one, and rapped on the side. In an instant, the back door swung open.

Peter and Trev jumped down first, shook Helena's hand, and turned to their crew. "Okay lads, all the boxes and tools inside first, softly, quickly, no talking, just like we practiced it."

In seconds, the empty Elgin boxes were being carried, or trundled on the four-wheel low-loader carts, through the loading door that Adam had just reopened. In two minutes, the dock was deserted.

Helena motioned to Adam to sit down with her. She had a picnic basket, coffee for herself, fresh squeezed orange juice for Adam. "The camera gig go okay?" Adam tipped his head towards the scanning security camera at the opposite end of the loading dock.

"Just like you taught me."

"Training pays. I wonder where I heard that one before?"

In a time that seemed too short, the "Conga Line" began to snake past, low-loaders wheeling silently by, up the ramp into the lorry, which then rocked softly side to side as the heavy boxes were slipped to the floor and secured, starting at the front, working towards the middle.

Adam, followed by Helena, trotted back along the line. He gave thumbs-up signs of encouragement. "Any problems?" Helena whispered after him.

"None, and there aren't going to be any."

"There's always…"

"I know, Helena – we've covered them."

"Well, if you have, then there won't be any problems. But if you have forgotten a single thing, that very same one will bite us."

"That some sort of law of your spy craft?"

"You could put it that way."

"I know the engineer's version of it. The worst that can happen, will always happen, unless you prevent it."

"Sure," Helena agreed, "same idea."

Athanassios watched most of the boxing-up of his Treasures, but then the stress of his week overwhelmed him. He knew that there was a very comfortable cabin behind the driver's seat in their lorry, and he repaired to it. The bed was comfortable, and he thought, "I will have a short nap." He had instead fallen deeply asleep.

The Elgins crew did not notice the strange bearded man in flowing robes and tall hat walking against their flow. Nor did he know with any certainty just what was going on.

These crates and low loaders are not the ones for my Treasures.

Adam was with Peter in the Duveen Gallery as the last of the large sculptures were being raised on the lifting arbours, and lowered lovingly into their prefabricated crates. They were ten minutes ahead of schedule, but the Expected Unexpected was even then walking up behind them. Athanassios' mental image as he came into the strange room was that of a line of ants carrying their leaves back to the nest. It wasn't the Exhibition Hall at all!

Adam caught movement in the corner of his eye, turned his head, then for an instant stared incredulously at the now very familiar face, bobbing its way along the line towards him. Adam rushed forward.

"Father Athanassios, yes, well, let's go back now, just this way." Adam tried to turn his man, but he stopped, firmly rooted to the marble earth beneath his feet.

The good Father was staring open mouthed at the progression of giant ants going about their work. His mental images rearranged themselves as the last wisps of sleep dropped from his eyes. The only thing he said was, "Ah. I see."

His whiskers had been itching the whole time since the dinner, his inside bells ringing as if for a major festival. So this was it. The

Marbles were on their way back to Greece. The immensity of this realization rocked him, and then swelled his heart to bursting.

He took Adam's hand and pressed it white, knuckles popping. "I hope I haven't ruined anything. What do you want me to do?"

Adam almost lost his balance, so dramatically had his fears been erased. "Well, uh, let me think. The cameras are disabled, nobody knows you are here, and our crew will be in France by midday tomorrow, nobody to identify you. Come on!"

Adam led his charge back through their loading door, along the dock, to the other end. He took out his trusty QC, released the security lock, and slipped the latch, peering in through a crack. The party beyond was in full swing, lubricated by freely flowing wine, and the guards were in the midst of it, backs turned.

"Slide back in there, Father, have a glass of wine, and stick with your plans, whatever they were. Good luck."

"Godspeed, Adam." With that, Father Athanassios slipped through the door. Adam closed it behind him, wiping his sweat-beaded brow.

Peter trotted up behind him. "Wow, that was a close one. What did the geezer say?"

"'Godspeed'. It was a heart-thumper, but we're okay on this."

"Good lad." Peter slapped his back, "Like we said, if the Unexpected happens outside our plans, we call the play as we see it."

"That's exactly how it came down, Peter. How're we doing?"

"Five minutes to go, ten minutes under schedule."

Irini had been on duty in the pedimental sculptures annex to the Duveen Gallery, keeping an eye on the clock, doing odd jobs such as checking that the next case was right side up, facing the correct direction, and that its lid was ready to drop on and be nailed down.

As the last box was trundled away, the crew as they had rehearsed, followed it out of the hall. Irini made to do the same, but Helena was moving against the current and came towards her. "Irini, great job."

"Yes, ten minutes under schedule. The crew said it was actually easier here than in the warehouse. All the pieces fit exactly, thanks to our friends over at the Slade." Irini and Adam had kept the drawings the young sculptors had made, on which the measurements for the supports inside the boxes had been calculated and written out. They were in themselves works of art.

"Irini, I have decided to change tactics, and wanted to ask if you would agree to it."

"You're the boss, Helena."

"No, this goes beyond that, so it is voluntary. I want you to remain here and keep an eye on things after we go."

"I think Adam would say something like, 'Wow!'"

"I think he would, and that he may say something about me that's less polite."

"Yes, I think so and maybe me too."

"I wouldn't blame either of you, but that's my request. Here's the reason. Something might still go wrong. There could be a moment when an insider in here could make a difference. I know it may *seem* unlikely, but before you ask, my tummy talks to me sometimes."

"Damn, another sacrifice. I was looking forward to an end to all this." Irini's hands swept around the echoing, empty room.

"And to pick up your life with Adam. I know." Helena patted Irini gently on the shoulder.

Irini raised her head, and looked at Helena. There was something in her eyes, an extra gold-flecked gleam, a deep mystery. Helena whispered a nod in response.

"Okay, Adam will have my head, but okay. I'll cover the retreat."

"I'll take care of Adam, and it will work out. Thank you."

Helena then visited each of the three guards. "As you have drawn the short straws, gentlemen, you must stay here until midnight. Your pay packet has the extra-duty payment we agreed. There will be a blue Rolls Royce in front at midnight. Simply walk out the employee's door, salute the guard if he is there, and get into the car. The man inside will see to it that you rejoin your mates on Eurostar. Is all that understood?"

Each had answered, "Yes." The plan had been rehearsed so many times that tonight had seemed to many of them, just another rehearsal, and easier than most.

By staying behind, they assured that the security control centre would not notice anything until after midnight, when the keys stopped turning in the guard boxes.

With that, Helena turned on her heels, and strode quickly across the dusty floor, some of that dust 2,500 years old, unintentionally rubbed from the Marbles, the same ones that the eyes of Pericles had touched, and the hands of Pheidias had fashioned.

The legitimate Treasures team had been queued up, and then filed out the staff access door from the garage. They had each received an extra, unexpected envelope, with several weeks' salary in cash, as a tax-free tip. They would soon know why, but none of them suffered any more than questioning by the police, and the generous payment was more than fair compensation.

The Elgins team followed, all sporting their badges, turned in to the guard waiting outside. They had received a thick envelope that included their payment, which for most of them was some years of income, plus tickets on the 06:00 Eurostar to Paris with hotel vouchers. They would join their wives and sweethearts who had spent the evening in a safe place, already ensconced in the Tourist Bus now waiting in the street outside the museum. They would slumber together in it, and then they would be off to the City of Lights. Peter shook Trev's hand for the last time, for a while, then his friend and crew boss turned, and was the last out.

Helena said, "Peter, Adam, you're going to the airport with Charon, blue Rolls Royce in front. No baddies out there, but we want you under cover."

"Not in the lorry?" Peter questioned.

"Small change of plans – more secure this way – Adam's hot, and we don't want you exposed either, Peter."

"Okay." They shook hands, and went through the small door, shutting it with a metallic clang behind them.

Helena then went under the camera, raised the ladder once again, switched the splitter to "source", and took down the Sony. This was necessary so that the control centre would now see the entirely legitimate departure of the Treasures of Mount Athos. Helena checked that the door back into the Exhibition Hall was locked, and then crossed the loading dock.

She stopped, and looked across the room. The camera was swinging mindlessly back and forth in its programmed orbit. There was still time for her to change her mind about this last, and most extraordinary, cusp in her plan.

She crossed her fingers behind her back for luck, and rapped on the door. A sleepy pair of drivers sloughed off their naps, and gave the thumbs up.

"Other truck lads, hop down, and let's clear this load out of here to you know where." They dutifully grabbed their duffel bags and map cases, jumped down, and crossed back along the dock.

Chapter 25

The Flight

Boomerangs!

Helena sat tensely in the jump seat, the two drivers sitting, as they would have done in an aircraft, as pilot and co-pilot. The lead driver checked his watch. "Heavy traffic for this time of night. I estimate we will lose ten minutes on our predicted time."

"It's okay, as you see, we finished with nearly an hour in hand. So long as we are airborne by midnight."

The traffic finally cleared, the drivers made no errors in reaching the freight area, and were directed to the aircraft. It was a new Greek Air Force C-17 Globemaster. The rear-loading ramp was already down, and at least thirty Greek Army personnel were lined up waiting. The driver backed up to the ramp accurately on the first try, and the ground crew had the truck open, and its ramp down before Helena's feet hit the ground.

The 56 frieze cases were hand-carried, four men, one to a corner, directly into the aircraft, while the heavier Elgins were rolled on pneumatic-tired forklifts. The packing and loading at the museum end had required an hour and a quarter, give or take, the job here was done in less than ten minutes.

Helena spoke to the drivers. "Take the lorry and the rest of its load, as scheduled, back to Greece. It's vital to be across the channel before dawn. No rush after that."

"Yes, Miss Helena."

Peter and Adam got out of the Rolls, saluted Charon, and came across the tarmac to watch the parade. Then, a minute or so before it was finished, they walked up the ramp into the bowels of one of the world's largest aircraft, and took their bucket seats just behind the pilot's compartment.

The pilot came back and shook hands. "Miss Helena, we are ready to roll. Flying time, five hours, more or less. Do you confirm the longer flight path over international waters all the way?

"I do. Take her up!"

Athens Control: tensed faces strained as their video monitor, relayed directly from the aircraft, showed the plane lifting off, turning southwest, and gaining altitude as the lights of London fell astern.

"Blast." The cleaning lady, a Mrs Georgina Hardy, uttered her number one curse. She was, above all, a polite woman. "Out of toilet paper." She shut the cabinet that was normally overflowing with the stuff, and made her way towards the master store, pushing her cart in front of her. Her card opened the door to the same workroom that Adam had toiled in for so many months, and she approached another door. Her key opened it, and she heaped up as much toilet paper as her cart would carry, and then a few more rolls for good measure balanced precariously on top. "Might as well put some in my stockroom."

She retraced her steps, humming idly to herself. As she turned the corner, three rolls of paper tumbled off the top, two landing on their flat ends, but the third gaily rolled away towards the Duveen Gallery. She gave chase, and almost had it, then accidentally kicked it instead. It would have been a "goal of the week" if there had been a camera running, but they had been disabled by Adam. The errant roll wobbled its way out into the middle of the Gallery, spun around, and settled on the dusty marble. She bent over and picked it up, rubbed her back as she straightened, and walked out of the Gallery.

Then Mrs Hardy stopped, and cocked her head to one side. She thought to herself, "Floor's dirty, now who's forgotten this time?" She turned and went back. There was dust everywhere. She began to sense that something else was not quite right. Then she pressed her fist between her teeth, "Lord in heaven!" and ran from the room.

Athens Control: "Prime Minister, our air force fighter escort flight is airborne, rendezvous estimated at 50 nautical miles this side of Gibraltar."
"Excellent."

Gibraltar Royal Air Force Base: "Scramble, scramble, this is not a drill!!" The klaxon then cleared its throat and commenced its raucous, punctuated howls. The flight of UK Fighters was soon off the ground at Gibraltar, heading west towards their rendezvous target, shockingly described as a "Greek Air Force C-17" on an eastward course, approaching the Pillars of Hercules.

The RAF squadron leader squawked, "Confirm, *Greek* Air Force?"

Helena was asleep in a hammock, rocking her like a baby. Adam and Peter were simply staring into space out the window.

"Whoosh!"

"Hey, Adam, did you see that?"

Adam turned to the window. "Whoosh!"

"Cripes, that was close. What the hell?"

The pilot opened the door, plugged in a microphone, and hit a switch. "… at once. Turn back to London at once!"

The pilot depressed the "send" button and said, "Identify yourselves. This is not a hostile aircraft."

"Royal Air Force. Turn back at once." Crackled from the speaker.

Peter grabbed the microphone, and motioned to Adam to get Helena. "Which Royal Air Force?" Peter and everyone else had heard the accent, but it bought time.

"British, you fool! Turn back or else!"

Peter said, "This is a Greek Air Force plane, on official business."

"Crap!" the British voice replied, "you are carrying stolen property. Turn back…" The transmission ceased in mid sentence.

"What's all this?" Helena yawned.

Peter said, "British fighters, ordering us to return, or else."

"They won't do anything rash. Give me the mike."

"Helena Katsis here, who are you?"

"Group Captain Macintyre. My orders are to turn you back, or…"

"Orders from whom, exactly?"

"My boss, the Prime Minister."

"You know you are not going to do anything foolish, so keep calm. I'll pass this to my boss, the Greek Prime Minister."

The very same chose that moment to chime in on the plane's secure satellite circuit. "Helena, what's happening?"

She told him. He replied, "The British Prime Minister has been on the phone to me. Needless to say he's a bit upset. We're talking again in ten minutes. Stay on course. Ignore threats for now. Out."

A sea of long faces surrounded the table in Number Ten Downing Street. "Prime Minister, the Elgin Marbles were stolen from the British Museum last evening, and are now bound for Greece in a Greek Air Force Transport. Present location just entering the western approaches to the Mediterranean Sea. They are in international airspace and have been so since departure from Heathrow." The defence minister was terse, and accurate, as always.

"Get me the Greek Prime Minister, now!" The speaker crackled, and then made a perfect circuit. "Turn your plane back."

"Why would I do a stupid thing like that?"

"Let me count the ways. One, you are in violation of international law."

"Untrue. We are recovering stolen property."

"That issue was settled, by your own statement. I have it here in front of me, less than a year ago, Greece accepted that Britain acquired the Marbles legally."

"My statements, whether quoted correctly or not, are not admissible in court. Remember the UNESCO directive."

"Melina's folly, you mean."

The huff in the Greek Prime Minister's voice could be heard clearly. "Let's try to keep this civil. I have a copy of that UN directive right in front…"

"Second, we are holding your Treasures of Mount Athos, and their guardian, a certain gentleman of the clergy."

"Blackmail, now is it, Prime Minister. I didn't think you grew up in the gutter."

"Look who's talking. Listen, my political life is on the line here."

This caused the Greek Prime Minister to pause. If true, he knew his opposite number well enough to realize that he would not stop at much if anything. "I don't think so. The public opinion polls are still over 60% in favour of returning…"

"Don't play games with me. Send them back or else." The Prime Minister of Great Britain broke the circuit. He beckoned decisively to the defence minister, who handed him a small black box. He manually keyed a message into it. The encryption and transmission systems were such that no third party could possibly see it, now or ever, including those in this room and the intelligence services.

Group Captain Macintyre's matching black box echoed: "Turn them back or shoot them down." It was validated by the same level of security and confirmation as would accompany the decision to launch nuclear weapons. He knew it was his career to disobey, but also understood that to obey was probably a war crime that could be tried outside Great Britain under the heaviest penalties. Everyone concerned was now between their various rocks and hard places.

The Group Captain spoke to the Greek pilot, and they established a close link by hand-held infrared transmission between the cockpits, reminiscent of the flash-lanterns still used by the Navy. The British fighter came along side, and took up station, so that they could communicate on a secure circuit. The pilot called Helena to the cockpit, and handed her the black box. She knew what it was instantly. "Any way to record this, any way at all?"

Her pilot shook his head. "We could make a system that would do it, but what's the point? The rationale is secure communication with our enemies. It's new anyway, no time for countermeasures. Our own little 'White House Hotline' like the bad old days with the Soviets."

"Thank you, yes, the theory being that if we can talk and not be overheard, maybe errors can be stopped in time. I think this is different."

The little device flashed, "Turn Back or be Shot Down."

Helena keyed back, "I don't think so, but I'll push it upstairs."

Gibraltar Control: "Battle Group of Greek fighters ahead of you, Group Leader, ETA 7 minutes."

The C-17's radio crackled: "Greek air force, ETA 6 minutes, Spiros sent me, tell Helena with a hug from him!"

Helena keyed for transmit, "You'll be a sight for sore eyes. We've got company, and I don't like the smell of it."

"Affirmative, but my nose can take it. I've dealt with worse."

Something clicked for Helena, and she smiled richly, and relaxed a touch. "Yes, I think I know you, by reputation at least."

"Spiros? Spinning his yarns, as usual?"

"Something like that."

"We'll swat the flies for you. Hold tight."

The Greek Prime Minister came on again, via secure satellite transmission. "Helena, they have the Mount Athos Treasures, and Athanassios, and are talking tough."

"The first is incorrect, they absolutely do *not* have them, repeat, do *not* have them; the second I'm not sure about. I wonder how serious they are?"

"The British Prime Minister is being advised to juice him. Apparently he was a witness."

Helena slapped her fist against the bulkhead. "That's true, but they wouldn't dare."

"I don't know, Helena..."

"Have they mentioned Irini?"

"No, why, isn't she with you?"

"No, sir, I left her covering our rear in London."

The Prime Minister did not ask if that had been wise, but his silence asked the question nevertheless. Both of them knew it, and that there was no answer. A command decision was a command decision, and the penalty of command was exacted when they went wrong.

The pilot pointed to a message on his communications console, which read, "Captain, we'll be with you in 3 minutes."

Helena continued, "Is the British P-M pulling any punches?"

"I don't think so, all the stops are out I'm sure."

"That's my view. We've received a closed-circuit you-know-what."

The Greek Prime Minister was silent again. "Ah, exactly so, a little accident, plane just dropped off the radar screen, most regrettable."

"Reinforcements are almost here."

"Somehow," the deep voice from the speaker sighed, "that doesn't make me feel more secure. It seemed like a good idea at the time."

"I don't believe they would do it, sir."

"They *probably* wouldn't," he said slowly. "Helena, how would you call it?"

She knew the Prime Minister was going by the book – give your field commanders the first shot on the final say, if they want it. She could pass the buck back to him, also by the book, her choice. There were several reasons why that was not the best idea. She had

313

information he did not have, and could not be given, for it was essential under her master plan that she and she alone possess it.

Without enough hesitation in the pilot's view, and therefore to his visible shock, she capitulated! "Call it off."

Their boss was silent for a very long time. "I'll get back to you."

"Prime Minister, Greek counterpart on the line."

"What can you offer me if I order the plane to turn back?"

"What do you need?"

"Pardons and safe passage for anyone I require, including all participants, perhaps others not known to you."

"Empty our jails of all the Greeks? No thank you."

"Be serious, I won't name anyone already in jail."

"Okay, agreed. Anything else?"

"Release the Treasures of Mount Athos, and the Archimandrite Athanassios, *immediately* the Marbles are back in the British Museum."

"Agreed. Do we have a deal?"

"Deal."

Their hearts were so heavy on the return to London that they were surprised the plane could stay in the air, and Helena had been forced to endure some of the hardest looks she had ever received.

Number Ten Downing Street

"Sir Robert Mansfield to see you, sir."

He strode into the room, speaking as he came, usually an offensive no-no. "Prime Minister, I'll get to the bottom of this in a trice. Let me juice them, all of them, and we'll get the goods on everyone right up to their bastard Prime Minister."

He was answered with a nod, and then a shake of the head. "Sir Robert, you are right, and you probably would. But," he sighed, "as satisfying as that would be, we really can't. I wanted you to hear it directly from me."

"Sir, there's still the matter of the Quantum Computer. I know we overlooked the museum, when it was staring us in the face."

"You can't be blamed for that."

"Thank you, but there's still the Computer, and it's a matter of top national security. I ask you to reconsider."

The Prime Minister hadn't got where he was by ignoring the advice of his top men, and he paused for thought. "I'll go this far, Sir Robert. I'll keep our options open for a time – but for now, no juice. And I must release the cleric, uh, Ark … what's his title?"

"Archimandrite, or some such ridiculous nonsense, Prime Minister."

"Yes, thank you, the Archimandrite Athanassios. We cannot hold him."

Sir Robert stroked his chin. "He's at most a witness, one of many. I have my little list of society offenders…"

"No, not for now, Sir Robert. I'll meet you half way, and think about the principal players – but simple witnesses, no, I can't authorize that. Deal?"

"Yes, Prime Minister!"

The plane came to a stop in front of a British Army lorry, and the Greek soldiers reversed the process of loading, using the same methods and tools. Adam, Helena, and Peter were standing behind their aircraft, watching the unloading. When it was finished, as they turned to board the plane, six uniformed police ran up to them. "Hold! Are you Adam Blix, Helena Katsis, and Peter Ryan?"

"We are, and we are leaving."

"You are under arrest. I have the warrants here. If you come quietly, I am advised that you will only be put under house arrest, for the time being."

They were hustled into a police car, Helena waving the Greek plane off, before anybody else changed their mind, and Greece had to go to war. They had perhaps narrowly averted that possibility over the Mediterranean, no reason to do otherwise here.

The senior officer turned back to them, "What's the address of your place?"

Helena thought fast. "I'll show you."

"I would prefer the address in advance."

Helena thought, "I'm sure you would." Then said, "Better I show you. Go first to Euston Square for now."

So they were hustled down the narrow steps and pushed through the door of Safe House One. She could have chosen number Two, but they needed equipment from here, as all their kit had been left behind on the plane. Given that they were to be arrested, it was lucky that they had left their bags aboard with all the evidence. Their Prime

Minister had said that they would be free to return. Evidently the British Prime Minister had gone back on his word. Why was it that Helena wasn't surprised? "Hah, should have foreseen that," she thought ruefully, marking herself down a point.

Chapter 26

The Return

Don't trust the Greeks even when bearing gifts in packing cases.

London, Saturday morning, 29 April, L+1

Sir Robert Mansfield was sitting in his office at MI5 headquarters, having been up most of the night since being awakened just before midnight by a call from the Prime Minister. His headache had slowly built up, and it was now pounding, threatening to get out of control. He gulped down another painkiller, and squinted at the clock: 8AM.

His speakerphone buzzed. "Director, there is a courier package for you downstairs at security reception."

"From whom?"

"Just a minute ... A doctor Adam Blix."

"What? Repeat that."

"Adam Blix."

"I'll be right down."

He signed for the package, and tore off his receipt. "When and where was this sent?"

The courier replied, "Heathrow airport, our office, uh, 10:55 last evening. Prepaid in cash."

"Thank you."

He turned to the security chief behind the counter. "Don't touch this. Get the bomb squad in here, and I mean yesterday."

Within a minute, a man rushed up opening his black bag on the run. "Where?"

"There."

"Stand back." He pulled on his helmet, the faceplate, and then went over the package with a device that looked like a barbecue fire-starter, the electric kind, with a loop of thick wire extending out of a box.

Another colleague hurried along, pushing a cart. He set a flat video screen on the counter facing away from one side of the package, and scanned the back with something that looked like a microphone. The screen immediately showed an x-ray like picture in vivid colours of the contents. He then shook his head. "Director, it's clean."

"Thank you." Still, Sir Robert approached it as if it were a poisonous snake. He slipped the catch on the webbed belt that secured the box, and opened the lid. There was a postcard of the Tower of London on top. "Thank you for the loan. It was very helpful. Good luck on the development. Doctor Adam Blix."

Sir Robert lifted the soft foam pad in the top, and read the label attached to the silver box inside. "My darling QC, give my regards to Sir Robert and the team. They will take good care of you. Love, Adam." It was the Quantum Computer! Sir Robert was more mystified than he had ever been at any time in his professional life.

He quickly figured it out, even through the deep haze of his throbbing headache. "So, it had been all about the museum, and *only* the museum from the start." It was the last scenario he would have thought of, and his headache began to lift, as he shook his head in wonder. He had occasionally felt respect for an opponent in the past, including the bad old Cold War days of his younger years in the service. It was a positive side of this otherwise often lonely life, a rare example of comradeship independent of affiliations. He was feeling it again for this man whom he had never met.

But they had failed despite everything. The Marbles secure in their cases were stacked along the walls in the gallery, and they had all the birds in a cage. He was looking forward to meeting them, particularly Adam, but also realized with a tinge of disappointment that it would now have to be a more cordial encounter than he had been planning only a few minutes before.

He swept back into his office, and called over his shoulder to his secretary. "Get me the P-M straight away, please."

Two London Bobbies stood guard at the top of the steps leading down to the basement flat in which Adam, Peter and Helena were under house arrest.

Helena had just finished, and removed the third encrypted backup disk of their records. "One disk for each of us. I think we should keep a record of all this, don't you? Okay, Adam, scrub them clean."

"At once." Adam called up the disk erasing software, and keyed it into execution. The hard disks of each computer were now buzzing contentedly as the software erased the whole disk ten times with random data. He knew once was not enough, because security agencies had subtle tools for extracting the last few levels of content despite any erasure. To simply order the files deleted was hopelessly inadequate, because any eight year-old could recover them. They had to be overwritten several times, and it would take a few minutes.

Meanwhile Helena was handing papers to Peter who was stuffing them into the ancient, coal burning central heating system as fast as the fire could consume them. "That's the last, Peter, thanks."

Adam was testing the backup set of secure, digital mobile telephones. "All okay, batteries fully charged." He tossed chargers into a spare backpack.

Helena broke open a sealed package. "Here are your new identities, memorize the names and birth dates, place of birth, and everything on the sheet of paper folded inside." Helena made coffee and served everyone. This menial task freed her mind, and she looked around the room, noting some minor items for the fire, and tossed them in.

Peter turned next to the delicate job of disarming the self-destruct system. He teased the necessary wires to the top of the connection box, and cut them in the correct order. Their lives all depended upon his memory. To have this on paper would have rendered the whole exercise meaningless. He made no mistake.

They finished off a light breakfast from the last of the stores. Helena rapped for attention on the table. "Okay, here's the play. Use disguise kits "C", then down the chute to the Underground. Adam, Peter, so, straight to Waterloo International and the ride on Eurostar that Adam booked online from here in the wee hours?"

"It's the 11:15," Adam agreed, "plenty of time."

Helena consulted her watch. "We have to be there at least thirty minutes early, to pick up the tickets, and meet their twenty minute limit on the gate. The timing is about right. We don't want to have to stand around much either. The odds are good. Let's do it."

Adam yanked at the guts of the refrigerator in the back of the room, and it all came out exactly as Peter had demonstrated during their first meeting. It seemed a lot longer than the ten months it had been. Peter went first, and then Helena. Adam did his best to pull the insides of the fridge back in as he hung over the lip of the slide, and succeeded pretty well. Then the three of them were in the closet at the bottom. They put on the fake London Underground uniforms hanging on hooks, and slid open the back panel slowly. A Metropolitan line train rushed past, then they stepped down onto the workmen's narrow edge of platform, and turned right to Euston Square station.

The "employees only" gate swung easily inward, and the trio made their way to the loos, dumped the uniforms in the waste containers, stuffing them well down with papers on top, and emerged into the station's concourse transformed. It was safest to proceed separately to Waterloo International.

Adam collected the three sets of tickets, and then sat down in the coffee shop. Each of his partners picked up theirs from the edge of the table. They had widely separated seats in the same car.

"Eurostar train number 1017, the 11:15 for Ashford, Lille International, and Paris Gare de Nord, is now closing. Please proceed through security to the platform."

Geoffrey Hayward stood on the loading dock as the drivers of the lorry swung up into the cab. He had personally checked that the shipment of the Treasures of Mount Athos was genuine, even demanding that one of the cases be opened. There was no real reason to take these precautions – only the one vehicle there – and the Elgins were safely stacked up in the Duveen Gallery after their short-lived flight towards Greece. When the case lid came off, he could plainly see the Icon lodged inside, its golden embellishments shining benignly back at them in the guard's light. The cases were counted, and checked off against the original manifest. Then the lorry backed out of bay number one into the parking area of the museum, and out into the street.

Archimandrite Athanassios shook Hayward's hand. He was booked on the Eurostar, under a changed reservation, at 2PM, for Paris, Marseilles, and then to Ancona in Italy, for the ferry crossing to Greece, and home.

He was not the same man he had been only a short week before. The stress had worn him down, and then, just as he was raised up by the prospect of the Marbles returning to Greece, he had been smashed down, held under house arrest for an interminable few hours, now released to make his lonely return home, feeling as defeated as the conspirators themselves must. He uttered a silent prayer for them, one of many to follow, turned, and walked out the door.

Sir Robert Mansfield greeted the two Bobbies, flashed his identification, and descended the steps to knock on the basement flat's door. After an interval, he knocked louder, then bent down and looked through the window. The lights were on, but the room was empty.

"Sergeant, break down this door!"

They could not have just disappeared. A cadre of police, and John Fiske with two new agents as partners, were searching the room for hidden doors and passageways. It was clear that their birds had not gone out the front door, and there were no other visible exits. A police sergeant was tugging at the refrigerator, trying to pull it out to have a look behind. "It's stuck, give me a hand." All of them together couldn't budge it.

John Fiske snapped his fingers. "It will be through there." He pointed inside the unit, grabbed the first shelf, and pulled to free it. The whole insides came out, spilling him on the ground as the astonished group peered into the dark hole behind.

Fiske, running on overdrive, opened his briefcase, took out his laptop computer, unplugged the other computers from their phone line, and plugged his into the same line. He then called a special MI5 program that interrogated the phone company. Fiske recognized the last number dialled as an Internet Service Provider. He then patched into their server, and displaying previously concealed brilliance, determined that their last Internet contact had been with Eurostar Reservations online.

"They've booked on Eurostar. Let's go."

HELENA TO IRINI
 CLEARED OUT OF SAFE HOUSE ONE
 11:15 EUROSTAR TO PARIS

Irini thought to herself, at least they are free. Helena will get them safely home. That was something. She felt disoriented, rudderless in a stormy cosmos of her own feelings. What should she do, if anything? Resume her life here? Give it up to follow Adam? Give him up? Escape? Was there any threat against her? She had promised Helena to watch things here until further notice, and she had not yet had the release from her. So she followed the plan and her agreed orders, bravely remaining at her post in the temporarily closed museum. Her office seemed strangely foreign, as did the silent halls and mute galleries that she wandered through, accompanied only by her thoughts and timeless ghosts.

As the train pulled into Ashford station, Helena was first at the door when it slid aside with a hiss of air pressure released. She looked forward along the platform, just in case, and her experienced eye caught the unmistakable body language of policemen boarding at the head of the train and moving down the platform towards them, their plain clothes not fooling her for an instant.

She gave a come-on sign with her first finger to Peter, who tapped Adam on the shoulder. They grabbed bags, and stepped off the rear of the train, hidden by the crowds of people boarding. Two things had saved them. First, the train was making a regular stop. It could have been a non-stop, therefore a non-scheduled police halt, in which case they would have been alone on the platform, and been scooped up. Second, First Class had been at the rear of the train, when it could have been at the front, straight into the net.

The three separated after Helena whispered "Asda!" to each of them. They managed to mingle with those seeing off friends and relatives, waving to the windows, and then exited the station with them as the train pulled out.

MI5 Headquarters, 2PM the same day

John Fiske reclined in his office chair, catching a well-earned kip. He rested only fitfully because of his frustration at the unanswered questions and escape of the suspects from his net. The police and his people were scouring the countryside in and around Ashford, but he didn't hold much hope. The whole business was so bizarre as to make any experience he brought to this job almost meaningless. There were no precedents. He was tracking British subjects, in Britain, and a Greek spy (his experience helped there but mainly by warning him against hoping for an easy catch), who were wanted for what? The Marbles were back. Their audacious plan had failed, torn from the jaws of success by Prime Ministerial hardball.

His main reasons for persisting were the more than vague aches in his heart left there by Irini (where is she in all of this if anywhere?) and the inexplicable disappearance of his two previous partners in circumstances that were incomprehensible in the extreme. What were the connections, the lifeblood of his and all police work?

He understood the Greek desire to have those sculptures back, and he now understood the Quantum Computer caper. Yet that was all ancient history, and it didn't fit. He felt he was missing a part of himself; there was a niggling something else.

He awoke with a start, a cold chill tingling his back and raising the hairs on his neck. He had suddenly thought of a possible connection, an alternate thread. It was almost too improbable to take seriously, but a connection was a connection, and it should be followed up. He picked up his telephone.

British Museum, 4PM the same day

Irini was sitting on a packing case in the Duveen Gallery, feeling shattered. Emily was with her, having stopped to offer consolation. She was sympathetic for her friend's obvious grief, and amazed by today's news of the Marbles' theft and return.

Suddenly, the staff door of the gallery burst open, and Geoffrey Hayward stood there, panting with exertion, bibulous and red-faced. His pale grey linen suit looked decidedly the worse for wear, and he threw them a tipsy smile, and burst out, "Oh – I'm suh happy that you're – both here."

He made his way to a packing case, and sat down heavily. "Been dragged away from my birf – day – party by dis bloody cop, or izz he MI5, Fiske, who's s'posed to be helpin us with sec – urty."

He glared around the Gallery, imagining it was full of John Fiskes. He wagged his finger at the walls, "Well, 'ere I am." He added defiantly. "Now, s'pose I must go through this ridic – ridic – pantomime of checkin'." He got up, and turned towards the case he had been sitting on, and tried to open it with his bare hands. "He was so insistent." He mumbled this more to himself than the others. Then, "Ouch!" he yelped. The director of the British Museum had proved that he bled like any other mortal man.

Emily moved forward, "Can I help you?"

"Get me a toolkit, quick." Hayward was rocking back and forth, nursing his hand, and tying it with a handkerchief.

Emily returned with a small crowbar.

He grumbled, " You do it, Emily, my dear."

She could see that he was in no fit state to open a can of beans. Without a further word, Emily bent forward across the packing case, inserted the crowbar under the lip of the lid, and prized it back. Irini came forward to help. The lid opened with an anguished squeal of released nails.

Emily looked inside, "See for yourself." After a silent pause, she gasped, "… Ah … yes…" then slammed the lid down, and began driving the nails home with the crowbar.

Irini stood dumbfounded as Emily finished resealing the case.

Hayward flapped his injured hand dismissively, "Well done." "Close the blasted thing up." He turned around. "Dank you laddies." Having made a weak attempt at gallantry he walked unsteadily towards the door, taking his champagne headache with him.

Emily struck the last nail home in the box, and with equal finality, in her life as she had known it. In that instant of fateful decision, she had become an accessory after the fact.

Irini shook her head in bewilderment. "I think you must come with me. Now. Right now."

HELENA TO IRINI
    OFF TRAIN AT ASHFORD
    COPS EVERYWHERE
    PICK US UP ASAP
        RSVP WHEN YOU CAN
IRINI TO HELENA
    ON THE WAY, EMILY STONE COMING WITH ME
    FORWARD TO CHARON
    PICKUP AT EMBASSY SAFE HOUSE IF POSSIBLE
    TRANSIT TO SAFE HOUSE TWO
    COVER OUR REAR IF POSSIBLE
CHARON TO IRINI VIA HELENA
    ON MY WAY
PLUTON TO HELENA
    ACROSS CHANNEL WITH TRUCK
    AWAITING INSTRUCTIONS
HELENA TO PLUTON
    CONTINUE ON AUTOROUTE UNTIL FURTHER NOTICE
    THEN HOLD AT QUIET AIRE AND ADVISE LOCATION
CHARON TO IRINI AND HELENA
    OUTSIDE MUSEUM IN ROLLER
    HAVE ACHILLES AND BAGS

"Irini, I must at least pack." Some of the practical exigencies were now occurring to Emily as they hurried across the museum concourse, the guard saluting them with a smile.

"I'm sorry, there is no time. Your things will be forwarded. You must trust me in this, and all else today."

Emily nodded, and struggled to keep up. A few minutes before, she thought she had understood everything in a blinding flash of insight, but now it was just a confusing jumble. It had all overtaken her, and she was sure of only the one truth, Irini was her lifebelt, and she must hang on for dear life.

Charon released the door locks, and they jumped in the back seat. Achilles, in his travelling box, delivered a resounding "meow" of gratitude for one familiarity in his equally disrupted life.

The Saturday traffic was forgiving, for a change, and they were at the entrance to Safe House Two in a few minutes. "Word to the wise, Irini. Leave immediately, before the vultures gather. I'll stay here as long as I can. Good luck."

She shook Charon's hand, grabbed Achilles' box, and stepped to the entrance, keying her code in the door lock. It released, and the three ascended the twelve flights on foot. Irini wanted to avoid that last Expected Unexpected, a lift that jammed half way up, or worse as she imagined it, if it had been placed under somebody else's control.

The room's door opened without difficulty, and Irini put Achilles down for a moment. The computer panel was all green, so she could be certain nobody had entered since they had last been there. Irini slipped the backup computer disk in her handbag, and commanded the computer system to "scrub clean and self-destruct".

There were only a few papers or other evidence about, and she stuffed all of it in a plastic bag, and then made one last tour around the room. Emily followed her with her eyes and helped gather without being told. One last check-up, then Irini pulled down the staircase, and nodded for Emily to follow. Irini threw the trash bag and handbags up onto the floor above, and climbed the ladder, Emily following. Then it was pulled up, and the hatch sealed, with a large, mechanical lever turned across it. "That will hold them for a while, if they come."

Emily was trying to take in the scene around her, the inflated roof above with the large balloon-like covered shape in the centre.

Irini pulled the release, and it snapped across the room, revealing the helicopter. It was beyond the last thing Emily could have imagined.

Irini commanded, "Help me throw the goodies in, then you sit in the right seat."

Irini dashed around to her side, and jumped in. Emily was safely aboard, so Irini could hit the master panel "on" button, lighting up a double-dozen lights and switches, and lastly the dome release. With a roar of flying jets, it flew over their heads, and landed against the outside of the building, a stiff breeze from the southwest adding impetus to the spectacle.

The blades were already spinning up from the compressed air starter; its hose released and snaked across the floor, as Irini hit the throttle. She reached up and flicked five switches, toggled another until the red light behind it turned yellow, and then green. The turbine caught at once, and the blades rose up as they gathered lift. Emily watched in fascinated awe.

With an ascending whine, accompanied by a "pocketa-pocketa" rhythm, Irini eased the joystick, watching the RPM dial in the centre left of the computer display. She remembered something her instructor had told her about takeoff in windy conditions, and held the craft down until the blade speed had reached the second green mark, then pulled up on the joystick. They leaped into the air, spinning left because Irini had also inadvertently twisted the joystick slightly counter clockwise, the command to rotate (yaw) the craft. The wind caught them, and they spun off the roof to the east, gaining altitude at an exhilarating rate. Each, Achilles included, prayed to whatever Supreme Being they hoped they knew.

Irini released her grip on the joystick, exactly as she had been trained to do, while still retaining a lift on the handle. It returned to neutral position, and the plane steadied on a northward course. Irini glanced at the compass, took her visual bearings on the London skyline, then twisted the joystick a touch to bring them slowly around to a south-eastward course. That would do for now at least. Takeoff was easy compared with landing, but that would come later, after the adrenaline rush had worn off. Meanwhile, her hands were shaking, and the aircraft, by computer transmission through the fly-by-wire control system, was vibrating in sympathetic synchrony.

A terse silence lay heavily between them. Emily thought, "Is this really happening to me? I could never have imagined that my career in museum work and the eighth century would end so. This is Ian Fleming, not Emily Stone!"

Achilles felt cat-like equivalents in his transporter on the back seat and gave a rising, guttural howl of protest.

Irini's phone chimed, and she spoke to Emily, "Please take that."

PETER TO IRINI
    GPS COORDINATES FOLLOW. ENTER IN COMPUTER
    IT WILL FLY YOU HERE

"Emily, when the coordinates appear on the screen, please enter them into the GPS system, that box between us, on top of the console. See it?"

"Yes." In a moment the phone spoke again, and Emily carefully entered the location on the keypad, and without being asked, checked that everything agreed to the last number and sign.

Irini held 2000 feet elevation, which she remembered from her navigation classes was the correct altitude. When the GPS green light started flashing, she engaged the auto-navigation. The screen in front of her asked, "Altitude, hold?" She keyed "Y" and "ENTER". The system responded by taking control of the aircraft.

"Whew." Emily then thanked Irini with a heartfelt, "well done" but her emotions cut off further conversation.

ATC Command Centre, SE England: "We have a low-flying aircraft not responding to Air Traffic Control."

"Log and file it." The chief controller replied, and then he remembered something that had come through a few hours back, a memo. He shuffled through the computer messages, and then it popped up on his screen. "Charlie, what's the Transponder ID?"

"AH403"

"Track it! I'll get back to you." He picked up his telephone. "Mr Fiske? Yes, we are tracking the type of aircraft on your alert. They're not in contact with ATC. Hang on. Charlie?"

"Gone off screen."

"Where?"

"Just this side of Ashford."

When the navigation computer bleeped at her, "Trajectory complete," she did what all pilots do as their first choice, and looked out the window. The GPS navigation unit continued to show range and course. She was a bit to the left, and twisted the top of the joystick ever so gently clockwise. The aircraft yawed a touch, and the indicator showed spot-on. Then she saw it, a large parking lot, with three tiny figures in the far corner waving to her. There was plenty of space to land, so Irini pressed down on the joystick to descend, release to hold altitude, and lift slightly to rise, forward to speed up, back to slow down. She did not realize either how recent this new fly by wire, CAP, Computer Aided Piloting system was, or that until its development, helicopters had been far more difficult to fly.

Though somewhat nervous, she had certainly done it a few times before, and the ship glided out over the parking lot, then hovered above the open area, descending easy-does-it in response to her soft touches on the joystick. With a slight bump, they touched down. Irini slammed her hand down on the top of the stick, and the craft stuck like a limpet to the ground. She pulled back on the stick, and the engine began to wind down.

Peter was animatedly waving his hands at her to keep the blades up, so Irini complied. The girls were directed to hop over into the back seats, and did so, Irini slumping forward in exhaustion. She consoled herself, "At least I have done my best."

Helena climbed over into the rear seat, patting Irini on the knee.

Peter jumped into the left, pilot's seat, Adam co-pilot in the right. Adam called back to Irini, "What's the ATC frequency down here?"

Then the terrible thought hit her. "Uh, sorry Peter, I didn't, I ah, forgot."

"Uh, Oh," Adam groaned, "they'll have spotted that for sure."

Peter grinned, "I doubt they will have called the cops, but we'll play it safe. We still have good light; we'll skim it under the radar." The engine whined up again, and Peter threw them into the sky on fast forward.

Chapter 27

Denouement

There are Old Pilots, and Bold Pilots, but no Old, Bold Pilots.

Irini, Emily, and Helena were squashed in the back seat, with Achilles in his cage across their knees. Helena gave Emily a little hug of encouragement. "Well done," she said with heartfelt admiration. Emily raised her eyebrows garnished with a slight smile, her mind full of what she had left behind, in her life, home and hearth. "Well," she thought, "it would be a new adventure, and maybe it is high time."

Helena mused to herself, "never prejudge people" and the thought of the Archimandrite also came into her mind. "And wasn't he a surprise." Helena now allowed herself a sigh of relieved satisfaction, and a deep smile suffused her face, one that surpassed that on the Sphinx for its timeless intensity.

Then quite unexpectedly she began to hum. Was it that Theodorakis theme Spiros had sung on the beach, their song? She gave a soft laugh. Emily, squashed between the two women, put it down to post-trauma reaction. Nobody else could hear.

Peter handled the helicopter as if he had been flying it all his life. The women in the back were too exhausted to really enjoy it. Adam let out a "Whoopee!" now and then as the balky little craft dodged between the low hills, hugging the ground, both keeping a sharp lookout for any cables or antennas. Then it was out over a choppy channel, literally skimming just above the waves.

Helena's cheerfulness again became apparent. What she felt was deeply at odds with the others. They could only wonder if all professional spies were like this.

ATC Southeast England: "I'm sorry, Mr Fiske, but they have not reappeared on radar. Landed for dinner, eh?" His laugh was not reciprocated on the telephone, which was slammed down.

PLUTON TO PETER
  GPS COORDINATES FOLLOW
WE ARE HOLDING AT AN AIRE EAST OF PARIS AS INSTRUCTED.

Peter landed the plane without incident, on a broad, grassy knoll, beside the Aire. They jumped aboard the lorry, stowing Achilles in the driver's sleeping area behind the passenger's bench seats.

The intercontinental truck pulled out onto the Autoroute that bypassed Paris to the east, on a direct course for Lyon and points south. Peter was on the phone, "Yes, that's what I said. Pick up the 'copter in that Aire. I'm sending you the coordinates, but I think you'll find it easier by name on a map. Deliver in Athens, chop-chop! Okay, Roger."

Helena was sitting in the jump seat between Pluton and a man she didn't know who was driving this shift. "Can you give me some ETAs, Pluton?"

"Sure, Pandora. We're going east around Paris, Lyon, Nice, then across Italy and down to Ancona, ETA no later than noon tomorrow, in good time for our booking on Blue Star, the first overnight ferry to Patras. If we are delayed, there are several others during the afternoon and early evening."

"Ventimiglia Carbinieri? Fiske here, MI5, Great Britain. Yes, good evening. I have the registration on a Greek lorry – yes, truck, camione, whatever – and I want you to call me the moment it passes through your checkpoint. There will be some readies, uh, lira, cash, money, in it for you. My agent will be parked on the French side in a yellow Porsche. Give him the high sign, and then call me. He has an envelope for you. Yes, goodbye."

Pluton shook Helena awake. "We're being followed, I think, since shortly after the Italian border." He tilted the outside mirror with its controls. "There, can you see him, a yellow Porsche."

Adam, wide-awake as usual in the early hours, said, "There's no reason, now. It has all been for nothing." Helena felt sorry for him in his discouragement, but it would soon be over.

"What do we do?"

"Nothing. That will attract the least suspicion." Helena then added, surprising everyone, "Try not to lose him!"

As the day progressed, Helena received a long sequence of messages. After each one she smiled enigmatically, and invariably hummed another Theodorakis song. It was beginning to get on Peter and Adam's nerves, while Irini and Emily exchanged questioning glances.

That Sunday afternoon, they rolled along the dockside of Ancona, looking for the Greek ferry to Patras, and then there she was. They had only been parked for a few minutes when the first officer beckoned that they follow him. Their truck was loaded first, well ahead of any other traffic, backed in just inside the doors to one side, so they would be the first off. Apparently it was to be the red carpet treatment, despite having lost, or was it just basic security for the original Athos treasures? Runner-up's privilege, but Peter and Adam would rather they had snuck in under cover of darkness.

It was five minutes to sailing time, and only the odd last-minute car was still rumbling over the gangway into the cavernous hold. Then three Port Authority Police cars came roaring around the corner of a freight shed, and stopped side by side with their front wheels on the gangway, the rear on the dock.

Helena, Peter, Adam and Emily had just been introduced to the captain on the bridge. A man jumped out of one of the cars, and ran forward, clutching a piece of paper in his hand.

Irini gasped, "God, Helena, that's Fiske! What the hell is he doing here?"

"If anybody knows, you do, Irini." Helena kidded. "If we wait, we'll soon know."

He arrived on the bridge panting, gulped when he saw Irini, and then again for Adam. "Captain, I've got an order from the Port Commander to search this vessel."

"Captain, I'll deal with this." Helena stepped forward. "You're on your own, Fiske, why I don't know. The museum director you pressurized yesterday has confirmed your question. As you well know, Irini and Emily here were also present. I've had the word several times from London. You have received recall orders. So shut up, pack up, and buzz off, sunshine."

"That's just it, only *they* checked the contents; he pinpointed Irini and Emily with stabs of his index finger. And the director," he spat this word on the floor, "was in his cups. I think the real Marbles are on board!"

"That's ridiculous," Adam stated flatly. "And I don't appreciate your attentions to Irini either, maybe that's the real reason, eh?"

"I've got the paper, and you can't sail without my signature."

"Helena," the Captain offered by way of information, "this Port Captain will sometimes issue one of these for a fee, or a favour, but that doesn't make it any less valid."

Fiske was smiling like a fat cat that had just caught the rat. "Gotcha!" his expression was saying.

"Fiske, this captain is going to raise that gangplank on my signal, and if you're still on it, I can't answer for the consequences."

"Uh, Helena, be…"

The captain was stopped by her eyes, flashing starry flecks from the reflected afternoon sun. Helena handed him her telephone. "Yes sir, Prime Minister, but…"

"Yes, Mr Anguelopoulos, I know you own the…"

The Captain shrugged helplessly.

"Fiske," Helena smiled dangerously, "I suggest you move it out, now. Call off your dogs."

He stood his ground.

Helena asked, "What is the hour, Captain?"

"A minute past sailing time."

The tiny mobile telephone was rasping the command, "Sail, sail 'er now, dammit!"

"Raise the Gangplank." Helena commanded.

The Captain shrugged again, this time with purpose, and signalled to the officer at the controls below. He had to repeat the gesture when the man pointed at the police cars. The Gangplank then began to lift, as the ship started backing away, the fronts of the Police Cars rising. The three occupants escaped before the angle was too great, but as the front wheels cleared the knife-edge of the steel platform, the three cars plunged into the sea.

"Mister Fiske, can you swim?"

"I can, why?"

"Yeoman, throw this man off my ship."

"Yessir."

British Museum, 4PM, Monday, L+3

Geoffrey Hayward scuttled back and forth like a peripatetic crab, pointing this way and that, and barking orders. This chair there, camera Three, overriding the cameraman, a yard this way, the lights redirected. He certainly saw himself as the director, and perhaps he was, for he knew that this was his grand moment.

The clock was edging to 4PM, and so he took the low stage with the presenter, who when the countdown was completed, made the introduction.

"Doctor Geoffrey Hayward, the Director of the British Museum, has a statement to make that is of interest to everyone in these British Islands. Dr Hayward."

"Ladies and Gentlemen, fellow countrymen and women, greetings from the British Museum. The Crime of the Century has been attempted against us, and it has failed." His hands swept the Duveen Gallery in an all-encompassing gesture. "The heinous theft from these hallowed precincts, carried out by despicable villains from Greece, was thwarted, in large part by the decisive actions of our Prime Minister.

"I therefore first wish to direct my appreciation, and on behalf of the British people, to him. In a few seconds, we will open the first case, and begin the restoration of these treasures to their rightful…"

A man was gesticulating wildly at Hayward, and his attention was diverted. The man rushed into the field of view of the camera, and whispered in the director's ear. A look of disbelief, and then horror swept the condescension from his face. "**What?**"

The man whispered again, "These are the copies, director."

"Impossible!" Hayward ran from the platform, the cameras following him, as he kneeled down at the side of the first box to be opened. He threw his hands up to heaven, and whimpered in the strident voice of a small child, yet loudly enough to be heard on-camera, around the room, across the nation, and overseas on BBC World television:

"My Marbles are Missing!"

At the BBC main studios in London, the director of programming on duty was staring in disbelief at the transmission. "Jeez, what a story!" A colleague signalled to him from the control room, motioning and mouthing the words, asking him to pick up the phone.

It was a call from the Greek television network, suggesting that he take their feed from the Hotbird satellite, with the unusual disclaimer that it would be free of charge, courtesy of the Greek government, and that their Prime Minister would shortly be on-camera with a statement.

"We interrupt this program to bring you a live news flash from Greece."

The camera in Athens was panning the streets, which seemed to be an undulating curtain of blue and white Greek flags. The ecstatic crowds were almost totally concealed by them, hardly a face to be seen. The expressed passions far exceeded that from the winning of a World Cup, plus a hundred Gold Medals in their beloved Olympics thrown in. It was infectious, exhilarating, wave upon wave, in a sea of emotion.

A large truck was slowly wending its way up a curved, cypress lined avenue, turning then at such an angle that the camera swung past the Acropolis and Parthenon high in the background, finally fixing on a modern structure of glass vaulting up into the heights, seeming to reach out to the ancient city above, golden in the setting sun's rays. The truck came to a halt, and five people jumped out, three women and two men.

The camera switched to a closer shot. Three other men entered the picture from the right, and all embraced each other in turn with bear hugs. The Prime Minister then lovingly herded them towards a dais in front of the museum. It was pandemonium for several minutes, despite his eloquent, as ever, hand signals requesting calm.

Then a hush swept like a summer breeze across the crowd, and the flags stilled, each flag bearer holding it low in front of him or her. Now the tens of thousands of proud, strong Greek faces could be seen. The camera scanned the scene, and then returned to the podium.

"Fellow Greeks." The amplified voice of the Prime Minister echoed from the Acropolis cliffs behind him, and spread out its welcoming arms to the world.

"We are honoured today by the bravery and brilliance of these people here beside me, and I introduce them with humble respect. I will mention their nationalities, for by no means are they all Greek! They have sacrificed much to be here, and to serve our country in the repatriation of our beloved and long lost Parthenon Marbles, which will be placed this very day in the New Parthenon Museum.

"Helena Katsis, Greek, a national heroine in other wars before this one, who led the team and directed this coup.

"Spiros Anguelopoulos, Greek national, the 'back room man' to the nation.

"Irini Baynes, United Kingdom national, half Greek by birth, our Inside Girl and a new Helen of Troy.

"Adam Blix, Unites States of America, who opened the doors as no man has ever opened them before.

"Peter Ryan, United Kingdom national, who lifted the Marbles, with help from many others of his countrymen, none of whom we will ever forget.

"Emily Stone, United Kingdom national, who was called at the last minute, and answered that call with fast thinking, and instant commitment to our cause.

"And here he comes now, just arrived back from his triumphant tour with his Treasures of Mount Athos, Archimandrite Athanassios, who also answered an unexpected call.

"All of the foreign nationals have sacrificed their very lives to be here, yes, their lives, for each one of them had a promising professional life of their own, that is now forever denied them in their home countries. This they willingly sacrificed for us. Do you welcome them here as Greeks, forever!" His arms swept the heavens, and then the platform.

There was no holding the crowd now, and it surged forward, a tidal wave of blue, the lighter, brighter blue of the Greek flag, contrasting with their deep hued Aegean far below, and the rich blue of the lightly cloud scudded sky above.

Reprise

When the ferryboat from Ancona to Patras reached international waters, two Greek Navy frigates took up station in convoy. It was then that Helena could call her team into the Captain's mess room to break the news. Helena looked each one straight in the eyes, in turn, including Adam and Peter. She then fixed on Irini, and Emily, whom she felt had figured out at least part of her ultimate plan. Helena's smile metamorphosed into laughter, then gushing tears of joy.

"We've won," she finally managed to gasp out, "the true Marbles are here with us, and Doctor Hayward has his excellent copies!"

Epilogue

The Prime Minister, together with all of the team he had introduced to the world, later repaired to Spiros' penthouse apartment. It was a wonderful, but exhausting moment, so a quiet interlude with convivial drinks was most welcome. They swapped a few brief tales and anecdotes from the enterprise and earlier days – for some of them, bygone days that would never be recaptured. They had answered the challenge, and triumphed. Had they languished in prison for years in the alternate fate, at least they would have done their best. Perhaps now everyone in the room understood this truth. The first rule of life is to live! And by so doing avoid the poisoned chalice of regrets.

Finally, they had to know, all of them, from the Prime Minister to Emily and Irini, the two who had glimpsed the truth, and acted on that revelation, yet had not been able to quite put it all together. It had been Helena's plan, and her command decisions so it was up to her. All heads turned, and she knew it was the moment.

"You have all now realized that the Marbles on the plane were not the originals, but the copies! I was the only person in the world who knew that, at least until after the fact, when Irini and Emily had an inkling of the truth for a second or two. This was a key to the plan."

Helena held up her hand to still the avalanche of questions on their lips. "I know what you are thinking. 'Helena was lucky. How could she know that the plane would be turned back?'"

She smiled. "I didn't, yet I wonder if any of you have actually worked out the alternative scenarios, as I did. I don't imply that you couldn't, nor than my plan was particularly difficult to figure out, but my training has always been to work *everything* out from *every* angle. When you do that any and all of you would have made the same command decisions. So here we go, please grant me just a moment's patience.

"Scenario One: The copy 'Marbles' on the aircraft reach Athens. Answer – leaving them safely concealed for the moment in their boxes, we present them to the world as the originals! Everyone will believe us. Eventually, the Treasures of Mount Athos will be released. Is anyone going to search that lorry any more assiduously than Hayward did when we left the British Museum with it Saturday midday? Unlikely, and the result is the same, the lorry trundles down to Athens, and then we send the copies back to Britain. I think I would have enjoyed that one the best, certainly more ironic.

"Scenario Two: The copy 'Marbles' on the aircraft are turned back, as indeed happened. They go back into the British Museum in their cases. The museum is predictably closed as a precaution, they are 'obviously the originals', who is going to suspect otherwise? I realize it almost came unglued (saved by Irini and Emily), because of that persistent English bulldog in the person of John Fiske. Still, he made a fatal error, and trusted the director to check it out. If it had been me, I'd have used my pass and done it myself, as he should have. But he didn't. *And by then, in any case, it was already too late*; the true Marbles were across the channel. There was some risk in all the scenarios. The real question is, 'Which one had the least?'"

She had to hold up her hand again. "Wait, there is more.

"Scenario Three: I put the real Marbles on the aircraft and they reach Greece, as everyone believed was the plan. Success. Or is it? I will come back to this issue.

"Scenario Four: I put the real Marbles on the aircraft, and they are turned back, as happened. Failure! Please also note carefully, in that case there is no way back, except to steal them again, and that would be impossible even on a holiday weekend.

"So the obvious scenario you all quite reasonably believed in along with everyone else, Three/Four, had a fatal risk built in. If it failed, there was no way back. Call it fifty-fifty, or ninety-ten in favour, there was a significant risk, and in the event, we see that it would have failed.

"By choosing scenario One/Two, we were odds on to win *either way.* There was a moment when I was standing on the loading dock, just before we were to leave for the airport. That was the turning point. The drivers were already sitting in the lorry with the original Elgins, and the copy Athos Treasures. All I had to do was let them go, and we have scenarios Three/Four. I chose to stick with my plan, and we left the museum with the copy Elgins, and the *original* Athos Treasures.

"Incidentally, that's why I had to send Peter and Adam to Heathrow in the Rolls. You would have instantly recognized that the wrong lorry had been taken out. Then you would have had to act the part, and all the rest. Better to have only one who knew. I'm sorry you had to suffer such pain of failure over the weekend, but it really was best." They were nodding agreement, and forgiveness.

"This plan also gave flexibility when we hit the crunch over the Mediterranean in the aircraft. Turning back was not a big risk at all. There was, of course, some risk. We could have been forced to unpack the second lorry. I felt all along that this was unlikely.

"I hedged those bets by having the Mount Athos Treasures copied in Thessalonica during the exhibition there – good copies. It was best to have the same contents, as much as possible. To implement the plan, both shipments had to have identical boxes, and manifests, packed with the Athos Treasures in the back of the lorries, the Elgins in the front under false labels. Adam and others had to do the boxes the hard way, and there were many other people who laboured long hours to make the two pieces fit together."

Adam finally got his question in. "So this was the plan from the beginning – everything duplicated – everything doubled? Our shipment as loaded in the museum was the original Elgins, plus the copy Treasures, the other had the original Treasures and copy Elgins? What I don't see is how the Elgin copies ended up in London. Oh," he answered his own question, "you simply sent them back to London with the Mount Athos originals, after we shipped them to Athens. I'm just dumb, that's all."

Helena came across to hug him. "The last thing we could ever accuse you of is that, my dear Adam, the magician. Without you, we would have had to kidnap at least a dozen people by force, and put them away for the weekend. Those are capital offences, life in prison, nasty, and people usually get hurt. Adam's QC was literally the key, without which we would not have succeeded, for I would not then have had the superior option of using scenarios One/Two.

"We would have been forced to go with Three/Four, so that with success, at least we all would be in the clear here in Greece. For example, Irini, I would not have had the benefit of leaving you behind, and you would have come with us. Her bravery in that will be remembered by all here.

"In the event, would we have engaged the RAF in an air battle? Could we take the chance they wouldn't shoot us down?" The Prime Minister was shaking his head in the negative. "Just so," Helena agreed, "and so we would have lost everything, the Marbles, and our freedom! We certainly would not have been granted house arrest, but locked up on capital kidnapping warrants, no doubt staring at prison bars for a long time, if not the rest of our lives.

"Everyone had critical roles, never forget it. My job was to plan, and I did my best. Your various jobs were all key, and you did your best. Let all the credits rest where they fall.

"Prime Minister, do you remember when I said to you from aboard the aircraft that the Brits did not have the Mount Athos Treasures?"

He nodded.

"Well, as you can now see, they didn't. I released the lorry, the one with the *Original* Athos Treasures at the airport, and it then left the country in the early hours of Saturday. So on that score we were safe either way. For you see, *if we had succeeded* with Scenario Three, the British might have held them hostage, or kept them!"

She turned to the group. "So, it was simple, and obvious. A lot of work, yet that's often the answer, the right plan, the best people, and simple, hard graft."

Spiros was shaking his head in frank admiration. "Say what she will, as modestly as she has, the plan was brilliant, and there is no substitute for that." The Prime Minister began the applause, and the room rocked with it for a very long series of curtain calls, everyone taking their figurative turns.

Suddenly Emily felt weak in the knees, and found she had lost her voice in the excitement. She could only tug at Spiros' sleeve and whisper, "Would it be possible to have a nice cup of tea?"

They had all overheard her plaintive call. The humour of the situation gradually captured everyone, and the laughter built up into monumental cascades of blessed release.

The Careers

The British authorities lifted Irini's pilot's license. Their excuse was the inadvertent failure on her final flight in England to contact and follow Air Traffic Control. The Greek minister of transport instantly issued her a replacement. The helicopter was back in Athens, with hundreds of corners of the vastness of Greece beckoning to them. It was a worthwhile compensation.

Adam and Irini married, the Prime Minister officiating at the civil ceremony in Spiros and Helena's penthouse. It was timed for the sunset over the Acropolis, now presiding over the full set of Pheidias' glorious Marbles.

Adam was appointed full professor of Computer Science at the University of Athens.

Irini was appointed first assistant curator of the New Parthenon Museum. She was also granted Greek citizenship.

Emily Stone became joint-curator of the National Museum of Archaeology, Athens.

Peter was offered a post in the Greek intelligence services. That required Greek citizenship. It was granted with honour by the Parliament for services to the nation.

Archimandrite Athanassios went back to his monastic life, but later wrote a best selling autobiography.

Spiros set up a new Film and Television company in London, and then Hollywood, specializing in face casting, headed by Trevor Green, in partnership with his son "Baby" Jim. They all made a grand success, and a fair return on their human and financial investments.

Charon had arranged for the forwarding of Emily Stone's household effects, which arrived to her joy in perfect condition. The same applied to Irini's possessions.

Achilles moulted in the Athenian heat, but then found the climate and surroundings entirely satisfactory. He often sunned himself on the ledge of the great windows in the penthouse overlooking the Acropolis.

Geoffrey Hayward was sacked forthwith by the Prime Minister because his popularity had dropped ten percent following the Marbles fiasco. He ended up running a newsagent's shop.

The Prime Minister of Great Britain was left fighting for his political life. A study by the School of Political Science at the LSE concluded that he had dropped 10 percent because of the Marbles, his party by 5 percent, and this threatened to wound him fatally, politically.

Transition

Some weeks later when Charon had returned from the cleanup in Britain, Spiros invited him, the Prime Minister, and Helena to an intimate dinner for four in the penthouse. It was a formal affair in the sense that all the stories and lies swapped that night were serious, and mostly true. After the final round of brandy had been passed, and the evening was complete, Charon rose from the couch, and went over to Helena, offering his hand to raise her from her chair.

"Helena, our Pandora of the Miracle of the Marbles, attend me." He then lifted his Circle of Ouroboros necklace over his head. "There comes a time in every life to pass the torch to the next generation. This is mine." He lowered it over her head, and lovingly adjusted it on her breast.

He nodded silently, turned and left the room, leaving his life behind as so many of the others had done.

Helena had tried to make a new career for herself, and now her future plans lay in tatters. A new version of the old life lay before her. She fingered the chain of office, tears dropping silently down upon it from overflowing eyes.

About the Author

The author was a principal navigator of Apollo to the moon at JPL NASA. He founded the highly successful Sage Software UK and has published widely in science He is a public lecturer, and has written two other novels.

This is the first book in his new trilogy:
The Circle of Ouroboros

He lives with his wife Sara Gill Costelloe-Muller in a medieval village in Southwest France. The author can be reached by e-mail: muller@tournesolbooks.com.

The author and *Pooh Bear*, the model for *Achilles* in the novel.
Photo: Sara Gill Costelloe-Muller